RIVER OF NIGHT

RIVER OF NIGHT

JOHN RINGO
& MIKE MASSA

RIVER OF NIGHT

A Baen Books Original

Baen Publishing Enterprises
P.O. Box 1403
Riverdale, NY 10471
www.baen.com

ISBN: 978-1-4814-8421-3

Cover art by Kurt Miller
Maps by Randy Asplund

First Baen printing, July 2019

Distributed by Simon & Schuster
1230 Avenue of the Americas
New York, NY 10020

Library of Congress Cataloging-in-Publication Data

Names: Ringo, John, 1963– author. | Massa, Mike, 1967– author.
Title: River of night / John Ringo, Mike Massa.
Description: Riverdale, NY : Baen, 2019. | Series: Black tide rising ; 7
Identifiers: LCCN 2019004660 | ISBN 9781481484213 (hardcover)
Subjects: | BISAC: FICTION / Science Fiction / Adventure. | FICTION / Science
    Fiction / General. | GSAFD: Adventure fiction. | Science fiction.
Classification: LCC PS3568.I577 R59 2019 | DDC 813/.54—dc23 LC record
available at https://lccn.loc.gov/2019004660

Pages by Joy Freeman (www.pagesbyjoy.com)
Printed in the United States of America
10 9 8 7 6 5 4 3 2 1

As always
For Captain Tamara Long, USAF
Born: May 12, 1979
Died: March 23, 2003, Afghanistan
You fly with the angels now.

And for
Lieutenant Kevin Partridge, USN (EOD)
1971–2017
Desert Storm
"All for one, one for all."

ACKNOWLEDGEMENTS

As ever, many thanks to our Alpha readers, including Griffin Barber, Roger Foss, Jack Clemons, Jay La Luz and Jamie Ibson. Thanks again to Mike Gantz for his guided tour of select TVA facilities along the Tennessee River. Thank you to Brandy "Tiny Fists of Death" Bolgeo, for design of a very cool, inexpensive electrical induction device. Ryan Johnson, founder of RMJ Tactical, spent an afternoon giving your authors a tour of his factory, looking at all the goodies—thank you, sir! Special thanks to Mr. Charles C. Williams, Jr., who very graciously loaned us the original surveys, design papers, and construction logs for the Watts Bar dam and generating plant. A big thank you also to Ginger Cochrane who alerted us to the existence of these invaluable reference materials. We were tempted to add lots of detail, because big honking dams are just cool, especially the turbines and power house assemblies. Additionally, special thanks to Mr. Bert Hickman, an electrical engineering specialist and Tesla coil expert with whom we consulted and who has personally designed and assembled some of the very special constructions in this novel. If anything, we understated what these genuinely powerful and quite real machines are capable of doing.

Any technical errors in the book are our fault, and not that of our long suffering experts.

And most of all, Thank You to all of you, our readers, who continue to enjoy the stories of the Black Tide.

Don't get bit!
John Ringo, Mike Massa
Chattanooga, TN
2019

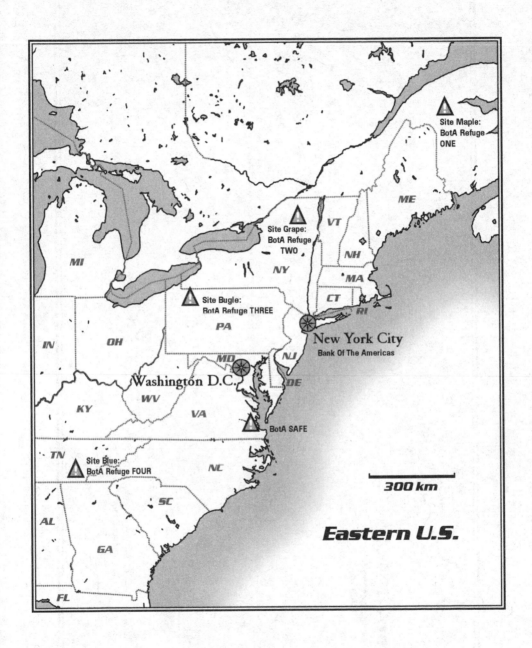

Site Maple:
BotA Refuge
ONE

Site Grape:
BotA Refuge
TWO

ME

VT

NH

MA

NY

Site Bugle:
BotA Refuge THREE

CT

RI

PA

New York City
Bank Of The Americas

IN

OH

MD

NJ

DE

Washington D.C.

WV

VA

KY

BotA SAFE

TN

Site Blue:
BotA Refuge FOUR

NC

MI

SC

AL

GA

300 km

Eastern U.S.

FL

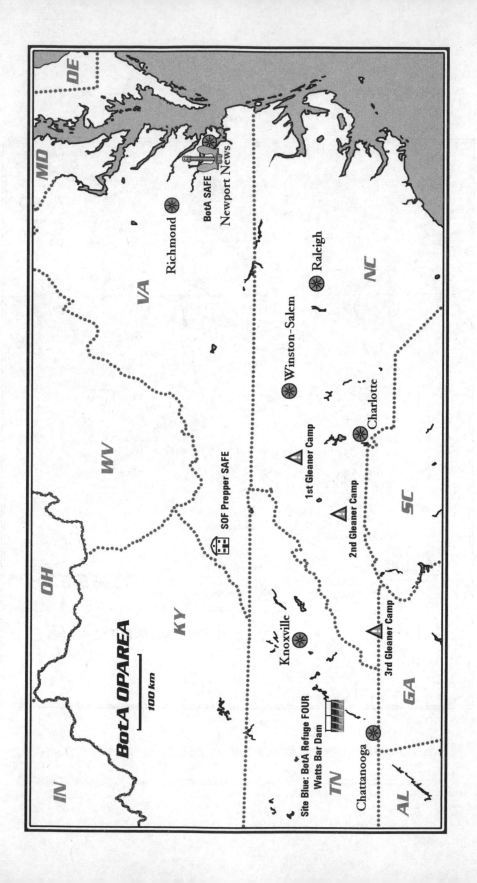

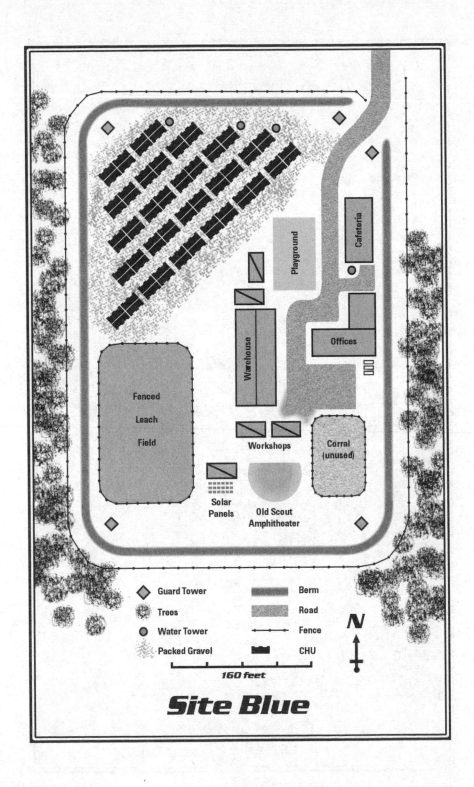

Solar Panels

Playground

Cafeteria

Warehouse

Offices

Fenced Leach Field

Workshops

Corral (unused)

Solar Panels

Old Scout Amphitheater

◆ Guard Tower
◉ Trees
● Water Tower
⬚ Packed Gravel

▬ Berm
▬ Road
•—• Fence
▪▪ CHU

N

160 feet

Site Blue

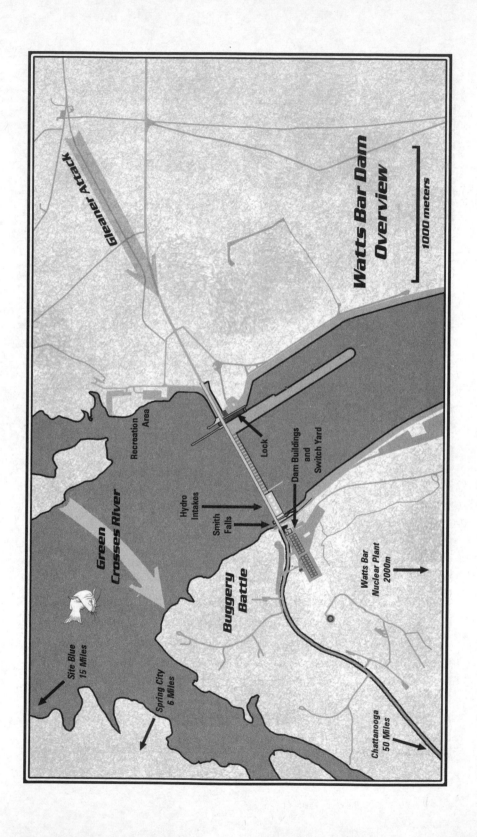

Gleaner Attack

Recreation Area

Green Crosses River

Hydro Intakes

Smith Falls

Lock

Dam Buildings and Switch Yard

Buggery Battle

Watts Bar Nuclear Plant 2000m

Site Blue 15 Miles

Spring City 6 Miles

Chattanooga 50 Miles

Watts Bar Dam Overview

1000 meters

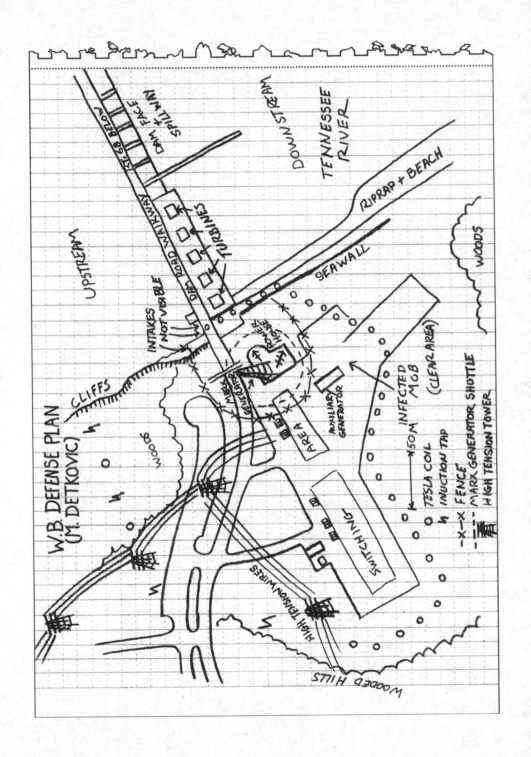

PROLOGUE

During the endgame of the Fall, state governments and major cities of the United States lost their ability to provide essential services to their populations. This development was accelerated by the degree to which each state and municipality relied on electrical power that was generated from feedstock, be it natural gas, coal or oil. A unique government corporation formed in 1933, the Tennessee Valley Authority, spanned seven southeastern states and operated a variety of power generation facilities, including traditional fossil-fueled plants as well as nuclear power plants and hydroelectric facilities.

These last had a dual role, providing not just immense amounts of electrical power, but also improving the navigability of the economically important Ohio and Tennessee Rivers as well as controlling the propensity of the region to severely flood during seasonal rains.

Unfortunately, all sophisticated equipment requires human supervision and periodic maintenance. As H7D3 took firm hold in the region, the nuclear plants were safely spun down to cold iron. The infrastructure necessary to move fuel to the traditionally powered generating facilities broke down, and these fossil-fuel plants also went dark. Solar facilities and hydroelectric sources of power lasted the longest of all. However, the chaos of the Fall, the desperation of operators trying to protect their families and the inevitable fighting over increasingly scarce resources also impacted these parts of the formerly vast network of power generation and distribution that was the TVA.

1

As the lights went out all over the world, the myriad ways that humans had shaped their world for convenience and entertainment were set afire, shattered or abandoned. As with any radical shift in the environment, there were adjustments. Domesticated animals that had become dependent on humans for their daily survival were rapidly converted into food by the dwindling numbers of healthy humans or by their far more numerous competitors, the infected. However, food animals and what stored crops existed were a limited resource, and the great civilization that was built on automation and sophisticated logistics crumbled into starving pockets of humanity.

It was the beginning of a new dark age and a bad time to be human.

On the other hand, there were winners *and* losers.

The lakes and rivers that dominated the Tennessee Valley region provided a ready source of water to the infected that slowly dispersed from the population centers. A huge number of the dead ended up in the river system, and from a strictly pragmatic view, they enriched the ecology.

Without any natural predators and now free of the bothersome humans, the channel catfish, the flatheads, and the mighty blues prospered, making the most of the expanded food sources so thoughtfully provided by their former hunters.

It might have sucked for everyone else, but it was a pretty good time to be a catfish.

CHAPTER 1

October 17th
Upper Chippokes Creek, the Chesapeake
Virginia

"When are we going to LEAVE this FUCKING house!" screamed Dina Bua, startling everyone around her.

Bua, a young and well-adjusted drama teacher at an expensive private boarding school, had started the trip south in a condition of shock. After her last minute attempt to escape New York City with some of her students had ended in a cannibalistic welter of blood, she'd nearly been run over by some speeding SUVs and then had been caught up in a second zombie attack and *then* a terrifying gun battle.

She had, understandably, nearly frozen in panic.

Huddled with one other teacher and their remaining three students, she'd obeyed the directions of their rather scary rescuers. The soldiers or mercenaries or whoever were clearly accustomed to working together. Despite her apprehensions about her saviors, the long boat ride had been a ticket out of a nightmare that had erased the only home she'd known. Arriving at the little house tucked into a tributary on the James River, the pressure of the emergency had been reduced and she'd appeared to recover somewhat. She'd repeatedly thanked the tall, handsome Bank of the Americas official who'd appeared to be in charge of original group of eight from the boat docks. She'd pledged to do anything to help.

Yet, Bua began to incrementally exhibit different symptoms of the strain she was under.

Long after everyone else had accepted the loss of the cell network and either turned their phones off, or left them on airplane mode in order preserve battery life while using them as music players, she would periodically stalk through the interior of the small house, her iPhone at arm's length over her head, hoping to see a single bar's worth of reception. After the water utilities failed, complicating the task of daily depilation, she'd tried mightily to use treated river water to complete her toilet and shave her legs. Through a quirk of oversight, a supply of artificial sweetener in their hideout had been overlooked so while others added "unhealthy refined white sugar" to their coffee, she'd complained about not being able to enjoy one of the few bright spots in an otherwise endless succession of identical days. Still, she'd complained quietly, mimicking the low profile that her fellow survivors practiced in order to avoid attracting the attention of hunting zombies or predatory survivors.

That is, she'd been quiet until now, when she just couldn't take it one more day and started screaming. And screaming.

So far their party had survived not due to firepower but from exercising absolute discretion. Anything else put the entire group at risk and everyone knew it.

Emily Bloome, the second schoolteacher, reached the screamer first. Driven to her knees by Bloome's tackle, Bua fought and bit like a woman possessed. Bloome rolled away clutching her face, but she had very competent back-up. Kaplan, the former spec-ops trooper turned bank security specialist and Risky, the unexpectedly capable gangster's moll, fell on Bua as though they'd rehearsed it many times, which in fact, they had.

A panicked schoolteacher was a new opponent for them, but just not in the same league as their previous wrestling matches wrangling hyperaggressive, zombified humans infected with the man-made plague virus called H7D3. A vicious arm bar that painfully threatened to dislocate Bua's elbow kept the panicking woman from bolting outside, and some duct tape and a belt sufficed to restrain the unhinged survivor while they fished some hemp rope out of a nearby gym bag.

"Is she infected?" Risky asked, sweeping her dark bangs out of her eyes. "She went wild so fast!"

Oldryskya "Risky" Khabayeva was an athletic five foot ten

inches tall, and appeared to be in her late twenties. Years ago, her youth and sex had been enough reason for the traffickers to keep her alive, but the supermodel good looks that prompted their efforts to sell her to an Italian-American gangster had led to their deaths.

It turned out that Frank Matricardi, the Jersey mobster who ran the Cosa Nova, had a real thing about human trafficking on his patch. So these particular kidnappers had, in the words of the head of the Family, been the subject of an *involuntary business merger* with Cosa Nova's waste management brand. Ultimately, their remains joined the ceaseless pre-Fall stream of garbage that flowed from New York City towards landfills in other states. Risky had been part of Matricardi's crew, first as an ornament, and later as a partner. They hadn't loved each other, but there'd been mutual respect, especially at the end.

After which she'd had the pleasure of killing Matricardi's murderer herself.

"Well, we've got all those patch kits just sitting there..." said Jim Kaplan, "Kapman" to his close friends. "Let's draw a little blood, shall we?"

The former Ranger—Green Beret, "unit name redacted—no such record exists"—trooper had been a security specialist inside Bank of the Americas' pandemic survival plan. Now he was one of the trusted enforcers living in the safe house along the Charles River, just west of Newport News. He stretched towards a kit bag, but stopped when his boss waved him off. Kaplan rubbed his sore leg instead. Three months on, and the gunshot wound he'd picked up on the way out of the maelstrom that had been the fall of New York remained only partially healed.

Risky had been teaching him yoga, of all things, so his flexibility was coming back, but he walked with a limp.

Tom Smith, the leader of this cheerful little band, squatted to look over the wild-eyed schoolteacher. She glared back silently, red-rimmed eyes perched above a duct tape smile.

"We've only got so many of the test kits," Tom said, shaking his head ruefully. "She doesn't have any secondary symptoms, so I think that she's just crackers for a bit."

Risky looked over from trussing the teacher around the knees. Tom noted that she was a dab hand with the rope.

His plan, *the plan*, Plan Zeus, had not included schoolteachers, or their students. His team was already supposed to be at one of Bank of the Americas' carefully sited and prepared long-term recovery centers. In *his* plan, they were supposed to be coordinating with surviving national authorities and reestablishing the economic framework that would keep their country alive. In *his* plan, there were supplies, communications, doctors, security, everything that a well-funded investment bank could lay hands on.

That *plan* . . . wasn't.

Instead, the former Managing Director for Security and Emergency Response for BotA was here, stranded with a motley collection of survivors, most of whom had never worked together, lacked formal training and, as they'd just experienced, were still dealing with the emotional shock and isolation of being trapped while all about them the United States, indeed the world, writhed in the final death throes of the deadly global plague.

"Let's see if I'm right," Tom said, visually inspecting Bua's hands and face. They'd learned the hard way about the dangers of a member of their party succumbing to the deadly symptoms of the zombie virus. He kept watching Bua, who'd closed her eyes and started breathing in a more controlled manner. "If she starts itching like crazy, or foaming at the mouth we'll try a test kit. Otherwise, we conserve what we have. We may need them soon enough and there's no way to get more."

He turned to survey the rest of his little band.

"You're going to have a black eye," Kaplan was saying as he looked at the other schoolteacher. He activated a pen light and shone it across his patient's face. "She tagged you pretty good. Let's see."

Emily Bloome might have been an educator too, but that was nearly all that she had in common with her shell-shocked fellow. Bua, Bloome and some of their students had been nearly run over by Tom's convoy as it had barreled to safety through rogue NYC cops, turncoat mobsters and thickening crowds of infected. Tom had watched her master her fear, keeping her focus on her three young charges. Even during the bad nights in their hideaway, she'd been an emotional stalwart, comforting the kids and organizing quiet activities.

She lowered her hand from her reddened eye, brushed a wing of dark hair back over one ear and glared at the bug-eyed woman next to her on the carpet.

"What the hell, Dina!" Bloome exclaimed, exhaling sharply. Then she looked at the her kids, cowering in the opposite corner of the room. She tried to reassure them, saying, "It's okay guys, Miss Dina is just scared."

The kids didn't relax. They'd seen people turn before and had a perfectly rational fear of being close to a possibly incipient cannibal.

"She's a fucking nutter," flatly stated Astroga. Cathe Astroga was one of the three National Guardmen who'd joined Smith's rag-tag band at the last concert in New York City on the night that the lights went out for the last time. The Army specialist casually slipped a taser back into her cargo pocket. "Damn, I wanted to see if these things still worked. Battery operated, you know."

"Astro, lay off, and go inventory," said Sergeant Copley wearily, too tired to muster the usual NCO discipline needed to corral his irrepressible subordinate. "I'll help."

A seasoned veteran of the wars in Afghanistan and Iraq, Copley had led the patrol that fought alongside the bank team. He'd been glad of the help of Smith's specialists as well as the extended Smith clan.

"C'mon," he added, standing to go into the other room. "Let's go."

The stocky sergeant chivvied the Specialist out the door in front of him. She paused at the doorway to give Bua a long meaningful look while patting her pocket.

Tom ignored the byplay, which he'd learned was the safest course when dealing with Astroga, who was the junior surviving representative of the U.S. Army and self-proclaimed "Global Leader of the E-4 Mafia." After they filed out, Tom remained squatting on his haunches. He looked at Bua.

"Dina," he said, getting her attention. "Hey!"

She opened her eyes and looked at him.

"Will you behave if I pull that tape off?" he asked, striving for nonthreatening sincerity. "I'll listen to everything you say, promise. I'll even untie enough rope to make you comfortable while we wait to see if this is just nerves. But you have to talk normally, no yelling. What do you say?"

"Mmmmmpf! Mwwwwwwwp-hmmmhmmmmmmn! Rumpfh Huuu! Rumpfh Huuu!"

"Yeah, that doesn't sound like a simple yes," Tom replied, glancing around. "Kap, give me a hand and we can drag her to the dining room where she can relax and we can still keep an eye on her. Check on her in a half an hour or so."

"Sure thing, Boss," Kaplan replied, but caught his eye and shot a glance at the back door. "After, let's talk."

"Now we're talking!" exclaimed the bearded scavenger as he pulled open a family room cupboard.

"Whatcha got, Ricky?" his companion said, sticking his head into the formerly well-appointed kitchen. Both ignored the drying corpse that sprawled in the breakfast nook, partially eaten. From the look of things, it was mostly smaller animals that had been at it. Experience had taught them it was usually the family dog.

"Top shelf! Some sealed bottles of whiskey, rum and some other stuff," Ricky said, and laid his pump shotgun on the brown swirls of the granite countertop, scratching the smooth finish. "Here, hold this open, wouldja, Freddo?"

"Dunno man," the second man replied, itching his own patchy facial hair. "Boss was pretty clear. First sweep is still going on for live ones and any zombies."

"Just one for a nip later then," Ricky said, selecting an engraved bottle. "I'll just grab a—"

"Wouldn't do that. He'll know," Freddo said confidently. "You saw what he did to the other guy."

"He didn't do anything. He didn't have to. That fucking ogre did it," Ricky said darkly.

"Same thing," came the reply. "You break the rules, I ain't gonna cover for you."

"Okay, okay," said the taller man, conceding the point. He shoved a few bottles back in the cabinet, leaving the others on the counter. "I'll come back for these when we do a proper gleaning. Let's clear the upstairs."

As they moved to the landing they heard a quiet rustle. Ricky put a hand up, and paused. Then he dashed upstairs to find a small dog bristling at him.

"Shit, just a dog," he said, casually raising his weapon and shooting the animal. Ricky didn't have formal training. Unlike the Hollywood fiction that perpetuated shotguns' reputations as "street sweepers," the weapons still required careful aim. His was bad enough that the shot didn't kill the pet outright. Instead, he nearly missed and only a single pellet struck home, severing the animal's spine. The resulting squealing from the mortally injured pet was piercing. Before he could shoot again a small form blurred out of a doorway and bounced off his knee.

"Don't you hurt Muffie!"

Ricky screamed, and short-stroked the shotgun, so that when he tried to shoot, he was treated to the loudest sound in any gunfight.

A resounding click.

Freddo made a long arm and plucked the child off his friend's leg. Despite being outmassed by a factor of five, the little red-headed boy made a creditable attempt to defend his pet. The kicking and gouging persisted even as the older man pinned him to the wall with one gloved hand.

"Settle down!" ordered Freddo, giving the little boy a quick shake. "Shut that dog up, will you?!"

Ricky quickly stepped on the small dog's head with one heavy boot, cutting off the noise.

"Damn, he scared the shit out of me," Ricky panted, bent over, one hand on the wall.

"I could tell, from the manly war cry you let out," Freddo said chuckling. "Nah, this kid's just scared. Maybe not as scared as you."

"Fuck you, Freddo," the scavenger replied, still panting. "Thought he was a zombie!"

"And if he was, you'd be dead now," Freddo said crossly, even as his arm shook with the continuing struggle of the child. He turned his attention to the captive. "Come on now, quiet!"

"Take him outside to the truck. He's a keeper," Ricky said. "I'll wait here for you to come back and we can finish the house."

Before Freddo could get all the way downstairs with his screaming, fighting captive, the front door swung open with a squeal. A very tall, very broad man entered, ducking his head under the frame. Freddo wasn't an Army guy, so he didn't know the names of all the guns that the newcomer wore, but he could count, and there were at least four.

The black submachine gun the man carried was dwarfed in his grip. His bulk was augmented by a very modern black plate-carrier from which hung an assortment of professionally appropriate equipment. Two large pistols were chest mounted in Kydex holsters. A handle for a long, wide-bladed knife, nearly the length of a machete, was balanced by the stock of a pistol grip shotgun that rose above the opposite shoulder. A matte black cranial helmet framed a pair of eyes so dark that they matched the black utilities that were the uniform of the uppermost tier of guards in their outfit.

He briefly locked eyes with Freddo. The big man's racial heritage wasn't obvious, apart from clearly being descended from mountain trolls. He considered the two irregulars and their squirming captive before scanning the rest of the room.

Noting an absence of any immediate threat, he stood to one side to make room for the next man.

Behind him strode a figure who looked small only in comparison to the monster that preceded him. He wore mud colored body armor over khaki trousers and a blue windbreaker. He bore a shoulder slung submachine gun and holstered pistol, but his hands were filled with a notebook and pen. Freddo knew the man only as Mr. Green. Green had captured him, recruited him, and given him a job.

Mr. Green also made the rules.

Freddo could tell that Mr. Green was an educated man. The fancy words, the organization, the regulations, all of it, were things that Freddo could never duplicate, but he also knew that every pack needed a leader. He couldn't easily articulate his reasoning but he was bright enough to know that his best chance in the current world of shit was to join the best pack under the smartest alpha-dog that he could find.

Green was smart enough for all of them. But he wasn't merely intelligent. The dispassionate look on Green's face as he glanced at Freddo, Ricky and their captive reminded the looter of a term his granddaddy had used to describe the local sheriff, renowned for his skill at catching—or dispatching—criminals.

A killing man.

"What was the shot?" demanded Green.

"Just a dog, sir," replied Freddo. "This kid's pet."

"Ah, very good," said Green, spying the new captive. "Give him to Loki here and continue the sweep."

"Uh, sir?" Ricky asked from the top of the staircase while Freddo gladly passed his struggling captive to the much taller bodyguard. "Why do we want kids? I mean, he's too young for the recreation hall, even for thems as like boys. And he's too small for useful work."

"Did I ask for questions?" replied Green. "Negative. When I want your questions, you'll hear me ask for them. Got that?"

"Uh, yessir," Ricky said carefully. "I didn't mean nuthin' by it."

"I guess you didn't," Green replied. "But I'm in a good mood, so I'll let you have your explanation. Your job's to clear houses. My job is to do the thinking. Do a good enough job and you get vaccine. Eventually. Continue to deliver and you get additional rewards. Don't . . . well, Mr. Loki or one of the Guard will do for you. Do I need to make an example to help you remember?"

The giant's eyes glinted when he heard his own name and he looked directly at Freddo.

Freddo gulped and backed up the stairs, something preventing him from willingly turning his back to Loki.

"No sir, definitely not!"

Green glanced about the room again. The damned alcohol bottles that Ricky had lined up on the counter stood out like a sore thumb.

Green favored both of his looters with a final knowing look and stepped back outside, followed by his hulking shadow.

The boy was fighting more feebly now, suspended at arm's length from one of Loki's ham-sized fists.

Risky watched Smith and Kaplan ease outside before she looked in on her wrestling partner. Bua was lying quietly on her side, still secured at the wrists, elbows, knees and ankles with sturdy rope. The teens were pointedly ignoring the tied-up teacher in the next room, and instead were clustered around Bloome, playing some card game on the beige carpet.

Risky stretched, easing the residual strain of wrestling with a potential infected. Her experience in the bank's Biological Emergency Response Teams had taught her that she could expect soreness once the adrenaline wore off. Until the pandemic struck, she'd been limited to a mostly decorative role as the "girlfriend" of the head of the Jersey-based Cosa Nova. However, thanks to her old boss's keen eye, she'd been seconded to the bank as part of a complicated four-way deal that saw BotA, city government, cops and the mob cooperate in an attempt to keep the lights on in New York City. Matricardi had spotted an opportunity to get closer to the head of the bank's head of security and sent her to do it.

Risky had immediately known that Tom Smith was no fool. The man hadn't required instructions and simple diagrams to understand why the Cosa Nova boss had sent Risky as his liaison. The obvious chemistry between them that neither dared to acknowledge was just, how-you-say, icing on the cakes.

Risky knew that Smith's world was now upside down. She also knew that she was a piece that didn't fit perfectly into his post-apocalyptic scenario. He'd made ruthless decisions in an instant when he had to, in order to save as much as he could for his own employer.

She snorted.

Bank of the Americas was—had been—as dangerous as any gang. They'd been the ones who'd started the unsanctioned harvesting of spinal tissue from infected humans. The resulting vaccine was just another part of Smith's plan.

She'd also seen Smith behave with grace, when he could afford to. The kids next door were one example. The fact that Bua was still breathing was another. Speaking of which, her shoulder was getting tight now. She stretched again, moving both shoulders deliberately, loosening her muscles while straining her T-shirt.

Across the room, she noticed Vinnie "Mouse Sacks" Dingatelli, one of the two surviving goons from Cosa Nova, glance away from her tightened clothing, guilty as hell.

Even though they'd worked for the same man before, she wasn't going to fully trust him anytime soon. To be fair he hadn't had a hand in the murder of the last boss of the Cosa Nova. As long as he followed Smith's lead, same as everyone else, she'd let him live.

However, Risky had kept the RPK that had done for Matricardi's traitorous second-in-command, and made sure that everyone knew it.

Bua moaned slightly, arresting the moll's attention.

She was pretty sure by now that the teacher wasn't infected. What she was, was scared. Lost. Without any foundation. Lonely.

Human things.

As good as Smith was at plans, he could lose sight of the human problems that were at the heart of everything. Not everyone was a soldier, corporate or otherwise.

She grabbed a windbreaker from the peg next to the door and headed outside to join the first two.

∾⊖∾

After a companionable silence, Tom got to the point.

"Okay," he said, facing his companion squarely. "What's on your mind, Kap?"

"Weather's turning, getting cooler," Kaplan replied. After a glance around the property, Kaplan returned his boss's look. "People are getting cooler too."

"We've had this conversation, Kap," Tom said, suppressing his obvious irritation.

"Tom, it's me, okay?" Kaplan replied earnestly. "You pay me for my opinions and I'm telling you that we can't stay here. It's not a smart play."

"What am I paying you with, again?" replied the taller man, flashing a wry grin. "I'll double it!"

No one had gotten paid since the Fall.

"The finest scavenged, room temperature Red Bull in all the land," Kaplan said, sharing the joke. Then he stepped closer, directly in front of his boss, and kept his voice low. "You know what I mean. Stop evading."

"There isn't exactly a playbook for this situation, Kap," the taller man said, folding his arms. "We were *supposed* to be at one of the refuge sites before everything went. We were *supposed* to have more and better situated refuges, for that matter. We weren't supposed to be marooned three hundred miles from the nearest long-term hide out, saddled with civilians and kids! Kids for chroissake!"

Like his subordinate, Tom kept his voice low. His sharp gestures and a hint of the Australian accent communicated his keen frustration as clearly as though he had yelled aloud.

"How soon can we move?" he continued. "Depends on the infected count and the road conditions. How far can we recce? Fuel's limited. This is a pile of piss, Kaplan! Zeus was never supposed to devolve this far!"

It wasn't their first time through this discussion. Each knew his lines.

"How far can we trust Fat Ralph and Sacks?" Kaplan said, naming the two former gangsters Tom had elected to keep alive despite the treachery of their former boss. A boss who had succeeded Matricardi as the surviving head of the Cosa Nova.

Briefly.

"How many supplies can we afford to use on scouting before we don't have enough to make it to Blue? The questions are a nested set of unknowns, Boss. I get it. I do. So does Gravy," he said, referring to Dave "Gravy" Durante, the second Bank security specialist and the only other member of the team that Tom trusted implicitly.

Kaplan turned so that they both faced the estuary, lowering his voice further.

"But I don't think that we can keep this entire group in this little house until first snowfall. That's what you're thinking, right?"

"It's still a solid idea, Kap," Tom replied, raising one hand in a frustrated wave. "Zombies might be scary cannibals that swarm in big numbers, but they're still just humans, most of them without clothes. Without tools and cooperative behaviors humans are remarkably fragile, slow, blind and easy to kill. Wait until winter and let the cold kill some and drive the rest into shelter. We'll have the road to ourselves and we can be at Site Blue in two, maybe three days. Week at the outside."

"We don't have that long," Risky's voice sounded behind them. Both men jumped.

"God-*damnit*, don't do that!" Kaplan said. Then he almost fumbled his first attempt to reholster the pistol that had appeared in his hand.

"We don't have anything like that long," Risky said, ignoring his comment and the gun. "And it's not so much about what's in cabin as what's outside."

"I'm listening," Tom said flatly. After the initial surprise, he hadn't reacted to her quiet approach.

Although he acknowledged Oldryskya's role in saving their collective skins, he'd elected to keep her at an arm's distance despite . . . everything. She'd run out on Tom's team before, prior to the Fall. Later she'd fought her way free of a kidnapping as the Cosa Nova mob devolved into fratricide. A happy side benefit was that she'd been able to return their stolen escape boat, but she was still an outsider whose first allegiance wasn't clear.

"The reason that schoolteacher is losing mind is because she doesn't see the point," Risky said, choosing her words carefully. She was conversational in English, despite it being a third language for her, or fourth if one counted "Jersey mobster" as its own dialect. "If everyone's dead, if it's really all gone, then why stay inside, why bother to live? Simple survival not enough."

"Simple survival looks pretty good, considering the alternative,"

Tom retorted. "We wait long enough for the cooler temps to drive most of the infected indoors, then we get to the refuge, take stock and, well..."

There was a brief silence.

"That's the point," Kaplan said. Rhetoric and allegory wasn't his strong suit, but he was trying. "You done good, Boss. Your plans, your vision got us out of a really bad spot. We're here, we're fed and safe, mostly. Out of sixty million people between Boston and Atlanta, how many can say that? Damn few. But being alive lets you think about what comes next. And what comes next is... well, suppose we get to the refuge. Then what?"

"We do our jobs," Tom said insistently, raising both hands in the air. "The mission is get to the Site, assess, protect and rebuild. That's what we do. Mind you, just getting there is enough to occupy us. Travel at day or night? Scavenge along the way? Do we bring trade goods? Where will survivors have clustered? Do we dare approach anyone? There are plenty of problems to solve, Kap."

"Biggest problem of all you don't mention," Risky wasn't going to be derailed. "Everyone needs a reason to live. Before, maybe it was money, or having family or making art. Those reasons don't matter anymore, not if everything is gone. Is all gone, yes?"

The conditions of the Fall had been clearly visible during their escape. The failing TV and radio broadcasts were plain. After a week or two, and by general agreement, the survivors had agreed to avoid talking about their families or what lay outside.

"Yeah," Tom said. He rolled one shoulder, stretching it as much to relieve his stress as loosen the an old injury. Then he looked towards the sluggish estuary that was slowly oozing by, ferrying the occasional bloated corpse to the Atlantic. "I think that it might be. Oh, there'll be small groups of survivors in lots of places. But organized government? I doubt that there's anything more than isolated military units, submarines for example. Probably military command centers like Cheyenne Mountain. Maybe even some science outposts, like McMurdo maybe."

"Nah," Kaplan replied, shaking his head. "Last transmission on the ten-meter from the Beeb said that infections were confirmed there."

McMurdo Station, far away in the Antarctic, had been one of the last scientific redoubts to go dark. Many hopes had been pinned on isolated groups of scientists who tried to produce a vaccine or a cure, laboring until the last lights were extinguished. How the disease had infiltrated a research station during the heart of Antarctic winter was just another mystery that would have to remain unsolved until the immediate challenge of survival was overcome.

"Ten meters?" asked Risky.

"A radio band, good for long distance," Tom answered. "In the right conditions, you can communicate thousands of miles with good gear and a school-taught comms guy. Something else we planned for but don't have. We have a couple of transceivers, but..."

All three fell silent. Listening to the number of active radio stations dwindle had been hard. A few times they had caught a last sign off as journalists or amateurs bid an empty channel goodbye. And good luck.

A long ululating howl sounded across the water.

"Hunter," Kap said dryly. "Best we get out of sight."

Their little house was tucked into trees well back from the creek. Tom had foreseen the need for waystations for any bank stragglers on the way to the long-term refuges. He had borrowed from his military training to find Selected Areas For Escape, or SAFEs. These were locations where the survivors could evade detection more easily, though they weren't truly *safe*. Their current house in coastal Virginia was completely shielded from the nearest road and the drive was blocked by heavy brush and ditches. During the first few weeks, car engines and a few boats had been audible. Then, occasional screams.

Tom had kept everyone inside until lately, and even now he sharply limited outside excursions. The competition for the external guard duty that rotated among the reliable members of their party was fierce.

The last month had been quiet, except for the hunt. Warm weather, mosquitoes and hunger kept the infected in motion. Like schools of sharks, the bands would be composed of relatively healthy zombies of the same approximate size. They seemed to prey on livestock, humans, pets, and occasionally each other.

"There's got to be a better reason, Tom," Risky said, motioning towards the dark water that oozed past. "Just being alive and leaving the world to that, it isn't enough to keep us together."

"I'll think about it," replied Tom.

"We'll all think about it," added Kaplan.

∽─⊖─∾

Sergeant "Worf" Copley was in a strange place. Oh, the SAFE wasn't bad as accommodations went. The actual immediate tactical environment wasn't too unusual in his experience.

Unconventional chain of command complete with admin pogues in charge? Yep.

Strap-hangers and civilians underfoot. Meh. You ever seen an embedded CNN camera crew?

Bitched up supply situation. It happens.

Living in cramped communal quarters for an extended period. The Army called that an ordinary Tuesday.

It was how he and his sole remaining subordinate had arrived here that was some next level bullshit. You could call it a long, strange trip, but that would be a charming understatement.

The experienced National Guard staff sergeant had been out of communication with higher since the harum-scarum withdrawal from Washington Square Park, shooting and meleeing infected all the way back to Bank of the Americas, where they found a no-shit for-real command post on Wall Street. *Wall-fucking-Street*! Then, marooned out of contact with higher, he'd directly negotiated a deal for vaccine with the civilian in charge—an action so far above his pay grade that he still had a nosebleed. Then he'd helped run a noncombatant evacuation from a twenty-million-dollar Park Avenue property, while keeping Specialist "I mean—it's a Faberge egg and it's just *sitting* there, Sergeant!" Astroga from helping herself to the semi-abandoned baubles in the mansions. Then he got into a running gun fight with cops and the FBI.

The F-fucking-B-fucking-I. Who, as it turned out, had fucking Stinger anti-air missiles, *because of course they did*!

Worf hadn't had the time to worry about shooting cops, but at least the moral quandary was clear. They'd been making a very sincere effort to shoot Mrs. Copley's little boy before he could return the favor. On that basis alone he just fought to keep himself and his little team alive. Finally, before he had time to process that fracas, there'd been another, rather one sided firefight at the docks, where Astroga had gotten shot. Her armor kept the rounds out, thank god.

It was nearly as much combat time as he had from two OIF deployments, combined. And about as satisfying.

About like a visit to the latrine on day six of an all MRE spreadable cheese diet—a lot of strain for very little output.

The Russian girl, Khabayeva, had saved all their asses, though. Then off they had gone, hey diddle diddle on a long ass boat trip. During the all night over-water transit Copley had been too damn tired to think it all through. Once he had made certain that Astroga was as comfortable as she could be with her bruised ribs, he had deployed his woobie and chimped down for nearly the entire boat ride.

Now they were in the bank's hideout.

At first, just the relief of being out of New York City was enough. Worf and the little band of bank survivors had lain up within a relatively short distance of a major naval base and listened to the VHF harbor traffic as ship after ship punched out, the fleet surging seaward as though it could outrun the land-based plague. Enough transmissions made it clear that the virus was already at sea.

He tried to imagine how he would fight zombies in a big steel squid bin. Pity those bastards.

Over in the corner, the tied-up schoolteacher had quieted. It was a classic case of freakout, no H7D3 virus required.

Astroga was chatting quietly with one of the schoolkids, and was kibbitzing their cards. Despite her unrecalcitrant pseudo-E4 attitude, Cathe Astroga had a surprisingly helpful manner with the young teens. Decent kids and their good attitudes had made it easy to like them.

Worf walked over to the wall and reapplied himself to the map pinned there. Even after a good long stare, none of their routes away from the SAFE looked particularly good.

"Whatcha doing?" Astroga said from his elbow, materializing suddenly. She called it one of her super powers.

"You know, you're gonna do that to some new NCO one day, and their gonna lose their shit," he answered, entirely too used to her little ways. "But, what I'm doing is looking at routes west. Sooner or later we have to drive out of here and it's going to be a mess."

"Big highway right there," the young private said, helpfully stabbing a finger at the blue line representing I-64. "Should take us west, no?"

"No," Copley replied seriously. "Think, Astro. Hampton Roads used to have more than a million and a half people and the only highway out is a two-lane interstate. It's going to be a parking lot of stopped cars. What we need are side roads. What we gotta do is stay away from anything but really small towns."

He tapped the indigo push pin almost three hundred miles west.

"Figure a week plus to get to Site Blue, maybe more," he said musingly, while considering another local road that was marked in a dashed line. "Maybe a lot more."

"Hey, Worf?" Astroga asked in a surprisingly small voice. "You figure that Gunner is gonna be there waiting, right?"

The last thing they had seen of Sergeant "Gunner" Randall, the third member of their New York city "presence" patrol, he'd been boarding one of the last helos scheduled to leave from the top floor of the bank. One bird had been shot down by an FBI Stinger. The resulting fireball had crashed back onto the roof, destroying a second aircraft still spooling up on the pad. They'd hoped that Gunner was in the one that got away.

They had to believe it.

"Hundred percent," Copley said, forcing a smile. "He made it, sure. He and that bank intel guy Rune are probably living the life of Riley in a camp full of high bred banker chicks, right?"

Astroga carefully did not sniff.

"Yeah, the lucky bastard."

CHAPTER 2

Site Blue (Bank Recovery Site Number Four)
Blue Ridge Mountains, Western Virginia

Paul was walking the perimeter.

His daily routine varied between leading patrols outside the wire, performing nighttime light discipline checks or pulling maintenance on their limited supply of equipment. There were other members of the ad hoc security team, even a few whose experience approached his, that could have performed the chore. Nonetheless, he always found time to stroll watchfully along the internal fenceline. It helped him maintain a sense of proportion. As tough as it was, things could have been worse.

He paused as the screams of a hunting pack carried across the valley. After the sound died he resumed his route.

Even though Site Blue, named for the Blue Ridge Mountains, had not been completed by the time of the Fall, it had begun with some clear advantages. Those advantages had been critical to preserving the smaller than expected group that sheltered there.

Site Blue was situated on the finger of a ridge overlooking a small lake, fed by a tributary of the Tennessee River. The land was anything but flat. The southern end of the Cumberland Valley was dominated by lines of steep, parallel ridges that were separated by cultivated land and small towns. Situated near the top of one such ridge, the site benefited from the elevation. Foraging zombies were disinclined to climb it and other survivors couldn't see their camp unless they were right on top of it.

Paul paused his walk and rubbed his smooth scalp. For the

moment his supply of disposables was holding out, but eventually he was going to have to figure out how to use a straight razor or let his hair grow back.

He looked over his shoulder, to where the camp blended into the hilltop. The earthen berm that was arranged like a horseshoe around the main facility dated to the origin of the camp as an old Scout lodge. As a result, there was a natural obstacle that prevented direct line of sight into the center of the camp. This reduced the chance of a light leak being detected from outside their hideaway at night.

Beyond the berm was a new narrow link-expandable fence. More expensive than chain-link, it was harder to climb. The bank prep team had placed it inside a treeline a few hundred yards from the berm. It constituted their first layer of barrier defense.

In the camp itself, a few buildings had been updated, though none were especially large or modern. The white painted communal eating hall had started life as the Scouts' cafeteria, so it included enough seating for three times their current number. The workshop was a converted barn that still had a packed dirt floor. The administration building had been a sales office, intended to sell the camp off in lots after the Scout facility closed for good. A long, low prefabricated building served as their warehouse, stuffed with more than a hundred pallets of FEMA meals, the civilian version of the military's reviled Meals Ready to Eat or MRE. It had taken less than a week for the survivors to rehash every MRE joke in existence.

A small collection of solar panels generated intermittent power sufficient to keep a bank of deep cycle marine batteries mostly charged. With those, limited electric lighting was permitted inside spaces with blackout curtains. Rows of tan Containerized Housing Units, or CHUs, were neatly arranged along gravel lanes just broad enough to accommodate a vehicle. BotA had found a literal shipload and acquired them for less than disposal cost during the American withdrawal as the wars in Iraq and Afghanistan wound down.

His old boss, Tom Smith, had sworn that they'd find a use for them, eventually. And so they had.

The full complement of bank staff had never been assigned since Blue was the least prepared of Bank of the Americas' refuges. The formal management structure that Smith had planned was never stood up. Since few of the senior bankers who were to be evacuated to Blue had arrived, the onsite survivors had created an ad hoc council to provide a way to organize the camp, apportioning work, distributing supplies and enforcing the rules that kept them all safe. As the senior-most surviving bank security representative, Paul attended both the informal daily morning breakfast coordination meeting as well as the bigger weekly Sunday get together.

He glanced back towards the camp, but it was still safely dark.

Zombies tracked light sources. So did other survivors. Both were dangerous.

Careful to avoid silhouetting himself against the skyline, Paul approached a short rise downhill from the fence and looked out, across the valley.

The dying light drew long shadows across his fields of view. No electric lights were visible anywhere. Humans instinctively feared the night. The infected, unless baited by artificial light or prey activity, tended to quiet down and stay near shelter during night hours. It was daylight that brought the greatest threat from zombies.

He sighed as he turned his steps back into the camp. The weekly meeting was in a few minutes. Paul had insisted on deferring major decisions until more bank staff showed up and, because of his role at the bank, he had gotten his way. After several weeks, however, he had begun considering the possibility that neither Smith nor anyone else was going to show.

Paul had spent all his time putting out fires, adjudicating minor disagreements, checking on critical supplies while trying to find things for the other survivors to do in order to keep them busy.

There were too many little crises every day. He'd been forced to ask one of the non-bank refugees for assistance. He knew entirely too much about Joanna Kohn to be comfortable around her. Formerly the director of NYC Office of Emergency Management, she'd been one quarter of the informal but powerful council that had coordinated efforts between the cops, Wall Street, the gangs and the City government. Apart from the locals in the camp, she'd built the next largest group of organized staff and had sufficient stature to make their joint decisions stick.

Despite her calculating nature, Paul had to acknowledge that it was her warning about the cops losing their minds that had let as many bank staff escape on what became the last day of New York.

The first day of the Fall.

Working with Kohn, whom he knew to be a murderer, wasn't his first choice. Or his fifty-first choice.

None of this was.

Paul knew that he was going to have to come up with something sooner or later. Maybe when things were more settled.

"Calm down, everyone," Tom instructed. "That means you too, kids."

Astroga used a gentle head chop to get the attention of a tow haired teen named Katrin. Worf looked on approvingly.

The three amigos, as Astroga had labeled them, continued to bounce back from the early terror of the escape from Manhattan. Katrin Jonsdottir was the obvious ringleader, her second was dark haired, crew-cutted Eric Swanson, and the last was Cheryl Blaine, a quiet redhead.

"I wanted all of us to hear this, so I even pulled in the usual guard," Tom said, referring to the twenty-four hour guard duty that rotated among the competent adults. "We've been waiting here for the situation to settle down, get clearer. The initial confusion, the explosion of infected and the breakdown of civil government has paused, or at least not gotten worse in the last month. So . . . it's time to tell you what I think we should do next."

"Are you going to be in charge forever?" Dina folded her arms petulantly across her chest. She'd calmed down a few hours after her break, but hadn't forgiven anyone for leaving her restrained for so long. "When do we get to vote? This is still a democracy, isn't it?"

"Okay, let's address that first," Tom replied. "There's no more United States, as we knew it. There's, as far as we can tell from here, no one left in charge anywhere. For the time being, the survivors in this little band have accepted that we need someone to be in charge and that I'm that someone. I'm not going to call for votes on every important decision. If you don't like that, I'll not stop anyone from leaving. However, I'll make the rules and my trusted team will enforce them." He paused and looked directly at Bua. "So, no. This isn't a democracy."

"Who says?" demanded the schoolteacher. "What kind of dictatorship is this? I have rights!"

"In order of your questions..." began Tom, "they say so."

He gestured to the little group of Bank of the Americas' staff.

Durante nodded and Kaplan smiled toothily. Risky and Copley flanked them, grim faced. All were fully armed.

"Hey, I do say so too," offered Astroga, looking up from her ever-present green notebook. "What he said."

"And no, you don't have any rights," Tom said, continuing with surprising gentleness. "None of us do. There are no cops. There aren't any courts. Civil rights, enforced by courts and policed by law enforcement, simply don't exist, at least for now. But, we can be responsible to each other. Or not."

He answered Bua forthrightly. "Do you want to leave?"

"I want to get out of here, yeah," Dina said, sniffing. "But doing anything alone is suicide and you know that."

"And that's the point," replied Tom, sighing. He looked around the rest of the room. The kids were clustered around Emily while Dina had segregated herself in a corner. "We've survived thus far by exercising discretion and patience. We aren't going to overcome our next set of problems using just superior firepower."

"Ha," Fat Ralph snorted. The youngest of the remaining Cosa Nova gangsters had been trying to fit in, but whether he was an asset or a liability remained a question. "There is no overkill, there's—"

"Yeah, yeah, we know the quote, Ralph," Durante said. "It comes from a comic strip. If that's where you get your tactical doctrine it explains why there's only two of you guys left."

Durante was the second of Tom's special hires, and his military resume was even more redacted than Kaplan's. Before the Fall, he'd been part of the original Biological Emergency Response Team, or BERT, that Bank of the Americas had fielded under Tom's leadership. Locating and capturing the infected that they needed had become routine. The actual "harvest"—extracting the still warm spinal tissue needed for manufacturing the attenuated live-virus vaccine production—hadn't.

But Tom, Kaplan and Durante had persisted, and trained others, like the NYPD.

And Ralph's old boss, the former head of the Cosa Nova organization.

Ralph subsided. His surviving friend, Vinnie Mouse Sacks, laughed quietly. Sacks, as he was previously known, never passed up a chance to stick it to someone else, perhaps because he had not yet escaped the insulting nickname that his old boss had stuck to him. Both men had mostly recovered from the gunshot wounds they had suffered during the fighting in the City.

"Moving on . . . the plan broadly is this," Tom resumed smoothly, and tapped a map of the southeastern U.S. "Our goal is to reach Bank of the Americas' Site Blue. It lies in Tennessee, four hundred miles west of our current location. Site Blue should have a large number of bank survivors. It'll have much more room, it's defensible and there should be some communications equipment. There should also be people that we can trust already there. Halfway there we'll try to stop at a place where I hope some of my friends are holed up, basically another SAFE, sort of like this one. I certainly don't intend to walk, so we are taking the two Suburbans that were cached here and will keep our eyes out for another vehicle."

He paused and used one finger to trace the route west.

"There are highways nearly the entire way, but . . ." he tapped the closest medium-sized city, Petersburg, and then a few others that lay westwards. ". . . they're close to population centers so we shouldn't expect that they will be passable."

He scanned his audience, reading hope in some faces, fear in others. "His" team kept their game faces on.

"Questions so far?" Tom offered.

"Is next SAFE also for Bank of the Americas?" Risky asked.

"No, it's a private connection, a sort of personal real estate investment from before," Tom said.

"I've got one," Emily said, tentatively raising her hand. "Can we vaccinate the kids?"

"That's a question, all right," Tom replied with pursed lips. "As some of you know, and the rest guessed, we have vaccine. What we don't have is a doctor who can evaluate if younger kids can tolerate the kind of vaccine that we've got. It isn't recommended for children because the vaccine contains attenuated live virus. It made my thirteen-year-old niece very ill, and she's about the same age as the kids with us. Also, we've been keeping the case cold using the vehicle batteries, but I don't know how long the vaccine will be good for. A competent doctor could tell us—and that is another reason to get to Site Blue."

"I got another, Boss," Durante said. "Day or night?"

"What Gravy means is whether we travel in the daytime or the nighttime." Tom nodded at Durante. "The answer is that we can do either, but there are pros and cons. Zombies and uninfected humans rely primarily on their vision. Night vision isn't magic, and performance of the goggles varies. You can still only see so far. The farther we can see, the more advance warning we have about a potential danger then the more time we'll have to decide when to push and when to run. And at night, any uninfected adversary will have an advantage, since we'll be moving into their space. At night we have less warning. Our natural advantage is that we're still thinkers and problem solvers while the infected aren't. I intend to use that. Thus we'll move during the day. We've got a few sets of night vision devices but batteries and spare parts are a question so we save them for emergencies."

"When do we leave?" piped up Risky.

"Day after tomorrow," Tom replied easily, "so start packing your personal gear, but pack light. Kaplan, you're on comms and navigation. Copley, food and water. Gravy, you're on weapons. Bring everything we have ammo for, including the Mk19 that we dragged here from New York."

"You sure, Boss?" Durante replied dubiously. "We've got almost no ammo for that pig, it takes forever to deploy and it's going to take up a lot of room just by itself."

"Thus, *packing light*," Tom said. "Better to have it and not need it than to need it and not have it."

"Hey, Boss!" Astroga nearly yelled, waving her hand in the air. "Really important question!"

"Oh?" Tom answered cautiously. "Go ahead."

"Road trips require music," she said. "What are the rules?"

"Oooh, music!" Katrin said enthusiastically, and started singing. "Party rock is in the house tonight! Everybody just have a good time!"

"Every day I'm shufflin'," chorused the other two middle schoolers, before standing and pumping their arms and skidding their feet on the carpet.

Astroga whipped her notebook about.

"LMFAO, check."

"Wait, what?" Copley inquired, looking back to Astroga. "No. Just no."

And the meeting ended on a higher note than Tom had expected.

∾ ⊖ ⇁

"Good evening, everyone," Joanna politely opened the meeting. "This is the second monthly anniversary of our safe exit from New York. On a terrible, terrible day, when so much went wrong, many sacrificed everything in order to evacuate as many others as possible. I propose a minute of silence to commemorate the fallen."

She bowed her head and murmurs sounded around the table as everyone else copied her example.

Joanna had carefully positioned herself in the ad hoc council from the outset, persuasively offering her experience in disaster management and recovery efforts. She'd actively pitched in at the start, but slowly withdrawn from the most demanding physical work, instead organizing the camp with the handful of other informal leaders. Camp meetings had been over attended at the start, but as the weeks passed, most staff had fallen away, tired or depressed. At this point, only a handful of bank staff still attended, and most of them were not Smith's people. All of Joanna's staff, both the old and the new, as well as some hangers-on were present.

The former head of New York Office of Emergency Management used the minute of silence to review the top points that she would bring to the others. After two months of waiting, of merely surviving, it was time to consider what their mission was to be.

And who would lead it.

Joanna had some ideas.

"Thank you," she said briskly. "We are in a strange time. While it has been necessary to gather ourselves and process what has happened, I think that we are overdue to take stock and determine what options, if any, we have. I have asked Kendra Jones, formerly of Bank of the Americas, to prepare a high level overview of just where we stand."

"Wait a minute!" Paul said, interrupting the city official. "What's this 'formerly' business. The bank is our employer. I'm the senior representative of the organization that arranged, funded and prepared this place. There is no 'formerly'!"

Joanna observed as Rune glared at Kendra and then back at Joanna herself.

"Paul, I think that your exclamation highlights the need to evaluate the situation realistically," Joanna said, gesturing with one hand up at the suddenly intense security officer. "I think that if you allow Kendra to proceed you will understand my point. Kendra, please?"

Kendra stood and riffled a sheaf of handwritten notes, avoiding meeting anyone else's eyes. Like the rest of the camp, she'd lost some weight due in part to the unavoidable food rationing. It made the angles of her face sharper.

"All right, from the top," Kendra said, with a look at Joanna, who smiled encouragingly. "Camp population is stable at ninety-six souls and we haven't had a walk-in in six weeks."

Kendra referred to the dozens of people who, attracted by the helicopter activity during the final days of the evacuation, had approached the main gate on foot or in private vehicles. By the time Paul had arrived in the last helo, they were already partially integrated into the fabric of the camp. Even more frustrating, he had been compelled to use much of their vaccine to inoculate the "walk-ins," if for no other reason than they were already inside the camp and they would be a tremendous danger should they turn. They were more than half of the camp now. Two of their leaders were present, sitting next to Kohn.

"I'll address the easy items first," Kendra referred to the next page. "Water is fine; between the well and the filtration system, we've enough water for drinking, cooking and washing. The vehicles, equipment and fuel are fine since we are only running them for brief periods to keep the batteries charged. Our communications watch reports no new transmissions and the major stations remain silent."

"Nothing at all?" asked Wilton, one of the two "walk-in" representatives.

"Nothing from any federal or state source since the start of the month," replied Kendra. "We had contact with Site Bugle during periods of ideal radio propagation through the end of September, but we haven't been in contact since."

"How hard are we trying?" the refugee demanded aggressively. "How often are we transmitting?"

"We're not transmitting," Paul replied forcefully. "During the Fall, there were hundreds, then dozens of stations all sharing information or calling for help. We still hear some stations like that but the number is steadily dropping. They've nothing to offer us nor we them, so there's no point. In order to avoid draining our batteries and to avoid getting DF'd we haven't been transmitting, on my authority."

"Dee-Effed?" Wilton said with a snort. "What the hell is that? And what authority do you have here, city boy?"

"He means that we could get found," Sergeant Cameron "Gunner" Randall spoke up, glaring at the civilian loudmouth. The tall Army National Guard had begun as a specialist, but his old patrol-mate Astroga had shotgunned some promotion paperwork when no one had been watching. Gunner had been pretty isolated since they'd landed, but nevertheless had been invaluable to Paul. Courtesy of his Army training, he was the primary radio operator. "You transmit long enough, or regularly enough, and someone else can triangulate our position and come a-calling, see?"

"Please!" Joanna said, her voice stopping the incipient argument. "Let us hear the rest of Kendra's report and then we can prioritize what we have to discuss."

"Umm," Kendra said, glancing back at her notes. "Look, there's more, but what it comes down to is food and medical. While we budgeted for more than twice our present number for a period of one year, this camp received neither the complete suite of equipment nor supplies. The initial plan included supplementing those supplies with locally sourced or internally grown crops. We aren't going to grow any meaningful amount of food until very late next spring, at the earliest. Even with our current two meals per day schedule, we'll reach spring with our long-term, shelf-stable food supplies entirely depleted."

Kendra looked around the table but there weren't many strong reactions. The basic math was already known to all present.

"Apart from basic first aid, a couple of trauma bags and the small remaining supply of vaccine, which we have to keep chilled, there are no medical supplies," Kendra said, this time looking across the table to Anderson, the OEM staffer who had begun operating an ad hoc clinic in the mornings. "We've got almost no antibiotics, no birth control, nothing beyond over the counter analgesics and no specialty trauma gear if we have a serious casualty. Worse, we don't have a qualified doctor, even though Gunner and Schweizer have some practical experience. There are currently no life threatening medical cases, but it looks like we do have several pregnancies, which thank God won't come to term till spring or later."

"Thank you, Kendra," Joanna said, and the bank analyst sank back into her seat as the OEM chief smoothly resumed control of the table and pivoted towards Rune. "Paul, as I noted at the start, it has been two months. We all recognize the amazing preparation and hard work that Bank of the Americas did to get

us here. We owe you and your team a tremendous debt, but...
there is no more OEM. And there is no more bank."

She paused for effect and then sharply rapped the table with
her knuckles.

"In fact, there may not be a government. We are on our own.
We will have to rely on what we can accomplish for ourselves for
the near future. No group of a hundred people can work efficiently
as a committee. We need to determine our own authority and
take steps to protect our little community. Does anyone disagree?"

Joanna scanned the table. She could see Rune still looking dag-
gers at his erstwhile subordinate who seemed equally determined
to not look at him.

Good.

She saw the doubt on a few new faces, but equally her private
staff appeared relaxed and confident.

Excellent.

"I propose that tonight we charter a council," Joanna declared.
"Each of our little communities will need to be represented. The
former bankers..." she gestured to Paul, "the former city staff..."
she laid a hand across her chest, "the persons from the previous
local community..." she smiled at Wilton, "...and specialists as
needed."

"I'm not saying no, Joanna," Rune said almost reluctantly as he
looked around the table and then back to her. "We need something, sure." His tone became skeptical. "What will *your* role be?"

"Someone has to help coordinate, to administrate the plan that
we all build together," Joanna said, successfully refraining from
smiling. "I am happy to serve in an acting capacity as we shake
the bugs out of our system. I would like to be able to ask for your
help. Perhaps you would consent to remain our head of security?"

She watched him think about it. He really didn't have a choice
and she knew it. He knew it too.

This was going to be fun.

"Get your ass in here, Biggs!" Loki said, holding the door for
a man with heavy facial tattoos. "You were supposed to be here
fifteen minutes ago!"

"Hey, it's all good, 'migo!" The smaller ex-con smiled ingratiat-
ingly, as he slid by, looking up at the much taller man. "Had to
sort out a little situation over at the Rec Hall, is all."

Biggs hitched suggestively at his belt as he leered at the table before hooking an office chair with his ankle and plopping into it.

"Enough!" Harlan Green ordered briskly. "This place is not a democracy. All of you took my deal. You joined our association on my terms. There will be discipline. Discipline means being on time."

Harlan ignored Biggs's prison yard patter as he consulted his wristwatch. The Patek Phillipe had a tan leather band that clashed with the adjacent bright red circlet of woven hair. He frowned and removed the watch before admiring his wrist again. Content, he then opened the notebook PC at his elbow. Around him, most of the meeting participants sat patiently.

They damned well should. They owed him their lives. Harlan had engineered the entire plan that had led to this meeting.

He'd built on his successful, initial recruiting *session* of prisoners from the State Penitentiary bus that had mysteriously crashed in a conveniently remote area. Those volunteers became his cadre, and helped with each successive round of *interviews*. With one exception, each person at the head table was a hand selected, carefully screened product of the American prison system. Not all of his initial recruits had made it this far. There had been some breakage.

One doesn't engineer a borderline catastrophic bus crash, let alone three or four, without casualties, naturally.

Speaking of which, Biggs hadn't stopped talking yet.

"Mr. Loki, if Mr. Biggs doesn't shut up by the time you draw, shoot him in the head," Harlan ordered.

Loki made a lightning draw from his chest rig and was on target a shade after Biggs's mouth clopped shut. The huge man preferred a big pistol, and his H&K Mk23 actually appeared to be a normally sized pistol in his oversized hands.

The violent elimination of one of the inner circle wasn't unknown, but no one had been culled in this manner in weeks. Everyone sat a little straighter. The men on either side of Biggs leaned away from him in involuntarily reflex.

"And if he opens his mouth again other than to answer a direct question from me," Harlan said, "you may shoot him without warning."

"Done, Mr. Green," replied Loki, his voice rumbling menacingly.

No one, and probably not any four of the inner circle, could take Loki in a straight up fight. Since Harlan had carefully avoided recruiting prisoners with shared gang affiliation or other documented ties to each other, he was confident that no one would stick their neck out for a relative stranger. By the time that they knew each other well enough for that to become possible, they would either have accepted his leadership or been *excused*.

Thus, if Biggs opened his mouth he would die.

Harlan didn't feel particularly strongly about it other way, as long as Biggs stayed quiet. None of the candidates meant to become his lieutenants meant especially much to him, apart from their utility. All of them were sociopaths; they'd been chosen for that very quality. That meant that they shared, to a certain extent, his lack of empathy for other people. However, they were also prone to rash action and could give in to their baser desires at inefficient moments.

That was fine, as long as it served his purpose. Otherwise, bang.

Replaceable.

He didn't feel bad about it, of course. They'd all been dead men in the supermax prison, so really he'd practically saved their lives, hadn't he?

From a very early date, it was obvious to Harlan that the H7D3 was a weapon. It became equally clear that the targets of the plague were broadly distributed and that barring some biological breakthrough, the disease was going to progress until it burnt its way across the entire planet. He ran some simulations through his own statistical models using datasets that he accessed somewhat *entrepreneurially*.

Yes indeed, the disease had shown every sign of winning. Harlan was a little jealous. Quite jealous.

Since it wouldn't do to be caught in the biological trap set by whoever it was, he intended to leverage the conditions surrounding the fall of the American system. That would require a team.

He would supply the brains.

The team would provide loyalty and muscle, but the right sorts.

Timing had been tricky. Too early and the law enforcement infrastructure would remain distressingly intact. Too late and both his recruits and his, well, call them his additional *conscripts* might be infected.

Once Harlan had equipped himself with sysadmin permissions

inside the Virginia Department of Corrections system, he'd scanned the general population and special holding areas of the supermax prison for candidates.

He had defined a specific profile. Sociopathic, but able to compensate somewhat. Intelligent, but not necessarily genius level. A record of some success, but not too much. Demonstrated capacity for violence tempered with control. In short, capable subordinates he could both motivate and reliably direct.

A simple Python script had narrowed thousands of names to a hundred or so. Creating prison transfer orders of those carefully selected inmates was equally straightforward.

Loki had been the real jewel. Formerly Senior Corrections Officer Gilmar Hadolfsen, his name had popped up on one of the database searches that Harlan had performed when scanning for the correctional staff that he wanted to *keep off* the transfer buses.

The senior prison guard's profile had been intriguing. His records reflected complaints of excessive force, suspicion of organizing and participating in no-holds cage fights with the prisoners and he had been the focus of several unfruitful internal affairs investigations. He had prior military service and time as a private military contractor, linked to third party rendition operations. A deeper search of his personal records and finances had strongly suggested that he was enjoying income outside the scope of his official prison salary. That degree of moral flexibility blended intriguingly with capability.

On a whim, Harlan had included him on the first set of recruits.

It turned out that they had some shared *interests*.

Which had worked out surprisingly well.

Though less well for most of the rest of that particular shipment.

"We're poised for growth," Harlan said, lecturing a very still audience, a few still eyeballing Loki's rock steady pistol hand. "We have the basics of what we need to establish ourselves as a successful replacement for local government. Each of you will have a territory and a team. Within your assigned territory you will rescue those that can provide useful work, or fight or . . . otherwise contribute to our plan. Our priority is to identify any surviving civic structures and replace them. We'll also organize the logistics necessary for food, clean water, sanitation, resupply and ahem, recreation."

This time there were a few low chuckles. Even Biggs smiled. With his mouth closed.

"Those logistics will rely on vehicles, fuel and clear roads," Harlan said, gesturing to the table that they shared. Gas station maps, cartographic maps, even a framed map of the regional voting districts were layered underneath pages of notes and a loose digital tablet. It was all about information. Information, control and vision.

He had vision, and to spare.

"We'll organize labor forces to clear at least a single lane on every major road everywhere that we take and hold territory." He looked at each person on his immediate staff. "For the nonce, you will principally work in pairs. Later, you'll own and boss your own crews. Right now, we'll continue to work in relatively close proximity to each other and we'll grow our labor pool. Questions?"

"I got one, Mr. Green," Eva O'Shannesy said, raising her hand even as she spoke. The sole woman among the senior crew, she was snake quick and perhaps more prone to violence than the rest. "Do you got a place where you plan to set up shop or is one spot as good as another?"

"That I do, Ms. O'Shannesy," Harlan replied matter-of-factly. "Eventually, we're going to need select a long-term base that is both defensible and has access to important resources. Fortunately, we'll have several options to explore soon enough. Meanwhile, mobility and productivity will remain our focus."

CHAPTER 3

In the months since they arrived, Paul and Kendra had been a sometimes item. It began as two people with a lot in common finding simple comfort in each other's company. She'd been scared and lonely and he had been lonely and, well, horny. Paul recognized that crises and catastrophes can stir human emotions and that he was as susceptible to it as the next man. So he decided to embrace the possibility that something might be there. He'd been delighted to find that he'd guessed right.

Since the meeting where Kendra had unexpectedly briefed the group on behalf of Kohn's big picture, that had ended. Up to that point, Paul allowed himself to feel closer to her. That made her decision hurt all the more.

They'd built a habit of sitting together before breakfast. They hadn't shared a bed in almost a week, but this ritual persisted, though the picnic table was damp and uncomfortably hard.

"How can you work for her, Jonesy?" Paul said, squeezing Kendra's hand as he spoke. "She's running a scam that will end up with her in charge, that's all!"

"Someone has to be in charge, Paul," Kendra said, her face miserable. "You won't do it. She will. She says that she can help us all work together. She's already figured out how to get the townies to genuinely contribute."

In the week since the initial acknowledgment that both central management and a plan beyond "wait for others from the bank to show up" was needed, Kohn had suggested and the council approved changes to their routine. One detail was to begin to carefully scout their immediate area, avoiding contact with anyone, but noting the location of possible supplies and other survivors.

"Once we are properly secure in our own right, we will again look to help as many others as we can," Kohn had proclaimed. "But first we must reestablish our own civilization."

"What about the bank, the long-term plan?" Paul replied insistently, squinting into the first orange rays of sunlight. "We're supposed to plan ahead. To be ready to rebuild."

"Bank?" Kendra said, yanking her hand away. "What bank? The bank that we last saw on fire?"

Stung, Paul reared back.

"The people that vaccinated you," he pointed out. "The people that evacuated you!"

"You mean the people that murdered plague victims and extorted me?" she replied, just as angry. "Oh, *those* people. *That* bank."

"I never exto—" Paul began.

"'What do you think Train Smith will do to someone who puts his plan at risk?'" Kendra said, not quite sing-songing his much earlier words back to him. "I didn't forget your warning. You shouldn't forget it either."

They stared at one another for a moment before Paul looked away.

"Yeah, I said it," he said, more softly. "And it was right. It was true. Then. If you'd tried, Smith would have locked you inside the building and no lie. And you powered through. You survived."

She didn't reply but scooted a little bit farther away from him.

The gray dawn was lightening faster and around them the camp was stirring. The breakfast crew was neatly stripping the prepacked meals from their containers and sorting them according to desirability. Condiments were placed in communal bowls to avoid wastage. The pots of water were waiting to boil.

Paul reached towards her lap, laying his hand on top of hers, without grabbing.

"I'm sorry that I scared you," he said, trying to reconnect. "I'm sorry that all this terrible stuff happened. Even the best possible decisions were sometimes not particularly good. But I know this..."

He struggled to find words as Kendra looked up into his face.

The Saint Joshua medallion that he'd given her swung from a chain he'd shortened for her, and caught his eye with a silver twinkle.

"When we are together, really together, I feel better," he said, attempting to finish his thought. "I don't want to lose that. You want to work with Kohn, well, okay. We've been working with her all along. But, you have to be careful about Kohn. She is... *not right*."

He tapped his own skull with one spatulate finger, emphasizing his point.

"Not right how, exactly?" Kendra said, sweeping a wing of hair back over one ear. "I know that she was involved in the vaccine production, but so were the cops, the bank, everyone."

"I mean, not quite right in the head," Paul answered. He slicked one hand over his scalp, self-consciously. "She has a record. She was convicted as a juvenile, but she did some terrible things. She doesn't really care about other people and I know that she's capable of cold-blooded violence. That's part of why she worked with Smith. He agonized about harvesting human spines. It bothered her not a whit."

"Do you have any proof?" replied Kendra. "She's always rational when I'm around her."

"I didn't say irrational," Paul answered, and then immediately regretted it. Every time they argued, Kendra would end by telling him that she was tired of him contradicting her. "I mean, being dangerous and being rational aren't mutually exclusive. Besides, there's no proof of anything anymore, not here at least."

"Then I should get the chance to judge what you think happened," Kendra said curtly and then stood. "And even then, she has a plan to find a way for us to survive with what we've got. That was good enough when it was 'Train' Smith making life or death decisions. Now that it's Kohn, you have cold feet?"

Paul didn't answer immediately because there was someone approaching.

The lean blonde woman was another New York City survivor. Smith had collected her from the disaster at Last Concert and offered her a seat out. Her boyfriend hadn't made it out of Washington Square. An oversize BotA sweatshirt hid most of her spare frame.

She stopped a few steps away and shot them a quick look from under her hood.

"Hi," she said, somewhat diffidently. "Ms. Kohn asked me to find you, Kendra. She asked if you could come see her after breakfast."

"Sure, I can do that, Christine," Kendra replied brightly as she held out her hand to the newcomer. "I was just going to go eat now. Join me?"

Paul watched them walk away, arm in arm.

Tom Smith squinted through the windshield and then back in his side mirrors. Both Chevys were a light metallic blue, and Durante was keeping the second vehicle an easy fifty meters back from the lead truck. The sun shone in the driver's side window as Tom headed south on the first leg of the trek, skirting Petersburg.

The group in the car was silent, looking at the wreckage of the civilization that lay along their route.

"Remember, keep your eyes peeled for a book store or a Walmart," Tom said, raising his voice over the stereo. They'd indulged the younger set on their music initially, and Tom was beginning to regret the decision.

"What?" someone asked from the back seat.

"I said," Tom said, twisting the volume knob down on the singer who was caterwauling about tanks and bombs and more bombs and guns. Once he was sure he could be understood, he repeated himself, "Check any strip malls or businesses you see for a book store or a Walmart."

Giving the passengers something to do would go part of the way of taking their mind off the depressingly common human carrion that littered the roadside. "We can use some paper maps."

"We've got that GPS, don't we?" replied Katrin, gesturing to a functioning Garmin handheld sitting in its dash cradle. "Can't we just use that?"

Katrin had continued to stay engaged with the adults of the party. All of the kids were missing their families, but Katrin and her sidekick Eric were bouncing back the fastest.

"Yeah, I know how to use my dad's," offered Eric, wistfully eyeing the stereo right next to the Garmin.

"I'm kind of with her, Boss," said Fat Ralph from the very rearmost seat. "Let's just get to your bank site, ASAP."

"I'm not going rely solely on GPS if I don't have to," said Tom, stretching and rolling his shoulders as he drove. "Frankly, I am not sure why this thing is still working."

"Why not?" asked Risky, riding shotgun. "The satellites have solar power, yes? They will run till they wear out."

"It isn't the satellites that I am surprised about, exactly," Tom said, glancing over for a moment. "The accuracy of each GPS satellite relies on getting precise clock updates and occasionally ephemeris corrections. Those come from ground stations. If the accuracy drops below a certain threshold figure, the receiver rejects the satellite."

He gestured with his chin at the GPS receiver, keeping both hands on the wheel as he smoothly dodged around a stalled school bus. He carefully avoided looking inside as they passed.

"That thing says we have a five-satellite fix. So, at least one or two of the ground stations are still up and manned by uninfected people. Places like Colorado Springs have stations, but also island bases like Kwajelin and Ascension. I am betting that is the answer. Whoa..."

He added that last as another naked infected loomed from behind a stopped big rig. It stretched for the SUV even as Tom adjusted their course to drive on the shoulder.

"Uggggh!" exclaimed Eric. "Can't we just, I don't know, shoot them or something?"

"Are not enough bullets anywhere that I know of for us to shoot all the zombies," Risky said as she looked over her left shoulder towards the teen who was craning her neck to see out the back window. "We must save bullets for emergencies."

The secondary road had plenty of stopped cars, but they maintained a comfortable twenty-mile-an-hour pace and the infected quickly lost interest, disappearing in the rear view mirror. Durante stayed in his wake.

Tom had spread his cadre of shooters across both cars and was driving the first shift personally. The car was tightly packed, and although the kids and teachers took up little room, the fully equipped adults were very bulky in their armor, festooned about with pouches and weapons.

"Um, Mr. Smith?" Dina Bua's voice came from the very rear of the vehicle. "Can we stop soon? I have to use the ladies'."

Before Tom could answer, someone else's voice rang out.

"Are you serious!" Cathe Astroga said, jumping in. "We haven't even been driving for forty-five minutes and everyone was told to go just before we left!"

"I didn't have to go then!" snapped Bua. "Besides, it's different, women—"

"You can take a leak when I do, lady!" Astroga said as she pulled a taser from her MOLLE. "Remember my leetle friend? She says you can wait another forty-five minutes!"

"Smith, are you going to let her keep threatening me!" demanded the irate schoolteacher. "Besides, you have to pull over now! I'm not even kidding!"

"Can't stop just now, but I'll watch for a suitable place," Tom said as he kept his eyes on the road. However, he reached for the handheld to let Durante know about a pending stop.

"Butchers?" wailed Bua, unfamiliar with Australian slang.

Risky unbuckled and turned around so she could look straight at the complainer.

"Look at me," Risky said very calmly. "I'm not driving for the next four hundred miles with you behaving like this. Your student is fine. I'm fine. Private, sorry, Specialist Astroga is fine."

"All of us are women," Risky continued. "You'll wait. And if you make Smith pull over, I'll ensure that you regret it."

"Yeah!" Astroga said, waggling the taser.

Tom hung his head just a minuscule amount.

Four hundred miles.

Eric stretched his arm out and turned the volume back up and the music filled the car again.

"What's in your head, in your head, zombie-zombie-zombiee-ee-eee!"

The town was quiet and the forty or so survivors were clustered on the steps of a local Civil War monument. They stood under the guns of the Green's crew, quietly looking around the security ring. The infected presence had been almost entirely shot out, and scores of naked, bloody corpses were in view. As ever, the stench of decomposition lay heavily on the square, adding to the oppressiveness of the southern humidity.

Eva O'Shannesy stood on the steps leading up from the bust of a long dead Confederate general. Her black outfit was dirty and there were some drying, red splashes on a heavy, long coat that she was experimenting with as improvised protection against bites. She'd learned that a coat was no protection if you weren't wearing it, so it stayed on despite the warmth of the day.

"Listen up, you primitive screwheads!" Eva said, holding the megaphone in one hand. "For those who haven't figured it out yet, there's new management here in the town of..."

She looked nonplussed for a moment, then leaned down towards Loki.

"Where are we, again?" she said, whispering.

"Gatlinburg," Loki answered impassively.

"The town of Gatlinburg," Eva said, addressing the audience again. "We're gonna be organizing things from now on. More people are on the way to live and work here, at least for a while. You're going to work here too. Mr. Green..."

She gestured to the slightly built, armored man already stalking the edge of the group of townsfolk. Green was inspecting the nervous crowd like a farmwife simultaneously eyeing her chickens while testing the edge on a carving knife. There was the usual distribution of survivors. They ranged from a superannuated grandmother type down to a few small children who sheltered in the arms of an attractive middle-aged woman whose blue dye job was growing out, revealing golden blonde hair.

"...has decided to place this town under his protection, and you'll benefit in the following ways." She started ticking off points on her fingers. "One. We'll kill all the zombies. Two. We'll protect you against anyone that tries to take your stuff or harm you. Three. We'll improve the food and medicine situation. Four. Shit, three is enough, don't you think?"

One man, braver or perhaps stupider than the rest, called out.

"What's it going to cost us?"

"I'm glad that you asked," Eva replied, smiling at the questioner. "Nothing's free in this world. We'll take what we need from whoever we must in order to carry out Mr. Green's promises to you. So, some of your personal belongings might be gleanings, see? Helps everyone stay alive. Share and share alike, right?"

"That's it, you just want some stuff?" the objector said, sounding pretty relieved. "There's all kinds of stuff. More stuff than people, in fact."

He wasn't wrong.

Everywhere that Harlan Green's growing raider parties went, they found a surfeit of durable supplies. Many, indeed most people were reaped by the zombie virus before they could eat all of their supplies or burn all of their fuel. Those that had lived long enough to exhaust their supplies usually died when looking for more. In long-term cases, food seemed to go first, then ammunition and fuel. Consumables weren't rare, but they were increasingly scarce.

But so-called valuables such as gold, jewelry or luxury cars? No one could eat diamond engagement rings or McLaren sport coupes. Help yourself. Take as many as you like. Cash? Mostly litter.

The circle of security included six of Green's lieutenants and another two dozen low ranking gunmen. These were early converts who were still on their best behavior. They had come from towns where the Gleaners had already passed. Their low numbers were offset by their armament, mostly consisting of break-open or pump shotguns. They lacked the full protection and armor of Green's inner circle, but their armament sufficed to clear low densities of zombie areas and intimidate other survivors.

Most pertinently, their shotguns weren't a real threat to the full plates that Green had already scavenged for his immediate staff, who also carried military grade weapons.

"Stuff? Well, about that," the sole female Gleaner said, drawling out her words. "What Mr. Green really needs is your work. So, he's gonna need you, personally."

She stabbed a gloved finger at the survivor and then people standing close to him. "And you, and you and..."

She searched the group of thirty survivors more closely, and picked out a rosy cheeked preteen boy.

"...and especially you." Eva smiled evilly.

"No, we are not listening to an extended didgeridoo solo!" Durante yelled, pounding his fist on the steering wheel.

"It's my turn to pick," answered Astroga, smirking. "And I pick this."

"A fifteen minute set of didgeridoo noise does *not* count as one song," Durante said angrily.

"Well, we could go back to 'Hey Jude,'" the specialist replied.

"Oh-my-God, Astroga!"

"Do you think that Risky holds a grudge?" Ralph said, whispering to Sacks. "She might think that we were backing Joey T. over the Boss."

The convoy had pulled over, inside a little copse of trees. The survivors had learned to take advantage of every stop to use the bathroom. Or in this case, the slit trench.

"Does the pope wear a funny hat?" the second former Cosa Nova shooter replied. "You dumbass, of course she holds a grudge. Hey, pass me that bag."

Sacks gestured to a kit bag from which a roll of TP printed with pink bears was peeking out.

"Sure, but I was just laying there, bleeding," said Fat Ralph, protesting. Fat Ralph was actually about thirty pounds lighter than he had been at the start of the boat ride. "It's not like I was Two-Tone, what lit up the dock with the machine gun, or Lugnut, what drove the boat."

"Yeah, you was practically a victim, right?" sneered Sacks. "The New Thing is dead. What we got here is a chance to go straight."

He glanced over the bushes that screened the latrine area that Durante had designated for the stop. No one seemed to be interested that the two of them were taking their time.

"We're on probation, see?" Sacks said, chopping the air with his good hand. "The next screwup and we aren't gonna get probation, if you know what I mean. Me? I'm gonna put out, get me a new name. This Smith guy is way smarter than Joey T."

He glanced over the bushes again.

"Yeah, but what if she gets, you know, mad? I don't want to get the chop like those other assholes what she blew away with that fucking RPK. I didn't even know she could shoot!"

Sacks glared at him and then looked over the hedge to see if anyone had overheard.

Risky was talking to Tom and the scary guy special forces dude named Durante. The three were standing in a building courtyard looking at bullet holes in the side of the second truck.

Sacks looked back at Ralph.

"Shut your fucking pie hole," he said. "How fucking stupid are you? She spent weeks with that Smith guy, rolling around in the BERTs. She made it through the fight with the cops. At least now you're smart enough to know not to piss her off."

He glanced again, and then shook the toilet paper at his companion.

"So don't fuck this up, *capisce*?"

~⊖~

Risky was making a point of listening into the impromptu war councils, and no one was objecting.

"We got lucky, Tom," Durante said as he ran his finger across the small hole in the front fender. "Small caliber. Poked a hole in the exhaust manifold, which won't stop the engine. That one..."

He pointed to a starred hole in the passenger's window.

"Even luckier. Six inches left or right and it's a head shot."

"No way to avoid it, Gravy," Smith said, rubbing his chin. "No road block, no warning shot, no signs, just the first impact and a few seconds later, the window."

"We need a plan for losing a vehicle," Risky said. "We need to know what we do if we get hit again. We need extra parts. The average distance per day is less than we expected."

She wrinkled her nose as the slow breeze brought the odor of decomposition from inside the adjacent structure. Their vehicles had remained outside, engines running, while the clearance team had swept the farmhouse, barn and sheds. There had been a medium sized family forted up inside, at least until one had turned and the rest had suicided. The compound made a nearly ideal lay-up point, screened from direct observation and yet equipped with adequate sight lines and internal space. There was even a hand pump fed well.

Kaplan was supervising Sacks and Fat Ralph as they used garbage cans to move the human remains into one room.

"I know, Risky," Tom said. It was the first time he'd used her nickname and she carefully concealed her reaction. Tom went on. "I really wanted another Suburban, but it isn't like we can go car shopping at the Chevy dealer."

The former residents of this farm had left behind several vehicles, including a Winnebago, a Volvo wagon and a really rusty Chrysler sedan. So far, no one had found the keys, not that the older cars' ignitions presented a real obstacle to hot-wiring.

"We want to get to our next SAFE as fast as we can." He held up one hand and began folding down fingers as he listed option. "So, do we drive the shortest route, probably with more risk? Do we look for more equipment or even people so mitigate that risk? Do we go in whatever direction we have to in order to push risk as close to zero as we can, and accept a longer route and more time on the road?"

He paused at the approach of Katrin, Eric and Cheryl, each walking awkwardly under the weight of a full five-gallon water can. Astroga walked at the end of the line, her rifle slung but with one hand on the pistol grip. She smiled as they drew near but didn't interrupt.

"We're not a war party," Gravy said as he patted the fender. "Lots of civilians with us. Slow and steady wins the race."

Risky didn't contradict him, but she didn't agree either.

"Let's get settled and then we can have a group meeting tonight before we turn in," Tom said and then faced the teens. "Hey, kids, can I give you a hand?"

Camp chores had to be completed before nightfall in order to avoid creating any light that would betray their presence to any hunting packs of infected.

Prior to last light, Smith called in the entire party.

"Okay everyone, we're having a quick briefing on how things went today and what to expect tomorrow," he stated. "After today's sniper, it's obvious we need to be ready for additional incidents. I asked Gravy and Kapman to put their heads together and come up with a balance of simplicity and efficiency. Both of them have worked extensively in the field and we'll all have a role to play."

He paused and looked at Durante.

"Things we did right," Durante said. "We didn't stop in the danger area and we got off the X when the sniper took his shots."

"What X do you speaking of?" Risky asked. "Like intersection?"

"The X is the spot where the enemy tries to pin you," Durante replied. "Special operations types, shooters in general, use the term to refer to the focal point of any ambush or attack."

"So get off the X means be anywhere but where enemy wants you?" Risky said. "And maybe the place where you want enemy to be?"

"Right, but you want to do it on purpose," Durante answered. "Today we got lucky, and while I'll take lucky over good any day, freaky stuff can happen in a fight. Luck always plays a role. Guns jam, engines stall on a bit of bad fuel or someone loses their mind and charges into the middle of the action. This time, luck means that the bullets didn't disable the Suburban or one of us. However, you can't always count on luck, so teams usually practice, a lot, to remove random change from the equation as much as possible."

"Like RN-Jesus?" offered Eric, wrinkling his nose.

"Who—what?" replied Durante, looking at the formerly chubby teen.

"He means 'Random Number Generator—Jesus,'" Astroga said, translating for Eric. "Kids and gamers use it to describe random weird stuff that happens in video games. The RNG part of the game creates a gotcha factor, and when it happens in your favor, it means video game Jesus, RN-Jesus, was looking out for you. Man, who doesn't know that?"

For the benefit of the kids, she silently mouthed "Old Dude" while pointing at Durante.

"Um, riggght. Moving on, we don't have the time or a place to practice," the tall security specialist said. "So the focus will be on having quick attach and release tow points rigged to drag a truck if we need to, spread loading both our weapon types and shooters and ensuring that we fill the driver spots with the most qualified people."

"What does that mean for us?" asked Emily. "I mean Dina, the kids and I don't shoot and we don't drive."

"Everyone's a spotter," Durante replied. "The kids have great eyes and during the morning drive, the drivers will explain how to call out directions from the trucks. Tom, Kap, Worf and I will rotate through the left seat. Risky, Astroga, Ralph and Sacks— sorry—Vinnie, will rotate at shotgun. We'll spread the remaining people among the trucks."

"That's it?" asked Vinnie. "I mean, no disrespect an' all, but we used'ta do more coordination than that just to drive into da' city, back with Matricardi."

"Like I said," Durante said, exasperated. "No. Time. To. Practice. The goal is to get to the next safe place as safely as we can. On a good day, we could be there in a few hours. With this mess…" He tossed his head to one side, indicating the world in general, "we're going to keep having to backtrack. It's worse than I expected, and so it's going to take longer. That means more gas. More clean water. And we need to keep our eyes open for maps because this digital crap isn't giving us any useful detail."

"We'll be considering a scavenging stop tomorrow," Tom said, punctuating Durante's comment. "If we see anything worth the delay."

Then he looked to Sacks. "Everyone is going to pull their weight," Tom said.

The swarthy Sicilian held his hands up, deprecatingly.

"Anything to add, Kap?" Tom said, looking back over to Kaplan.

"Nothing special," the shorter man said, shifting a toothpick to the other side of his mouth. "Everybody use the honey hole first thing in the morning. Last person fills it in. Keep your eyes open. Less useless yapping. Sing out if you see something."

Tom looked around the circle but no one signaled a desire to speak.

"Okay, then," he said, tapping Durante again. "Gravy has the watch schedule. Two awake at all times. Keep noise to a minimum. No unshielded white light. Everyone should get some rest while they can. No way to predict how much you'll get during the day."

Jason Young ignored the faint, ever present waft of rot. Ditto, biting insects. Hard-won practice also allowed him to ignore the physical discomfort of perching immobile in a tree for hours. The hunger was harder to suppress and threatened his focus. He'd learned that all the difficulties of the Fall could be navigated if you had clean water and a full stomach. Almost everything else was a luxury. Thirst and hunger drove hasty decisions and clouded judgment.

A single bad call could mean death, especially to a man traveling alone.

Jason, formerly a cop with the Williamsburg PD, had been traveling alone for a long time. He'd thought that the absence of human contact would bring peace, would allow him to forget some of his choices. But lately he'd begun to detach from reality a bit too much. Questioning why he was bothering to survive was one symptom.

Taking chances was another.

He willed the distractions away and focused, watching the end of the hunt.

They'd been at it for almost an hour.

Not far from his tree, two zombies continued to growl and snap at each other as they circled a third, which was crawling very slowly across the dry, crunchy grass in what previously had been a nicely groomed tot lot. The good news was that since no other infected had come to see what the fuss was about, these two were probably alone. The bad news was that they were between him and the buildings he intended to scout. Smaller towns were safer than larger cities, offering much easier routes in and if need be, out. However, zombies liked being indoors too. A few times, he'd stumbled across singletons and small groups and *very* quietly snuck away. During periods of quiet, they seemed to lapse into torpor unless roused, making them hard to detect until it was almost too late. Jason had stopped looking through ruins at night as a result.

Scouting the darkened interior of a building and waiting to see if you surprised a nest was...contrary to survival.

So far, the best way to check empty buildings seemed to be to watch them at daybreak. Generally, infected stirred at first light, some instinct tying their hunt to an older rhythm. Usually no movement meant no active zombies.

Mostly.

These foragers were unusually lively. One would charge a few steps, often earning a swipe from the prey, and then retreat. The second would ape the first. Lather, rinse and repeat. If one infected stopped to dispatch the weakening cripple, it would be vulnerable to the third.

The cycle had persisted longer than Jason expected.

"Way too much energy for anyone to have before coffee," he thought to himself. "I dub you hyper-gits Thing One and Thing Two." It was a rare bit of post-Fall humor for the lone man.

A few times Jason had wondered why he kept pushing in this godforsaken land. He'd turned his back on duty, everyone had; why keep fighting? It would be easy to let go. He still had some ammunition. He even had some rat poison that he used to salt the occasional fresh corpse, reducing the zombie population by a little more. He didn't have to eke out this life for...what? He couldn't say.

Yet he couldn't help pushing, every step taking him farther away from D.C. and the crawling suburbs that spread all around it. Every day farther away from the horror. At first, he had tried to help, here and there. Early on he had joined a missionary caravan as a guard. He narrowly escaped when it disintegrated in the middle of the night. He'd watched families turn, brother killing brother, like Cain murdering Abel. After that, he avoided other survivors. Mostly, he walked or cycled. In suburbs, there were plenty of bikes.

His calf throbbed. He ignored that too. Salvage from big hospitals was a no-go. He sampled smaller hospitals and clinics, eventually giving up. He told himself it was because the infected density was too high. Still, he tried not to think of the gruesome scenes where zombies had made kills in rooms with bed-ridden patients.

On the playground, the two hale zombies had decided to share the rations, but skipped the nicety of waiting for their prey to fully expire. He shut his ears to the sounds of the feast. Usually zombies were quiet, but when provoked they grunted, howled or roared inarticulately. They were still human animals. They could still scream. Especially when they were in pain.

Focus.

He considered his options. Use two of his remaining rounds and risk drawing zombies from farther away? Wait these two out and hope that they didn't lie up nearby? His stomach growled.

One of the big changes of the Fall was how quiet everything was. No motors, no air conditioning hum, no car stereo, no aircraft overhead, no muted freeway rushing in the distance, no TV droning through an open window.

Just the silence of a dead civilization. And the screams of the zombies' prey.

As the screaming tapered, Jason was startled by the sound of a car engine. Though it sounded surprisingly close, habit prevented him from jerking his head around. Sudden motion drew attention. Carefully, he used his eyes to scan for movement, but the foliage obstructed his view. The vehicle drew close enough that he could hear tires licking pavement. A car door opened.

"Just these two?" A man's voice, clear as a bell.

Below, Thing One lifted a blood-stained muzzle, growling over its meal.

"Gimme a sec. I'm looking." Another man. "Yeah, all I see are these two."

"Dump them, and we can scan for survivors from those trees up the hill."

Two muted bangs, and Thing Two looked up angrily as its erstwhile partner slumped across the eating area. Moments later, its head flew apart messily.

"Who's a good zombie?" cooed a new voice. A woman.

Jason held very still as cars doors slammed and the vehicle moved a short distance away before shutting down.

He considered his options.

These three seemed . . . competent.

CHAPTER 4

"This looks like every zombie show, ever," said Fat Ralph, remarking loudly on the condition of the convenience store. "Like that one about the sheriff that wakes up in the hospital, amirite?"

"Quiet, and stay alert," answered Tom. "Just because we haven't turned up any infected in the last few stops doesn't mean that there aren't any here."

The group had dipped southwards, detouring around Petersburg. As expected, Interstate Sixty-Four had been a parking lot of stopped cars, extending onto shoulders and overflowing onto the greenways. Even the state highways and routes were iffy, the key intersections blocked by tangles of burned and wrecked cars and trucks. The roadway was eerily quiet, populated only by the dead that remained in many vehicles, or laying outside them, where their picked-over corpses lay drying in the sun.

Missing were the howling mobs of infected that had chased their group out of New York City.

Tom had made an effort to use the highway, looking for a path that could accommodate their big SUVs. However, trying to squeeze past only served to disturb scavengers, and the flocks of crows that rose squawking into the air served to advertise the survivors' presence, something that the banker was trying to avoid. He moved off the interstate and made better, though very slow headway. The deliberate pace imposed by the poor road conditions, as well as Tom's innate caution, afforded the survivors the chance to study their navigation options, usually from a distance. They'd doubled-back often, avoiding any risk of confronting other survivors.

Once, they'd been warned away from a cross-roads. It had been guarded by a bunker made of white FEMA sandbags. An unseen guard, whose presence had to be inferred by the black snout of a rifle that had slowly emerged into view upon their cautious approach, didn't respond to their shouted queries. At least their equally careful retreat hadn't prompted any shooting, but it had cost them half a day of backing and filling as they tried to navigate around the road junction.

As a result, they'd stayed on side roads, and then side roads to the side roads. Tom looked at his handheld GPS and zoomed in on their location. Details were sparse, limited to what was included in the small-scale pre-loaded maps. The Garmin only offered the barest information, in this case a marked intersection and a symbol for fuel. Which was already obvious, given the fifty-foot-tall, red and blue Chevron sign looming overhead.

The good news about moving slowly was that they were burning a lot less fuel. The bad news was that the roundabout path forced them to cover a lot more ground, and that was eroding their fuel savings. So far, he'd been keeping the fuel tanks topped off with what they'd brought along. Scavenged fuel would require a gas additive to deal with any water contamination, which was something else he hoped to find in a fuel station.

He squinted down at the screen, fighting the glare of the hazy sunlight that washed out the details in the small display. What he really missed about paper maps, what galled him about using their digital replacement, was that he couldn't spread them out and really "see." In addition to keeping their supplies topped off and gleaning any new intelligence about the conditions ahead of them, what he really needed was some paper maps.

"Well, let's go then," Fat Ralph answered, exasperatedly. Tom shot the recruit a sharp glance. At least Ralph had kept his voice down this time. Tom held up one fist, the universal symbol for halting in place and being quiet. He'd taught everyone as much field craft as time and space permitted and this signal was easy for the gangster to remember, reinforced by a decade's worth of post 9/11 war movies and video games.

Tom performed a three-sixty scan. Over his shoulder, he took in the state of the rest of the party, leaning against the blue Suburbans. This particular kind of stop had become common enough that some of his ragged band had relaxed, perhaps dangerously so.

Tom had pulled the lead SUV around the side of the structure, facing back towards the access road and at least the gang was sticking close the trucks, watched over by Durante and Kaplan. The last thing Tom needed was for his group to scatter through the cluster of structures that marked this crossroads. Tom had decided to bring along the former mafioso in order to judge how much the knock-off Italian gangster had matured.

"All right, stay close," Tom said, preparing to enter. He kept his right hand on the pistol grip of his AR and pulled on the unbroken glass door with his left. Wonder of wonders, it was unlocked. He cautiously stepped inside and waved Fat Ralph along before holding up his hand again. Ralph quirked both eyebrows at him, puzzled at the stop-and-go.

"We wait a moment to let our eyes adjust to the light level," Tom said, keeping his voice low.

Ralph nodded, looking around. The unlit store had been hastily looted. Enough light filtered through the dirty glass storefront to reveal the racks of snacks and candy were bare. The dirty floor had enough wrappers to illustrate that previous visitors had begun eating on the spot. The formerly refrigerated cases were open, mostly empty and gave off a musty odor.

After a minute, Tom touched his partner on the shoulder, and led off. The cashier's station was open, and the empty cash register lay sideways on the floor.

Ralph leaned over the counter, and spotted the tobacco shelf and started dropping cans of smokeless tobacco into the empty laptop bag that he wore over his left shoulder.

Tom scanned the magazine rack. There weren't any maps. None of the papers or magazines post-dated their departure from New York, but on a whim Tom collected a three-month-old copy of the *Virginian Pilot*. The small electronics aisle remained pretty full, but without electricity, most of the items were useless.

Tom pointed to the lubricant selection and Ralph obediently grabbed some quart containers of oil before holding up a small red plastic bottle with a long neck, and shook it for Tom to see. Fuel stabilizer, check. Also, empty. Check.

"Let's see about the garage," Tom said, pointing to the door at the rear of the store.

He let Ralph lead off, this time.

Both men entered the larger and much darker space before

pausing to adjust to the light level. Once they gingerly navigated the two cement steps that led to the lower level, Sacks reached over and groped on the wall for the light switch, then stopped and gave Tom an embarrassed nod. At the very end of the space, one of the roll-up garage doors was cockeyed and partially raised. The furthest bottom edge of the door just kissed the ground, rising upwards to leave perhaps eighteen inches of daylight to illuminate the front section of that bay. As their eyes acclimated, four car hoists became visible, looming out of the deep shadows. The work bays were filled with equipment, the nearest hoist holding a still gleaming red Durango. The SUV was missing a wheel but otherwise seemed intact.

Tom took a step forward and his foot made a splashing sound. Rainwater had made it inside, and the floor sloped away towards the rear of the shop. He turned to Ralph to coordinate completing their sweep, but the man had spotted a rack of plastic bottles. Before Tom could grab his arm, the gangster splashed forward to check for stabilizer, and kicked a metal toolbox. The banging sound was very loud in the space.

Coming to rest, the tool box just barely touched a fifty-gallon drum, which rolled and knocked over another box. The succession of crashes was guaranteed to wake the dead.

Both men froze, listening. Nothing. Ralph turned a sickly smile towards his boss.

Just as Tom's pulse began to return to normal, both men heard a querulous growl.

The first zombie lurched out of the black shadows, and splashed directly towards the closest target. Fat Ralph threw himself backwards and Tom ducked to one side as the former gangster swept his new boss with his loaded rifle. Time abruptly slowed as Tom paused, assessing the situation.

The second hand on Tom's watch advanced one tick.

Ralph was scrabbling backwards, and Tom noted the man's fingers began to form into claws, seeking purchase on the water-slick concrete.

The infected was wading towards them in slow motion, perhaps thirty feet away.

As he watched, another infected loomed out from behind the last car hoist. A third silhouette joined the first two, then another pair. Tom knew, without looking, that he might still escape back through the door, leaving Ralph to get swarmed. But, despite being a pain in his ass, the former mobster was his man now. Ralph had taken his salt, and it was a two-way street.

So leaving him to die wasn't going to happen.

Tick. The second hand advanced again.

Twenty-five feet. The zombies' collective growling and keening filled the space, drowning out the sounds of their splashing progress.

Tom had heard the sound before, at Washington Square Park, and again, beneath his own building during their breakout from Manhattan. It was pure hunger, raw and red. It was the warning of the predator, signaling to the pack that there was fresh prey. It was the sound of the darkness come alive, penetrating some deeply buried species-subconscious where ancient humans built fires against the unknown.

Center mass wasn't enough. He needed stops and drops. That meant head and spine shots. The second hand on Tom's watch ticked for the third time, and Tom processed the angles, the distance and knew it would be a near thing.

Twenty feet.

On a battlefield every bit as dark as the Indonesian triple-canopy jungle in Timor where he was first blooded, Tom called on the same focus to surmount the ancestral fear. He noted his own emotions, shunting them aside, compartmentalizing everything but the need to service the targets in front of him. In that moment, as the zombies accelerated, closing the distance to their prey, Tom became nothing so much as the guidance system for the weapon he bore.

Before the watch ticked once more, he raised his custom AR and engaged.

Despite the poor lighting, the view through the Aimpoint had sufficed to center the bright red dot on the first zombie's chest. The first two rounds he fired into the infected's center of mass were attempts at a spine shot, but they only staggered his target. Tom adjusted and drilled his third round through the zombie's head. Instantly, it became a good zombie, bonelessly slumping in mid stride as its fellows narrowed the gap by another yard.

Fifteen feet. As the infected closed, the water became shallower, allowing increasingly faster movement.

The next infected was making good time, but the jerking gait forced on the zombie as it fought through the now shin deep water cost Tom the first shot. His disciplined second sight picture allowed him to find its head with the next round. His shots were coming closer together now.

Switch targets, the muzzle traversing with aching slowness.

Nine feet.

Shoot—shoot—shoot. Infected down. Tom's cadence was even faster, the Geissele trigger barely resetting before he released each subsequent bullet.

Six feet, a lunge away.

Shootshootshootshoot and one more round through an eye, instantly rag-dolling his target. It splashed face first into the water-covered floor.

The last infected closed all the way only to trip over the dead fellow at Tom's feet before sprawling gracelessly. Tom carefully moved back half a step so that his next round would bounce away, not towards Ralph or himself. Then he loosed the final bullet, which zipped through the crown of zombie's skull and against the cement underneath.

Tom heard the ricochet whine spitefully, but then there was only the splashing behind him as Ralph continued to flail backwards, heedless of muzzle discipline.

"Jesus goddamit whatthefuckwasthat!"

Tom didn't so much as glance behind him. He double-checked the room instead, sweeping carefully, finger off the trigger, head up.

He did have time for a comment, however.

"Mate, if I turn around and that fooking gun is sweeping across me again," Tom said, in a perfectly calm voice. "You're going to eat it, flash suppressor first. Believe."

Shouts from outside finally penetrated his combat focus. Mechanically he replaced the partially spent magazine in his rifle as Ralph picked himself all the way up, very deliberately, even exaggeratedly keeping his rifle muzzle down the entire time.

Tom wasn't worried about a sweep now; no man is as careful as someone who has broken the first rule and been called on it.

"Two friendlies, coming in!" Durante's voice rang out from the front of the store, warning the pair of the approach of friendlies. "Tom, you okay?"

"In here, Gravy!" Tom replied sharply. He slid the old magazine inside the open neck of his blouse and then studied his empty left hand. It was steady for now, but he could feel the adrenaline still coursing through his body.

He knew from experience that in a minute or three, he was going to have a few residual shakes.

Just like the old days.

The view from the silver and navy blue Crown Vic with Virginia State Trooper markings was just like the old days. Except for the novel sensation of sitting in the back.

Jason patted the cracked upholstery as the car ghosted along the two-lane state road. Back seat or not, this still beat walking. Looking around, he noted that his seat mate was scooted as far from Jason as the cabin permitted.

"Hey, could you lower the window a bit on my side?" he asked the wheel man. A rosary was knotted around the rear view mirror, and the shortened swing of the crucifix caught Jason's eyes for a moment before he met the driver's squint in the mirror. The driver, sporting a shaven head, dismissed Young before looking at the other figure in the back and raising his eyebrows in an obvious question.

"It's cool, Dragon," the woman to Jason's right answered. "He's not going to jump from a moving car. And he smells like actual shit."

"You're in charge, Eva," the driver answered, lowering the window. Then he replaced his blue latex-gloved hand back on the wheel, and refocused on the road ahead.

Jason immediately enjoyed the rush of cool fall air. He noted, for the umpteenth time, that the road they were using was remarkably clear of wrecks, garbage and bodies.

"Sorry," she said, looking over her passenger without any shame. "You smell worse than I thought—and it's even more like ass with the windows up. It's probably been a while since you had a shower, right?"

"You could say that," Jason replied. "Since, well, since before I got to Richmond."

Richmond was two weeks' worth of careful hiking to the east. His last real shower had been the morning that he walked out of the apartment that belonged to his infected patrol partner. He'd never looked back.

Not till now.

Jason had spent much of the morning shadowing the newcomers from a distance. Seeing the strangers cooperating, sharing what was clearly an improvised uniform and most of all, killing his arch enemy, the infected, had stirred intense feelings in Jason. He'd watched as the three scouted and dispatched several more infected. The internal argument about joining up with anyone again had been fierce.

In the end, simple human loneliness had won out, and he'd very carefully called out to them while they ate lunch in their car.

The entire "getting-to-know-you" dance had been akin to two porcupines sizing each other up before mating. Slow and gingerly steps had led to a surprisingly civilized conversation, led by the woman. She'd introduced herself as one Miss Eva O'Shannesy. Once he'd cleared and safed his Remington 700, she even let him hold onto it, earning a couple of surprised looks from the other two.

Jason had been on his own for so long that the presence of three other people, armed and apparently organized, was making every cop-sense he possessed go off incessantly. Despite the softness of the ride and the emotional comfort of still being armed, he was sitting on the edge of his seat.

Metaphorically speaking.

He patted the pliable upholstery again.

Still, every time he looked up his personal alarms sounded, because even the has-been ex-cop could see that this trio wasn't quite the land-based version of the Cajun Navy that he'd first assumed.

"Uh-huh," Miss Eva replied. "Well, like I said, we're always looking for talent, the Gleaners I mean. We have a pretty strong team already, but our boss, the governor, doesn't hold nothing against anyone. He knows that just surviving this far means that a body is pretty competent. And he likes cops, soldiers, doctors, medics, engineers and so on, if they have the right mindset."

"Like how?" Jason asked casually, looking out his own window as he said it.

"Hey," Eva said, getting his attention.

Jason looked over to see her studying him.

"The way you're patting the seat, you're either a con or a cop," she said. "And even after all the shit you've probably been through, you don't have the eyes of a con."

Jason studied her in turn, then the two up front. All three had stripped off the heavy, mustard yellow fireman's turn-out coats, gloves and what looked like bicycling helmets that they'd worn during their sweep. Underneath they wore blue jeans, blue T-shirts and boots. Both men had slid their rifles into improvised plastic sleeves that were pop-riveted to handy interior surfaces, but they retained pistols and knives.

When they took their gear off, the obvious prison ink and long hair had been a dead giveaway. Much more puzzling was that the driver had forearm tats that included ornate Chinese hanzi and what looked like a winged snake coiling out of his collar while the other had the roman numeral thirteen inked onto the nape of his neck.

It didn't take a genius to know that the Triad and MS-13 weren't natural allies.

Eva, sitting to his right, had reslung her weapon, and kept it casually pointed across the compartment. The muzzle didn't quite cover him. She watched him carefully.

"We take all kinds," she said, smiling. "But there's a mandatory interview first."

"Who with?" Jason replied, essaying a smile.

"With the guy in charge," Eva answered. "Governor Harlan Green. And you don't want to judge him by us and you don't want to lie. He can tell."

"How'd he get those two to work together?" Jason asked, deciding to take a little risk. Hell, if they'd wanted to, they could've shot him back in town.

"Mr. Green is a no-shit *genius*," Eva said, emphasizing her words unironically. "Somehow, very early in the plague, he figured it out. He was some sort of hacker mastermind who did some shady shit back when we had an Internet. When he saw how it was going and where it would end, he took steps to put together a team."

"A team of ex-cons?"

"Well, we're only *ex*-cons by courtesy," she said, keeping her right hand on her rifle's pistol grip. "You might say we were released early on Mr. Green's recognizance."

There were chuckles from the driver. The dark haired man who rode shotgun said nothing, but his shoulders shook with silent laughter.

"He supplies the smarts and the plan," Miss Eva went on.

"Okay, I'll bite," the ex-cop said to the somewhat ex-con next to him. "What's his plan?"

"I don't know the details yet, because I don't need to know," Eva answered unwaveringly. "But I know this. He's gonna save the world, or at least our little part of it."

"No, you can't kill her, Astro," Copley said wearily. "You made the rules and she's following them."

"But, but—" Astroga replied, sputtering. "It's not music!"

"Feeed theee woorld," Bua sang, defiantly staring at her Army nemesis while she stretched the lyrics for all they were worth. "Let them know it's Christmas time again. Fee-aWWWK!"

"It's not even Thanksgiving yet!" Astroga yelled at the top of her lungs, lunging over the bench seat for the speaker wire jacked into Bua's iPhone. "And that's not music! It's an abomination!"

"Don't make me stop this car!" Kaplan said, warningly. "I will stop it! I don't like it either, but it ain't any worse than the crap you picked!"

"Astro!" Copley reeled her back in by one ankle. "Square your shit away, Specialist!"

"It's not even— Wait," Astroga stopped in mid re-lunge. "You called me Specialist!"

"Oh shit," the Army sergeant released his hold on her ankle and she sat back, smiling. "Yeah. Yeah, I did."

"Ha!" his subordinate said with an air of satisfaction, now ignoring Bua. "You recognized the new rank. That makes it official. Even more official."

Astroga's highly irregular promotion scheme during the evacuation from New York had involved access to an Army headquarters shared drive, an open laser printer, a clipboard and a National Guard general in dissociative shock. She'd arranged for a bump upwards for her and their now missing comrade. No one had really challenged her so far.

And his use of the appropriated rank just permanently legitimized it in her eyes.

"You know what, this calls for a celebration! Hit it, Bua!" she said, poised for some quality seat dancing. "I'll even join you!"

"Feeed theee woorld..."

"This is so much worse than I expected," lamented the senior NCO.

Tertiary Powerhouse Control Room,
Tennessee Valley Authority, Region II
Watts Bar TN

"That ended better than I expected," Stantz said, leaning across the table with a grunt of effort. "Hey Phil, stay on, wouldja?"

Pre-Plague, TVA staff meetings ended noisily, as management and line personnel hustled back to their actual jobs, usually indulging in a little banter on their way back to their offices or trucks.

This time a sort of stunned silence drifted across the half full meeting hall. Since this was the TVA, with power and to spare, the room was brightly lit. The mood, however, was dark. The announcement of the presumed loss of another dam control center, this time the Nickajack, just two stops downstream from Stantz's own location near Watts Bar, had dispirited many.

Mike Stantz, the unassuming regional General Manager for Power Transmission, spared a glance for the relatively few people in the room. Social distancing rules had been mandated by TVA headquarters in Knoxville only weeks after the plague had been formally declared as a pandemic by the CDC. Between folks who had been infected and the long ago announced option to attend meetings by phone, the headcount for the meetings was lighter than he had ever seen it.

In this case, exactly three of them remained at Watts Bar.

Bill Rush, the longtime watershed management officer for Nickajack and Chickamauga reservoirs, slapped his hand down on the table. The sharp smack caused his table mate to glare at him.

"Give it a rest, Bill!" ordered Mike. At fifty-three, he was among the oldest of the line managers, having dedicated his entire post-Navy career to the TVA. Like most of the full time employees of the public corporation, the mission came first, last and always for Mike.

He didn't have a lot patience for unproductive posturing, especially as it pertained to the crisis.

"Give it a rest?" Rush began to yell, but lowered his voice with an effort. "Six nuclear fueled generating plants, thirty hydroelectric dams, fifteen gas or cogen plants, plus the dinky solar and wind stuff and they want us to walk away?"

"Stop exaggerating, Rush," Brandy Bolgeo said pointedly. "No one said to walk away. They said to take steps to preserve the generation and distribution infrastructure while we *still* have the people to do it. We don't know what happened at Nickajack or Chickamauga. All we could see was a lot of smoke over their facilities and now all we know is that they aren't answering the phone anymore."

Bolgeo was an up-and-coming engineer who had been moved, somewhat against her will, into a junior management role in the Distribution division. After a great series of interviews, Mike had offered her a relocation package back to Tennessee and away from California taxes and crumbling infrastructure. Her masters in Electrical Engineering was only a few years old but Mike was confident that Bolgeo could manage the living fossils, all male, that populated her department. Most of them were almost ungovernable, but they usually had the grace and experience to be right every time.

Bill Rush had missed that memo.

"That's my point," Bill said. Clearly still upset, he managed to not raise his voice this time. "They're giving up. They aren't fighting it anymore."

Mike sympathized with Bill. Everyone was upset and with reason. The unprecedented spread of H7D3 was terrifying. Like many industries, electrical utilities had a real-time view of demand for their product. The amount of electricity demanded by the grid had begun dropping slowly at the two week mark into the plague. The trend had accelerated as retail and industrial consumers scaled back how much electricity they used.

Four months on, and the flow of gas and coal for the conventional generating plants was all but exhausted.

"No one is giving up," Bolgeo said. "We've been going since the cities went dark. We kept going when most of the load evaporated. Now we must prepare to address all the possible outcomes. I'm just pleasantly surprised our 'end of the world' plan is working at all."

"Failing to plan is planning to fail," Mike retorted. He knew that despite her technical skills, Bolgeo was still a *newish* employee, having been at TVA less than a decade. "Both of you know that making, managing and distributing power is our religion. We are the Mormon Church of prepared public utilities. We've got a plan for everything. All we had to do was dust off our zombie apocalypse plan. It wasn't even particularly complicated."

"Says you," Bolgeo replied. "You're not fighting kudzu that grows sixty feet a season. Three months without treatment and line tension is already approaching limits in some places. If we weren't at the start of the winter season we'd have a problem starting right now. Come next summer, Katie-bar-the-door!"

"Phil, you still on the phone?" Mike asked as he leaned closer to the black tabletop speaker.

"Yup," Mike's deputy replied. TVA had redundant, internal communications networks, dating back to the Cold War. The phone and cell network problems that had already made the retail networks unworkable weren't a showstopper and all the dam locations were connected on lines wholly separate from the legacy Ma Bell network.

"It's time to finish the consolidation," Mike said. "Use the big truck to check the yards at the gas and cogen plants. All of them, even if they've been picked over. Inventory any remaining spare parts, fencing, raw materials, all of it. I want every spare transformer, power supply, every reel of primary conduit and cable, all of it. Bar stock, round stock, bigs and smalls. Put as much as you can in the yards next at Chickamauga dam and Watts Bar dam. What doesn't fit there goes into the repair yard outside Unit One at Watts Bar," he added, referring to the nuclear plant that lay on the Tennessee river north of Chattanooga.

"What about Sequoyah?" Phil asked, referring to the second nuclear plant in the immediate area.

"Both nuke plants already sealed and they're responsible for their own spares," Mike said. "If they don't already have it inside their fenceline, they aren't gonna get it. If you try to get in, you're gonna get shot. But we've got Watts Bar. We can park extra stuff on the repair pad there."

The TVA had been slowly finishing Unit Two at the nuclear plant referred to by Mike, but NRC permitting, intermittent protests and congressional deal making had slowed the process to a standstill. Now, absent a miracle, it wasn't ever going to be complete.

"So are you walking away from the gas plants?" Rush demanded. He scratched his ribs fiercely.

"Makes sense," Bolgeo said, nodding in approval. "The fossil plants need to be supplied externally, and the flow of feedstock stopped weeks ago. Whatever they managed to build up outside is either gone or about to be gone. The nuke plants are already spun down to cold iron. That leaves the dams and those are easy to defend."

"Well, *easier*," Mike added. "We can move supplies by boat if we have to, and no one has seen a zombie swimming so far. It's about planning ahead."

"No!" Rush yelled this time. "No, we don't give up! We protect the gas—wait—what's—we doann't..."

He stood and started tearing at this shirt, still yelling incoherently.

Mike reached into his waistband and withdrew his concealed sidearm. Despite his carry permit, unauthorized possession of a firearm in TVA offices or on TVA property was a firing offense.

He'd been carrying every day since the announcement of the plague.

Failing to plan was planning to fail.

His sole surprise was when Bolgeo beat him to the shot.

CHAPTER 5

"Relax, Mr. Young," Harlan Green instructed his newest guest. "Ms. Eva has already passed to me a précis of your biography, shared by you during your return from her latest run. Although this is in the nature of an interview, I think that it'll go better if you aren't sitting on the edge of your chair, ready to spring into action at any moment. If I weren't interested in you personally, you would already have ceased to be a *factor*."

And isn't that a warming, reassuring statement of welcome. Jason thought. His glance roved around the surprisingly well-appointed room, pausing on the truly enormous and well-armed man by the doorway before he looked back at his host. At this point, he was so deeply in any potential trap that being ready to jump out of his chair was pointless. With a deliberate effort, he forced himself to relax and lean back in the admittedly very comfortable easy chair.

It was harder than he expected.

The military atmosphere that greeted him when his new companions drove into the Gleaner camp was startling. It was clean, for one thing. They had an actual armored truck from the Army, for another. Everyone seemed busy, even the obvious low-ranking laborers digging a ditch or washing vehicles.

"There you go," Green said, smiling. "May I offer you a refreshment? We've a wide variety to choose from."

"Water, just some clean water," Jason replied. "If this is an interview, I might as well keep a clear head."

"Of course," his host said, lifting the cover on a small insulated bucket. "Ice?"

"You have ice!?" Jason said, trying not to squeak. "I mean. Sure, ice is fine."

"This is our second encampment," Green said as gestured about with the ice tongs. "We have been here a while, though it's nearly time to move on. However, our group has grown and we've been able to add a few refinements. Right, Mr. Loki?"

"Right, Governor Green," rumbled the huge man.

Green smiled unctuously and dropped a few perfect ice cubes into an ordinary water tumbler before filling it from a beautiful crystal pitcher.

"We're successfully producing limited electrical power running on a combination of generator sets and solar panels," Green elaborated, passing the glass to his guest. "Maintaining cold storage is important for our supply of vaccine. We've actually had to recreate some bureaucracy just to administrate our collection of personnel and equipment, so obtaining computers and people proficient in their use has been necessary as well."

"Vaccine?" Jason said, unable to keep his features smooth. "How are you producing it?"

"We aren't, not any longer," Green said, pouring himself a few ounces of a brilliant amber liquid. He sniffed his crystal highball glass appreciatively. "Before the collapse I worked with a laboratory partner to collect and attenuate live virus. A few organizations were using that method, though the federal government didn't attempt production until it was much too late. It involved killing infected humans for their tissue."

"I heard about it, but I thought it was just rumors," the former cop replied.

"Of course you did," Green said, swirling his drink. He gestured with the glass. "Balvenie. The fifty-year-old limited reserve in the original crystal. Before the virus was released a single presentation set would've cost upwards of thirty thousand dollars. Now I can collect it from a ruined estate for free. A cheap high proof vodka is actually more useful now—disinfection and so forth. The price of things has changed, Mr. Young. And while the vaccine is very, very useful, it isn't particularly critical to my plans anymore."

"How can it not be critical?" Jason said, carefully *not* raising his voice. "You could've saved a lot of people! Ones with important skills."

"*Could have* is the operative phrase, Mr. Young," Green said, raising one finger in ritual protest. "At this time, nearly everyone has been exposed to the virus that is going to be exposed to the virus. The calculus is clear. Fifteen percent of those exposed die. Three quarters become mostly insensate cannibals and the remainder recover and . . . live. Of course, the surviving ten percent is being rather heavily winnowed by the current harsh conditions. That's where I come in. And perhaps you, as well."

Jason drank some ice water, marveling at the feeling of refreshment that a simple cold beverage was creating. Still, he held his peace. He might not be a cop any longer, but letting suspects talk at their own pace without interruption was practically the first thing that he had learned as a rookie.

"From the beginning I required my associates to have a certain skillset," Green said and looked back towards his guard. "Mr. Loki here is a former law enforcement officer, like yourself. His assistance has been invaluable as we managed certain members of our team."

"Eva, Miss, said that you recruited from prisons?" Jason said. It wasn't really a question. "Convicts and cops aren't known for being on good terms. Why pick them to begin with?"

"I needed the nucleus of a team I could rely upon," Green answered, gesturing towards Loki. "Even as the pandemic progressed, my forecasts predicted the fabric of our old society would wear completely through. Criminals aren't without a code, Mr. Young. They merely have a very different code from those you call civilians."

"Do you mind if I asked how you got started?" the cop asked. "You're pretty far along and it hasn't been even four months since I left metro D.C.—you even have an MRAP outside."

"I don't mind, Mr. Young," Green replied, smiling. "A lot can happen in a few months and I'm not your average criminal. Make no error, by the standards of the recently expired civilization, I am a criminal. I laundered digital funds transfers for anyone that could pay my fees. I hacked into every level of government and law enforcement networks, I funded and later directly participated in the illegal collection of human tissue to manufacture vaccine. But by the standards of the world-that-is, I'm just a survivor."

He chuckled.

"A very well equipped survivor, with access to some military grade equipment that had been seconded to a local police department, courtesy of the now expired War on Terror. More importantly, I have the only organization that is clearing zombies, reestablishing the road network and enforcing any kind of discipline. At the final analysis, I am still just a survivor."

"I see," Jason said. "That's a lot to take in. But your system is already working. Why me?"

"As we move forward, my organization will require new skills in order to succeed," Green said, gesturing expansively with his glass. "As we transition from simple clearance and asset collection, we will have to create a different framework for governance. The communities that we rebuild will need some symbols of reassurance. The presence of former law enforcement personnel will be attractive to certain kinds of survivors. A sort of familiar symbolism, you see. In addition, some of my existing team exhibit a certain overenthusiastic moral flexibility and that requires... the occasional enforcement of a Gleaner boundary, as it were."

"What kind of boundaries are we talking about, Mr. Green?" Jason said, falling naturally into the cadence of his host.

"Excellent question," Green replied, setting his drink down with a slight click. He steepled his fingers and leaned back in his chair. "Boundaries. Well, whichever boundary I select, and drawn to whichever extent I dictate at whatever time I choose. In general my goal is to preserve life and well-being where I can. However, I have no intention of reestablishing some sort of illusory representative government. I mean to be in charge. Mine will be the first word, and the last word and my Guards..." he inclined his head towards Loki's bulk "...will be my sword."

"That doesn't seem too drastic, given the current conditions," Jason said, reflecting for a moment before continuing. "This is the first organized group that I've seen so far. But there's got to be more to it than that, no?"

"Tell me, Mr. Young," Green countered. "Are you a particularly religious man?"

"Parochial school as a kid," Jason replied honestly. "Not so much as an adult. Law enforcement can make you question the concept of a god."

"Just so. Our current total personnel at this base, from laborers to entertainers to technicians and Gleaners, is just under three hundred and fifty," Green said with a smile. "About that many again are living in the original areas where we found them, maintaining our presence at potentially important points. You see, when you have less than ten percent of the population to work with, and little industrial age machinery on hand, what works is feudalism. And the true authority is the feudal lord, not God."

"So when you say 'governor' what you really mean is 'baron,' right?" Jason asked, finally grasping what his host was selling.

"Baron, count, duke, prince," Green replied cheerfully. "Who knows? What I know is that in order to save even a quarter of the survivors I've encountered since the collapse of civil authority, a form of governance rather less random than democracy and much less benevolent than religion is required. And I say this from experience: if the old American government had acted quickly and decisively, they could've saved much more. They might even remain relevant."

"A quarter?" Jason was still digesting the implications of Green's . . . confession? He finally asked. "What of the rest?"

"They weren't required for our operations," the would-be king, warlord or dictator-for-life answered, quite simply. "And I couldn't leave them behind me."

There was a pause in the conversation while Green allowed Jason to consider that tidbit.

"Eva explained about your name, the Gleaners," Jason said, electing to pursue a different tack. "Is that an official label or just your team's nickname for themselves?"

"Gleaning was the old practice of carefully searching an already harvested field for useful bits of the original crop," his host replied before collecting his whiskey and sipping again. His smile was distorted by the rim of the crystal glass, making his teeth seem abnormally large. "Sometimes the bits you find are edible, lifesaving. Other times they are rotten, dangerous. Very dangerous. This virus has already reaped its harvest. We now look for what's left. What's valuable. What I value most is people. I mean to rebuild civilization, Mr. Young. What I need to know is if you are as useful a bit of gleaning as you appear to be."

The interview went on for a few hours. Green carefully interrogated him, not just about what Jason had seen during his journey from the Washington D.C. area, but about the decisions he'd made as he fought to survive. He probed rather more deeply about Jason's reasons for walking away from his job, from the city and ultimately from his police partner. Neither the details of his decision to honor his infected partner's dying wish for a quick death nor his ultimate decision that it was every person for themselves had occasioned a comment from Green. Even Jason's Irish Catholic roots came in for discussion, not that Jason, a self-described Easter and Christmas Catholic, was especially devout.

Green had closed with a provocative statement, signaling the end of the meeting.

"You seem to have decided that the world was over and therefore, your responsibility was over. I am telling you that a new world will rise from the wreckage. You'll have to decide if you want to be a part of it. In the meantime, Mr. Loki here will further orient you."

The giant standing behind Jason rumbled affirmatively.

"He'll insert you into our organization. You'll get an escort for a few days while you look around and regain some amount of personal equanimity. You won't be armed, of course. I give my team considerable latitude, but I expect complete loyalty and obedience. After you clean up and get used to eating regularly, I may have a little job to do, and you can help. It might go a little way towards earning yourself a place among my people. Or not."

Tom's close call in the garage had become a minor matter of contention. It was time for a formal debrief, Bank of the Americas-style.

"Go on," Tom said, turning to place his back to the counter of the farm kitchen they'd used overnight. He jumped up and twisted around to use the countertop as a seat. "Gimme the rest, because so far this isn't news."

"The first thing that's going to help is realizing that we're not fighting people," Kaplan said, writing on the white painted wall with a piece of charcoal that he'd scavenged from their breakfast fire. "They're human all right, with the same physiology, the same autonomic nervous system, but they don't think like they used to, not like us. The tactics that we've drilled during our entire lives are bass-ackwards now."

"Yeah, yeah," Durante replied, leaning against the far wall. "Stealth is the first lesson. We get it, that's how we survived in the old SAFE."

"We're used to being tactical," Kaplan went on. He drew a long straight line at shoulder height, horizontal to the floor and put an X at one end, labeling it "Kap." "We're taught to be silent, to see without being seen, that the first person to be spotted gets dead."

Most of the survivors were either in the surprisingly clean house, or taking care of last minute post-breakfast chores before they loaded up and hit the road again. A few poked their heads in and began quietly listening.

"Thing is, when we get sneaky, we sneak right into the zombies' turf, and let them choose the distance of the engagement," Kaplan said, drawing another X midway down the wall. He labeled it "twenty-one feet." "When we let them get within twenty or thirty feet, we're relearning the Tueller rule all over again."

"Okay, I'll geek," Worf said. "What does a physicist have to do with zombies? We're going to nuke them now? If this is up for a vote, I vote no."

"That's Teller," Tom said, without turning his head. "He said *Tueller*. American cop who made the case that once a man with a blade closes within twenty-one feet of a gunman, the gunman has a second to a second and a half to draw and shoot to stop the attacker before the shooter is eating steel."

"That *rule* is so much bullshit," Durante scoffed, still holding up the wall, crossing one leg over the other. "The distance is an approximation. The time is an approximation. The level of competency Tueller specified is an approxi—"

"The *point*, Gravy," Kaplan said, cutting his teammate off, "is that once zombies get close enough, you're gonna get dogpiled and shooting contact distance with a rifle is *hard*. We need something else. And before you say pistols are the answer, Tom's little rodeo where we got the Durango doesn't help that argument. If they'd run into a few more infected, they would've gotten bit, and vaccine or no vaccine, your nose ain't gonna grow back, or any other soft bits neither."

"We're wearing armor, no?" Risky pointed out. Behind her, Vinnie winced and nervously stroked his proud Roman nose.

"Yeah, armor that's good against guns, but that has limited protection against half a dozen infected trying to eat your face." Kaplan continued, adding a long pointy knife in the hand of his stick figure avatar. He added a few drops of what was presumably blood dripping into a puddle. "We need more complete coverage in order to be bite resistant. That way, getting dogpiled isn't the end. Not if you're covered up, have pistols and a machete, and you can keep your head."

"Rain gear is too light," Tom said, pulling at his chin. "Leather is heavy. Neoprene is hot. MOPP gear is heavy and hot."

Tom was referring to the military Mission Oriented Protective Posture gear worn when biological or chemical weapons were expected or suspected.

"But okay, I see your point, we need a different armor concept," he added.

"We can sort out the armor by scavenging," Kaplan said, riffing off his boss's interest. "What we need to think about is making noise on purpose before we go into any more dark rooms. The groups of live infected we've seen have all had two things in common so far. They tend to like dark spaces, usually inside, and they are near water. So, if we're thinking about going into a house or near water, we should make noise and let them come to us, so we can use distance to take maximum advantage of our ranged weapons."

"Look, I like getting stuck in as much as the next guy," Durante said in a reasonable tone. "But if you put enough armor on to cover every extremity, you're gonna be slow, noisy and a pushover for the first nonzombie gunman you come across. And if everywhere you go you start ringing the dinner bell, you're calling the infected. That means dozens, maybe hundreds of infected. And this is the really dangerous bit: sooner or later that's going to get noticed by someone who *isn't* infected."

"We're going to have to mix it up," Tom said, breaking in. "I see your point about going into potential close-quarter combat blind. We'll adapt our procedures."

"How about spears?" Ralph asked. "The old boss, he was always talking about pig hunting with great big stickers, boar spears. Nice long spear would keep a zombie off you better than a knife."

That stopped everyone from speaking for a moment, surprised at the actually useful contribution from an unexpected quarter.

"That's . . . actually interesting, Ralph, thanks," Tom said, eyeing his clearance partner from the day before. "It almost makes up for nearly shooting me yesterday."

Ralph began to smile widely.

"I said *almost*," Tom added, before continuing. "Seriously, we need to observe all the safety rules *all* of the time. The Big Four are always in effect, got it?"

He was referring to the pre-Fall rules of fundamental firearms safety.

The ex-gangster looked sheepishly around the room and then at his shoes. Everyone had heard the story of how he'd panicked in the darkness. It was...embarrassing. Dutifully, he began to mumble.

"Every gun is loaded, all da' time, don't aim at nothin' you ain't gonna kill..." he began.

"Booger hooks off the bang switch unless you're about to shoot and know what's behind your target!" the three teenagers caroled loudly from the sidelines. Apparently one of Astroga's lessons had stuck.

"I'm not going to beat your ass, Ralph," Tom said, favoring Astroga with a tight little grin. "I'm going to do something worse. At our next camp, you're going to be teaching a formal firearms safety class, for everyone, including the kids, who have clearly been learning from Astroga already. Your students will also include Ms. Bua. If anyone fails to pass the quiz that *I* will administer afterwards, you're eating the vegetarian omelet meals out of every case of MREs we have till they do pass. Do not mistake my resolve."

"Boss!" Ralph protested, suddenly over his embarrassment. "They smell like puke and taste like ass!"

Astroga made a capella retching sounds.

"Yep, the good ole Vomlet," Copley said raising a hand to his temple as if trying to think. "You better teach me right. I hate those things. Oh, oh, I feel a memory lapse coming on!"

"And that's the point," Tom said. "Gravy, Kap, load 'em up."

He watched as his trusted lieutenants briskly moved out, herding the civilians toward the vehicles. He rocked back and forth on his feet, satisfied with the progress of his little group. They'd made a couple of mistakes, but things were looking up.

"There is no way to tell how much gleaning you can get of these podunk towns, Boss!" Biggs said, complaining again. "Some places you might find ten survivors. Out of that you might have two or three worth feeding. Other places you can't find anything worth the time to collar 'em up or the gas to bring 'em back."

Biggs was keeping his voice down, keeping the exchange private despite the open setting. The town of Laurel wasn't much more than a slightly built-up crossroads.

"Did you sweep the entire town, Mr. Biggs?" Harlan asked.

"Naw, Mr. Green," the broader man said, chewing on a candy bar with his mouth open. "It was the second place we hit and we'd already mostly filled the trucks, so when I saw you coming I stopped, figured we'd finish after talking to you."

Harlan dropped his initial appraisal of the prisoners that he had to convert into productive assets and rounded on Biggs.

"You left the town incompletely secured after you took people out?" he asked mildly. "You left potential assets behind armed with knowledge of our tactics and awareness of our operations? And you plan to go back?"

"Sure, Boss," Biggs, replied, spraying a few bits of candy bar. "Soon as we drop this batch off."

Sometimes the inability of these convicts to think past the next day blinded them to the consequences of their actions. Harlan made a mental note to address this in future recruiting. In Biggs's case, he couldn't think past his next meal. If the ex-con wasn't a perfectly aggressive, somewhat biddable creature, Harlan would've already liquidated him. Lesson learned.

Harlan deliberately relaxed, striving for control. Hasty decisions yielded suboptimal results. Biggs was what he was, and no more. The self-styled governor returned to his scan of the new batch of potential recruits.

"Standard priority selection for the assets that we extract from recovered towns goes to mechanics, engineers, doctors and... entertainers," he asked skeptically. "Do any of these three fall into those categories, Mr. Biggs?"

He didn't have to point to the three men in question.

"Well, no doctors or engineers, but the older guy says that he's rebuilt classic cars," answered Biggs.

"Classic cars? How many nineteen fifty-five Thunderbirds are we operating at this time, Mr. Biggs?"

"Hey, he's as close to a mechanic as I have found!" Biggs protested vehemently. A few bits of snack food joined the remnants of chocolate that already decorated his beard. "If he doesn't work out, we can use him for something else."

"Really, Mr. Biggs?" Harlan said, pausing in front of the older tall man with a silver crew cut. "And why's that?"

"Huh?"

"What qualities does he seem to have that made it worthwhile to, as you say, 'waste the gas to bring him in'?"

Harlan awaited a response, noting the bloody cut across the captive's forehead, the watchful eyes, and the captive's carefully closed expression.

Biggs appeared to be getting agitated. He swallowed and looked around the crossroads for inspiration.

"Ah, he looked older, maybe not as hot headed as some of the younger men, you know," he said, offering the explanation in apologetic tones. "Also, we brought back a woman from the same place. Daughter-in-law, I think. Figures, it gives him a reason to make nice, not make trouble?"

Harlan looked over Biggs's shoulder and noted the expression on the face of Biggs's deputy. Davy Khorbish, another recruit from Green's prison bus scheme, was listening intently. A black swastika tat crept out of his collar and up the front of his throat. He was staring hard at the back of Biggs's head.

Harlan walked around the end of the short coffle of three able-bodied men, striding until he stopped on the opposite side of the original subject of his examination. Loki, like a massive threatening shadow, strode behind him.

Internally, Harlan Green sighed. His lieutenants varied in their treatment of new inductees to their system. Sometimes solo captures were stuffed into the back of a truck under guard. Larger numbers of recruits, especially men, were handled more cautiously. Adults were usually tied together. Biggs had a thing for making sure that new people felt the weight of their new position so he kept them chained neck to neck with one hand cuffed to the coffle chain, leaving the other free for balance. It was a humiliating position and didn't do much to incline inductees to cooperate.

It was clear that Biggs had missed an important detail. One that Harlan Green had not.

An object lesson was required.

Again.

This was going to compromise the reliability of this batch of prisoners, but if Harlan couldn't effectively delegate the basics of screening and collection, then his organization could not scale. And it had to scale, quickly.

"So you're claiming that you personally examined the prisoner—carefully?" Harlan turned very deliberately to look at Biggs as he asked the next question. "Did you ask your deputy, the deputy that *I* appointed, for his opinion?"

Khorbish's eyes glittered.

"Well, sorta. But look, this dude, uh, I mean, he's healthy enough," Biggs said, swinging a "starter" made of knotted line against the prisoner's thigh. "Plenty of muscle for an older dude. Minimum, he can farm, or fetch and carry, or push cars off the road. Lots of cars to clear, Boss. I mean, Governor."

"What do you think?" Green addressed Khorbish for the first time.

"Dude is trouble," the shorter ex-con replied. "I smelt it. Tole' Biggs. Said we should grease'm. Biggs said to shut up, that the dude was good labor material—would work hard."

Green turned back to the object of their scrutiny. After a further moment of appraisal he made up his mind.

"And would you do that for us?" Harlan said, addressing the erect man directly. "Are you going to work cooperatively, contribute to the new community?"

Hard, pale blue eyes met the mild inquisitive gaze of the mastermind, but the man held his peace and nodded.

"Really?" Harlan said, extending his hand and slid the sleeve on the man's torn work shirt higher, fully exposing the man's forearm. It was decorated with a muddy, aging tattoo of a helmeted bulldog smoking a cigar. "I rather don't think so. Mr. Loki, if you please."

Loki stepped laterally, ensuring that nothing valuable was on the other side of the gray-haired veteran. As fast as a man could blink, he drew his pistol and shot the prisoner in the head. The fresh corpse fell, dragging the other two chained men to their knees. A child screamed in the background.

"If you'd an ounce of imagination, you would have smelled the imprint that military service leaves on some men," Harlan said, ignoring the screams of surprise. He carefully stepped away from the growing pool of blood and faced Biggs. "If you'd consulted seriously with the partner that I assigned, you might've looked more closely. Had you bothered to check, you would've found the tattoo. You might've remembered my orders about law enforcement and military types. As long as they don't actively resist, you keep them separate and under individual guard until I can personally inspect them. This one would never have worked for us after the way you treated him. The woman's family is dead, yes? Dead from your operation? Instead of a potentially valuable asset, what you *made* for me, what you've wasted my time on, is just another corpse, in a world already full of corpses. Making more is easy. *Very easy.* Do you understand?"

"Maybe. I mean, uh, yes!" protested the ex-con, staring at the body laying at his feet. "But, you got to make an impression, and if they fight, well, you can't leave resistance behind. But you can't just waste my gleanings! That's my money! We got rights, like you said!"

He subsided as Loki loomed behind Green.

Khorbish carefully slid out from behind Biggs.

"Rights?" answered Harlan. He looked first at Biggs, and fought his impulse to slap the stupid candy bar out of his hand. He then nodded at the assembled group. "What you have are responsibilities. To me," he said, tapping his own chest. A gleaming woven bracelet of fine fibers gleamed with blue and golden highlights against his narrow wrist.

"To them," he said, gesturing to Eva, Loki and the other lieutenants.

"You even have a responsibility to the new recruits that we glean from this benighted countryside."

His arm movement expanded to take in the huddle of chained men, the kids who were sobbing and the few women under guard.

"But you speak of *your* rights," Harlan said, eyes glinting. He stepped closer to Biggs, purposefully invading the other man's space, close enough that he was confident that Biggs could feel his boss's breath on his face. Harlan lowered his voice, ensuring that only the ex-con could hear him. "I'm leaving this convoy. I've other teams to govern. After this fuck up, Biggs, you'll immediately return to base camp with the gleanings accumulated so far. I can't babysit you, Biggs. I'll let you come back but it will be your last chance, Mr. Biggs. Your very. Last. Chance. When you return, you'll complete the sweep and never, ever leave a job half done again. To do so is to risk this entire plan. Now apologize to me in a nice clear voice, so everyone can hear."

Harlan Green gestured casually as he stepped back, the movement of his arm encompassing the numerous Gleaners, the workgang and the newest prisoners.

"Make them believe it," he said.

Biggs's eyes flickered to Loki for a moment, but he didn't even hesitate. His posture remained upright and he raised his voice for the benefit of the large crowd, while looking directly at Harlan.

"Governor Green, I humbly apologize for wasting your time with that trash. It won't happen again," he enunciated carefully.

Harlan looked at him for several long moments. Despite Biggs's outward calm, the open collar of his looted shirt revealed skin that was darkening with a suffusion of blood, making his facial tattoos and neck harder to distinguish.

Which was fine. Anger and fear were Green's tools-in-trade.

Green made sure that Biggs felt his regard and then turned to address the entire assembly, focusing on the newest raw material. A few steps away, the corpse was still leaking onto the pebbled, gray pavement.

"My name is Governor Green," he began, framed against the dark clouds overhead. "I'm the head of the new civil government in this area. Let me explain how your life has changed."

October 29th
Cumberland Uplands, western Virginia
The Twelve Gauge Ranch

Robbie Robbins inhaled mightily, enjoying the scent of fresh cut timber and crisp fall air. Then he mopped his brow with a dull OD green bandanna that he produced from a hip pocket. Once his hands were dry and *clean-ish*, he produced a can of Copenhagen and with an unthinking but expert flick of the wrist he settled the tobacco in a compact mass before packing a generous wad into his cheek.

He and his teammates hadn't been able to operate the portable sawmill for months, lest the din attract unwelcome and ravenous guests. However, early in the crisis, the heavily wooded pocket valley had rung with the snarl of chainsaws and ripsaws as they harvested lumber from their property. He sighed, enjoying the cool numbing sensation of his fresh dip, and surveyed the pile of freshly re-stacked, seasoning lumber that he had salvaged from a dead pecan tree months back. The work was worthwhile, and the resulting couple hundred board feet were stacked out of the weather, continuing to season into very nice furniture grade material. He'd even set aside a dozen stock blanks for the ranch's gunroom.

By reflex, he turned to scan his surroundings, taking in the fruits of the last five years of his labor. The existing prefab structures had already been connected to the county grid, but had been improved and expanded by contractors selected for discretion. His group of fellow investors had also paid to update the leach field and installed a large propane fuel system. Likewise the small wind turbine mounted on an adjustable mast. The seasonal truck garden surrounded by an eight-foot deer fence didn't make the ranch self-sufficient, but it helped. They even had a decent four-lane range good out to three hundred meters. In theory, the families that had formed the limited liability real estate investment firm and acquired the previously run-down property in the ranch were each supposed to take their turn in residence. In practice, the Robbins family had stayed for nearly five years so far, homeschooling their four kids and systematically renovating the estate, one project at a time. Most of the investors summered at the ranch, which had enough room for all the grownups, and in good weather, plenty of tent space for the kids. Some investors had never lived "in" at all, but contributed in other ways.

They'd all been carefully selected after much mutual evaluation. The group ran heavily to retired members of the U.S. Special Operations Command Association and its auxiliaries.

Rob snorted as he thought about the Aussie specops troop turned banker that was their silent partner. Smith had always been unlikely to leave New York City and the ready supply of feminine company that it had represented. He'd certainly helped with the financing though. They hadn't heard from Smith or any of their City connections in over ten weeks. The last of their association arrived at the refuge two months prior, leaving a third of the group unaccounted for.

Rob appreciated the presence of his teammates and their families; there was greater safety in numbers. Pre-Plague, solo prepping had been all the rage and much money had changed hands for this gadget or that bit of apocalyptic kit. The truth was that mutually supporting communities and mastering the fundamentals of shelter, water and security were far more important than any high-speed, low-drag gear. Of course, if you *had* mastered the basic, special purpose kit could make a difference.

He grinned. *His* group had more than mastered the basics.

The group had selected western Virginia for a variety of reasons, though compromises had been made.

There was no point in buying in the Midwest when the majority had day jobs on or near the Boston–New York–D.C. axis, for example. Not to mention that the Feds controlled water rights on everything west of the Mississippi.

The vets had pooled their interest and their resources. Rob had learned that the only thing that preppers liked as much as prepping was *arguing* about prepping. After debating an apparently infinite number of variables such as growing season duration, proximity to a trauma facility and the potential for future development and others ad nauseam, they'd finally pulled the trigger on a large plot of land.

The investors had deliberately picked a spot that was not too close to the interstate and then groomed the access road so that all-wheel drive was required to navigate some carefully tailored obstacles. The difficult and extended driveway dissuaded lookie-loos and represented just one layer of a passive defense that shielded their get-away from prying eyes. The location was in a triangle between two small rivers. In the event that social conditions deteriorated so badly that the rule of law was no longer respected, bridges across each waterway could be dropped, preventing most access by vehicles. There was also a ford that could be used in an emergency, and was known only to the locals. No one was going to find this place without a map.

Rob wasn't particularly antisocial, but he would've been lying, pre-Plague, if he told anyone that he wasn't a little paranoid about things.

And look at that—all of sudden who was looking like a prescient genius?

Ha!

Having a place that didn't rely solely on the grid generated some peace of mind. He inhaled deeply again and glanced at the sky. The clouds were lined up in endless gray-white ranks. Time to get moving again; there were plenty of chores to get done and a trip into town to complete before dark.

He heard a low growling coming from the woodline, not even thirty meters away. As quickly as a stooping raptor, he pivoted his head and drew his ever-present side-arm. The infected that emerged from the shadows was a large male. This one appeared to have been feeding well. The dirty skin was mostly free of open sores and there were no obvious wounds. As it neared, the infected accelerated from a quick walk into a jog.

Rob had already lined up the Glock. The big Gemtech can still allowed use of iron sights, but in the last year Rob had invested in a *very* expensive prototype holo sight, a concession to his middle-aged eyes. As the infected reached a full sprint, the tall former CAG operator completed the trigger stroke and the infected dove into the dirt a few feet short of its intended meal.

Rob kept the gun on the unmoving zombie as he scanned the treeline for any additional threats. His kill had been alone; the steep approaches to the ranch dissuaded most infected from wandering upwards when easier meals could be had for less effort.

"Maybe they've eaten out the lowlands?" Rob muttered. "Sucks to be them."

In an effort to stave off boredom and forestall arguments, Tom had been rotating passengers among the three vehicles. Today he was again driving the lead Suburban, but this time he was the lone male in the big SUV. Risky was riding shotgun, one hand maintaining control of the AR casually lying between her legs, muzzle down on the floor pan. Astroga was tutoring two of the 'tweens, Jonsdottir and Blaine, in the dark arts of the E-4 Mafia. Bloom and Bua filled the crowded third-row seat of the SUV, alternately arguing or pointedly ignoring one another. All of this was set to a succession of late nineties pop music.

Tom was irritated, and neither the so-called music nor the bickering were helping. Rounding the next turn, he jumped on the brakes, biting back a curse. The passengers didn't refrain.

"What the hell, Smith!" Bua yelled from the back seat. "How about warning us before you do that!"

He sighed inaudibly. She still hadn't forgiven him for leaving her restrained during her break with reality in the SAFE.

"Should be wearing your seatbelt, dummy," Astroga said, tugging on the strap that had locked her in place during the sudden stop. "SOP is briefed every morning."

"Oh, you think you're pretty smart don't you, you little fascist runt..."

Tom ignored the incipient fight behind him, and scanned the road.

For every five miles of westward progress made, he'd been compelled to backtrack as much as three times that distance, threading the convoy through wrecks, abandoned roadblocks and on one occasion, as they crossed a tributary of the Tennessee, several hundred infected.

This time, he'd stopped just short of another impassable clot of cars. The jumbled wrecks, some blackened with fire damage, blocked not only the two-lane state road but also the drainage ditches and fields extending to either side. Tom checked both sides of the state highway. Even the big-wheeled trucks and 4x4 jeeps that had ventured off the hardpan were sunk in soft mud up to their floor pans. A few decomposing bodies added their redolence to the grim scene.

He plucked the handheld radio from the cup holder.

"Turn it around, Kap, Gravy," he said into the handheld radio. "We'll try the last fork to the north and give it another go."

The radio emitted short bursts of static as the other drivers broke squelch to acknowledge the order.

Inside the car, Risky had turned around to adjudicate the growing argument. Astroga was still taunting Bua while Bloome held her seat mate by the waist, preventing her from climbing over the seat-back in front of her.

No one was paying the least bit of attention to security, the *one* critical thing that he asked of his car-mates.

"Enough!" Tom yelled, his booming voice cutting through the growing din. "That's it! I can't threaten to stop the car, because we got somewhere to be."

He punched the stereo button with one thick finger, and the pop singer's endless request "to call her, maybe" was cut mercifully short.

"But the music goes off, and stays off until you all grow up, do your job and"—he squinted at Astroga—"stop instigating fights."

There was a brief silence. Jonsdottir scooted all the way against the door and Bloome tugged Bua back onto the bench seat. No one met Tom's look. Well, almost no one.

"Me, sir?" replied Astroga, wide-eyed. "I was just sitting here—"

"Off!" Tom repeated. "It stays off."

He got the unwieldy SUV turned around and a few moments later all three vehicles were picking their way back the way they'd come.

Tom knew his passengers by now. The drill was well practiced. *In three, two, one...*

"Mr. Smith, is it okay if we talk?" Astroga asked politely. "As long as we maintain our security scan?"

Tom grunted neutrally, which was all that the juniormost Army soldier needed.

"Because I've been thinking," Astroga continued, "and you being the expert, maybe you can answer this question that's started bugging me. I figure that this emergency is going to go on for a long time. We are gonna have to build everything back up, but before we do that, we have to clear out all the zombies, and there's steps before that."

"Make it march, Astro," Tom said, keeping his eyes front. He smelled a rat.

"So the question is: what's the best sort of man to have with you during the zombie apocalypse? For aspiring, independent women like us?"

Meeting her eyes in the rear-view, Tom raised his eyebrows.

"My going-in position is that the definition of a good man has changed," she added helpfully. "What do we want from a man, now? With all this?"

She gestured towards her window.

"We're not having that conversation, Astro," Tom replied sternly, returning his eyes to the road. "Ask me la—"

"Is interesting question," Risky said with a sideways look at her driver. "In Manhattan, it was all about money. Money not so important now. What does a good man have to bring to table?"

"Respect," said Christine.

"Guns," Astroga countered. "Big guns!"

"Yeah, is he cute?" Jonsdottir added, flexing a slender biceps. "A cute prince, with big guns, like in the movie."

"The other kind of guns, silly," Astroga said. "Sheesh."

"He's supposed to be good in bed?" said Cheryl, drawing verbal admonishments from a couple of adults before collecting a head chop from Astroga. She indignantly waved a wrinkled fashion magazine that sported a lurid cover and added, "What? Its says so right here in the survey results!"

"Must look healthy, no biting!" Risky said, looking at the cover. Tom saw her quirk an eyebrow in his direction as she added, "Maybe nibbling is fine."

A few more suggestions originated from the back seat, and in short order the participants were getting titters, and finally an outright belly laugh all around.

"Can we drop the subject?" Tom said, clearing his throat.

Whether the exchange was morale-boosting humor or not, a few of the ideas were a bit . . . specific. He felt a warmth spreading across his face and hoped that his tan covered what he suspected was the start of a blush.

"So you've got a *healthy* guy in mind," Astroga replied, ignoring Smith and turning to Risky. "How do you let him know that you're interested?"

"Smile at him a lot," offered Jonsdottir.

"Act like you need help," Blaine offered.

"No, never that," Risky said. "Offer help instead."

"What do you mean?" asked Bloome. "What kind of help, Risky?"

"Like Specialist Astroga said, it's different world now," Risky said. "Best kind of man not just interested in nice makeup and a good body," she added, turning to look at both teens, who were listening carefully for a change. "If you find man that makes that priority, look for different man. World was never perfectly safe. This especially true for the physically weak, and sorry, but is fact that average woman is much weaker than average man."

There was an offended huffing sound from the very back row.

"There is reason that men and women have different events in sports," Risky replied, dismissing the implied objection. "The world is not, how you say, inherently equal, no matter what the weak wish. Old civilization had problems, but the old, the young and the weak were protected from the worst threats. Now, is even worse for women—no police, infected everywhere. But any man worth having wants more than good-looking woman who only needs protecting. He wants partner who can carry her share, cover his back with rifle and is not afraid of blood. You don't want prince who will come rescue you—you want man who puts strong woman over woman who asks for help all the time. He will want decisive woman, not wishy-washy supermodel who can't decide what salad to order."

"Yeah, girl power!" enthused the teens.

"Does not come automatically," Risky said, smiling to soften her words. "If you want power, must accept problems of responsibility. But we will teach you. Right, Specialist?"

"You betcha," Astroga replied. There was a longish pause. Tom knew this part of the script, too.

Three, two, one . . .

"Mr. Smith, if I change the music, can we turn the tunes back on?"

CHAPTER 6

The fitful breeze stirred a fading American flag and rattled the halyard against the aluminum flagpole.

Another small Southern town, of the kind Tom and the rest had seen several times before.

The sameness was simultaneously comforting and unsettling. There were the usual two churches, elementary school and a medium sized chain supermarket. There might be a hardware store. A pharmacist. An auto shop. Perhaps two hundred homes, ranging from double-wides to stick-built construction.

The usual number of long dead bodies in view, usually recognizable because of the remnants of clothes, especially shoes, that marked each person's final resting place.

Total silence, save for the occasional bird call.

"What do you think, Boss?" Kaplan inquired. "Nothing has moved in the last half hour. Around or through?"

"Not sure, Kap," Tom said, lowering the binoculars and squinted at the early afternoon sun. "I don't really want to backtrack. The last good lay-up spot was two hours back. I hate to give up that much ground. I think that the main road looks clear enough to get through without detouring or pushing. Map says we can find a camp spot about another hour up the line."

Most of the party was staying in the SUVs, including their newest acquisition, the Dodge, below the line of sight to the town, hidden by the gentle rise of the road that they had followed. Drivers remained behind each wheel, and the passenger side doors were open on the first two vehicles, just in case Tom and Kaplan had to scamper back in a hurry.

"Wouldn't mind a look see," the security specialist said thoughtfully. "If we see a lot of infected, we just drive on. No infected—we can take a look for salvage. I wouldn't mind a hose pump for transferring fuel."

Many abandoned vehicles still had partially full tanks, but Smith insisted on topping off their tanks whenever they could and siphoning gasoline was a hated chore. The rubber hose method had been their standby. However, Tom suspected that the gas stations they passed had plenty of fuel. Without electricity to power the main pumps, there was no way to get at it unless they found a manually operated pump.

Tom took another look through the glasses and considered.

"Right," he said decisively. "We go through."

For the sake of security and the comfort of human contact, the drivers had instinctively parked together in front of the hardware store. Tom ordered most of the staff to stay with the vehicles, armed and watchful. Meanwhile, two pairs would scout Ace Hardware and the grocery, respectively.

Tom took Worf into the grocery. They ghosted through the aisles, stepping gingerly in part to avoid making noise but principally because the volume of remains was impressive.

"Why so many bones?" Worf said wonderingly. "Why choose to die here?"

Tom bent and picked up a polymer framed pistol, the slide locked back on an empty magazine. He held it for the other man to see. A few empty pistol magazines peeked out from the litter.

"They were fighting over the supplies," he said. "This must have been the first place everyone decided to go when they ran out. Maybe this guy..."

Tom nudged a clothed skeleton, mostly complete except for the upper skull and one arm. The chest and legs were somewhat protected by an equipment vest and heavy trousers. Despite the decomposition, it had clearly been a really big man. Incongruously, a velcro patch of a small white rabbit armed with a switch blade gleamed on the vest, below the remains of dry yellow beard.

"...decided to protect what he was buying, or looting."

"I see a fair bit of brass," Worf said, pointing at scores of spent cartridges scattered on the dirty floor. "Must have been a real rodeo here, at the end. Not gonna lie—not sorry I missed it."

Tom followed the gesture and then did a double-take.

"Now that..." Tom said, leaning over and shaking garbage from a small axe "...is worth the salvage."

"R-M-J," spelled out Worf, reading the logo. "Shit. That's a six-hundred-dollar tomahawk! How did that end up here?"

"Finders keepers," Smith said. "This thing can chop through nearly anything."

The tomahawk was anodized steel, Despite the lack of maintenance, the sharpened edge still gleamed. Opposite the blade was a wicked spike, sharpened on both sides and curving gently back towards his hand. Green paracord served as a grip. Tom bounced the handle a few times contemplatively and then unstrapped the sheath that still adorned the corpse's vest.

"Thanks, mate," he said, saluting the single battered corpse.

One aisle over, Tom heard Worf inhale sharply.

"If you liked that, you're gonna love this."

Tom turned a corner and found the floor carpeted with skeletal remains. The vinyl flooring was nearly completely obscured by the bodies, or rather, parts of bodies. Few clothes were visible in the light that filtered through the front of the store.

"Whoa," Worf breathed quietly. "That's a lot of bones."

"No clothes," Tom said dispassionately. "The bodies are disarticulated. Brought here and eaten post-mortem. It was a larder while the water lasted."

He looked down the adjoining line of shelves. They were bare but the floor was ankle deep with chewed plastic bottles. He picked one up and read the brand name.

"Looks like the zombies like expensive designer bottled water, too," he said. "Liked it enough to chew their way into the bottles to get a drink."

"You can't bite through a plastic bottle!" Worf said, objecting quietly. "No way!"

"Apparently you can if you're thirsty enough," answered Tom. He glanced back at the bone pile. "Looks like this was the buffet area."

"Where did they all go?" Worf asked.

"They're animals," Tom replied. "They go where there's water, food and shelter. But not here, not anymore."

Having swept the aisles from one end, they paused near the back of the store. There was a set of swinging doors to the rear stockroom, but they clearly had been closed for some time, blocked by refuse that was piled against them.

"Okay. Let's fill a bag with any canned stuff that looks useful and get out," Tom said. "I'm about rea—"

Outside, shots rang out.

"Eva, don't forget!" Biggs blustered. "My town, my gleanings! You're just here to help and advise."

"Sure thing, Biggs," the slender brunette answered nonchalantly. "It has nothing to do with Mr. Green wondering if you are an asset or a liability, right? Whatever you gotta tell yourself. Just remember that Green sent me along to keep an eye on you."

She tugged at the heavy fireman's coat. What she really needed was something for a female firefighter, but so far she was making do with a men's extra small. Clearing towns was as much about making sure that you didn't get swarmed and bit by infected as it was finding and "rescuing uninfected survivors." She wore her armor on the inside of the coat. Only the lieutenants had both proper body armor and vaccine, so working hard enough to earn the heavy clothing was literally a matter of life and death for their recruits. Even for the vaccinated, avoiding bites was helpful. The vaccine didn't protect against the plethora of really disgusting bacteria found in the average human's mouth, let alone a carrion-eating shambler.

However, the huge crowds of zombies that had been common at the start of the Fall seemed to have left this town on their own.

The Gleaners had found that absent a water source, most infected would decamp from their old homes and spend their time closer to the many lakes, rivers and creeks that were common in the area. Still, you could run into a pack unexpectedly. All it took was a windmill-filled water tank or a cattle pond.

Somewhere, there was going to be a *really* big swarm, but it wasn't here. That was good enough for the Gleaners.

"On your last visit, how far did you get before you fucked up?" she asked Biggs, completely unintimidated by his size. Of course, her right hand stayed on her rifle's pistol grip.

"Maybe a third of the place," he growled. "Up ahead a few blocks."

"Let's just do the sweep and move on," Eva said, adding, "I want to get back before dark."

Biggs nodded and raised his fist over his head, pumping it once. The line of forty or so men waiting next to the parked convoy left their vehicles and began sweeping through the outlying homes of the abandoned town. Khorbish took station on the side farthest from the leader.

As the line of armed men combed through the town, the labor gang of fifty chained men were lashed into position. As they reached each successive abandoned car they would release the brakes and push it clear of the road. Locked vehicles were dealt with simply by smashing windows. Tangles of vehicles were either pulled apart or shoved by main force using the reinforced winches and bumpers of the semi tractor wreckers salvaged by the Gleaners.

The occasional single zombie lurched into view, stirred to action by noise or disturbed by scavengers, only to be dropped at close range.

On the second block, they hit pay dirt.

A whoop went up, and one of the men came outside, carrying a middling sized child under one arm. The girl fought and kicked ineffectually as the sweeper brought her over to the center where Biggs and Eva waited.

"Fresh as a daisy!" exclaimed the man, presenting his find to the field boss as Khorbish trotted up, drawn by the commotion.

"Well, that's not too bad," Biggs said, his eyes alight. "Any more like this?"

"Nah, Boss, just the one," the sweeper replied as his boss took possession of his prize.

Eva considered the young girl at close range. She was remarkably clean and her blonde hair was tied back in two braids. Perhaps ten years old, she kept swinging her fists against Biggs's leg and side, but the thick clothing and armor mitigated her ferocity.

"Man, this one is a peach!" Biggs crowed. "Just the right size for the rec hall. Betcha she smells good enough to eat!"

He leaned down to sniff the girl's hair.

The short girl reared back and unhesitatingly latched onto his ear, blood spurting from her lips.

Biggs screamed and straightened, raising her into the air even as his gloved fists struck her loose. The little girl was thrown several feet away, but hit the ground and rolled to her feet. She immediately began to sprint away, towards the center of the uncleared town.

Eva laughed into her fist as Biggs clapped his right hand to his bleeding ear, and clumsily tried to cross draw his pistol with his left. Khorbish smiled appreciatively. Even the sweeper was laughing, but he turned to recapture the girl.

Biggs finally made the draw and aimed his pistol at the small form darting between two houses and fired several rounds.

"FUCKING LITTLE BITCH BIT ME! F-FUCKING KILL HER!" Biggs screamed as Khorbish grabbed the pistol hand and forced it down. The two men struggled for a moment before Biggs shook free, glaring.

"Don't shoot her, you idiot!" Eva yelled. "The kids belong to Green. We'll run her down, she can't get far."

She turned to the rank-and-file Gleaners that were hovering a few feet away, having paused when the shots were fired.

"Well? Get after her!"

Kaplan had drawn the hardware store and asked Vinnie to accompany him. The place was thoroughly picked over.

They were examining a foot-operated inflatable pool pump to determine its suitability for fuel recovery when they heard shots.

"Come on!" yelled Kaplan. He sprinted back towards the cars.

Exiting the front of the store he surveyed the scene. Concerned faces looked first his way, and then towards the grocery as Smith and Worf exited. One of the teens pointed down the street where a small figure was sprinting hard. Another figure hove into view, then another and another. They were all clothed, and presumably, not infected. They chased the runner.

Kaplan snapped his M4 up and flipped the 3x magnifier into place behind his red dot Aimpoint. The figures jumped in size.

A little blonde girl chased by...dudes in fireman's coats?

Armed men in firefighter turnout coats.

"On me," Kaplan ordered his wingman and ran across the street.

Hank was a loner. Despite his study of country music, playing football, and some bitching tats, he had never made any strong friends after high school. When the zombie plague came, he got sick, just like Mama and Pop. But they died while he lived.

The few survivors in his little town had *still* kept their distance when he emerged, gaunt, and starving. Popular he might never be, but Hank was canny. Pop's old M1 carbine did for the occasional zombie until the new folks showed up a month back.

When the Gleaners rolled through and offered him a probationary place in their new world he'd said "Fuck yeah!" It wasn't the vaccine they held out since he figured he was immune now. But to be part of something, maybe something big?

Oh, hell yes.

So when the top dog got his ear bit by the itty bitty girl and that scary bitch Eva said fetch!—well, Hank was gonna fetch.

Little girl had some wheels on her, that was for sure.

Suddenly he spotted movement ahead of her. More Gleaners?

Wrong clothes.

And better guns.

Risky was standing next to the second Suburban when she heard the shots.

"Where did that come from?" she snapped, dropping her right hand to her rifle's grip. "Anyone see anything?"

She watched Durante grab a radio but before he could make the call, movement in the grocery revealed Tom and Worf stepping out.

She followed Katrin's pointing arm when the 'tween pointed out the window at a small speeding figure being chased first by one, and then three adult men. The running shape resolved into a small girl in blue jeans. Risky watched the runner cover the last twenty-five meters, the girl's braids snapping like short bullwhips in her wake.

And then the little girl ran straight to Risky and grabbed her by the waist.

"Don't let them touch me!" she wailed.

Tom's head was on a swivel. Every minute an additional armed fireman, or whatever they were, was joining the armed gathering a couple of short blocks away. There was a lot of gesturing and pointing. One of them had a radio.

"Everyone behind the vehicles," he ordered briskly. "Drivers start the engines. No one shoots."

He turned to Risky.

"What's going on?" he demanded.

Risky was squatting on her heels, trying to talk to the incoherent little girl. The girl's face and collar was covered in blood.

"Is she infected?" Smith asked, alarmed.

"Shh, shh little one," said Risky, crooning to the sobbing child. "I'll protect you. What's wrong? Why do you run?"

The little girl didn't release the adult, but buried her face in Risky's hair, bloodying it in the process.

"Shhhh. Look at me." Risky took the girl by the shoulders and examined her closely, checking her eyes and hands for the telltale tremors of H7D3. Seeing none, she tried again.

"What's the matter?"

"They're going to take me away!" the girl replied, still sobbing.

"What?" asked Risky, suddenly intent. "Who?"

"The bad firemen! They killed everyone and came back to take me. The big one said I smell nice, but he's mean!"

A loud yell carried from down the block.

"Hey you. In the cars. Give us the girl!"

Risky looked directly at Tom. Her eyes looked like something a gazelle might see, just as a lioness closed the distance.

Hank held the radio a little farther from his ear.

"What do you mean, you don't have her?" came Biggs's voice. "Why the fuck not!?"

"There's more people," the new Gleaner said, stammering. "Strangers. They got her!"

"What?!" the radio blared. "Who? Never mind! I'm on my way!"

This was not according to plan.

Maybe if Hank got the girl back...

"Hey, you!" he yelled. "In the cars. Give us the girl!"

Tom looked at Risky once more.

Given the set of her jaw, it seemed unlikely that she was going to relinquish the girl without a fight, or at least a very convincing explanation. The kid was still clinging to Risky, who moved her around the SUV to shelter behind the front wheel.

"Kap, how many?" he asked, without looking up.

"Seven," came the reply. "Eight now. Nine. They all have longs."

Tom considered just loading the trucks and running away.

But this was the first organized group that they had seen since New York. Information was worth more than gold.

"Send someone over," he said, yelling back up the street. "No guns. We don't want any mistakes."

A voice very different from the first roared back.

"Fuck that shit. She belongs to me!"

A taller, thicker figure began stumping towards the bank survivors.

Tom could see even more men appearing and starting to filter to the sides, taking position behind cars and dumpsters.

"Kap," he ordered. "On me. Durante, put together a firing line. Risky, Worf, watch the sides. Everyone else keep your head down. We're gonna try to talk our way out of this."

"The girl's not for giving back," Risky said flatly.

"She isn't worth our lives," Tom replied tersely, his eyes on the group of men. "No time now, take position."

He could see that their position was untenable. The bank survivors' vehicles were the extent of their cover and they were severely outnumbered. Tom's eyes flicked back and forth, weighing options, and then refocused on the approaching strangers. At this point, the options were to talk it out or start a drama in the middle of the street.

He flicked his eyes back towards the nearest group. The biggest was clutching the side of his head. He was also yelling at a shorter man, presumably his subordinate, judging from the amount of cursing and cuffing.

Okay.

Tom would try to smooth things over.

The big one in the middle was bleeding heavily from under a bandage that he held to the side of his head. He seemed pretty upset about it. The bright red stains continued along a well-equipped equipment harness and further down the side of his fireman's coat.

His hands were empty, but he bore both a rifle and a pistol.

"Hello," began Tom, mildly. "My name is—"

"Don't fucking care, prick," the bleeding man snarled out of a face covered in prison ink. He advanced a step. "Gimme the girl now! She fucking bit my ear off and no one does that!"

"And what do you do that she needed to bite ear?" Risky said, suddenly standing next to Tom, quivering in anger. "Big strong man couldn't keep terrible scary girl from attacking him?"

"Uh, Risky, would you . . ." Tom began to say, trying to keep the impending violence from actually igniting.

"Shut up, bitch, or you are next!"

❧ ⊖ ❧

Durante had shaken the two Cosa Nova men into a line, their rifles shouldered at the low ready but out of sight behind the SUVs. He glanced over at Worf, who had been listening to the exchange.

The Guardsman drew one finger across his throat.

Durante recognized the signal.

In reply Durante flashed back his favorite, the extended middle finger covered by the opposing palm.

Meaning, "Cover me, we're about to get fucked."

Worf just looked mystified.

Right, Smith's little classes hadn't gotten to advanced hand and arm signals yet.

Durante looked back towards the nervous men lined up behind the angry bleeding shouter.

They wouldn't be a problem.

He evaluated the dozen plus guns that were a short block away. He could also see movement just ahead of their flanks. Kaplan was one car over, bent halfway over, but tautly examining the evolving tactical picture. Even more men were filtering in from the sides.

He glanced over at Gravy and shook his head.

They were really exposed here.

"Tom," Durante said conversationally, "we need to get a move on."

Vinnie was excited. This was going to be a chance to show the new boss that he was a good guy. That he was dependable. He fiddled with his rifle out of nervousness.

His magazine dropped out of his magwell and clattered loudly, just beneath the bumper.

Hank was excited. He was standing right up front, with the boss. With the important people. The other side had some guns but so far there was just yelling.

He heard a loud clatter of metal and a curved magazine of bullets rattled into view, next to the SUV. He raised his rifle out of instinct and aimed under the car.

Biggs heard the clatter and looked under the truck, seeing a rifle magazine and the barrel of an M4. He registered one of his men aiming at an unseen threat. He dropped his ear bandage and drove his hand towards his holstered pistol.

∽ ⊖ ∾

Eva was fuming that Biggs, the idiot, wouldn't answer his god-damn radio. As Khorbish plopped down beside her and aimed through his own rifle scope, Eva watched the confrontation unfold. The small group of people weren't backing down. If everything went to hell, Biggs was going to be left holding the bag, all by himself.

Out in the open.

Eva's eyes widened in appreciation.

"Hey, Khorbish, how do you feel about a promotion?" she said, nodding towards the pending confrontation. "That asshole is about to get us into a gunfight, and there he is, right in the middle of the road."

Khorbish looked at her uncomprehendingly for a moment, and then smiled nastily. He reset his cheek weld and aimed in.

"On my go," Eva said. "We gotta make sure that negotiations break down at the right moment, no?" Then she smiled a little and aimed at the tall stranger in front of Biggs, sliding the safety to the fire position. She took a deep breath, let about half trickle out through her nose and permitted the front sight to sharpen against the blurry tan outlines of the target's chest. As soon as she saw sudden movement, she completed the trigger stroke.

Durante heard the clatter. Knew exactly what it was. Knew exactly what was going to happen.

He'd carefully maintained the lowest profile he could, exposing no more than a part of his cranial and one eye. Even as the first inbound round cracked, Durante snapped his rifle up and starting servicing targets, dropping the first man to move and smoothly pivoting outwards and picking up as many hits as he could before hell cut loose.

In the first second he had sent rounds through the first three heads, swinging right to left.

Out of the corner of his eye he saw Tom stagger and then Risky yanked the boss backwards.

Somehow, Biggs wasn't hit in the initial fusillade. He got his pistol up and shot over the suddenly prone man who had been arguing with him. His pistol bullet dug into the black macadam several yards away. He began to aim the pistol again but he saw movement to his left.

As he turned, he felt a solid punch to his back, accompanied by sharp lance of pain.

Confused, Biggs turned his head back to the nearest SUV in time to watch a rifle barrel foreshorten. The muzzle flash yel—

Panicked by the incoming fire, and desperate to fire back, Vinnie finally reseated his magazine and stood to fire. He began yanking the trigger, randomly shooting at the buildings and the flashes which he could see about a block away. His aggression was faultless. Unfortunately, his tactical acumen was not.

Vinnie was fully upright and got off several shots before he absorbed three rounds nearly simultaneously. His armor stopped the two rifle rounds, which left nothing more significant than shallow craters, but a shotgun pellet creased the skin over his collar bone, creating intense pain and a nonlethal bloody gash.

"What the fuck?!"

Vinnie Mouse Sacks sank to one knee, looking for the source of the sudden burning pain in his neck and shoulder. Unfortunately, this left his head above the SUV's hood. His skull intercepted a fourth round and he dropped with limp finality.

Fat Ralph gaped at the body of his friend, but ducked lower, demonstrating somewhat better tactical judgment.

Tom felt the bullet impact on his chestplate in a sort of clinical way. He continued to raise his rifle but someone grabbed the carry handle on the back of his plate carrier and violently tugged him backwards. Reflexively he reacted by pushing with his legs in the same direction, jackknifing in the direction of the pull. As though he were in slow motion, he could hear individual rounds impacting against the SUVs, one every few moments. As soon as he was in cover, Risky began pulling at his armor, desperate to assess his injury.

He shook himself and twisted left and right. No pain, no heat. The armor had kept the round out.

"I'm fine," he insisted. "No penetration. Take a position!"

"Are you sure?" Risky said, pausing her fevered tearing at his velcro closures. Seeing his calm eyes, she inexplicably flared in sudden anger. "Fine!"

She left him and crawled to the next wheel over.

Tom glanced under the truck, but all the nearer attackers were down, along with the screamer, who was missing most of the back of his skull.

Worf, Astroga and Gravy were in view, all prone, angled behind the vehicles. Their rifles popped in syncopated time, but their lack of rhythm didn't reduce the effectiveness of their fire. After the initial blast of incoming fire, relatively few bullets were still hitting their vehicles. Kaplan had paused shooting, like Tom, and was evaluating the battle.

Even so, it was time to move. They had to get off the X, and right now.

"Mount up!" Tom yelled as loudly as he could. He double-checked himself for injuries, but couldn't see any blood. "Get in and drive! GO!"

Over his shoulder he saw Risky pushing their own kids and the rescuee into the first Suburban. One of its tires hissed as the run-flat compound tried to plug multiple leaks.

"Kap!" he yelled, waving his arm to get the shooter's attention. "Drive! GO! I'll cover."

Kaplan gave him an exasperated look but dropped his rifle on its sling and swung behind the wheel as Tom continued to fire on their attackers a block away. Judging from the number of muzzle flashes that winked across his front and sides, the volume of fire should have been really heavy. Yet, most of the rounds must have been very badly aimed, or they would all be dead by now.

The first Suburban made a tight turn and scraped past a stop sign, shedding a rear view mirror as Kaplan punched the truck out of the ambush.

Ralph was trying to shove the limp bulk of his dead friend into the backseat, but couldn't get the leverage he needed. Screaming from the interior greeted his bloody efforts as gray and yellow brain matter smeared on the upholstery.

"Leave it, he's gone!" Tom ordered. "Get in and shoot!"

With a horrified look at the ruin of Vinnie's head, Ralph let go of the body and closed the door on the terrified rear passengers. He jumped into the front passenger seat of the truck as Tom finished his mag dump and hopped behind the wheel of the big SUV. Worf continued shooting from an open window, risking the exposure in order to keep rounds moving downrange.

"Gravy, GO!" Tom yelled at Durante. "Mount up and follow me!"

Durante was laying down final suppressive fire as fast as he could but glanced up at Tom's desperate yell.

Tom shifted into reverse, mashed the gasoline pedal and the big engine roared in low gear as the fat tires drove the truck backwards. He accelerated backwards, alternately looking over his shoulder at their escape route and then back over the hood towards their last SUV. He saw Durante stagger as he got into the red Durango, but nonetheless slam the driver's door shut. Moments later, the Dodge began backing up as fast as Durante could push it, before spinning around in a violent turn and accelerating again.

Tom's eyes flicked back to the rear window as his own truck approached fifty miles an hour. He kept his hands light on the wheel in order to avoid over controlling the big truck. A single twitch would cost him steering authority and then roll the vehicle. He turned his head forward in time to see Durante, leaning into the Dodge's steering wheel, catch up to the first two trucks.

The Suburban's windshield caught another round, and one of the kids screamed anew.

Dave Durante knew that he had taken the round in a bad place. He felt the searing icy pain of the initial impact as the lucky shot caught him just under the lip of his armor plate, entering his lower back two inches from his spine. He felt his left leg go numb, but was close enough to the Dodge to lever himself inside by main strength.

"Get your seatbelts on!" he commanded his passengers. Emily Bloome turned to click the belt on her charge and then herself. Her eyes were huge in Gravy's rear view mirror.

Combat adrenaline had gotten him into the car and now it got them off the X. He pinned the accelerator to the floor, smoking the tires as he backed up as fast as he could. At a wide spot in the next intersection Gravy smoothly pulled the car through a J turn, spinning the steering wheel first one way and then reversing it, simultaneously popping the automatic transmission into drive.

A wave of pain swept through his body as he straightened out.

He was bleeding badly, a hot sour sensation boiling in his abdomen. Looking down, he saw that his lap was red with blood. A few more rounds splattered against the sheet metal, but he could see the edge of town. They were almost clear.

But instead of elation, Durante felt a wave of pain and nausea that seemed to tighten his skin all over his body. With startling suddenness his vision began to blur, graying around the edges.

He leaned onto the wheel and tried to steer smoothly but over corrected. He reversed his turn, and over compensated again. Looking up, Durante saw that he was going to strike a guard rail. He stabbed the brake and jerked the wheel, but too late.

Blackness.

Eva stopped shooting and kept her head down. As return fire tapered, she was in greater danger of catching a ricochet courtesy of the atrocious marksmanship of the Gleaners foot soldiers. She counted on the other Gleaners to reflexively return fire and continue until either they ran out of ammunition or the strangers managed to run away.

She heard engines roar and she peeked around her cover.

The red SUV was last to back away, and as she watched, the driver managed a skillful reverse, shifted into forward and sped forward.

The Gleaners could barely hit a vehicle at rest. Shooting at the trucks now was just an exercise in turning ammunition into noise.

"Cease fire!" she yelled. "Cease fire! Cease fire!"

She turned to Khorbish.

"Get the rest of these asses to stop shooting—they're just wasting ammo at this point!"

Khorbish nodded and started yelling and cuffing the nearest shooters.

Still in sight, the red SUV followed the bigger trucks. All three vehicles were approaching freeway speeds. She watched the convoy pass the edge of the town proper when the last truck began to weave a bit. Without warning it crunched against a guardrail and pirouetted into the ditch about a quarter mile from the fight.

"Cease fire!" she yelled again.

She had to repeat herself several times until the fire stopped. She eyeballed the wreck. One of the bigger SUVs had pulled up.

Interesting.

Behind the Gleaners some infected began to trickle in, and the shooting started again.

Tom watched the Durango rock to a halt. He ruthlessly suppressed his fear and anger. Even as he smashed the brake pedal to the floor, he issued directions.

"Ralph, grab the radio," Tom ordered. "Tell Kap we got a crash, we're stopping. Worf, I need cover fire right away. Once I stop, organize a firing line and deny the road to anyone that shows up."

"Check," Sergeant Copley said. His tone was all business.

"O-okay," Fat Ralph stuttered as the abused transmission clunked back into drive.

Moments later Tom drew abreast of the crash. He ran to the ruined vehicle. The acrid scent of coolant was distinctive as the radiator fluid from a smashed radiator splashed across the hot engine.

He could hear one of the kids crying inside and tore at the airbags that obscured his view. When he found Durante he tried to understand what he was seeing.

Modern passenger vehicles are engineered to be highly resistant to impact damage from front and rear collisions. The sheet metal that makes up the unibody is designed and assembled so that it crumples inwards, absorbing and dispersing the huge amounts of kinetic energy created when a fast, heavy vehicle is stopped almost instantaneously. The passenger occupied space is further protected by a special cage of thicker metal, intended to prevent a phenomenon that pre-Fall automotive collision experts antiseptically labeled a "compartment intrusion."

In short, modern vehicles could take enormous amounts of damage while keeping their occupants alive, if not uninjured.

Had Dave Durante actually struck the rail squarely, the crumple design would have worked as intended, preserving the integrity of the passenger compartment. The airbag deployment would have reduced internal trauma even further. Instead, his last ditch effort to avoid the collision changed the impact aspect of the Dodge in important ways.

First, the sudden braking made the front of the car dip slightly. This permitted the rail to impact just above the bumper, engaging the sheet metal of the hood and fender instead. Second, the last moment course correction changed the impact from a full front aspect collision to a different sort of accident, labeled by those same cheerful automotive experts as a "short overlap impact." This denied the crumple zone geometry a chance to protect the driver and permitted the full force of the impact to focus on a single concentrated part of the SUV's body, the driver side window pillar.

The end result was that Dave blearily regained consciousness to find his view blocked by the white fabric of the now flaccid airbag. He reflexively attempted to swipe it aside with his left hand but his arm wouldn't move properly. He looked down to find the dashboard in his lap and his left leg twisted into the firewall at an impossible angle. He waited for the pain, but only the throbbing in his stomach was perceptible.

He squinted his eyes and years later opened them again. This time he saw Tom staring at him.

"God-damn it, Gravy!" Smith said urgently. "Can you hear me? We have to get you out."

Smith swiftly cut away the air bag with a folding knife and then blanched at what he had revealed.

"That bad?" said Dave, coughing. "You should see your face."

Blood trickled from his mouth.

"Jesus." Smith turned to yell over his shoulder only to bump into Kaplan who had run up, rifle in one hand and a trauma bag in the other.

"Hey Gravy, you just fucking around or wha..." Kaplan's comment died away. "Aw, fuck, Gravy. Jesus."

"Ha," Dave tried to chuckle. "I don't think that He's here, just now."

"How do we cut him out?" asked Kaplan. "If we take the leg he'll bleed out."

"No one is taking my leg!" he wheezed, squinting as the pain began to bloom up his broken arm. "Get the kids out. Gimme a rifle and go."

Risky appeared in Dave's vision as she moved to help the battered passengers out.

"Maybe we can dismount the seat from the pan..." Tom said, leaning into the back seat area, desperately trying to come up with a solution.

Kaplan's head jerked up as they all heard a bullet snap overhead.

"These fuckers ain't giving up, Tom."

"Buy me time," Smith ordered, his voice harsh. "Okay Gravy, what we're going to do is—"

"Tom, just give me a rifle and go," Dave said, wearily cutting him off. "I'm hit bad. My leg was gone before I piled this shitheap up. Losing blood. That's why I dumped it. No point. Just let me do my thing and buy you time."

"What?" Smith stopped trying to muscle the seat from behind and turned to look more closely and the bullet wound. Underneath Durante blood was pooling in the ruined seat. "Shit, how bad?"

"Gut shot," Dave stated, his voice beginning to fade a little. "Maybe some splinters in the spine. No feeling in the leg."

Smith rummaged urgently in the trauma kit, plastic wrapping and gauze flying haphazardly. He popped the fasteners on the body armor and opened Dave's shirt. Locating the messy exit wound, he immediately packed it with a blood clotting bandage, drawing a pained grunt from Durante.

"The damage is inside, Tom," Dave heard Risky as she handed tape to Smith, one piece at time. "The bleeding will continue, we don't know how bad."

"She's right," the wounded man said, looking up at his friends. "Give me a weapon."

"Gravy, I can't—" Smith began, but Risky leaned back into Durante's field of view, handing another open package of blot clot to Smith.

Behind her, he could hear a rifle popping rounds too quickly to be accurate. There was a pause and Gravy distantly heard Kaplan correcting Fat Ralph's shooting.

"Tom, we can't stay," Risky said gently. "We must go. Let him have what he wants." She looked at Dave. "Dave, I'm so sorry."

She leaned over Durante and kissed his forehead.

"Godspeed, Horatius."

Dave smiled. "I got the first kiss after all."

It wasn't a bad way to go. This was all right. He looked towards Smith in time to see his friend's face change.

Smith had looked up from the wounds in Dave's abdomen and turned to face Risky, his face terrible, angry.

"*You*," Smith said, packing pain and anger into a single syllable. "You and that girl."

"Smith. Smith. TOM!" The unexpected strength in Dave's voice cut through Smith's anger.

Smith looked back at Dave.

"Stop it," the trapped man said, his voice husky with pain. "She's right. I woulda done the same thing if I had the balls. Saving little girls is what we're supposed to do, Tom."

He began to cough, hacking sounds wracking his chest.

"Save the rest, leave me," he said, spitting blood on the airbag, making a crimson splash on the white fabric. "It's the right call. You know it is."

Dave exchanged a look with his friend for a long moment. Two friendly rifles were barking now, their cadence growing in urgency. Another round snapped overhead.

"See you, Risky," Dave offered. Straightening, she looked at him again, her violet eyes sad. Then she turned and trotted away.

"You too, Tom," Dave added.

A long moment passed. The sharp metallic impact of a round striking one of their vehicles prompted a short heartfelt monosyllable from Fat Ralph, unseen behind them.

"Everyone back in the trucks," Smith ordered, keeping his eyes on Gravy's.

Letting his own AR hang by the sling, he reached for Dave's weapon. He automatically performed a chamber and safety check to confirm that it was loaded, ensured that the optics were intact and then laid the pistol grip in Durante's right hand.

"See you in hell, Boss," Dave said. "Can't be worse than here."

"Save me a spot," Smith answered, and looked at his friend's face for a long final moment. "I'll be along presently."

Then Smith straightened, blinked twice and turned to jog back to the remaining vehicles.

By touch, Dave flicked the safety on his AR off safe. Then he looked up at the ceiling of his SUV, and took slow measured breaths, willing energy into his good arm.

CHAPTER 7

"Tell me again," Harlan Green said patiently. "How many people did you see, exactly?"

"I only saw a few!" stuttered Freddo. His strategy of staying firmly in the middle of the Gleaner pack had been intended to keep him from being noticed too often. During their disastrous fight earlier in the day that strategy had only ensured that he survived to be interrogated by Green, which was terrifying all by itself. "Maybe five people with guns? Three cars, one crashed."

"Yes, you've said that already," replied Harlan patiently. "Did you talk to the survivor in the crashed car?"

"No," Freddo twisted his hands together. "He was already hurt. When he started shooting again, everyone just shot the car until he was mostly in pieces. Even so, he killed Hank! Hank was my friend!"

Harlan regarded the nervous man quietly.

"Mr. Green, I think that Fred here will immediately tell us if he remembers anything else," Eva said, interceding in a respectful tone. "Right, Freddo?"

"Right!" stammered the terrified man. "Anything I think of, it's yours!"

"Of course it is," agreed Harlan. "Mr. Loki, perhaps you could show Mr. Fred the parlor. Once we're done, you might walk him over to the rec hall. He seems to be in need of some reassurance."

"Oh, that's all right. I don't . . ." Fred said, but subsided as Loki stood and opened the office door, holding a hand out to indicate that the smaller man should go.

With a quick look around the room, Freddo scuttled out.

Stooping slightly under the average height ceiling, Loki carefully closed the door and returned to the table.

The dim light filtering from outside was considerably augmented by two LED camp lanterns. They cast a bright white light. Batteries were not yet in short supply, but eventually they would run out.

"Miss Eva, one moment while I make a note," Harlan spoke sideways as he located the bulleted list of prioritized salvage.

"Here we go," he thoughtfully checked an existing entry. "Tri-fuel lanterns and stoves. Seventeen in inventory. Excellent."

He turned to face his subordinates squarely.

"I'm very sorry about Biggs, Mr. Green," Khorbish said, beginning his own apology, but Harlan shook his head.

"Mr. Biggs was no great personal loss," he said, waving away the man's first concern. "On the other hand, he was a symbol of my authority. He was representing me. Us. The organization. And we were beaten. Publicly."

"I don't think that the group that got away is going to challenge your authority," Eva said carefully. "And we held the town afterwards."

"The girl," Loki rumbled. "They took the gleanings. Our people saw them do it."

Khorbish winced.

"Just so," Harlan replied, with an approving glance at the much larger man. "And we lost significant strength and commensurate group confidence. That can't be allowed to stand. What else can you tell me?"

"The group we hit is pretty organized," Khorbish offered. "They could shoot, they moved faster than expected and when one vehicle wrecked the others came back to rescue them. Well, all but the first headshot at the intersection and the other guy that got trapped in the wreck."

Green looked thoughtful as he digested this.

"Did you get anything else from the wreckage?" he asked.

"What wasn't crushed or shot up, sure," Eva said. "Clothes, some food and cooking gear, an intact fuel can. Some good body armor, a couple pistols and a rifle that we took off the dead guy. Some maps."

"The weapons?" the mastermind asked, raising an eyebrow towards the former prison guard.

"They had armory tags for something called BotA BERT," the

big man answered. He unslung a rifle and handed it to his boss. "Made by Daniel Defense—expensive, not just a generic carbine with some aftermarket upgrades. Above average optics. I'll add it and the other useful stuff to inventory."

"BotA. I see," Harlan stood the rifle against his desk and returned his attention to the woman. "And the maps? Show me."

Eva produced a canvas case and unfolded the bloodstained cover. Harlan took it from her and closely examined the map, unfolding it further. Carrying it over to the wall, he spread it against the map already pinned there, comparing the two.

"Hmm," Harlan maintained his study for some minutes, then transferred some markings to the larger map. "Well. Isn't that interesting." Returning to the table, he rapidly wrote on a yellow pad of stick-on notes while they watched.

"What didja find?" Khorbish blurted, unable to wait any longer.

Green noted Ms. Eva's annoyed glance at her compatriot.

He then turned to Khorbish, regarding him levelly, and gestured to the large map that he had previously taped to the wall of the office. Additional yellow notes were sprinkled liberally across its surface, highlighting points of special interest.

"We're continuing to clear our way west and north," he said, standing with his hands on his hips, looking at the map. "There are extended clear driving lanes, double lanes in places, to the south and back the way we came. What else do you see?"

"We're about to hit a river up north," Eva said as she moved to stand next to Khorbish. "A couple of towns and a big city. Not huge, but still bigger than we've hit so far. Figure, lots more zombies."

"What do we find on rivers?" Harlan Green tapped the winding blue ribbon of the Tennessee River. "What were they used for?"

Both lieutenants leaned closer, looking at the newest pen marks on the map.

"What's a Thunder Blast?" Eva asked, annoying him.

"Not that," said Harlan curtly. "Underneath."

"Aaah," said Khorbish, exhaling slowly. "Interesting."

"Just so," Harlan regarded him approvingly. "And someone else appears to think it's interesting too."

He turned to Eva this time.

"Miss Eva, you brought back what, two dozen effectives from your little adventure?"

"Sixteen worth keeping," Eva said, turning from the map. "Five dead. Seven seriously injured. Twelve more that aren't good for anything but simple guarding or basic labor."

"Not bad," Harlan replied. "I'll call a general meeting, but after Mr. Loki reviews your assessment the two of you may pick the most useful of remaining crew from Mr. Biggs's group. Ms. Eva, you will prepare for a reconnaissance to the northeast. Mr. Khorbish, your group will evaluate the river crossings to the northwest. Before departure, both of you will conduct local sweeps by way of shaking down your groups. But after that, you'll help me learn just what this map's former owners thought to be so interesting."

Loki closed the door behind the exiting duo. His eyes lingered for a moment on the woman's backside...but no. He understood Green's rules very well. Miss Eva might become one of his lieutenants, off limits.

If she continued to deliver.

Green himself continued to look at the map.

"Those two are gonna fight," Loki stated flatly.

"Almost like I'm planning it that way," Green replied, without turning around. "If they each survive long enough."

"The little man, Khorbish, he's clever, but a weasel," Loki said before adding, "But like you said before, we need smart people, people that we can trust."

"I need the right leaders to fill my Guards," Green said, turning to look up at his trusted subordinate. "And I've only one of you. The markings on that rifle that you evaluated was owned by something called a Biological Emergency Response Team— apparently one from a New York–based bank. They aren't here by accident and if they lived this long they aren't stupid."

"Eva's smart," Loki said. "At least as smart as I am. Quick, too. She can handle the men. Even money says Eva is going to kill the weasel while they compete for Biggs's spot."

"Maybe. Maybe not, Mr. Loki," Green replied. "It's time for Officer Young to step up. Assign him to Eva's team. She can evaluate how he shapes in the field and if he's going to be an asset. And I think that while Khorbish and our Miss Eva compete to prove their worth to take Biggs's share, you and I will prepare for a little wanderjahr about the territory. I think that we'll profit by not leaving the most important job to someone else."

Loki continued to watch as Green studied the map and traced several roads eastward. After a bit Green spoke over his shoulder.

"Now, be a good man and pick us out one for after dessert," Green said, his eyes never leaving the object of his study. "Maybe the one with the lovely eyes. Drug your choice well. I don't feel like wrestling."

Loki grinned at his boss's shoulders.

The job did have some satisfying perks.

Reaching for the easily visible carrion floating just out of reach, the zombie lost its footing on the steep rock-covered shore along the dammed reservoir and tumbled into the water.

"Back in the day, I never thought that I'd get sick of the view across the river," said Mike Stantz. "But I have to say, I've had just about enough."

The days of dressing sharply were well behind the senior Tennessee Valley Authority officer. His jeans were stained, his work shirt wrinkled and his boots were muddy.

The few remaining TVA staff were secure inside the fenceline at the hydroelectric facility or ensconced in neighboring Spring City.

The dark green Tennessee River lapped gently along the inside face of the dam. Bodies bobbed along the dam wall, herded by the consistent breeze and riding buoyantly as an inevitable result of decomposition. Downstream, migratory seabirds wheeled and dipped, white plumage flashing as they fed on bait fish that were stunned by the impellers that powered the mighty generators.

Enough infected fell from the dam roadway or tumbled into the lake upstream to ensure that the supply of dead bodies was refreshed, despite the scavenging ranks of infected that patrolled the riverbank in full view of the concrete observation platform that jutted out from the shore-side lockhouse. One infected, weakened by hunger, was trying to crawl out of the water while fending off another, more powerful zombie who was drawn by the splash.

"I'd say, 'eww'—" Brandy Bolgeo replied, "but watching a zombie drown doesn't even make my gross-a-meter twitch anymore."

Each dam along the river included a large canal lock that could be flooded or pumped out to raise and lower river traffic, such as barges and tugs. Before the Fall, this arrangement connected the Tennessee River westwards to the Ohio and Mississippi, and southwards directly to Alabama and the Gulf of Mexico. Even though river traffic had fallen precipitously during the economic slowdown, each canal lock still had accumulations of barge trains and tugs that had been stranded when the lock system ceased operations.

The long expanse of visible shoreline was dotted with moving shapes, all of them infected, who searched the riverbank for food. In front of their vantage point, the hale zombie first pulled its weakened cousin from the water, and then attacked from behind, burying its teeth in the soft flesh of the neck. The matted beard of the attacking infected suddenly ran with dark red blood.

"Yep, but just when you think it's over," Stantz said with the merest hint of humor, "they step it up a notch."

"Is it...um?" asked his teammate.

"Dinner and a date, apparently," Mike said as he implacably observed the grotesque scene. "Happens."

Below, the feeding infected was simultaneously attempting to copulate with its prey. Biological incompatibility didn't appear to be an inhibitor.

"Ugh," Brandy said. "I wish we could just shoot them all."

"Not enough bullets in the world," Mike said, turning away. "We had thousands of rounds of ammunition, sure. We used most of it just clearing the small part of Spring City that we held on to, never mind trying to clear the dam or any of that."

He pointed towards the cooling towers of the nearby Watts Bar nuclear generating plant. The wispy white condensate that used to hover over the towers was missing. Quiescent, the towers were a mute reminder of the power of the Fallen civilization.

"Do you think anyone is still alive in there?" Brandy followed his glance.

"Maybe," mused Mike. "There hasn't been external communications in months. The diesels went quiet almost two months ago. There hasn't been a catastrophic nuclear accident or, believe me, we would have known it by now. We didn't see anyone on our last foray into their equipment yard for that rough terrain crane. No one has come out, and the grounds are crawling. But they lasted long enough to do their job and shut it all down."

The Watts Bar and nearby Soddy Daisy nuclear plants had been part of an extensive power generation infrastructure along the Tennessee Valley. As far as they could tell, the dam that they protected was the only remaining operating plant within any knowable distance.

"No, the nuke plant is fine, it's the dam I worry about," he continued, fretting. "The maintenance is going undone because we can't get to the parts that need attention."

He looked at the dam lock, which in normal times was used to raise or lower barge traffic between the upper lake and the river below the dam. The lock motors had seized during the confusion surrounding the early Fall. That same confusion had damaged a lot of the exterior bits of infrastructure, like the crane that adjusted the critical trash racks. Large coarse screens that fit into grooves along the upper side of the generator house, the racks kept oversized logs and well, trash, from entering the dam intakes and damaging or worse, fouling the turbines themselves.

"I can live with a dinged turbine blade," he said, gesturing angrily. "But a fouled assembly means burning out the windings and rotors. They're the heart of the dam. If we lose those, there's no point."

Brandy followed his gestures, pensively cupping her chin and calculating the risks, as best she could.

Zombies didn't swim, or least wouldn't swim very far. Corpses had begun to accumulate in the raft of debris along the upstream face of the dam. Occasionally, one of the mostly naked, bloated corpses would sink. At flood, a turbine drank in sixty thousand gallons of water *a second*. And there were five of them, although only two were at risk. When each corpse hit the turbine it was moving at thirty miles an hour. The turbines that spun the mighty generator would burp a dirty cloud of offal into the spillway downstream, gladdening the migratory seabirds that had previously relied on a less frequent diet of small fish.

"So far, so good, right?" she finally asked. "The deaders are mostly naked and the turbines haven't even hiccupped."

"For now," Stantz replied darkly. "Not forever. Come the rainy season, were going to get a lot more debris, and the turbines can't digest a tree."

"I can't believe how many infected there are," Bolgeo said, wondering aloud to distract Stantz from something that they couldn't chance. "And we're only seeing a fraction of the horde."

"They're filtering in along the shore from the metro area," Mike replied, referring to nearby Chattanooga. "We are effing lucky that it's nearly sixty miles away or we would've been overrun in the first few days."

"We're damned lucky that you started getting us all organized when you did, or no one would have lived this long," Brandy replied. "The power has kept us alive. It's the only thing that made it possible."

Stantz had used his authority and remaining staff to isolate and reinforce the dam's critical components, including a small landing area that they used to beach their boats. Roads remained impassable, but Spring City was a brief boat drive away.

Much farther downstream, the fall of Chattanooga had finally been precipitated by a sudden mass of refugees pouring along the I-24 from Nashville. Overnight the infection rate had shot through the roof. Hardy communities east and south tried to block roads with varying degrees of success. Stantz's early preparations had paid off tremendously. Key among them had been cutting State Route 27, the principal road from Chattanooga into the immediate area of the nuke and hydro plants.

"Such of us as are left," Mike said grimly. "We lost two more Springers yesterday. Old lady Johnson insisted on feeding her 'family' and she fell off the container wall into the infected. Jimmy leaned too far trying to save her and was snatched off."

"What was she thinking!" exclaimed Brandy. "Just . . . damn it."

Almost ten percent of the people who contracted H7D3 pulled all the way through without turning. Mrs. Johnson had been one of the few older people in nearby Spring City who had weathered the virus's flu symptoms. Many of her extended family had lived as well, but as mindless carnivores who prowled the edges of the wall formed by shipping containers that Stantz's crew had emplaced during the early, desperate days of the Fall. Behind the barrier sheltered a small oasis on the edge of Spring City. Extending to the lake shore, it ensured that Mike and his few remaining technicians could commute by boat to check on the dam and the power house. By traveling after dark, they minimized the number of infected attracted by movement.

"She was thinking that she needed to take care of her people," Mike said, shaking his head. "And even though she died doing it, you can bet that someone will continue the practice. Christian charity, etc."

"There are still enough of us to protect the plant, the switching yard, the town and keep us fed," Brandy said flatly. "But not if we keep losing people. How long do we hold on? And what if the number of zombies goes up?"

It really wasn't a question, but Stantz answered anyway.

"We hold for as long as it takes," Mike said, scanning the area again. He ignored the growling and wet tearing sounds originating in the disgusting scene right in front of them. "As long as we have to. And I've got some ideas."

Downstream the water was briefly stained an unnatural color and the terns rose into the sky again, screeching happily.

Paul Rune picked his way through the local high school, scavenging for Kohn's prioritized items. The heat and insects had already had their way with the people that had died inside, so the smell wasn't too bad. He carefully didn't examine the classrooms other than to ensure that none held live infected. Though the school had been evacuated well before the Fall there were plenty of human remains, and they were somehow especially eerie in a school setting. Behind him, his wingman lagged, though he held his pike at the high ready, blade angled up and ferrule nearly dragging on the blue tiled floor.

"Jackson, move up," Paul ordered the townie in a low tone of voice. "All we need on this sweep is to confirm there aren't any infected and see if we can locate the school dispensary."

"This place gives me the creeps," mumbled Jackson. "I had a nephew that used to go to school here. Haven't seen him since."

"I'll say I'm sorry for your loss later, when I mean it," replied Paul in a very soft tone. "Just now I am a little too focused to give a shit. And you should be too."

The former intel analyst scanned the hallway and held up one hand.

"Okay, hold up."

He slowly eased forward to look left and right at the hallway intersection. The one-story school appeared deserted, but they had deliberately avoided making noise in order to conduct the recon without stirring a large number of infected. It was still even money on whether or not they might hit a nest.

Survivors and foragers had both reported that infected would tend to group up in shelters and appear to doze, perhaps saving energy. So far, there wasn't much understanding on the how or the why.

"I don't get why we're looking through a school?" said Jackson, complaining. "We don't need school supplies."

"Were you asleep in the briefi—never mind," Paul said, biting back his frustration. It was up to him to teach these handless cows how to fight and survive. Damnit, Smith should have been here by now. He would've organized this mob in a day. Paul stopped moving and let the second man catch all the way up to him.

"Keeping your voice down doesn't mean whispering like you are in a theater," Paul said, speaking softly in order to illustrate his point. "Just use a very low volume and pitch so that your voice doesn't carry. Now the point of our jaunt into this little corner of heaven is to locate and recover medical supplies, so the school dispensary is a target. Second, this place has a shop class, so we can identify tools for a later sweep. Third, we are looking for paper maps of the surrounding area. Lastly, we are checking for survivors and measuring the density of infected."

"And another thing, fuck this spear shit," his wingman said, persisting. "We have guns, why are we using freaking spears?"

"We don't have unlimited ammunition and guns are loud. Loud equals zombies. Like your voice. Now shut it."

So far, they hadn't found a thing, including any infected. Paul was feeling pretty relieved.

Naturally, that meant that it was time for a zombie.

A bank of open wall lockers and trash broke up the infected's profile, so Paul almost missed the first stirrings as it turned its head, spotting him.

This one must have been a football player. The tall, long-haired male was gaunt, but huge muscles still padded its shoulders and arms.

"Pikes!" Paul ordered, taking three long steps forward. He used the momentum of his charge to bury his spear in the infected's throat, socketing the weapon all the way up to the crossbar, fully eighteen inches past the needle sharp tip.

The zombie didn't get out more than the beginning of a querulous growl before it choked on its own blood and dropped, clawing at the pike shaft.

"Whataya waiting for?" Paul asked forcefully as he kept his

weight on the infected, pinning it to the floor. "Put your pike into the head and finish it!"

Even as the townie moved up, Paul heard another growl, this time from a classroom a door down.

Lovely.

From the bench seat, Risky could see the back of Tom's head.

She'd spent the day during the flight from the disastrous reconnaissance with her arms around the newest addition to their group. She'd finally persuaded the girl to share her name: Elpis Ambrosio—Elf for short. The grade-schooler had sobbed quietly into Risky's ribs, her face pressed into the rough Cordura fabric of the older woman's plate carrier. Eventually Elf fell asleep and, rather than risk waking her, Risky held still, braced against the inside of the car door. She carefully avoided looking at the rear view mirror, avoiding any eye contact with Tom.

She felt as though her heart had been torn to pieces.

It ached for the little girl's fear and pain, which resonated with Risky. The refugee had obviously lost her family. She'd been traumatized by her capture, however brief. Finally, she was thrown among strangers. Risky could empathize, understanding precisely what Elf felt as only another survivor could.

Risky was grateful for the temporary preoccupation of caring for the girl, because it distracted her from the second stab to her heart. The onetime mobster's moll had bonded with Durante strongly, as only comrades who'd shared danger could. His patience, his counsel and his obvious allegiance to Tom made the loss of Durante hurt all the more.

Durante had been special.

Perhaps most of all, her heart broke when she remembered the look in Tom Smith's eyes when she'd pointed out the inevitable, that they had to leave Durante behind. And she knew that Tom blamed her for the fight. From their first meeting she'd acknowledged his attractiveness. In the months since, she had come to see Tom as a paladin who was holding firm to his oath of allegiance, heedless of cost and alternatives, well past the point that any reasonable person would persist. That quality had saved them all.

She didn't just want him, she respected him. Knowing that he felt her responsible for Durante was an intense, painful ache. Acknowledging that he was right doubled it.

Still, she knew that her decision to save the girl was the right one. There hadn't been any good decisions available. Durante himself had said that the best definition for combat was a fight where one could do everything right and still die.

The enemy always got a vote.

Risky knew that as their world fell ever deeper under the assault of the virus Tom would continue to honor his word. He would put his promise to his former employer foremost, even if there was no more bank left to rescue. Risky knew, *knew* deep inside, that saving something that didn't really exist any longer wasn't the answer.

Maybe there was an alternative, something that else that Smith could consider worthy of his oath. Maybe.

Outside, the ruined countryside flowed past, a repeating loop of fire-blackened buildings, tangles of ruined vehicles and the occasional infected lurching into view before disappearing into the distance, behind them.

And now she knew that there were even worse monsters just out of sight, for now.

Though it cost her any chance to reach him, she knew that she could never, would *never* leave a child to the beast that they had slain in the first exchange of fire. A world where that transaction was satisfactory wasn't any world that Risky wanted to live in.

The dying light that filtered through the pines flickered on the inside of her window. She looked ahead, at the reflection of Tom in the driver side window. The mirror image of his face rapidly alternated between shadow and light.

The depleted two-vehicle convoy pressed on for a few hours, passengers and drivers alike anxiously scanning for signs of pursuit. As the shadows lengthened over the road, she watched Tom reach for the handheld radio to warn Kaplan that they were going to pull over for a map check, make repairs and prepare for the next leg of driving.

They found a truckers' rest area that was sparsely populated by a few burned out vehicles, including the skeleton of one that had been driven into the restroom building, burning it too. The driver was still in his seat, but no one commented on it, or seemed particularly disturbed.

While Smith awaited full dark, the group set security, quietly ate and replaced damaged tires. Risky watched Tom and Kaplan don peculiar cranials that vaguely resembled bicycle helmets. Once they snapped the night vision devices onto a clip, each swung the electronic devices upwards and Tom circled the group up for a quick brief.

"There isn't any point in waiting here for that group to pursue," Smith announced. "The risk of driving at night is outweighed by our need to completely break contact. Once we pass a few more major interchanges any pursuer will have difficulty guessing at our direction of travel."

"How far to the next place we can stop?" asked Dina petulantly.

"Pre-Fall, I woulda said that it's an hour, maybe two till we reach the next SAFE," Smith said patiently. "Now? A day? Day and a half?"

"This is *such* bullshit," the schoolteacher said, folding her arms across her chest.

"You want to stay here?" Emily offered. "The men we fought were collecting camp followers, like an old-fashioned army. Despite your age, you might qualify."

"Savage!" chirped the short soldier, holding a fist bump out to Emily, who stared at it, nonplussed.

"Oh, you bitch!" said Dina Bua, her hands balling into fists. "You did not just—"

"Aaaand you two are riding in separate cars from now on." Smith sighed. "Astroga, you got Bua. Emily, you and the kids are in the back of my vehicle. We're going to be really squeezed together for the next day or so, so we'll have to work at getting along."

Smith eyeballed Bua meaningfully and then consulted his watch. "We're going to leave after full dark, call it thirty minutes or so. Be ready and loaded in twenty-five."

"Okay, sweetheart," Astroga said, grabbing Bua's elbow. "There is a bush over here with our names on it."

Risky watched Bua try to jerk away from the shorter soldier, only to be surprised when Astroga yanked back, twice as hard. The specialist easily persuaded the former schoolteacher to keep the peace, and the rest of the group dispersed.

Risky waited a few moments and then walked up to Smith. She looked at him closely. Despite the fatigue that she knew he must be feeling, he seemed alert and focused. His eyes swiveled as he watched her approach.

"Miss Khabayeva?" he asked professionally.

"Busy now, I understand," she said carefully. "But I want to tell you that I want to talk to you, really talk, when we reach the next place where we have room and space to breathe. Yes?"

He looked at her carefully, his face still.

"Of course," Smith replied finally. "When we have room and space."

"Excuse me, Mr. Smith?" Emily said, approaching within a few steps. "I think that you need to take a look at this."

Katrin was supporting Eric, who was clutching his stomach.

"Hello folks," Tom asked, looking at the pair with raised eyebrows. "What's the problem?"

"My stomach hurts and..." Eric began, but subsided, his face red.

"He had an accident in the car," explained Katrin. "He's vomiting and he has cramps real bad and he's been going to the bathroom since we stopped."

Tom looked at the two, nonplussed, then frowned.

"Eric, have you been only drinking the water that we give you and washing your hands every couple hours?" he asked.

"I, I think so," the miserable boy said, then clutched his stomach even tighter. "I got to go!"

He ran behind some bushes while his classmates looked on helplessly.

"E. coli, I think," Emily stated flatly. "Maybe something worse. No way to be certain."

"I want you to wash your hands right now," Emily said, turning to the remaining teens. "Use the wet wipes that smell funny," she added, referring to the ammonia towelettes. "Stay out of the car till I clean it."

Tom waited until the kids walked over to the back of the truck.

"If we're lucky, it's only food poisoning," he said in a low voice. "With all the decomposition and the poor field sanitation, it could be dysentery—hell, it could even be cholera. Either way, keep him hydrated. We've got to keep moving, so the truck is going to get bad. Can you help him?"

"Yes," Emily said, nodding firmly. Retching sounds sounded behind the bushes. "Looks like I'm on."

"Is Bua going to be any help?" Tom replied, jutting his chin towards the latrine area, where the second schoolteacher was hastily emerging.

Emily looked over and shook her head.

"I can't see how," she said.

"Tell me about it," Tom said, under his breath.

Joanna Kohn was quite satisfied with her agenda for the meeting so far. Very little material progress had been made, but the framework for success was in place, and that was what mattered.

The first crisis to confront the newly arrived survivors at Site Blue had been the unexpected departure of the helicopter that originally fetched them. Although the oh-so smart Smith had thought ahead to providing for the pilots' families, the end game chaos had prevented the neat pairing of routes and aircrew to the refuges where their dependents were already sheltering. The last Joanna, or anyone else for that matter, saw of their sole aviation asset was the pilot in *their* helicopter fluttering north to Pennsylvania and Site Bugle.

That unpleasant surprise had spawned the very first structured camp meeting. Initially, Joanna had permitted Rune to run the semiorganized chaos that the previously transported bank staff had perpetuated. Thus were born the daily, weekly and monthly meetings necessary to coordinate the survival activities of the camp.

Joanna had watched Rune flounder, administratively out of his depth. He had deferred, eventually, to her guidance. Joanna had refined the meetings, spawning a feeling of normalcy. It was almost like the apocalypse hadn't yet occurred. She chaired the renamed weekly Executive Coordination Committee as the acting administrator. Symbols mattered, and she'd briskly moved to legitimize her eventual, permanent status. One such was sitting at the head of a green baize-covered table while receiving reports and recommendations and dispensing direction and resources. That process was now underway for today's meeting, and she'd allowed Rune to have the floor.

"There was limited infected presence in the school," the former banker said, continuing his report. "We found a small amount of analgesics and other first aid level materials. The shop was intact and well stocked. Most of the equipment operates on two hundred twenty volts, and we aren't well provisioned for that, yet."

There were nods around the table. He looked up towards the head chair. Joanna smiled warmly at him.

"Ah—we moved to the local pharmacy next," Rune said, hurrying to consult his notes. "It was already looted, but we recovered several kilos of drugs for evaluation and possible retention. I couldn't be sure, but it appeared that their compounding facility had been modified for vaccine production. Some of the equipment as well as the remains in the refrigeration units were consistent with an ad hoc vaccine lab."

"Remains?" asked Christine.

"The evidence was consistent with the presence of human spinal tissue in various stages of processing," he answered.

"Did you find vaccine?" Joanna said, suddenly very focused.

"The building had no power of course, but despite the condition of the remaining material, the setup strongly suggested that the lab was abandoned before production was at any scale," he carefully replied, before continuing. "I also grabbed some reference books. We located two more survivors who elected to return with us. They're in General Processing now."

Rune referred to the large semipermanent tent where recent arrivals were temporarily billeted as they were evaluated for health, skills and needs.

"One dental hygienist and her teenage son," he said, concluding his report.

"Is she familiar with the operation of dental X-ray equipment?" asked Joanna. "That could become key, no?"

"We have the detailed process for creating attenuated vaccine," answered the former bank intel chief. "We still lack the specialized supplies, equipment and the expertise to create it safely. And of course, there is no certain way to test vaccine, if we could make it. In theory, a sufficiently advanced dental X-ray machine could meter radiation precisely enough to work, but it requires maintenance, calibration..."

"You are right, Paul," Joanna said, waving the issue away. "A challenge for a different day. Still, well done on the personnel rescue. How do the pharmacological recovery efforts proceed?"

"I looked at drugs and equipment that Paul's team recovered, Ms. Kohn," said Ken Schweizer. The former OEM analyst had grown his beard out, and he affected a beaded chin braid that bobbed as he respectfully nodded. "Much of the lab equipment was clearly in use for illegal narcotics. Some of the precursors might have value. Most of the other salvage duplicates what we already have. However, one new item is a supply of Cipro. It's an excellent broad spectrum antibiotic and it isn't too temperature sensitive. We can use that to treat the new townies who have symptoms consistent with dysentery."

Joanna thought about that. She liked asking questions. If nothing else, it kept other people reacting to her. And occasionally she learned something.

"Dysentery is quite serious, is it not?" she asked. "I seem to recall that it can be deadly if untreated. Highly communicable too, no?"

"Yes, ma'am," answered Schweizer. "It spreads via contaminated water, usually as a result of poor latrine discipline, a failure to properly sterilize potable water or exercise personal hygiene. In the nineteenth century dysentery killed millions. We're living in conditions not unlike that time period."

"So how do we head that off?" Joanna asked, slightly alarmed. "Everyone has to be convinced that safety measures against this disease are for the good of all. Paul, as head of our security, what do you recommend?"

"I agree that the risk of disease is potentially serious, so we need to continue to enforce basic camp sanitation," Paul said. Joanna could tell that he hadn't anticipated this question. "Um, the kitchen staff have to ensure that all drinking and cooking water is brought to a rolling boil for ten minutes and that all utensils be likewise cleaned. Maybe people who are found slacking on the rules have to perform extra guard duty, or perhaps contribute to projects for the Improvements Group?"

Non-skilled survivors as well as everyone not on critical duty took turns expanding the cultivated area or raising the height of the earthen palisade. It was back-breaking labor on scant calories.

"Could someone actually die from dysentery, Ken?" Joanna said, letting her eyes grow a little wide as she glanced around the table, stopping at Paul. "If it can be lethal, then perhaps the measures to encourage mutual safety should have some...bite? There are security implications, are there not?"

"I'll think it over and have some options for you soon, Joanna," Paul answered uneasily. "It is really just a matter of education."

"Thank you, Paul," Joanna said, favoring him with another smile. "Speaking of which, is the Education Committee ready for their update?"

"Good morning, Coordinator Kohn," said Christine, beginning

her own report. "The Education Committee has outlined a general curriculum for our school age survivors. While we don't have textbooks, we do have adults skilled in many areas now important to our survival. The absence of conventional educational infrastructure actually presents an opportunity to bypass some of the hierarchical, promotion based grade levels of mass education in favor of a customized approach that can address the needs of every child, individually."

"Wait a moment," Paul said, interrupting. "There are a couple of elementary schools full of books and other supplies. As few kids as we have, it wouldn't be a problem to—"

"Thank you, Paul," Joanna said, cutting him off smoothly. "I would like to hear the rest of Christine's suggestions. We are just outlining some possibilities, after all."

"And Christine, dear," Joanna said, turning back to the original speaker. "Thank you for the courtesy, but I am only the Acting Coordinator, until we have a chance to establish something less... *field expedient*. Please, finish what you were saying."

"As I was saying..." Christine said, shooting Paul an icy look. "We can tailor outreach for each school-age child. We don't have to repeat the errors of the old system."

"I could not agree with you more," breathed Joanna. "These fresh ideas make me eager to start as soon as possible, once the idea is more developed and reviewed by the Executive Committee in detail."

"Um, don't you think that the parents should be involved?" said Paul, interjecting again. "After all, these are their children we're talking about, aren't they."

"Of course," Joanna said soothingly. "But in a sense, they are all our children, whom we must protect and succor if we are to raise a new civilization. As few as there are, perhaps they should reflect more than just the values of happenstance parents. But, before that, we will need a safe way to inoculate them against the still lethal virus."

Cutting off further debate, Joanna opened a new topic.

"Kendra, what do you have for our Research report?"

"Good afternoon Acting Coordinator Kohn," Kendra said, sparing a smile for Christine who was just seating herself again. "We're lucky that the salvage parties located Ms. Warmbier, the dental hygienist. She's aware of several clinics which may have the model of X-ray machine which might be adapted to vaccine production. Paul's school and pharmacy sweeps located much of the initial laboratory equipment that we need but there is still some hardware outstanding, notably a medical grade centrifuge."

"Once we have that, can we proceed?" Joanna asked, steepling her fingers.

"No, not really," Kendra replied. "We really need a laboratory scientist with a background in virology, a filter medium and a means to test the vaccine, once we produce it. Even if we can match the bank's quality, it's still an attenuated live virus vaccine, not suitable for younger children. Much more time will be required to produce a killed vaccine, and for that we will need proper growth mediums, even more precision filtration, viral growth enzymes and other items."

The meeting went on for another hour as details about vaccine production for both attenuated and killed vaccine were explained. By the close of the meeting, Joanna successfully maneuvered Paul into agreeing to search explicitly for a lab tech and an M.D. He had looked a little uncomfortable but Joanna felt that was more of an advantage than it was a potential problem.

She liked her men a little uncomfortable. It was quite acceptable.

CHAPTER 8

Eva didn't like meetings. She'd say this for the head of the Gleaners, though. Harlan Green kept things short and sharp. Around the table Harlan's immediate coterie was uncharacteristically attentive. In contrast, Eva's attitude seemed negligent, one leg propped over the arm rest of her chair, but her notes were comprehensive.

The Virginia state correctional facility that had housed the second set of Gleaner recruits included a women's wing. A fair proportion of prisoners had improved their education for the purposes of researching their appeals. Eva had been no different. The self-taught ability to make neat and accurate notes was a natural fit to her new role as one of the Governor's Guard, as Green had come to style his inner circle of subordinates.

During the early days of the Gleaners she, Khorbish and others had been set to some independent tasks. There had been early and obvious tests for loyalty and applied problem solving. All the successes ended in creative and often violent solutions. The failed tests generally just ended violently.

The half a dozen survivors were by now well past that screening, having long ago received their vaccine. They graduated from running very small teams whose tasks ranged from reconnaissance and zombie removal to independently taking small towns and bossing road clearance labor gangs.

After the haul that her new team had collected during their shakedown patrols, she figured that Green would cut her a little leeway. Her boss was all about results.

She looked around the room casually. Khorbish sneered when he noted her glance.

His team had done almost as well as hers.

Almost.

"You all know your parts now," Eva listened as Green lectured. "We'll continue to move north towards our longer term base. Everyone will continue to sweep for useful recruits and laborers. Do not get weighed down with crap. Consult the list of prioritized salvage. Keep the roads that we control clear. Some of our teams will conduct special tasks for me, the rest will continue with the plan. Questions?"

Eva didn't really expect any questions, but with this group . . .

"Yeah, I got one," said Dragon. The burly, smooth-scalped man with the dragon neck tattoo and the thing for blue latex gloves raised a hand. "When and where do we get to finally the place where you give me one of these satripey things?"

"Sa-tra-py."

Eva could tell that just correcting the pronunciation irritated Green. The boss went on.

"It means the territory that you'll run for me. As I've explained more than once, we will expand, your territory will grow and I'll assign lieutenants under you. Eventually."

"Sure, sure," the questioner replied. "No disrespect, Mr. Green, you said that before but what I'm saying is *when*? My team has found a lot of quality goods, really good loot, but instead you tell us to clean roads or bring you back different kinds of people. What good stuff we find—well, you're keeping it back here while we hang our asses out there."

He gestured broadly beyond the room.

"Again, no disrespect, but some of the road crew and lower level people are asking the same questions. We need to know enough to keep the good ones in line and the trim the rest, like you say."

Green stared hard at the man who returned his look evenly without looking away.

Eva tracked the exchange. Thanks to the map that she had recovered and which Greene had interpreted before showing Khorbish and herself, she knew a little, okay, a *lot* more than everyone else. She didn't know for certain why Green wasn't telling all of them the complete story about the bankers, if that was what they were, who'd shot up their foraging party. It might be as simple as Green's recognition that knowledge is power.

She watched Green come to a decision. She also noted that Loki was poised, his right hand empty and relaxed.

"Hmmm," Green said, rubbing his chin. "Reasonable. I can give you a sense of strategy and timing."

He took a couple of steps and wheeled, arms folded against his chest.

"We need a permanent base from which to expand. A base that we can use to establish control. It should have easy access to the things that we need, like water, power and...other survivors. It has to be small enough that we can clear the zombies from the immediate area, persuade and manage the survivors and still be defensible enough that we can hold it against any newcomers. Lastly, it should allow us to expand without moving again."

He paused and raised one hand upwards.

"As for when: the seasons matter," he said, pinning his questioner by eye. "I want to establish us in a new base before the first frost. We want to be in position, indoors before the winter weather complicates further gleaning. When spring comes, we'll need to have the nucleus of the labor force, technicians and soldiers necessary to set our community up for the following year. All that takes precedence over electronics, or gold, or recreational drugs. That is why I want you to bring me high quality recruits and why we keep pushing down the road. Now does that answer your question?"

"Sorta," Mr. Dragon replied. "For now, I guess."

Eva smiled. She knew what was coming. It was nice to know a little more than everyone else.

"Gentlemen and lady," Green said, nodding towards Eva, then tapped on the large map. "There are a number of candidate sites. When I have determined the best options, we'll move there. Now, if there are no further questions, carry out your tasking."

"That's a LOT of zombies," Brandy said in an artificially normal tone of voice. "How many do you think that is?"

"The way they move around I don't think that we can get an exact number," replied Mike in an offhand way. "Call it six or seven thousand. What matters is that many could actually just push the fencing over, if they ever came at it at the same time. The first several ranks would be so much mashed strawberry gelatin, mind. Still, our fence can't hold that kind of mass. So priority number one is not attracting attention."

"That many?" Brandy said, looking back across the dam and then back at the road leading south to Chattanooga. "How are you getting seven thousand from that?"

"Count the number in an imaginary box that's about the size of a football field," Mike replied, squinting back at the mass of infected. "Then multiply by the number of football fields that are in view."

The infected were clustering in groups, walking along the fence, across the dam, along the shore—in short, everywhere that the technicians could see. A sort of low growling was audible, like the idling of a distant chain saw. Remnants of uniforms were visible, though most were naked or nearly so. Many of the infected had open sores or partially healed wounds. Skin infections seemed to be common.

"Could be worse," he said distractedly. "If the H7D3 infection rate in Chattanooga is the same as it is here, then more than two hundred and fifty thousand zombies started out and so far, less than ten percent of them survived to reach this far."

"So..." his aide said, "You've, ah, you got a plan, right? For if they decide that they really want, um, in?"

"Well, what I've got is an idea," the stout engineer said, rubbing his chin. "And maybe some prototypes. You know those really big transformers that we stocked in the repair yard?"

"Sure," Brady said uncertainly. "Um, so we are gonna repair them to death?"

"Nope," Mike replied, frowning. "Well, in a manner of speaking. What we do have is a lot of power and no customers. I figure that we can do more with it than we have been."

"Oh!" Brandy exclaimed. "An electric fence. Duh! I should have through of that."

"Well, sure," Mike gave her a little side eye. "Except electric fences are boring. First, we have to see how many really big capacitors we have."

Tom kept his speed down. The cloudy night was profoundly dark, unlit by either artificial light or stars. Even the dash instruments were turned off in order to avoid glare on the night vision goggles which he wore. In the days since the loss of his second, the depleted convoy had pressed on, driving at night as well as day time, extending the distance between any possible pursuit. Behind him, the emotionally exhausted passengers were squeezed together, sleeping fitfully.

Tom was exhausted too. He knew from experience that he could last up to three days with scant rest. After that, decision making and motor skills would erode past the level of usefulness.

Tomorrow would be the third day.

More than the lack of sleep, more than the anger over the loss of Gravy, the sense of being alone weighed on him. Every decision that he made carried life or death consequences, and there was no respite in sight. Tom couldn't remember the last time he could just . . . stop.

Beside him, Risky swayed slightly, belted into the front passenger seat.

Though his NODs painted a bright green and black picture, he knew from experience that judging relative distances through the device was tricky, at best. The decision to purchase the very expensive, top of the line military night vision devices that he now wore had been a good one. However, it felt as though it had been made by a different person a lifetime ago.

Thankfully, the road was mostly clear and the two Suburbans were able to stay on the blacktop most of the time, easing the task of driving.

It also allowed Tom time to reflect.

Outwardly he gave no sign about the turmoil and grief that ate at his conscience. Tom knew that he had been utterly responsible for Durante's death. He wanted to rewind the day, to return to the decision to stop at that stupid town.

He replayed every decision. Every possible inflection point. The endless balancing of time and resources against risk.

Tom suppressed a sigh. Fuck melodrama.

It was no use feeling sorry for himself. It didn't matter that he hadn't thought through the worst case scenario back when he was the cock of the walk. He took the deal with the bank and his word was his life. Maybe he could relax a bit once they gained the security of Site Blue.

Occasionally an obstacle or route detail would interrupt his silent self-recriminations. They occasioned short radio alerts to Kaplan, driving the trail vehicle, and punctuated Tom's long watch. Without either routine vehicle traffic or anyone actively working to keep the road clear, a surprising amount of debris was accumulating on the roadbed. Rather than risk damage or a puncture, Tom slowed down to a walking pace in order to navigate the road when it wasn't certain that the way was clear. In the brief stretches that were completely open, he could maintain a slightly higher speed and return to thinking.

There was no calculus where Tom could find an answer other than his own culpability for their losses.

There was no scenario, short of dying, where he didn't have to continue to shoulder the responsibility.

The long night wore on.

Near morning the radio, turned down to preserve battery life, broke squelch.

"Thunder, dawn is coming up," Kaplan said. "Let's start looking for a spot to lay up."

Risky woke as the Suburban subsided, coming fully to rest. The vehicle was still dark and quiet, but a lightening of the eastern sky signaled the start of another day of survival. Behind her, the kids began to stir.

She turned her head, watching Tom scan the area through the four-barreled night vision rig that was clipped to his cranial. It gave him a slightly insectoid appearance, as the green phosphor glow from the image intensifiers scattered light against his face.

She felt, rather than saw, his fingers double-check the position of the lighting switch. In addition to blinding himself if the interior lit when then doors open, a sudden flash of artificial light would betray their exact location to any observers, sentient or otherwise.

"Everyone stay put until I check the area," Smith ordered. "Back in a moment."

He didn't ask Risky to back him up, so presumably he intended to collect Kaplan and give their stopping place a once over for infected or other survivors. She couldn't make out their surroundings yet.

"Miss Risky?" asked Elf. "Can we get out? I have to go."

"Hold on a few minutes. Mr. Smith is checking to make sure that it is safe, first. When you get out, stay with Katrin."

The newest survivor much preferred the company of the younger members of the party. Katrin and Eric had taken her under their wing, but Elf also tried to stay close to Risky.

Risky reached between her legs and double-checked the position of the safety on her muzzle-down M4. She flexed her feet to work out the tightness in her calves.

"Damn, it stinks in here," said Dina Bua from the rear bench seat.

The confined space of the car actually wasn't too bad, compared to some of the places that the survivors had encountered. The sour redolence of body odor clashed with the chemical fragrance of baby wipes. Eric's unfortunate "tummy trouble" hadn't helped either.

It didn't really bother Risky overmuch since she was preoccupied thinking about her pending chat with Smith. The sky continued to lighten as the rest of the occupants fidgeted uncomfortably. Nearly twenty minutes passed during which the fidgeting grew into near panic as the passengers waited for the all clear and a chance to race for the nearest bush.

Tom loomed into view and tapped the passenger's side window. When she looked up he gave her the thumbs-up and turned away again.

"All right, you can get out now," she announced to the rest of the passengers.

Outside, she noted that either Tom or Kaplan had set a sentry facing the way they came. The needful rotated through the designated latrine area while others prepared a makeshift meal on the tailgate of the second Suburban. The sun was coming up like thunder, and Risky could now make out that they were on some sort of scenic overlook. Below them she saw another valley through which a large interstate ran. A small town clustered around the visible offramp.

Kaplan and Tom were looking at a map as Risky approached.

"I'm pretty sure we're in the right spot," Kaplan said, agreeing with something Tom said. "That should be a town called Smyth, but I am not anxious to go into the valley and look for a name, if you catch my meaning. Still, this is a different map than the one Gravy showed me. The scale is off. The ranch might be another five miles or another ten. It isn't marked as clearly on this one so I can't tell."

"Okay," Tom replied. "I'll wait and you get the other map out.

I'm planning on talking to Risky anyhow and everyone is glad for a break out of the trucks."

"It was Gravy's map," Kaplan said. "I. Don't. Have it. I thought you..."

The two men stared at each other for a moment.

Risky realized that they were talking about a map that had been in the wrecked Dodge.

"We got the kids' bags, and some other stuff—" She started to say.

"Gravy had a map case, about so big," Kaplan said, holding his hands apart in the shape of a paperback book. "Plastic cover. You'd know it if you had seen it. The SAFE was just circled. But it had everything else on it, labeled. Site Blue, the different dams, our route, National Guard armories, everything."

They looked at each other again and without a word began searching first one truck and then the other. A quarter hour later, the ransacking was complete.

No map case.

"So the map and everything on it is at the wreck," Tom said meditatively. "That's... not good."

"Was at the wreck," Kaplan said, correcting his boss. "Yeah, everything. Figures. We weren't thinking about sanitizing our gear. This hasn't ever been an op. We have been in bugout boogie mode but without worrying about any OPFOR."

Kaplan's voice was calm but he betrayed his concern by lapsing into milspeak.

OPFOR referred to Opposition Forces. If fighting the infected wasn't enough, now they had to account for the existence and motivations of an organized hostile force as they continued their trek to Site Blue.

"So, who is OPFOR?" Risky asked. "Apart from kidnappers of children, that is?"

"The next thing is to get to the ranch," Tom said, ignoring the question. "Once we get there, we refit and resupply. Two-Ton and the gang might have intel on conditions around here."

He looked at Risky directly.

"Is the girl okay?"

"Her name is Elf," she replied tartly. "She is physically okay. A little shaken, I think. She's staying close to me or the other kids for now."

Tom looked over her shoulder at the group. Some were still eating. Astroga, who had the watch, was demonstrating malfunction drills for Fat Ralph. Smith looked back down at the town below.

"Right, then we get a move on," he said, rolling his shoulder and cracking his neck. "With a little luck, we get there by lunch." He strode back towards the lead car.

Risky had remained poised to continue talking. Kaplan carefully declined to notice and walked towards Astroga.

Risky watched Tom's receding back and refrained from gritting her teeth.

CHAPTER 9

The access road was unexpectedly difficult. The Suburban had to be carefully diverted around or in some cases, eased across large, jagged rocks. There were unaccountably steep sections and one stretch that appeared to have washed out despite any evidence of a drainage or a stream uphill.

In the end, they had to move the emptied vehicles one at a time, while Tom and Kaplan alternated between driving or being a road guide.

"Your friends have a shit road, Tom," said Kaplan.

"That's the point," retorted Tom. "You have to *want* to get up this road. Casual tourists and refugees in anything but a dedicated four-wheel drive wouldn't persist."

Just past a sharp bend they had to halt in front of an unexpected sort of obstruction.

"I think you misread the map, sir," said Astroga helpfully. "It's okay, happens a lot to officers." She snapped her fingers at a nearby middle schooler. "Take a note."

Eric flipped open a familiar, small green notebook and began writing while Astroga dictated.

"Number fifty-eight: officers will always misread the map and should rely on E-4 navigational expertise."

"Isn't that your notebook, Astro?" Tom commented, with a glance Eric.

"Yessir," she answered. "But now I got people for that."

"Ex-per-tise," mumbled Eric. He looked up. "Does that word end in 'se' or 'ze'?"

"Never mind," Tom said. "Here's what you put down."

Behind him the first SUV audibly scraped past a boulder. Tom elected not to look over his shoulder.

The entire party was staring at the obstacle that blocked further progress.

A tall chain-link gate, reinforced with crossmembers, barred the road at the point of their further travel. A bright white sign was wired to the gate. The legend was picked out in bold black letters. It warned against touching the fence without opening Master Switch #12, and appeared to belong to something called the Interbureau Liaison Agency, Bio-ecological Research Division. It went on to specify the gate for dropping off radioactive material, an exposure limit to same and pledged that Americans' taxes were being well spent. The last bit made Tom snort.

"Are you sure, Boss?" Worf said dubiously. He had taken to using the same title for Tom as the bank team. "This looks some kind of official installation."

The faces behind Worf looked more worried than puzzled.

"I'm pretty sure," Tom leaned back from reading the sign and examined the wire-topped chain-link fence more closely. Neither the sign nor the new installation were things he'd seen on his last visit long ago. The sturdy obstruction disappeared into the woods on both sides of the road. Deep drainage ditches complicated the task of anyone who might try to bypass the gate. "The guy that runs this has a sense of humor. This feels like something he would do."

A small junction box was mounted on the gate post. He popped the lid, revealing a button and a small grille.

"Everyone stay cool and mount back up," Tom said decisively, pressing the exposed button. "Two-Ton, this is Thunder at the gate," he said, and after waiting a beat, he repeated the call again.

A minute later the grille issued tinny scratches.

"Thunder, that you?"

"Yeah, it's me, with friends," Tom said, releasing the button as he finished talking.

"Did you bring my hat?" the voice inquired.

"Yeah, I brought the Eagles hat you wanted," Tom replied.

"That's got to be a code, right?" In the car Worf looked at Kaplan.

"Yeah, a real simple one," Kaplan answered, turning the engine on. "The challenger asks for an in-extremis verification, in order to see if we are forcing Tom to get us inside. Tom answers with a sports team whose color corresponds to our situation. The New York Eagles have green jerseys. Green means everything is legit."

"That's pretty cool, actually," Astroga piped up from the last bench seat. "Gotta remember that one."

"How about that handle?" Worf asked, leaning back in his seat. "Thunder? How do you suppose the Boss caught that handle?"

"The whole nickname is Thunderblast," Kaplan mused. "That one I don't know. Way too cheesy to be legit though. There gotta be a story. He prefers 'Train,' so we all call him Thunder."

A loud buzz sounded and the gate slid aside while the motor hummed efficiently.

"This guy has power, whoever he is," Astroga observed. "I'll offer free handies to that voice if they have hot water showers and they're ready to share."

Worf rolled his eyes.

The road improved remarkably just past the gate and the vehicle ascended past a few more twists and turns before being halted by a single empty-handed man. Tall, the ruddy faced man was another member of the shaved head and a sharp beard club. His hands were empty, but otherwise he wore a complete set of up-to-date tactical equipment, including a very short black rifle hanging from a friction strap.

"Only one guard?" Worf said critically. "Seems a little…light."

"Left side, in the trees," Kaplan said, grunting. "Dirt mound with dark green moss. See the bipod? That's a belt fed. You can count on more than one if Tom's description of this crew was accurate."

"Not seeing i…." Word said, but then paused. "Wait, ah. Got it. Nice camo. Gotta love competent allies. They really *are* allies, right?"

"Tom?" the man called out as the lead SUV stopped short. "That really you?"

Tom eased his door open with no particular haste, keeping his hands well in view. He paused for a moment to inhale. The pines scented the air, and that simple breath made him feel a little better.

"Yeah, Robby," he replied. "It's me. And some friends. Mind if we unass? Everyone is carrying, except for the kids, but I vouch for all of us."

"You close the gate behind you?" asked Robbins as he walked up to Tom.

"We aren't barbarians, Two-Ton," Tom said reassuringly, before taking Robby's hand and embracing quickly. One good thump on the back and the men broke back apart, beaming. "We even covered up our tracks from the main road so no one will spot recent activity."

"I guess you SAS pretty boys are all right after all," Robbins replied before putting two fingers in his mouth and whistling impossibly loud before waving his left hand in a circle over his head. "Bring it in!"

Twenty meters away from one side of the track, four shapes stood up. Clad in shaggy overgarments the same color as the earth, their outlines were further blurred with layers of vegetation and burlap. They collected some burdens whose familiar shape jogged Tom's memory, before picking their way over to the group that was eagerly piling out of the two Suburbans.

"Where did you get those museum pieces?" Tom asked, indicating the large machine guns dating to the Second World War. A particularly broad-shouldered young man carried his burden easily over his shoulder, one hand negligently balancing the barrel. A smaller figure next to him unceremoniously dumped two green ammunition cans on the ground and then swept its head gear off, revealing a raven-haired, fresh-faced teenage girl. As she scanned the newcomers with an intelligent look, a second, similarly encumbered pair walked up behind the first.

"Meet my oldest, Jordan," said the proud father. "Wants to be an electrical engineer. The tall oaf is my son Jake—call him Junior—and that is his 'leetle fren.'"

"Is that a replica Browning?" asked Kaplan.

"Replica?" replied Robbins Senior. "Bite your tongue! I picked up some M1919 parts kits from that crazy guy in southern Indiana that you turned me onto a few years back. A little welding, a little machining and we have a proper light machine gun without all the bothersome paperwork. I even chambered 'em in seven six two by fifty-one."

"I wouldn't call a thirty cal light, but..." Tom said jokingly. He knew from personal experience that the weapon was very heavy, but if the weight bothered Junior, it wasn't obvious. A hard-hitting weapon, the Browning was still in use in many developing nations where their SAS had conducted training.

Tom paused, reflecting that he now aspired to live in a developing nation.

"Well, hellooo, Mr. Fancy Pants!" the second gunner said, striding up. "Where are those sexy five-thousand-dollar suits that I heard you bankers were wearing?"

"'Lo, Half Ass," Tom replied, looking down ruefully at his stained plate carrier, but then extended a hand to the new man. "Good to see you! Are Sarah and kids with you?"

"Yep," said Dave Pascoe. "We've got parts of five families here, but a few never made it."

Pascoe was considerably shorter than the others, but nearly as broad as he was tall. If the bulk of the machine gun that he cradled was an effort, there was no sign of it on his cheerful face.

"Whoa, boys," interjected Robbins. "Let's debrief somewhere besides the main road. Dave, Junior, get the guns back to the ready service locker. I'll..."

A brief swirl in the debarking passengers caught the attention of the reunited comrades.

"Where's the bathroom?" Dina said, pushing her way up to the main group, addressing Tom personally. She looked at the heavily armed reception crew and blanched. "Wait, machine guns? Is that even legal?!"

"One of yours, Thunder?" Robbins said, regarding her in alarm.

"It's a long story," Tom sighed. "Astroga! Come take care of this."

"Oh, I am so going to tase you now!" the short Army specialist said, stumping forward. "I told you to wait with us back here, and I turn my back for one... Hey hey, nice belt-fed! Not as big as mine, but you know..." She regarded the first machine gun team with a bright smile.

"What?" stammered Junior.

"I've gotta take care of this person for a sec..." she added as she grabbed Bua by the elbow, ignoring a squawk of protest. "Maybe later you can let me shoot that? Say, do you have any hot showers?"

"If my dad says so," replied Junior in a doubtful tone. "And, duh."

"Oooh, you're my new best friend!" Astroga said over her shoulder as she towed Bua back to the truck.

"Right. Everyone move up to the main house," Junior's father said. "First stop is the barn for clean-up. We'll get some coffee and snacks going in a second and you..." he indicated Tom "...can brief me. Then I'll show you around, give you a feel for the place."

"'Preciate it, Rob," Tom replied, rubbing a hand across his face. "Really. Everyone's farking stuffed just now. We could all use a shower and a lie down."

"You're all tired and you could use some sleep, check," Robbins answered, clapping one hand on his friend's shoulder. "That we can do."

"After the debrief, Robbie. I've got to fill you in."

The Gleaner vehicles covered nearly eighty miles in the two hours of driving.

"How do you keep the roads so clear?" Jason said while looking out the windows of the diesel six pack Ford. He hadn't been in a powered vehicle in months. "The easy going makes a huge difference."

"Our Mr. Green is a student of history," Eva O'Shannesy replied from the front passenger seat. "He understands that clear roads give us a big advantage. It can take us weeks to clear a road outwards, but once we have it cleaned up, we can return almost as fast as you could in the old days—you know, before zombies. Anyway, we use labor gangs from the survivors that we pick up. We try to save the families intact if we can. Doesn't always happen."

"Why not? Who wouldn't want to be rescued?"

"Well, that's a good question." O'Shannesy said, flashing him a grin over her shoulder. "See, we don't exactly give them the option. If the adults fight, we kill them. Most of the healthy orphans under twelve or so go to the farm. Moderate labor and so on, but their real purpose is to give the women something to do, someone to care for. The dear children are easy to like and so the women who bond with them are less likely to run or make trouble. In a few years, the best of them will grow up as Gleaners."

"That's..." Jason said before pausing to consider the least negative thing that he could say. "...efficient."

"You can say the rest," O'Shannesy replied while keeping her eyes to the front this time. "It's brutal. It's logical. It advances our plan. And really, I've got to give Green props—he understands human nature very well. But, anyhow—the men we rescue have options. If they're family men, then they're highly motivated to get with the program. Their families might even be allowed to stay intact. Their kids get protection and light work. The teens perform harder labor, but nothing brutal. Their women don't work in the Rec Hall."

"Rec Hall?" asked Jason. "What's that?"

"Short for recreation hall," she said, pointing out a turn to the driver, then continued. "Use your imagination. Single men on higher risk duty, or any of the Guard, have access to the recreation hall."

The vehicle leaned into the turn and then pulled over to allow the next six vehicles past. As the converted wrecker with a five-hundred-gallon diesel tank on the bed rumbled by they joined the end of the procession.

"We rotate the lead car duty," O'Shannesy commented in answer to Jason's raised eyebrow. "Sometimes the locals leave presents for us, caltrops mostly, after we pass through. Too much land to comprehensively sweep. This way the lead vehicle crew is more likely to be fresh and paying attention, plus we each have an equal shot at getting wrecked. Lost a few trucks that way."

"So Mr. Green meets with resistance," the ex-cop said. "How does he deal with it?"

"This area is clear," the Gleaner officer said as she tried to unfold a map. "Has been for a fair bit. Back in the day though, he would find kids that lived in the immediate area and strap them to the hood of the lead car. Any wreck and *pow*, they catch it first. Cut back on incidents and random sniping by a factor of four."

"Huh," Jason replied. "That's . . ."

"Efficient." O'Shannesy said laconically. "Yeah, we covered that already."

Tom blearily sipped his coffee as his old friend finished talking.

"We're pretty well set here, as you can see," Robbins said, finishing the short version of the ranch orientation brief and was understandably proud of their achievements. "Even with your extra dozen or so, we can maintain here through the winter. The infected have never crossed the fenceline and we don't give them any reasons to be curious about what lies uphill. Once winter is over, and we're past the frost line, I figure the number of zombies will be dramatically lower."

He folded his arms across his chest while the newcomers sipped hot coffee, stretching their legs out from the simple picnic style bench tables that lined one wall of a surprising large barn.

"Maybe," replied Tom. "Maybe not. We can guess about the resilience of infected, but we don't really know. We're still trying to get a feel for behaviors. However, we weren't planning on here staying very long. Now I don't know if you should stay either."

"What possible reason could there be to leave here, now?" Robbins said, puzzled. "Great sightlines, decent sensors, plenty of supplies, safe haven from the infected through the winter?"

"I was planning on pushing through to the refuge that Bank of the Americas built before the Fall," Tom said by way of explanation. "Site Blue. But we got hit on the way here. Lost two people. Lost some gear. Lost the maps that mark our route and plans."

"You marked our ranch on a map and then...lost it," Robbins said, his voice gaining volume as he spoke each word. "Tell me you are making this shit up, Smith."

"Was not his fault," Risky said, stepping up next to Tom. "The first group of people we see in months are chasing little girl. Want to take her. We rescue, then they fight. We shoot and run, but Durante died. Another one too."

"Gravy Durante bought it?" exclaimed Pascoe. "Oh man, he was one hard snake. How'd he go?"

"Meeting engagement," Tom said, shrugging. He tried for a matter-of-fact tone, but his voice caught as he explained further. "Tried for a parley, but it dropped in the dunny. Gravy caught a round under his armor on the exfil, wrecked his ride. Couldn't get him out, his leg was wound into the wreckage. Left him to delay pursuit while we ran. His choice."

"Correlation of force?" Robbins demanded.

"Adverse," Tom replied. "And our training level was poor. Is poor. No unit articulation."

"Ground?" Pascoe said, speaking up.

"Channeled terrain," Tom said flatly. "One way out, one way in. They had mixed small arms, heavy on shotties. OPFOR was four, maybe five times our strength. And now we've got to assume that whoever they're working for has the information on the map. All of it. Even the important stuff."

"That was pretty, uh," Pascoe said, searching for a diplomatic phrase. "Uh—"

"Fucking careless, is what!" Robbins shouted, his face reddening. "What else could they have gotten that is as important as this place? Our families are here!"

"They might or might not have the location of this place, but they definitely have the location of the bank refuge," Tom said as he ticked off the details. "They have the some details on the inventory that I expect to find there. They know that I was thinking long term about restoring a source of power generation somewhere in the Tennessee Valley. They got the location of a couple possible military supply points for the National Guard. I think that is enough, don't you?"

"The guy I shot didn't seem all that bright, Boss," Kaplan said. "I can't see someone like him developing useful intel from our rubbish."

"Thanks for that, Kap," Tom said. "It isn't the meathead we shot, it's his boss that I'm thinking of. Rob is right."

"You're fucked," Robbins said, standing up. "And now you have probably fucked us."

"I know," Tom replied. He considered attempting a sincerely apology but he was just too tired. He settled for trying to hide the exhaustion in his voice. "But we have a few advantages. I didn't write *everything* down."

Debbie Robbins was a professional homemaker, presiding over a household of four active kids, two of them grown to adult size. Peacemaking was her middle name.

"He's practically dead on his feet, Rob," she said, laying a cool hand on her husband's arm. "Everyone needs some rest. We can hear him out tonight, dear heart," Debbie said, scanning the new group, stopping at Tom. Her eyes grew stony. "And if he doesn't have some good answers, then you can shoot him."

CHAPTER 10

It was nightfall, and the combined parties, including Tom's group and Robbins's extended clan, had closed the doors to the big barn, which was the only place large enough to accommodate everyone not on security watch. Preventing a light leak was important at night and Tom was pleased to note the discipline exercised by his former mates. Tempers as well as the temperature had subsided considerably by the time that Tom finished outlining his plan.

The assembled clans and the bank survivors had watched the principals bat the ideas back and forth for an hour. The audience's collective head swung back and forth as though they were watching center court at Wimbledon.

"So let me see if I got this right," Robbins said, still skeptical. "After we sort out teams, step one is to evacuate this ranch while you link up with your banker buddies at their ritzy refuge. That site is at least three, maybe five days away and you haven't had any contact with them in almost four months. Meanwhile, we drag our collective asses through the zombie-infested Cumberland Valley for up to another week and find a spot to cross the Tennessee and secure a hydroelectric power plant. Which may or may not be working. And we do this while potentially being chased by a larger force of unknown origin and unknown capabilities. And all because you think that they know where this place"—he smacked the tabletop with a palm—"is located. Because you lost a map."

"Enough with the crook!" Tom said angrily. "You've only mentioned the map what, eight times? No matter how sorry I am, I can't rewind the crash, Robbie! And if I could, I'd fooking well save Gravy first, wouldn't I!"

"All right, all right, everyone take a breath," Debbie ordered. She looked back at her husband and when he remained quiet, she gave Tom a little "come on" gesture.

He inhaled once, in-out, keeping his hands palm down on the table before continuing.

"I've been thinking about it a lot," Tom explained again. "Our bank plan was to hunker down and wait for someone else to fix stuff. The bank fallback points aren't really redoubts—they are interim way stations for some key people and data. You can't restart a civilization without a bank."

"Umm, I'm pretty sure that you can," Robbins said.

"Actually, no, you can't," Tom said insistently. "At least not any civilization that you want to live in. Call it a bank, call it an agricultural cooperative, call it an infrastructure restoration agency—someone has to manage the money. Literally. What do we use for currency? How do you arrange a loan? Who establishes and enforces exchange rates? Do you have any idea how big the infrastructure projects to get this country running again are going to be? Trust me, you are going to need an economic system which doesn't rely on trading wheat for iron for sugar and so on. It took hundreds of years to get from feudalism and chattel slavery to something like a modern economic system. Do you want to wait that long? Do you want your kids growing up in that?"

"Tommy, we're just parts of five families, with kids," Robbins replied, before pulling a familiar disc-shaped green can out of his pocket. He delivered several brisk taps to the lid, tamping down the dip tobacco. "We aren't Delta, we aren't FEMA and we aren't the freaking Justice League. We aren't going to be able to restart civilization. Somewhere else, someone else with the right people and gear is already on it."

"You didn't see New York burn," Tom said. He didn't have the tobacco ritual to relax himself, so he strained to sound reasonable. "You haven't driven a few hundred miles, which by the way is about the minimum distance to start getting used to decaying corpses everywhere, looking at the wreckage of the country. It looks like pictures of Rwanda in '94, but with Americans, Robbie. The radio spectrum is dark, the sky is empty and there is no civil authority anywhere. Whenever I haven't been cursing whoever started this shit show I've been trying to bully around or over all the opposition in order to live up to my promises. I *am* going to redeem my word one way or the other. Long term, that means restarting everything."

Robbins just sighed eloquently.

"Robby, we need a hydro plant because any credible plan to jumpstart our bit of civilization requires large scale power," Tom said, rehashing the main points of his strategy for what felt like the tenth time. "The only plant that we can 'fuel' is a hydro plant, of which there are several in the Tennessee Valley. I've got to get to Site Blue in order to warn them and ultimately prep it for a move, too. I'm nervous about leaving you here because of the map. Yes, that we left in a wreck. And yes, that was my fault. Doesn't change what we have to do now, though."

Robbins sat and glowered at his own map, which was spread across the table. His skepticism didn't require words. The distances on the map, the risk to their families, the unknowns—those had all been discussed in detail. He squinted over at his old teammate.

"I didn't say that there aren't details to work out," Tom said, moving papers away so that only the empty brown tabletop stretched between himself and Robbins. "But, the alternative is to wait here until we are invested by a superior force, and then get into a gun fight on someone else's terms while your family is supplying some of the foot soldiers. Even if those particular bad guys never show, how many years do you want to wait before you believe that there might not be anyone else coming?"

He glanced across the barn at the table where Worf, Astroga, Ralph and Eric were being run through a class on the antique machine gun by Junior. The tall, broad-shouldered youth was developing a progressively goofier expression as Astroga asked questions from close range. The younger daughter Jordan, who had been the ammo bearer for her brother, was at the briefing table sharing a bench with her parents. She also shared their same skeptical look.

"I agree with Robbie," Pascoe said, squinting at Tom. "You done fucked up, Thomas. But that doesn't mean that I have any better ideas."

"Wait a minute, Davey!" Robbins said angrily. "You're ready to pull up sticks and take our families on the road, out there?!"

"In case you forgot, Rob," Dave Pascoe said, then spit into an empty beer can, "Smitty was the man who gave us all the heads-up that got us here before the virus spread. Took a mite of risk doing that, too. He ain't said anything about it yet, but I'll bet my last roll of Cope that he also toted along vaccine for everyone." He looked back over at Tom. "Right?"

"We have vaccine," Tom admitted. "We've followed the refrigeration protocol so it should be good. Can't recommend it for anyone under twelve, ten at the lowest."

"Better than nothin'," Pascoe said, grinning at his old teammate. "Like that vaccine, a lot of really useful stuff, infrastructure, is going to go bad without someone to tend it. Better we try to get to some of it sooner than later."

"Given the scenario that we find ourselves in, Tom, what we need is time," Robbins Senior said as he looked first at Pascoe and then at Tom. "The tangos that you bumped into could be heading this way right now, correct?"

"Yes," Tom answered. "But we bloodied them pretty good. If they were going to pursue instantly, we would have seen them already. While things get sorted for the move here, we can send a couple of teams to double back till one or both are in contact and delay the shit out of them. If we give them a second bloody nose, I think that they will chase us in order to defeat us in detail this time."

He leaned over the map, and started tracing routes between the camp, Site Blue and the nearest dam.

"So we make two teams. Put some demo and say, four shooters in each truck. We'll retreat towards Blue while you head for the plant. Each scout truck covers one of the possible approaches to Blue. If we stumble into them unexpectedly, we can run faster than they can push, so we buy you time. If they chase us all the way to Blue, they bounce off the Site's defenses, and we still buy you time."

"How do we coordinate?" queried Pascoe.

"Mostly, we don't," Tom said. "The ridges limit VHF to line of sight. HF might work if we can get a decent antenna, good tropospheric conditions and an operator that knows his ass from a hole in the ground. We can set up a comms window once a day or so, but don't count on it unless we can get to a high point, or we're really close. On your end, start at Fort Loudon, then Watts Bar and Chickamauga. There's one more past Chattanooga, but getting that close to a city is dangerous. If the first three are clearly beyond restart, then come back here. We'll do the same."

"Delaying tactics are supposed to be a specops specialty," Matt Detkovic said, suddenly speaking up. "That's your thing."

Detkovic was a member of their little brotherhood, but his family hadn't made it to the refuge unscathed. He'd taken the necessary actions to keep his wife from harming anyone after she turned, and as a result of heroic efforts, he hadn't lost any of their large brood on the way to the refuge.

"Strictly speaking, the Australian SAS prefers the word 'commando,'" Tom replied mildly. "But I agree. You were First Group at Fort Lewis, right?" He referred to the U.S. Army First Special Forces Group which, pre-Fall, had been based outside Seattle.

"Yeah, and I was an combat engineer before that. E-9 when I got out," Detkovic said, looking around the barn. "Who do you think built all this, and trained all the kids?" A chorus of groans and jeers sounded. "Well, me and some of these slack-ass no-loads."

"Well, Sarn-Major, welcome to the zombie war," Tom said, essaying a smile. "We can plan for a few more hours, then get some more sleep. I'll pick the scouts while Robbie, Kap and you organize the movement for everyone else. A day of prep, maybe two, and we hit the road. Rendezvous at the river in a week or so."

"Fucking SAS," Robbins said, scowling at his guest and then turned to his wife. "What do you think, Deb? Shoot him or feed him?"

She pursed her lips and looked from her son who was balancing on the edge of his seat and then back to Tom's face. Her gray eyes were level. "We try it his way. I can always shoot him later."

"Okay, show me where on the Tennessee," Rob growled at Tom.

"Here," Tom said, stabbing the map on the table. "We've got some options, but I figure we try this place first. Little place called Spring City. Right next to Watts Bar hydroelectric power plant."

"Okay, your turn, kid," Robbins Junior said to Eric.

The Robbins family maintained an armory for all of the families, but a few of the recent arrivals had expressed an interest in learning how to use a couple of the more unusual items, including the large antique machine gun that had caught their eye during the arrival of Smith's wandering band.

In the background, Copley and Pascoe were overseeing a fundamentals of combat shooting class for the older kids.

Worf, Astroga and Ralph had rapidly grasped the fundamentals of reloading the M1919 as well as clearing basic feed jams but neither Katrin's nor Eric's obvious interest was buttressed by any previous experience. Still, they'd stepped up, and Eric went first.

The gangly middle schooler was about the size of his adopted mentor, Astroga, but lacked any of her confidence. He hesitantly grasped the weapon, pulling the stock to himself as the weight remained on the workshop table. As his hands sought the feed tray cover latch, Astroga slapped his hand.

"What's the first thing that you always do with a weapon?" she demanded.

"Uh," Eric stammered, obviously nervous about being the focus of the attention of three adults.

"You wanted to learn," Astroga added. "Settle down and remember. We already covered this during range time with the M4s."

"Check to see that it's on safe," he replied.

"Right, so do it," she said encouragingly. "And?"

"Visually inspect to see if it's unloaded," he replied, darting a look at Junior, whose intimidating teenage scowl deepened.

The lesson proceeded and Eric's hands became a little more confident.

"I want to stay with you, Miss Risky!" Elf was not happy about the plan.

Once the combined group had accepted Smith's leadership, the preparations had moved forward quickly, and within two days the scout teams were set to depart. Elf, the 'tweens and the other children were going to stay an additional day at the ranch while the balance of the households were packed and winterized. The ranchers and the noncombatants from the original bank party would be in the main group that proceeded towards the river, led by Kaplan and Robbins. Meanwhile, Smith had composed two smaller groups entirely made up of fighters. In addition to gathering intelligence his teams would find ways to discourage or at least delay possible pursuit.

"I'll only be gone for a short while," Risky said, reassuring the diminutive girl. "Mr. Smith and his friends are going to protect us and I'm going to help them. I'll only be gone a few days, I promise."

Risky looked up and saw Katrin watching with sad eyes.

"Will you take her? I have to go," Risky said as she gently untangled Elf's hands from her shirt. "Katrin will care for you until I'm back, little one."

Unbidden, vivid memories and emotions swelled inside her. Risky's eyes brimmed while she fought to keep a smile on her face, watching the teen lead their newest rescuee away.

Standing, she spotted Smith finishing a conversation. Risky sighed. The only times to approach Tom Smith were always going to be either inconvenient or awkward. Squaring her shoulders, she marched over.

"Hi Risky," Tom said, looking up. "Are you still sure that you want to come with the second blocking group?"

"Why not?" she replied. "Makes most sense. Durante trained me himself. We have worked together. I'm, how you say, 'readin' for team procedures from BERT. But before we go, you and I need to talk."

She watched Tom's light brown eyes widen a trifle at the sound of her last words.

Infected attacking? Smith would keep calm. Evacuate the bank? Smith was relaxed in the clutch. But pre-Fall or post-Fall; why is it that a woman's informing a man that it was time to talk would consistently inspire that kind of reaction?

"I must say something, Tom. Even though it cost Dave his life, I don't regret saving Elf. But I'm so very sorry that he died. I know that he was your friend."

"Gravy was my friend, yes," Smith said carefully. "But he was my responsibility. The girl, however tragic her situation, was not my responsibility. Not until you made her our problem. I know that you feel bad about Durante's death, but he was. My. Responsibility. And you made a decision about that without asking me. Without asking him."

"Tom, look!" Risky gestured towards the corner in the barn where Katrin and Cheryl were hanging out, attempting to pull the newest refugee into their play. "What do you see?"

Smith looked at Risky, then back at the kids. They were sitting around the children's table. Jonsdottir was weaving a circlet of flowers and trying the fit on Elf's head.

"They're kids, Risky," Smith said, shaking his head. "They're just goofing around. I don't see what you mean."

"All four are orphans, Tom," she said gently. "They know it.

I understand about your responsibility. To the people that you brought out of New York. To bank. But if you complete bank arrangements and those orphans all die, is it truly honorable? Why feel bound to some promise when what's real, when what is *right now* has changed so much?"

"I haven't changed. I *will* live up to my agreement," Smith said. Only a slight strain betrayed Smith's frustration with the implication that he might somehow not honor the bargain that he made with BotA. "What on earth makes you think that I won't?"

"That's just it," Risky said. "I know that you will. My question is what do you owe a dead person?"

"Risky, I just don't understand what you are asking. Who's dead—besides Durante?"

"What I'm saying is that the bank, as you knew it, the way it was when you worked there, it's gone..." Risky ignored his jibe about their dead with an effort. "There's no bank. There's just some scattered and scared people who *used* to work for your bank. There's some digital records about who owed money to who. But the system that moved money around and made the economy work? The system that we fought to protect long enough for someone, anyone, to find a better alternative to the vaccine we made, or even a cure—that system? Is dead."

As she spoke, Risky felt the rightness of her words. She pushed away her anger at an unfair world which seemed at every step to only grow worse. Risky knew better than to expect fairness. Fairness, justice, even basic survival—these were things that she, they, would have to build. These were things that one fought for. Again, her tired eyes began to brighten with incipient tears and both her articles and pronouns suffered.

"What we have is this!" She tapped herself on the chest. "And this!" She lightly poked his sternum and then made a short gesture to the side where others were carefully *not* listening. "All them including those we rescue. Protecting is honorable course. Your plan to rebuild, to turn on power and kill infected, that plan is plan worth fighting and dying for, not helping some escaped banker count money while world burns. Why go to Site Blue at all?!"

"I can't walk away from Site Blue, Risky," Tom said gently. He stepped a little closer. "Paul is there, other people that I'm responsible for. I pledged to do everything that I could to save the bank. The people who followed my plan believed in me. I've got to redeem my word to my satisfaction—even if no one else sees me do it. Or agrees."

Risky watched him search for words.

"I knew that I was writing a blank check when I took the bank's salt." He chuckled for a moment. "Blank check. Heh. So, I'm going to see this through."

Risky felt, rather than watched, as Tom drew close enough to hold her hands. At this distance, she could see that his eyes were speckled with gold.

"After that, then maybe there is something else for me to focus on. Maybe someone else."

"Oh!" Before replying, Risky swallowed and schooled her features at his revelation, though her hands trembled slightly in Tom's warm grasp. "Oh. Is not the ordinary world any longer, Thomas. We can't count on later. There isn't time to wait for dinner invitation. I know that you can't walk away from your duty, even if I think it is stupid. That's part of my problem. Is part of the reason that I brought the boat back. I think that you're the right person."

Tears glittered in her eyes.

"Risky, I am very sorry that I am making you upset," Tom said, as they both continued to ignore their audience. She felt his grip tighten as he squeezed her hands. He searched her eyes. "But what do you think that I'm the person for, if not to live up to my word? To save everyone? To kill all the infected? To be with?"

"Yes," she said, taking a deep breath and exhaling slowly through her nose. "Yes. All of it. For now, we get to Site Blue. You redeem word. Then we talk about the rest. Make promise that you won't die being brave and stupid! Agree?"

"I promise to try," Tom replied, letting go of her hands to hug her softly, as though she were spun glass.

"Try hard!" Risky said, getting the last word, and then she fiercely returned his embrace.

The homestead smoldered in the background. It was a testament to the horrors that had become commonplace that no one blinked at the smell of what was literally a funeral pyre for most of the family that had declined their invitation to join the Gleaners.

After a brief exchange of shots convinced Eva that taking the house wasn't worth the casualties, she had ordered the house fired. The one Gleaner casualty wasn't too bad, despite his hollering as his wound was dressed.

Jason had worked his way forward alongside another of the original Gleaner Guard whose thick, almost squat appearance had prompted the former cop to mentally dubbed him "Short Round," even though he heard others call him Dragon. Like the other Guards, his equipment was several notches up from that of the average Gleaner. Still, it had required three of their improvised incendiaries before the roof properly caught fire. Then they had sat back while the house burned, expecting the survivors to bolt.

The ex-cop had watched the windows and doors from an improvised hide and waited until the second floor sniper used the same window once too often. Jason knew he wouldn't forget the sight picture through his variable power Leupold scope, the crisp release of the trigger, the briefest blossom of red against the white-haired man's work shirt.

As the roof began to collapse, an older woman and teenage girl had run out, their hair smoldering. No one else tried to escape. Briefly, Jason had heard a church hymn being sung inside.

Eva had inspected the new captives before questioning them, almost gently. Jason saw that her demeanor was not unkindly and he'd relaxed.

Briefly.

Then Eva had turned the mother over to the convoy's rank and file. The new victim didn't start screaming until they threw her daughter onto the ground next to her.

Afterwards, the Gleaners took advantage of the open-sided barn to eat in the shade and perform simple maintenance before resuming their route.

Jason was certain that his growing moral flexibility wouldn't stretch to actual participation, so he had elected to excuse himself from the just concluded public rapes. Shooting an armed combatant was one thing. What followed was revolting. In the scheme that Green had built, it was as necessary as the rest, perhaps. Despite the absence of any objection at his abstinence, Jason saw a few speculative looks came his way. Even after the horror of metro D.C. during the height of the plague, the mercy killing of his partner and all the rest, he wasn't fully comfortable with...all this.

Green had a plan to get to some kind of civilization and his was the only organized group, though.

Jason was familiar with the adage about eggs and omelets. In a broken world with billions dead, the means justified the ends, right? Even God had turned his back. And he wasn't a cop anymore. Not his problem. He just had to keep repeating that to himself. He'd get around to believing eventually.

Meanwhile, he tried to continue to get a feeling for what he had to work with. He laid down his Colt Enhanced Patrol Rifle, no doubt scavenged by the Gleaners from an abandoned police vehicle. He pushed out the takedown pins and levered open the receiver marked "Law Enforcement Use Only." The little auto sear modification that he'd fashioned from stiff wire was black with carbon. In fact, the entire fire control group was dirty, probably due to the Russian ammunition they'd been using.

"What's with the blue latex gloves all the time, man?" Jason said as he reached for the rags next to where Short Round was cleaning a rifle on a workbench.

The Gleaner had actually worn the gloves during the fight but afterwards carefully stripped them off before beginning to work on his rifle.

"Are you seriously asking me if I am from the Triads because I'm Asian?" Short Round said, giving the cleaning rod a vicious twist. "Zombie apocalypse or not, that's some fucked up stereotyping, *man!*"

"Easy, easy!" Jason replied, holding up his hands placatingly. "The neck tattoo, the occasional bit of Chinese slang, the fact that almost all of the people that Green pulled off the prison buses were from organized crime of one sort of another, you know..."

The other man squinted at him for a moment.

"Whatever," he said as he changed out the jag for a bore brush. "Nah. What Mr. Green did was different. He went looking for bad motherfuckers. Like, everyone was handpicked because we're special. Me? I was actually sort of a cop, like Loki."

"Yeah?" Jason said, fighting to keep his face straight. "What branch?"

"DHS, man! Homeland Fucking Security!" Short Round said, tapping his chest. "I was a TSA officer. You know, airports, trains, that sort of thing. I had a sweet gig in Atlanta, running a crew at Hatfield. We made decent money on the side, but the great thing was picking out some fine thing coming through security. Make like she set off the explosives residue detector—scare them good. The younger, the better, you know? The teenage ones without parents were the best. Flash the blue gloves at them, take them in the exam room and hooo-eeee!"

He made a suggestive motion with his fist.

"Uh-huh," Jason said as he decided that skepticism was the safest response. After all, a quick headshot would prompt questions from the rest of this crew. "And that qualified you for Green?"

"Nah," the former TSA agent replied with a shrug. "Guy on my crew got careless. Got caught stealing penny ante shit by the straights, then flipped and gave state's evidence. Couldn't have that. Once I posted bail, me and the crew paid him and his old lady a visit. Made a point of explaining why we wuz angry. Skinned that bitch and made him watch. Blue gloves handy for that too."

"So then you got caught?"

"No man, ain't you listening?" Short Round said as he began assembling his weapon. "After, we decided to lean on the TSA supervisor who objected to our little ways. Turned out he was some kind of gun nut. Shot back, the fucker! Then the cops came, and it was all done. Damn shame. It was a good gig. Anyhow, I plead out for murder two, figured parole in maybe fifteen years and bam! Zombie apocalypse. Next thing, I'm on a bus somewhere in this shit state and it wrecks. There's Mr. Green and his fucking scary dog Loki and they're offering me a job. Like I don't know what would happen if I said no."

"So the tattoo?" prompted the ex-cop.

"Man, I was in prison," Short Round said with a grunt. "You never been inside? You gotta pick a side. You gotta run with your pack. The White Resistance wasn't gonna take me, and them MS13 fuckers were straight up crazy in groups. You know I ain't black, so what does that leave?"

"Cool story, bro," Jason said. He didn't think that the Gleaner would catch the lack of sincerity. "If I see any blue gloves I'll grab them for you."

"Yeah?" Short Round squinted again, checking to see if the new guy was being sarcastic. Then he smiled briefly. "Thanks, man!"

Paul Rune's early, personal efforts at using polearms had been surprisingly successful.

Despite the store of ammunition that Smith had transported to Site Blue prior to the Fall, Paul knew that it couldn't last forever. As a result, he had proposed creating more hand weapons to eliminate infected. Somewhat to his surprise, Kohn had enthusiastically backed the project.

To start he had made a demi-pike, nearly an assegai. Working with a local refugee and the tools recovered from a smithy, and after much trial and error over the previous month, they had forged a scavenged shovel blade into a long, leaf-bladed lance head. Fitted onto a shortened but reinforced shovel handle, it was light enough to be wielded one handed and remained handy in the tighter confines of a building. Their recce to the high school had proven that.

In order to ward off the infected while he was making with the stabby-stabby, Paul also built a plywood shield. It didn't have to resist other weapons but merely keep the teeth and lethally dirty fingernails of the infected away long enough for the deep, broad wounds he planned to inflict to bleed out his targets. A jury-rigged steam box helped him shape quarter-inch plywood into a form akin to a Roman kite shield. More scavenged material, this time the thin metal thresholds from the doors of destroyed homes, served to protect the edges of the shields and improve their stiffness.

Covered from throat to shin, a line of shield-bearing men could hold off infected across a narrow front, while using overhand stabs of their assegais to mortally injure or outright kill infected.

Paul had trained the few remaining BotA security staff into the nucleus of his recovery team. A few dry runs had been followed by testing the concept in very low concentrations of infected. With sufficiently heavy clothing, gloves and face protection, even a large number of infected really struggled to kill or seriously injure the fighters, so long as they kept their heads. Of course, if the fight went for a ball of chalk—as his old boss used to say—then they could fall back on firearms and shoot their way clear.

Paul felt that close-quarter shooting was best left to the professionals, and didn't want to use that as a fallback unless in dire straits. What he needed now was to expand the group, broaden his shield wall and build something to protect his flanks.

It was time to go back to Acting Administrator Kohn for another favor.

∽⊖∾

Kendra looked up when she heard his voice. It was Paul's turn to deliver the Security Committee's report. She'd stopped seeing him after he criticized her support of Kohn. She hadn't been certain if their connection was purely situational, a by-product of stress and fear. It might have been more than that, but Kendra was scared of being vulnerable, of relying on any part of the plan that had so clearly come apart. She folded her arms across her chest and shoved the memory of his arms around her away until the ache of missing him faded.

She watched Paul stand and update the usual figures for a few minutes.

"Our supplies of ammunition and spare parts are not unlimited," Paul said, completing his otherwise routine presentation. "But the infected represent a limited risk as long as we can select the ground and avoid getting buried in a large mob. Edged weapons and shields are much more cost effective and using them in other than emergencies will prolong the supply critical items, especially ammunition and weapons parts."

"Is the risk to your team quite high if you only use swords and shields, Paul?" asked Kohn. "Although the camp population is healthy, there are only so many people which are emotionally and physically qualified for such a role."

"Well, pikes and shields actually," Paul said, ever the pedant. "And no, it isn't without risk, Ms. Kohn. Nothing we do, including just sitting on our hands, is risk free. We've already lost a few people using existing methods. However, whatever number we dedicate, the training will have to be physically rigorous. Additional food will be needed for the participants—at least those that stay with it."

"We are all subject to rationing, Paul," Kohn said reasonably. "Forming an elite cadre and rewarding them with more rations seems counter to our message that all should contribute equally. That all benefit equally."

"Well..." The former intel officer drew out the first syllable, something that Kendra knew was a precursor to his infuriating habit of lecturing. She knew that Paul was about to step into a philosophical minefield which could only derail his real purpose at the meeting. She mentally grimaced as Paul continued.

"It isn't about rewarding the deserving, Administrator Kohn. Using a shield and a spear will require very heavy conditioning. For example, we'll improve leg strength and overall cardio by requiring trainees to advance in a line with their shields interlocked as they shove heavy boxes full of rocks along a dirt track. We'll have them thrust weighted spears into hay bales for hundreds, perhaps thousands of repetitions every day."

"And how long do you propose to train?" followed up a skeptical Christine. The former refugee had become an integral part of Kohn's growing team.

"Several hours a day," replied Paul. "I'll be happy enough if we retain half of our initial volunteers. Despite the difficulty, we'll realize several advantages in the long run, not the least of which will be a big reduction in friendly fire incidents."

Several refugees had been either rescued with existing gunshot wounds or had suffered gunshots during clearance and salvage operations. Paul had told Kendra that, the state of training being what it was, the danger from friendly yet panicked fire was at least as great as the actual risk from infected. He routinely forbade his teams to patrol with a round up the spout. Sometimes they even listened.

"How will you ensure that we have diverse representation on these teams who you propose to award greater rations?" Christine queried puckishly. "It sounds like your physical requirements are designed to favor men."

"Attacking zombies only come in one flavor," Paul said. "The hungry-all-the-time, largely oblivious to normal levels of pain and hysterically strong variety. They aren't sorted into 'great big zombies' for big men to fight, 'medium sized zombies' that anyone can fight and 'teeny tiny baby zombies' that even a bureaucrat ca—"

"That is not helpful, Paul!" Kohn said, sharply cutting across his reply. She paused and composed her voice. "What if we lose the only formally trained security staff that we have? Where do we replace them?"

"We have lots of wa—sorry, townies added to our team," Paul said. Kendra immediately noted a few audible inhalations and several angry looks. "What? What did I say?"

"The respectful term for recently arrived refugees who are sheltering in the camp is displaced persons," Christine replied acidly. "To use that other label is to deny them their humanity and unperson them. Disgraceful!"

In addition to her role as chair of the Education Committee, Christine had been the founding member of the Site Blue

Diversity Council. As more local refugees had joined the camp, it had begun to skew the demographics of the original urban transportee population towards a more rural mix. The council was established to address that troubling change, among others.

"It was this committee that changed the nomenclature from the original 'walk-ins,' which was perfectly descriptive," Paul said in protest. The temperature in the room perceptibly dropped as Paul's use of an even more forbidden word sparked additional audible inhalations of outrage.

Kendra knew that Paul had really put his foot in it. She'd gone on a few scavenging runs outside the camp. Out there, some brutal realities never stopped demanding a survivor's attention. Inside the camp, away from the horrors that Paul had described, alternative viewpoints had flourished. Based on emotion and identity, these popular positions were an occasionally frustrating, if perfectly understandable dynamic. She didn't buy all the way in, but she sympathized.

Well, a little.

"We're not going to accept the labeling conventions of the now thankfully *extinct* white male-dominated patriarchy—" Christine said, launching into full tirade mode before Paul cut her off.

"Are you *serious*? First, the zombies don't care about color, they just want fresh meat," he said, waving one dark-skinned forearm in the air. "Second, black guy here? One of the few left around? Like I was saying, we can ask for help from the new folks and incorporate them in the training, but that will mean time away from other projects."

"You're just participating in the system that—"

"Christine, one moment," Kohn said, cutting through the angry hubbub on her side of the table. "Paul, thank you. The Committee will take your request under advisement. Prepare a list of potential additional recruits and continue training with the people that you have. For the moment let us refrain from requirements that cut into our supply situation. Leave the list of required resources with us after the meeting. In a broad sense, I think that your concept makes sense..."

Kendra noted that a few of the administrator's erstwhile allies shot Kohn some side eye at that last statement. Kohn didn't react, but Kendra knew from experience that Kohn somehow seemed to notice everything.

After the meeting, Kendra approached Rune. It was time. She grabbed her sorrow and screwed it down tightly, to get through this.

"Hi, Paul," she said simply.

"Hi, Kendra!" Paul said, smiling warmly. "Hey, I'm free, do you want to grab some dinner? I could use the company after that crazy meeting."

"I've got some things to do," she replied, watching his face fall. "I just wanted to tell you that you're doing a good job and I appreciate it."

She leaned forward to give him a short, hard hug and, feeling her eyes blur with tears she quickly stepped away. She left him looking entirely confused and oblivious to the medallion that she'd just returned to his pocket.

As oblivious as he was to Kohn, still shuffling papers and making notes, while her eyes flicked about the large meeting room.

CHAPTER 11

"That's more than I had expected," Tom said, passing the binoculars to Pascoe.

"Mmm," the grizzled vet hummed a bit while he counted. "Eight vehicles. Figure maybe forty shooters. Fifty tops. That's bad odds."

"Vehicle ambush takes care of that," Junior said with a snort. "Two machine guns and we torch the entire group."

In addition to the RPK and all its remaining ammunition, Tom had sweet talked Robbins Sr. into the grudging loan of one of the heavy World War Two relics.

"I like it!" enthused Fat Ralph.

"They're armed and mobile," Pascoe said, reminding them. "We might get them to deploy, and then they pin us long enough to allow half the survivors to pick a flank and shoot us to shit. No thanks."

The young teenager looked angrily at the two older men but didn't say anything else.

"We're buying time, Junior," Tom said as he borrowed the glasses back. "We don't want to try to wipe them out, just delay them. They're going to have to cross that bridge we came over a few miles back. What we do is..."

"Boss, this is lead." O'Shannesy's radio startled Jason who had been zoning out, watching the monotonous view of unreaped corn fields sweep past.

"Go ahead," she replied.

"Got a bridge coming up. Blow across or prepare for deliberate crossing?"

"Wait one," O'Shannesy said, consulting her map. "We're well outside the cleared zone. Pick a spot and deploy."

"Copy."

As the convoy slowed and stopped, she studied the crossing, only a hundred meters away. It looked . . . clean. Usually choke points like crossings were blocked with vehicles and wreckage. This two-lane bridge spanned a dirty brown stream and it was clear, though she could see a car in the stream bed and a few more pushed off to one side.

"What's up, Boss?" her deputy said, walking up to check on the delay. He ignored Jason.

"Doesn't feel right." O'Shannesy said musingly. "Bridge is too clean and we didn't clean it. We'll set up here and you take a team across on foot to check the bridge and the intersection. If you see single zombies just shoot them. If you get a bunch, run back while we advance and we'll take them from a distance."

"Got it, Boss," the deputy said without hesitation.

"Problem?" asked Jason.

"Don't know." O'Shannesy said frankly. "We've done a bunch of these. I get a feeling sometimes. We aren't on a schedule—so no need to plunge forward. All I want to do is localize whoever we ran into at the town, scout some spots that Green highlighted and then get back. We can probably make our radio window tonight, if we find a high point on the far side. So that means getting across."

Jason looked around the valley they were in. Surrounded by gray limestone escarpments, the team's handheld radios weren't much good for other than short distances. The longer range of their one HF radio should reach camp, but it took a while to set up and needed good elevation.

He cast his eyes about for a route upwards while the foot team moved forward.

"Hold the wall!" Paul yelled in order to be heard over the din of the pack of infected that surged from the hospital's lower floors. "Brace yourself and just stab. Between shields, like we practiced!"

A few semi-dry runs had made short shrift of the small numbers of infected remaining in the mostly cleared crossroad hamlets and small towns within a short distance of Site Blue. Overall, the ammunition preservation strategy had borne fruit. As a result, the Executive Committee had approved his concept and directed that they continue the previously agreed salvage schedule.

The still missing components needed for vaccine production were doubtless a big part of the reason. With a little luck, itself a rare commodity, he hoped to complete their search for a functioning high velocity centrifuge as well as filtration media. His team had successfully infiltrated the regional medical center. A key advantage was the relative silence of the shield-and-pike method of clearance.

Once inside, his picked squad of a dozen had managed to dispatch the smaller clusters of infected by blocking the broad hallways of the medical facility and piling corpses up in front of them. However, the number of infected had steadily climbed until the Site Blue team was forced backwards. The remaining Bank staff seemed steady, but the new recruits were visibly wavering. To this point, they hadn't attracted the attention of more than a few infected at a time.

But that had changed.

"Second rank, aimed fire, now!" Paul ordered. They'd attracted far more infected than forecast. As a result, he'd resorted to using firearms in order to control the flood of zombies. The bright white splashes of light from the tactical flashlights intermittently lit a sea of bobbing heads as even more infected packed the corridor. Shooting past the heads of the shielded men, the team briefly relieved some of the pressure, until the infected started to clamber over their own dead.

"Where they all coming from?" screamed his squad leader, barely making himself heard over the crashing gunfire and the howling mob. Paul yelled his reply, trying to estimate the number of infected in view. It far exceeded the most pessimistic estimates in his worst-case scenario.

On the far right, the muzzle blast of a rifle fired right next to the shield wall caused the man anchoring the flank to flinch. His stance only faltered for a moment. It was enough for his shield to dip and an infected grabbed the upper edge, yanking it down and out of line. That pikeman instinctively drove his weapon into the target, but managed to get the broad leaf blade hung up on rib cage of the violently jerking infected. The matted, filthy beard parted in an unheard scream of pain. Spittle flew from the reeking maw and the faltering shield man bashed the zombie's face again. The shield boss splintered yellowed teeth and the infected disappeared into the bloody tangle of offal that delimited the forward line of defense.

"Shields up, close ranks!" Paul yelled. He knew that if they lost the wall it would come down to hand-to-hand and, despite the defenders' protective clothing, the sheer mass of the infected would be deadly. "One step back, hut! And hut, and hut!"

Still too many infected.

Paul knew that he had to drop the pressure right away. The shield bearers simply weren't in the physical condition to melee for so long.

"Pistols!" Paul yelled hoarsely.

It was a desperation move. The pikemen maintained their shield wall, dropped their polearms and drew their sidearms. Paul needed to reestablish enough space to allow his fumbling right side to reset. However, they only had as long as their ammunition lasted. Pistol fire from the shield line lashed out, dropping many infected, but the rate of fire was very rapid.

Too rapid to be efficient.

The spearman who'd almost lost his shield tried to do too many things at once. He fumbled his mag change, began to reach for his dropped magazine, then changed his mind and holstered. As he braced to raise his shield again, an injured infected tripped him up and he went down in a clump.

Immediately three infected piled on, tearing at his equipment and heavy clothing. Paul watched helplessly as even more infected joined, drawn by the man's frantic struggles to escape.

Given the level of team's training, there was no way to reverse the direction of the shield line. Recovering him was out of the question, but perhaps they could shoot the zombies off him. Paul drew his own pistol. In concert with others in the second line, he tried to carefully shoot the infected mobbing his downed man. The stricken shieldman fought, his knife flashing over and over but suddenly the plastic bicycle helmet that he wore flew off as a "friendly" pistol round cratered the plastic.

"Withdraw!" Paul didn't waste time mourning. There would be time later.

As they backed through the doorway at the end of the hall, men peeled off and reformed. Unfortunately, this meant that fewer were holding back the same number of infected. The pressure was enormous and the team was being forced through the door like toothpaste from a tube.

"Still too many!" his assistant yelled. "We have to pull out!"

"We'll retreat back to the front entrance!" Paul yelled back. "We've got to delay the mob long enough to break contact and get on the trucks." Hundreds of infected were hammering at the remaining handful of men holding the shieldwall. The white-faced men had reholstered their clocked out pistols and now grunted with effort as they pushed back against a wall of screaming, growling predators.

Paul and the squad leader stepped forward to begin a rapid series of single shots. As he did so, Paul activated his weapon light and was able to steady it long enough to *really* scan the corridor. For a moment, his heart seized. The number of infected had grown beyond his worst nightmare. Behind the depleted group of infected blocked by Paul's shieldwall, a fresh mob numbering more than a thousand surged forward, filling the length and breadth of the long corridor. Holding back those kinds of numbers with gun fire would be like trying to restrain the incoming tide by throwing rocks at the surf.

The men already through the chokepoint, like Paul, could probably make it to safety. The men in the shieldwall would be doomed if he waited any longer.

"Everyone back! NOW!"

The remaining shield wall disintegrated as the new wave of infected struck and Paul screamed his last command.

"RUN!"

Tom had watched as the adversary's foot patrol approached the bridge on foot. Cautiously, they probed forward.

"Well, that tears it," Tom said conversationally. "Wasted our best demo and we're not even going to get a single vehicle. Let's mount back up and use some of the ANFO from the ranch to collapse that cut."

He referred to a narrow cut in a rocky hillside that they had passed even earlier. Junior's dad had pre-prepared modestly sized ammonium nitrate charges, packaged in the bright orange plastic buckets from the local hardware superstore. One or two of these, fused with an old-fashioned slow match, would suffice for what Tom had in mind. Covering the road with rocky debris would compel the Gleaners to backtrack and allow his party to keep their distance. They would continue to draw the Gleaners away from the families' camp.

"Junior, Dave, get back to the truck," Tom said without taking eyes off the developing scene. "I'll initiate electrically from here. They'll have to ford downstream or go all the way to the next bridge. Either way, plenty of time to rig the pass."

Despite the beginnings of a protest, Pascoe towed the younger, if bigger, young man downslope towards their truck.

A few hundred meters in the other direction, well below Tom, a small party stumbled across the stream and started pointing at the underside of the bridge.

Well, shit.

He hated to use one of their few remotely ignited charges for nothing more than a delaying tactic, but he had committed to the bridge. The remotes had the advantage of omitting wires, making them easier to conceal. Additionally, timing was simpler since he could wait for the proper moment to explode the charge.

But, Murphy always takes a cut. Tom's gamble hadn't paid off, so he was only going to get a few individuals, not a truck.

Lesson learned there. Or relearned, as it were.

Chagrined, he dug the firing remote out of his pocket and lifted the safe and arming switch cover. With a second glance to check that their adversaries were within the blast radius, he pressed the button, sending a radio frequency signal to the waiting charge. The signal was designed to close a small circuit, allowing a battery to very rapidly heat the bridge wires in the detonator. Acting just like the element of an old-fashioned incandescent light bulb, the wires would ignite a chemical explosive that was very sensitive to heat. In turn, that very small explosion would ignite the secondary, or booster charge. The booster created a much larger, sharper explosion which would detonate the main charge.

Of course, all of this happened much faster than a human could blink.

Except that it didn't.

Nothing. Could be a slow detonator. Tom waited.

And waited.

Misfire. Damn it.

He stowed the remote and positioned his carbine. The range was a bit long, but all he expected to do now was to make them deploy, slowing their advance and buying some time.

Through his optic he selected one figure who was staring curiously at the underside of the bridge. Four hundred meters. The bullet would drop more than a foot over that distance. He repeated the familiar shooter's mantra as adjusted his point of aim in order to compensate.

"Front sight focus, breathe in, slowly exhale and squeeze..."

Paul squeezed the door knob in his right hand as he paused in front of Kohn's door. The growth in camp population meant that nearly all the CHUs were shared, so having a private office with a door had become a pearl of great price. The acting administrator had made a show of accepting the office from her fawning staff. Paul knew that it was a symbol of her power. He released the doorknob, swallowed and knocked.

The medical center salvage mission had been a barely mitigated disaster. The most recent losses on the clearance mission had further reduced the original security staff to less than a handful. In contrast, Kohn's coterie had grown. The original city staff, new refugees, commodity analysts from the bank and now, even Kendra were firmly embracing her leadership and a promise of collaborative safety.

He had already compiled the after action report. Three missing, presumed dead. Two more dead of their wounds. More seriously injured, including a few gunshot wounds. The Executive Committee would meet tonight to receive his verbal digest, but he wanted to pre-brief Kohn.

He recognized that he was delaying. Like it or not, Kohn was in charge. He knocked a second time with two firm raps to the door.

"Please come in," answered a familiar contralto.

Joanna was seated, but stood to reveal that instead of the usual dove gray trousers that matched her uniform tunic, she wore a knee-length pleated A-line skirt in the same color. She came forward across the reclaimed carpet, circling the desk, and took Paul's hands in her own.

"I am so glad that you have safely returned, Paul," she said with a barely perceptible catch in her voice. "We have all been so very worried about the risks that you take."

"Um." Paul searched for a response to this unexpected reception. "I'm very sorry, Ms. Kohn. You know by now that we lost two of the wounded. Septic shock. Four are badly wounded and may not recover to the point of returning to the team. We took on a target that was just too big. The risks of using only small teams and not investing in realistic training were eventually going to catch up with us."

"Of course, Paul." She pulled him into one the chairs that faced the desk before taking the adjacent one. Her hold on his hand didn't waver. "You must call me Joanna in a time like this. The loss of the team members is a terrible tragedy. You were right about the risks. You must forgive yourself!"

"Ah, well, sure?" Paul said, feeling a little whiplashed by the way the conversation was developing. "Like I tried to explain, inevitable. I feel badly about it, but honestly, there wasn't a lot that we could do. We had to enter the building to search for the centrifuge and filtration gel. Our numbers were limited. Sooner or later we were going to end up in a close-quarters fight without enough ammunition or shooters. That day arrived early, is all."

Joanna scooted her already close chair a fraction of an inch closer, and crossed her legs. The motion flashed a surprising amount of thigh in Paul's peripheral vision.

"I, I would like to propose the formation of a larger, dedicated security group which I can train up," Paul said, startled by the unexpected display. He attempted to rally and continue with his brief. "The current policy enforcing the rotation of personnel prevents anyone from establishing the base of experience which becomes critical during an in extremis event. This reduces the effectiveness of our salvage sweeps and if we ever have to truly defend this camp, it'll reduce our combat power there, as well. We need a larger security group, trained to a higher standard."

"Well, Paul, I am *certainly* open to reopening that line of thought..." Kohn said as she moved one warm hand to lay manicured fingers on his forearm. "We were together at the start of New York's response to this threat and we can understand each other like so few others can. Really, we should work more closely together, after all. We can lead this group to be the start of a new recovery for humanity."

"Well, that's the idea, Ms. Kohn," Paul tried to shield himself with the formalities that had become commonplace. Was it his imagination or could he actually feel her body heat across the narrowing gap that separated their chairs?

"Joanna, Paul. And I need your support too," Joanna said, not quite purring. "If we could amend the Operating Rules, several options become more accessible to the Council. It would be easier to expand your security team, selectively improve and increase rations and so on."

"You can't change the Rules without a unanimous vote, Joanna," replied Paul. He could see her game now. "The Council must sit a bank representative. As I've stated in my objections for the record—"

"Now, Paul," Joanna dropped her hand to Paul's upper thigh, where it rested lightly. "I am aware that your relationship with Ms. Jones ended some time ago. I have been alone since the start. It is fitting that the two principal leaders who were together at the start continue to . . . *support* one another, do you not agree?"

Her finger tips beat a brief tattoo. On the material of his trousers. On the worn, thin material of his trousers.

Paul abruptly stood up, appalled by the implications of her offer and by the uncomfortable if involuntary response of his libido. He hadn't had a woman in a long time—well, a long time for him. Way too long, his libido assured him. In fact, this new direction that Kohn was proposing seemed just dandy to his libido.

Kohn wasn't unattractive physically. In a flash, his libido helpfully noted that she was fit, smart and apparently kinda into him. She was just creepy as hell. And she was a murderer.

"I think you misunderstand my position, Ms. Kohn," Paul said as firmly as he could, even as he jammed his hands into his trouser pockets. "I'm not going to change my position on the Camp Rules. They're there for a reason. And . . . I'm not interested in other than a professional relationship."

"Paul, you do not seem quite sure." She stood up with him, noting the position of his hands. A smile crept across her face. "In fact, you seem of two minds . . ."

"It's. Not. Going to happen," he said as his anger asserted itself. "I've known for a long time about your record as a juvenile. About murdering your friends with a crowbar. About your boyfriend who died in a freak fall down marble stairs, his head so damaged that he must've fallen two, maybe three times. Some other deaths around you that remain question marks. Tom Smith knew, and he convinced me that we needed someone like you, in fact, particularly like you, if we were going to save the city. And we saw how that worked."

"Paul, the partnership between the City and the bank worked quite . . . well." Joanna didn't bother to repress a smirk. If his revelations disturbed her, it wasn't evident. "We survived. Civilization may yet survive. Expressly because Smith knew, like I know and in your heart, like you know—the end will justify any means needed to get there."

She inched a bit closer, her chest only a few inches from Paul's. He noted the motion of her blouse. It strongly suggested that she hadn't bothered with a, ah, foundation garment.

Her voice lowered a bit.

"And we all used the same vaccine," she said huskily. "We all have the same guilty knowledge. Would you give up your protection from the virus just because of the source?"

"Yeah, we all used the same vaccine, Joanna," Paul said angrily as he stepped farther back. "The difference is that I saw Tom throw up almost every day, sick from running the whole bloody mess. It was required to survive. Meanwhile, you slept like a baby. And that's the difference. So you and I . . . no. Never. Work with you to advance the Site? Yes. Get personal with you? I'd sooner fuck a bag of scorpions."

"Oh, I see," Kohn said as her face slid into immobility, her eyes calculating. "And my offer?"

"I'll continue to support the refuge and your role as *Acting* Administrator," Paul said, keeping his hands in his trouser pockets. "However, the Site Charter and the Rules are clear. At some point soon, we need to establish permanent governance and a permanent coordinator. Which may or may not be you."

Kohn regarded Paul at close range, looking first into one eye, then the other.

"I do see." She spun on her heels and stalked back to her desk, the gray skirt swishing pertly side to side.

Paul noticed.

God-damned libido.

"That will be all, Mr. Rune," Kohn said, her voice perfectly composed. "Please close the door behind you."

Paul stepped backwards, keeping his eyes on Kohn. In turn she ignored him, and sat, opening the same red folder that she had closed upon his entry.

He felt for the doorknob behind him before turning and then retreated, swiftly closing the barrier that separated them.

CHAPTER 12

"I'm getting really tired of all the fucking zombies," declared Rob Robbins, Sr.

They had departed the ranch shortly after the two bank SUVs had moved out on their delaying mission. Despite difficult roads, Kaplan's experience to date had improved their navigation and they'd made better time than the original group. One thing that both trips had in common, however, was the number of infected that stood in their way.

"This ain't shit," Kaplan said. "You shoulda seen New York on the way out. Now that was a lot. This is just the most that we've seen so far today. Still not too bad, though."

The first candidate dam had been a bust. Every fence had been knocked flat, infected buildings with open doors and broken windows and what appeared to be fire damage to the critical forest of high tension wires in the switching yard.

Now they'd pulled up well short of the second candidate. The group was able to surveil the Watts Bar installation while remaining hidden from direct view by an old multiple car crash cluttering the state highway on the opposite side of the river. Both men ignored the ever present corpses that were still in some of the vehicles. The light breeze was pleasant since the work of scavengers and months of weather had eliminated nearly all the odors of decomposition.

The state road descended the wooded hill where they were paused, eventually crossing the dam itself. Spanning the blue-green lake visible upstream, the dam bisected the river. Infected were in full view everywhere. Dozens appeared to be combing the near and far banks of the Tennessee. More were in motion near an RV park on their side of the river. Even more were on the dam itself, including the nearside dock mechanism.

"So, think that we could we crush through?" replied Robbins.

"Well, the numbers are pretty dense," Kaplan said, calculating. "For every infected that you can see, there might be four or five that you can't. Once we start making noise, those pop up. But take a look at the far side."

Kaplan referred to unpainted concrete building that bore a large blue TVA logo across the top floor. The three-story structure resembled a blockhouse. Behind it, enclosed in a smaller fenced area, was a large complex of masts, wires and high power lines.

"Well, we aren't getting across that dam unless we use the trucks," Robbins said appraisingly. "Lotsa zombies, but it looks like there is a watch tower and a heavy fence. I think that we can make it."

"That's not what I mean," Kaplan said. "No infected in view on the far side of the fence. No broken windows, all the doors are shut, no fire damage. I hate to offer any optimism, but it actually looks intact. Might even be occupied."

"Hmm," Robbins raised his binoculars and leaned across the hood of a burned-out pickup while he scanned the far bank. "Yeah. It looks . . . intact. In fact, look over there, on the right side. The fence extends to the water line." He continued to look before excitedly adding, "There's a boat!"

"So . . . probably occupied," replied Kaplan. He scratched his chin reflectively and looked at the scene a bit more. "I sure wouldn't appreciate it if I'd gone to the trouble to set up a defense, maintain the electric plant and then some assholes crashed through my fence and made a ruckus big enough to draw every zombie for a mile in every direction."

"How do we get in?" Robbins retorted. He gestured back towards their convoy where every able bodied adult was pulling security. "The easiest way in is straight through. Our collective ass is flapping in the wind out here!"

"We approach from the other side," Kaplan said confidently. "We go around, probably upstream and make an approach. And we ask nicely."

"Okay," Robbins replied. "Only let's not dally. How do you figure the other guys are doing?"

⚬⚬ ⊖ ⚬⚬

"We would be doing a lot better if Miss Eva would just grow a pair and turn us loose," opined Dragon AKA Short Round, eliciting a quiet round of dirty sniggering. "Ain't more than a couple of dudes staying just out of sight. Attack them again, in force, and we push right through. Cost us something, sure, but then we nail 'em! Then we can get back to camp and live a little better!"

A general round of assenting grumbles met his complaint. The Gleaner convoy had been playing cat to the harassers' mouse. In addition to the man shot at the first bridge, they'd been forced to leave one truck behind when a sudden avalanche had catapulted heavy boulders onto the narrow mountain road. In exchange they had twice wasted ammunition hosing down the suspected locations of their tormentors, each time after only catching the merest glimpse of their enemy.

Circled up in a clearing well away from the main road, they were eating canned rations instead of the hot meals that were the norm in the main base. The intermittent autumn rain wasn't helping morale, either.

"You volunteering to be the first guy in the charge?" Jason said. He didn't expect an answer, and Short Round didn't disappoint, choosing to stare at his bootlaces.

Jason looked over his shoulder at the command car where their leader was looking at two different maps. He hooked a thumb in her direction. "I think that Eva is doing exactly what Mr. Green directed. If she hadn't stopped at the first bridge, their bomb could have wrecked half the convoy. We don't even know how strong these guys are. They got unlucky twice. Push into them, on their ground, maybe their luck turns."

"So what's the point?" the ex-con said, grousing as he slid his blue-gloved hands along his rifle. "What we doing here?"

"We're looking for where these assholes come from," Jason said, trying for the confident tone that his old watch commander had used in the squad bullpen. "Then we push, or maybe go back for everyone else."

"Hmmmf," was Short Round's only reply.

"Hnnnnng!" Tom tried to hold still as Pascoe fished around in his shoulder for a bit of a round that had fragmented against a rock where he sheltered before spitting metal slivers into his deltoid. "Stop playing with it and just get it outta me!"

"Heh heh," Pascoe spit tobacco to one side, then resumed his work. "That's what she said."

"How you doing, Boss?" Junior said as he walked up. "Sounds kinda...bad."

"Sssa!" Tom exhaled during a particular deep dig and glared at his helper. "It's not bad. The armor kept the rounds out. I just caught some jacket metal and Dave here is playing at panning for gold."

"You know, the more you keep talking and moving the harder this is for me," the former SF medic said lightly. "I'm a little out of practice though, so I don't mind trying a few times. Keeps my hand in, like."

"Okay, I'll hold sti—gahhhh," Tom said as the probe returned to work. He resolutely declined to watch what Pascoe was doing. "Just finish already!"

"Anyhow, if we just set a really solid ambush, like I have been saying, we can riddle these dudes," Robbins Junior said. He had been bending everyone's ear about taking the offensive. "You don't have to stay behind to get shot at every time."

Tom glared sideways. He had tried for a second shot at the bridge and barely ducked in time avoid the large but thankfully diffuse storm of fire that their opponents had used to sweep the ridge where he lay.

"Not up for discussion," Tom gritted out.

"But, I'm sure tha—" the younger man said as he tried to explain himself.

"What part of not now isn't clear!" Tom twisted to face Junior. "Owwww!"

A renewed rush of blood stained the formerly white battle dressing that Pascoe had taped under the wound. Tom looked at it and then away, breathing through his nose.

"Is it supposed to bleed like that?" Junior said, observing with keen-eyed interest. "You look a little gray."

Carefully *only* turning his head this time, Tom leveled a very flat stare on the younger man.

"Why don't you check the perimeter again, shorty?" Pascoe said firmly. "We don't want to distract the boss while I'm working. Besides, I might have to practice on you next if you keep this up."

"Okay, okay," Robbins Junior said, turning away. "I'm just trying to help. Dad has been teaching me this stuff for years. I swear..."

His grumbling faded as he stepped away.

"Kid might not be wrong, Train," said Pascoe as soon as the teen was out of earshot. "Pick our ground, set up a nice kill zone, we could bloody their nose enough that they stop chasing."

"Maybe, maybe not, Davey," replied Tom. "If we'd a trained group instead of a teenager and Fat Ralph, if we weren't risking Robbie's kid, maybe I'd try. All it takes is one slip, one bad roll and we get gobbled up, even by amateurs like this."

"Only room for one boss, and you're it," answered Pascoe. "Ooh, look! There's a little more jacket metal in the muscle. Gimme!"

It was time for a shower and some sleep.

Paul stepped into his CHU. The heavy blackout drapes that he had improvised in order to make it easier to sleep during daylight hours were drawn shut. He quickly closed the door in order to preserve the cooler interior temperature and began to step across to the window to get some more light.

"Uunnh!" Paul grunted as he doubled over, absorbing a powerful blow across his abdomen.

He collapsed to one knee, but drove upwards into the direction of the attack, only to absorb another blow, from the rear this time, to his kidney. Excruciating pain momentarily prevented coherent thought.

Someone swept his legs from beneath him and he sprawled on his back. Heavy, painful weights pinned his wrists and shins. Dry fabric was shoved into his mouth, immediately starting a king-sized case of cotton mouth.

The drapes were swept open and he saw two "walk-ins," both burly farmer types. One kneeled across both of Paul's wrists, painfully mashing the small bones together. The second kneeled astride his ankles. Schweizer also stared at him, one booted foot braced against Paul's hip.

"Shoulda taken the deal, Rune," he said with a grim smile. "I don't have to like this, but it is necessary. Sorry."

Schweizer leaned down and delivered a short, chopping right to Paul's temple. Amidst a shooting burst of pain and sparks, the world went gray for a moment. Distantly Paul felt some kind of restraints being applied to his wrists. As his vision sharpened, he watched Schweizer withdraw a flat, black plastic case from his jacket. He opened it to reveal a serried row of syringes. He withdrew one that was loaded with what looked like water.

Paul struggled mightily as he felt the sting of the needle.

A rush of heat flooded across his skin and his heart began to pound. He tried to turn his head towards Schweizer but his muscles stopped obeying—

"Okay guys, I got to go," Kendra said as she pushed back her chair as her table companions made the usual farewells. Paul's CHU was only a short walk away. Everyone had heard how the salvage team had returned, savaged from their last mission. She'd seen Paul, still in his blood-spattered equipment, go to meet Joanna. By now he would be finished.

He might appreciate it if she just stopped by to say hi. A friendly face. Nothing more.

Smiling, she left the dining facility and turned down the path towards his room.

Ahead, the door to the CHU exploded open, banging against the railing like a gunshot.

"Hold onto his feet, dammit!"

She could make out several men trying to control the spastic kicking and bucking of . . . Paul?

"What the fuck are you doing!" she yelled as she charged forward, just as Ken Schweizer blocked her way.

"He's infected, Kendra! Stay back!"

She tried to dance around the outstretched arms of the taller man. She could see that Paul was gagged and his arms were tied but he was screaming into a gag and fighting his bonds. His skin was flushed, his eyes were hugely bloodshot and the Saint Joshua's medal that she'd returned to him danced on its chain as the group struggled to manage him.

"He's vaccinated!" she protested, trying to side step around him. "He can't be infected!"

"Kendra!" Joanna said, materializing beside her. "Let them take him to the clinic. He needs help right now!"

"How did this happen?" Kendra yelled again, but then allowed Joanna to ease her aside as the team of men maneuvered Paul towards the clinic. He fought and kicked, but without any perceptible control or skill. As his gag slipped, he began trying to bite the men holding his arms, causing a brief panic till another man could get the familiar stiff fabric of a Kevlar snake bag over his head. Growls and yells emanated from the off-white sack as the group renewed their progress towards the medical office.

"Paul felt very guilty about the loss of the people on the vaccine supply run," Joanna said as she slipped an arm around Kendra's shoulders and steered her in the wake of the lurching group. "He knew how badly we needed vaccine for the recent arrivals. We had some vaccine of unknown quality that he had recovered earlier. On his own cognizance he elected to try it."

"That doesn't make sense!" Kendra said, watching the procession fight to get Paul into the double CHU that was the new dispensary. "He was already vaccinated. How would a new vaccination be judged good or not?"

"I told Paul that I did not agree, that we needed him more than ever," explained Joanna. "He felt that it was safe enough since he was vaccinated. He expected the bona-fides of the recovered medicine would be apparent either way. No reaction would mean that the vaccine was either counterfeit or denatured from improper temperature storage. A very slight allergic reaction would mean that the vaccine was attenuated but sufficient to provoke the immune system."

"So how is he sick?" Kendra almost yelled. "You saw that! It wasn't either of those things!"

"Either what he injected himself with was a new strain of the virus or . . ." Joanna paused, appearing to consider a new, unpalatable possibility.

"Or what, damn it!"

"Or the vaccine that the bank made wasn't that effective after all," concluded Joanna.

"No physical evidence, understood ma'am," Schweizer said. He didn't click his heels, but the rigidity of his frame would have done credit to any Wehrmacht sergeant.

The figure at the desk sat in shadow. Methodically, she rapped a knuckle against the blotter.

Tap. Pause. Tap.

"Once you have disposed of the body, the displaced persons who aided you in Rune's quarters will be assigned to high-risk duties, yes?"

"I'm running the security since Rune became ill, ma'am," Schweizer assured Kohn. "It will be arranged."

"Very good, Ken." Tap, tap. "That is all."

"Well, don't that beat all?" said Eva. "Not exactly subtle, are they."

There was a tangle of tree trunks dropped across the road. The green foliage and white heartwood visible betrayed the newness of the obstacle, which was layered over an old three-car wreck. The Gleaner convoy had stopped short of the crossroads that lay ahead. A few others stood behind her while the rest stayed mounted up.

"There's a bit of a gap between the wrecks and that gas station," said Jason as he scanned in turn. "We could squeeze the wrecker through that, and the rest can make it no problem."

"Almost like they left that hole for us to use," Eva said flatly, as she scanned ahead and then squinted at the sky. "The last two times they carefully hid explosives. Now they are practically waving a big sign that says 'Easy place to drive through!' That's a hard pass, thank you."

"So, what are we gonna do then, Miss Eva?" asked Short Round respectfully. "We could push right through that roadblock, if you want!"

"We're gonna camp," Eva said firmly. "Let's go back a bit. We'll stop just outside long rifle shot and build some fires. Finally eat some hot food. Let them see us relax. Then sometime after midnight, we are gonna set some of our folks in the vehicles while the rest go with me for a little walk."

"In the dark?" asked a voice from the rear of the group. "Who's crazy enough to go walking in the dark with zombies?"

"Exactly my point," Eva said with a toothy grin. "I'm betting that our friends that prepared that innocent looking roadblock are going to wait to see what we are going to do in the morning."

"Yeah, they aren't moving," said Junior. "Trucks are pulled up in a circle and looks like they are planning to settle in. Told you that we could have hit them at that last bridge. These trees are way too obvious."

He handed the binoculars he was using to another rancher.

"I keep telling you Junior, the plan is to delay them for now,"

Pascoe said wearily. "We're buying time. If they want to camp, great. After we hold them for a night, we can scamper another five miles down the road and blow the bridge. By the time they detour around that, we should be at the bank's camp."

He looked over back downhill, but their vehicle was out of sight. Smith was fiddling with their radio since the distance to Site Blue was short enough that a transmission might get through.

In theory.

"Now go let Smith know what they are doing. We're gonna have to keep an eye on them overnight."

Jason had never spent any time in the military. Despite that lack, he was reasonably confident that their group would wake up everything within a hundred yards of the path. If their opponents had been made of dry sticks, the Gleaners would already rule the world, considering their unerring ability to loudly snap every single one in the state.

Thankfully, there was almost no talking. Or cigarette smoking. Eva had promised a painful death to any that fucked up and lived through the aftermath. Between that and the desire of their merry band of cutthroats to close with the little party that had been harrying the Gleaners for four days, the mood was upbeat and the noise discipline as good as it was going to get.

Everyone was ready to get stuck in. Even Eva finally seemed optimistic.

Her instructions had been basic.

"No point in a fancy plan. We stay together so that we don't end up ambushing ourselves or getting lost. Just have the guys walk up on the side where we think that those assholes are sleeping. As soon as we find them, we get in a long line and push forward, shooting. If they start shooting at us first, we just have everyone rush in and we use our numbers to roll over them. Meanwhile, the trucks push up the road. Keep the guys in the back from shooting the rest of us up front. Make them spread to the sides when the time comes, understand?"

She had also set Jason at the rear in order to ensure that no one strayed, either accidentally or deliberately, He couldn't fault any of her logic.

Logic or no, it took a surprisingly long time to walk the half mile. The heavy cloud cover made for a dark night, so when the line jerked to a halt he naturally bumped into the man ahead of him.

Then he heard some loud shouts from the front of the column.

Junior and Pascoe had the midnight to two watch. Situated at the edge of a small copse overlooking the crossroads, the pair lay behind Junior's leetle fren'. Although he had been teaching Smith and Ralph the manual of arms for the weapon, Junior remained the most proficient gunner for the antique machine gun.

It wasn't unusual to hear the occasional zombie wander within hearing distance. This night was no different. A single infected, as far as they could tell, had drifted across their front a few times. So far, they had elected to let it pass unmolested. Lacking both a keen sense of smell and night vision, zombies were ineffective nighttime hunters, cuing on movement and sound. Simply keeping your nerve and holding still allowed the survivors to defer encounters with individual infected as well as small groups.

However, the noise level was picking up. It sounded like a larger group this time.

"What do you think?" Junior whispered, nudging Pascoe as the crunching drew closer. "Are they on the trail?"

"Sounds like it," Pascoe said with a worried look towards their little laager, just out of sight. "I hate to give away our position, but I don't want to wrestle with a lot of zombies and the big gun will chop them up good. I'll initiate and you can use the flash to aim in."

As Pascoe began to aim towards the sound, there was a thump, an inarticulate but clearly querulous growl and finally a shout of alarm.

That wasn't an infected.

Being woken from a sound sleep by the sound of nearby fully automatic fire is a very unpleasant experience. Even after the recent gunfights, and despite not being fully asleep, Tom still spasmed in alarm when he was roused. The heavy chugging of Junior's weapon was distinctive, sounding like nothing else in the Fallen world.

He rolled over to see Ralph's wide open eyes at close range.

"Start the truck!" Tom yelled. "Lights off, keep it running and be ready to punch it when we get back."

Without waiting to acknowledge Fat Ralph's shaky nod, Tom shrugged into his plate carrier and grabbed his rifle and ran for the short path that led to the observation post. Ahead, the bass timbre of the vintage machine gun had been joined by a growing rattle of what had to be return fire. As he pounded into direct line of sight of the firing position, the gunner finished his first belt. Absent the overwhelming bass of the thirty cal, Tom noted three things immediately: first, his tinnitus had once again been stimulated to a fine, fresh high pitched whine. Second, despite the strength of the tinnitus, he could still hear the sharp popping of several rifles. And over it all, the building sound of howling.

As Junior began to reload, Tom dove into a prone position and immediately starting shooting into the center of a group that had been lit by the muzzle flash of the big gun. To his right, he could hear Pascoe cursing as he tried to neatly flake out a second belt. His hearing was too far gone for him to make out the clicking and racking sounds that Junior must have been making as he frantically tried to reload the gun under stress.

Tom knew that there were several qualities of infantry combat that could not be appreciated until they were experienced. Among them was a truism—that in combat even simple things become very, very hard. Junior had likely been drilled on reloading and clearing malfunctions hundreds of times by his veteran father. He was good enough to have familiarized the other members of the team on the gun. None of that could prepare him for the shattering experience of shooting at men, being shot at, and still calmly, precisely reloading a finicky mechanism. It didn't help that dark shapes, both howling infected and screaming men, loomed in the darkness.

"Get that gun up, Pascoe!" Tom yelled, adding, "Changing mags!"

Before he could insert a fresh magazine in the well of his rifle, an infected, drawn by movement and sound, sprinted towards him. It stumbled short of its target, tripping into the gun pit and falling across Junior and Pascoe. Tom made a fast draw with his pistol and simultaneously jumped onto the infected's back, pinning it with his knees. Despite his desperate haste, he very carefully placed his Sig-Sauer pistol in contact distance of the thrashing infected's head, where it lay between Pascoe and Junior, before safely drilling a round through its skull and then into the dirt beneath.

The sound of incoming fire increased. Tom felt first a punch on his chest plate and then the now familiar impact of a bullet, accompanied immediately afterwards by a freezing sensation on his leg, as he absorbed another wound in his left thigh.

"It's jammed!" cried Junior desperately, hammering at the feed tray.

"Leave it, run!" screamed Pascoe. He raised to one knee and fired single shots as rapidly as he could reacquire each subsequent sight picture.

Simultaneously a knot of infected ran into the pit.

Instantly Tom was in the zone. His pistol came up, the front sight post covered the zombie's center of mass and Tom stroked the trigger four times before the target stumbled. Tom pivoted fractionally, delivering another series of rounds into the closest infected before it too dropped. The next infected closed all the way and bit Tom's plate carrier, helpfully holding mostly still as Tom jammed his Sig against its chest, emptying the magazine.

"Tom, get the kid out of here!" Pascoe screamed, but Tom still had company.

He tore the RMJ hawk out of the Kydex sheath which he'd slung below his plate carrier. It came free in his hand and he began using short, economical strokes. He deliberately rejected the temptation to take a really big swing that might bury his weapon in a target for too long. The paracord handle stayed firm in his grip despite the blood that started to cover everything.

Another infected loomed out of the darkness and he tore out its throat with an efficient forehand stroke. A screaming man stumbled against his shin, hag-ridden by a zombie that bit at his shoulder. Tom hacked downwards, killing the man first with a blow to the back of the neck, and then spun the hawk to take the zombie in one eye with the spike. A sudden hot wetness splashed across his face, as the arterial blood from the gaping wounds briefly jetted in all directions.

"Tom, we ARE leaving!" Pascoe yelled, trying to tow the teen-ager away from the stubborn machine gun.

Tom joined him as they dragged Junior backwards. As the boy finally lurched into a crouch, abandoning his father's weapon, Tom heard Pascoe's firing resume, but the despite the very large amount of enemy fire, surprisingly few rounds were actually striking near them.

"Pascoe, go dark!" Tom ordered.

It wasn't Tom's first rodeo and he knew how confusing night-time engagements could be. Their best chance was to deny the numerically superior enemy an aiming point. The teen was already moving down the trail, as ordered.

The two of them stumbled after Junior, Pascoe running into every branch, and falling down more than once.

Tom's M4 banged against his hips and back as it dangled on its sling. He held onto his tomahawk, but used his empty hand to grab Pascoe and half drag him the remaining distance to the truck despite the growing burning in his leg.

Behind them, firing continued as their assailants continued to shoot towards both zombies and their now departed prey. The screams from the injured men were nearly indistinguishable from those of the zombies.

Jason couldn't hear or see any more incoming fire.

"Cease fire!" he began repeating at the top of his lungs. He could barely hear his own voice over the ringing in his ears. "Cease fire! Cease fire!"

A mere two dozen repetitions were required to get most of the Gleaners to stop shooting, only to start again when one man shot a still mobile zombie. Jason had to repeat the drill, twice more, before silence finally reigned. Jason pulled the remaining men into a single line, spread in a shallow C shape across the front of place where the machine gun had been. After a few silent minutes, he made half the survivors slowly stand, and walk forward.

The gun was still there, as were several dead or mostly dead zombies, one of their own men—who was most definitely dead—a lot of blood.

And exactly zero enemy.

Well, fuck.

CHAPTER 13

The bag over Paul's head was speckled with blood.

"Do zombies even sleep?" asked the newly appointed security guard. "This guy has been limp for hours."

"After we confirmed the diagnosis I had him tranked," Schweizer said, lowering the tailgate on the diesel pickup. "Just get him off the truck. We're the only three that know the whole story. We dump him, you shoot him and we go, right?"

"Whoa, what? Why didn't we just do this at camp?" whined the former townie. "Just bury his ass in the ditch outside the gate, like any other shambler."

"The administrator doesn't want a martyr, considering that he cost us so many lives," said the manager by way of explanation. "Out of sight, out of mind. This place is nice and anonymous. No memorial. He can just fade away."

"You shoot him then," retorted the guard. "This is fucked up enough, I ain't gonna murder this asshole. We held him down for you back in the camp. I figured it was a simple takeover, beat his ass and move on. I didn't know you were getting him killed."

"You think that you can back out now?" Schweizer said, resting his right hand on his pistol. The other two men were armed, but as in any pack, the pecking order was clear. "I'm not asking you to hate him. But I'm telling you: just get him off the fucking truck. Drag him inside and get rid of him. Leave the body for scavengers and off we go."

The two men eyed their new boss. Kohn was the undisputed

master of the camp and Schweizer was her man. There wasn't any upside to making an issue of this.

At the moment.

"Sure, sure," said the first. He turned to his companion. "Grab his feet and we'll tote him inside, no sweat."

Rune's slack body was unceremoniously dumped on the ground. Situated on a crossroads, the nondescript town was at the edge of the cleared zone around Site Blue. Zombies regularly filtered in. Either the feral dogs or infected could be relied upon to clean up any remains.

The two men grabbed Rune's feet and towed him inside while Schweizer clambered back in the truck.

Inside they stopped in what had been a convenience store.

"How do you want to do this?" asked the first.

"I don't," replied the second. "You talked me into this bullshit, you do it." Suiting action to temperament he immediately walked out.

The first rolled his eyes. He drew his pistol and aimed it at the prone figure. Long seconds went by.

Killing another person is *hard*.

Pre-Plague, it was a well-established axiom that most rank and file soldiers will actively work to *not* shoot their opponents, even in the heat of battle. In other than special operations units, the majority of soldiers wouldn't shoot, or would shoot to miss. Outside combat, it's an even rarer person who can initiate lethal violence. Psychopaths aside, there is simply too strong an inhibition to killing. Executing an unresisting human, absent a strong compulsion such as revenge, is simply not possible for normally socialized humans.

Despite the horror of the Fall, most survivors were pretty normal. They were traumatized, sure. Often desperate, certainly. But they were ordinary rural and exurban folk who were just trying to cope. Unless you started the Fall as a sociopathic murderer, one usually did not become a emotionless killer afterwards. Kill attacking infected? Yep. Drop the hammer on someone you know to be a sentient human? At a time when humans were edging towards extinction? When that person was helpless?

Just.

No.

This new guard had been an ordinary exurban dad, then a scavenger, and then had briefly trained under the supervision of the same man he was supposed to shoot. He was no better equipped to murder in cold blood than any other average man.

He willed his disobedient finger to squeeze. The muzzle of the pistol wavered back and forth. The guard literally closed his eyes.

Outside, Schweizer watched the first guard walk out and stand by the tailgate. One minute went by. Five. Just as he was about to get out and stomp inside there was a single gunshot. Moments later the second guard exited, looking ashen. He walked towards the truck and nodded his head.

Good enough.

Schweizer cranked the engine over and waited for his newly initiated staff to get aboard.

Kendra stared at her coffee cup. Paul had loved coffee. Other customers in the dining facility respected her space, allowing her to brood alone. Joanna had allowed her several days to compose herself after the patch test on Paul had come back positive for H7D3. After the obvious diagnosis was confirmed, the security team...disposed of the new zombie.

Kendra didn't want to know.

She felt like a different person, now. Her skin felt different. Her clothes, which hadn't changed, were unfamiliar. The very color of what should be well-remembered surroundings appeared to be fundamentally different. Somehow.

Kendra didn't know what this meant. Was she insane?

Did it matter?

She casually wondered what kind of person she was becoming in this place.

"Hey," Christine said, sliding onto the bench alongside Kendra. "Ms. Kohn wants you."

"No, she doesn't," Kendra replied flatly. "She said to take a few days."

"Kendra, that was almost two weeks ago. You have been coming in here, ordering coffee, watching it cool and afterwards, walking the fenceline, every day for twelve days," Christine said, pausing. "Look, I know ho—"

"Don't even say it," Kendra said, turning empty eyes towards the skinny blonde, who was leaning as far away as she could. "Just don't. I'll go see Kohn in a bit."

Christine bit her lip and nodded. She got up and swiftly walked out. Normally, hurting Christine's feelings—really anyone's feelings—would have bothered Kendra.

She shrugged mentally.

Apparently, she was becoming the kind of person who didn't give a fuck about that anymore.

She shoved her cold coffee away and stood.

Prior to Paul's death, Kendra had always felt that the office of the camp administrator was mostly theater. She felt that the building layers of bureaucracy were equal parts playacting and self-aggrandizement. Sheepishly, she admitted that she sort of went along because that kind of hierarchical structure was familiar, even a little comforting.

It was what she *knew*.

Now she felt empty. The kabuki dance of guards at the Administration building and the secretary that warded Kohn's door neither impressed nor reassured her. They were just things.

Not even particularly important things.

Kohn rose from behind her desk as Kendra knocked and stepped inside.

"Kendra, please sit down!" Kohn's said, her voice low and pleasant. "I am sorry that I had to disturb you."

They sat in two salvaged easy chairs, separated by a brown drum table. What looked like a genuine inlaid antique had been decorated with a hand-painted acrylic fleur de lis garnished in turn with violet flowers. Their garishness was lost on Kendra, who stared between her boots.

"I know that you are still processing our loss," Kohn said.

"*Our* loss?" Kendra said, looking up, her eyes suddenly bright with unshed tears. "*Whose* loss?"

"I know that you cared about him, Kendra," the administrator said soothingly. "But we all depended upon him. Even if you feel like you lost the most, we all lost something."

Kendra's eyes focused past Kohn, looking at the interior wall of the office, a mere thousand meters away.

"I asked two of our staff to attend to Paul respectfully," said Kohn after a very long pause. "I have a report that they did not. It...bothers me. However, I cannot take direct action for myself."

"Attend?" Kendra said, her attention riveted. She leaned forward, her teeth unconsciously bared. "Does that fucking mean what I think it means?"

"Yes," Kohn replied, instinctively leaning away a fraction of an inch before she grimaced for a moment and sat straight, schooling her calm mask back into place. "We had to euthanize Paul. I gave the orders, regretfully, but I gave them. I know that you might choose to hate me for that. It was necessary. He was infected. He had turned. You saw."

"I know. I saw," Kendra said, her voice cracking slightly. "So?"

"The two I trusted appear to have..." there was a slight hesitation. "...not followed my orders to the letter. There is a reasonable suspicion that they shot Paul out of hand. For sport."

"WHAT?" Kendra said, exploding upright. "Who?!"

"Two recent immigrants to the camp who were failed trainees for Paul's project," Kohn said. "They were trying out to replace our security losses, which are grievous. We need all the help that we can get. However, I need you more. If we are to work together, then I have to let you do this. I cannot hide it. If you choose to take action—well, it is yours to take. For the long term, for the greater good, we must have discipline. You worked in the security department of Bank of the Americas. Your actions will be accepted. You will enforce discipline. The rules of the camp that I administrate will be for all."

"What are their names?" Kendra said. Moments ago, her eyes had brimmed with tears. Now they were hard. "And where are they, specifically?"

"Schweizer has the names," Kohn replied. "I will direct him to give them to you."

Tom had ordered Ralph not to stop at the last bridge on the route to Site Blue. The only hale member of their little team was their least experienced man and Tom didn't really trust him to set the remaining orange bucket demolition charges, even under supervision. They would rely on speed to beat their pursuers to Site Blue.

If they continued to pursue, that is.

Tom had gotten lucky. The leg wound was mostly superficial,

but he had disinfected and bandaged himself in order to give the wound a chance to knit.

Pascoe was worse off. He would probably keep his eye, but wooden splinters from a bullet impact on the trunk they'd used for a shooting rest had driven into his eyes, nose and mouth. The swelling was comical. When it receded they would know more about his long-term outlook.

Tom turned and looked into the back seat while Fat Ralph drove.

"So, how does everyone feel about a leisurely drive straight through to Site Blue?"

His gaze lingered on a glum-faced Junior, whose thigh was bandaged. The quadriceps had deep scratches and lacerations from the zombie attack and the opposite calf had caught three shotgun pellets, two of which remained in the muscle.

Pascoe shared the rear seat.

"Hot damn, we're back in the cars!" Pascoe said jauntily. Beneath the bandaged eyes, his bright white teeth gleamed. "I love a good vehicle patrol! Let's do this forever!"

"Better than walking around, getting shot and bit," offered Junior.

"Fuckin' A," said Fat Ralph, who kept his eyes on the nice smooth road. "Fucking. A. Love me a road trip."

Eva had been hit twice, but she lived, which is more than a dozen of her team could say. Her gunshot injury was severe, but Jason personally hooked up a blood expander and disinfected the wound. The Gleaners' surgeon might be able to save her.

"I'm fucked," Eva said flatly, eyeing the hole in her gut in the gray light of morning.

"Missed the spine," replied Jason. "Missed the great blood vessels too, or you would already be dead. Worth fixing, unless you want to stay here?"

"Nah, not that," the Gleaner lieutenant said from between clenched teeth. "Green. Load me up. Leave the bodies, bring the machine gun they had, maybe I can explain how I fucked this up and he'll let me live."

Amazingly, Short Round had lived unscathed, despite his apparent eagerness to close with the shooters. Jason directed survivors of the attack to strip the bodies of the fallen. Intermittently, they had to shoot infected that wandered out of the treeline and followed them back to the trucks.

The dead were left where they lay, but the severe wounds made recovering equipment messy. The fresh carrion was a draw for infected as well.

Jason found Short Round disentangling a Franchi shotgun from the intestines of its previous bearer. This was complicated due to the additional zombie corpse that had two hands full of entrails; apparently it had been killed even as it fed.

"So, still anxious to mix it up with these guys?" Jason inquired pleasantly.

"Fuck that noise," the Gleaner said as he glowered at Jason, who wore an innocent expression. "Let's get the fuck back to camp."

"Taking your time, waiting things out a bit always beats staring at your own guts," Jason replied with a glance at the tangled remains. "Even for a minute."

"Yeah," Short Round said as he surveyed the littered corpses and then his ruined blue gloves. "Even for a minute."

"Remember to be polite, Robbie," Kaplan admonished. "I don't want to have to fight our way out."

After crossing upstream and pondering the best way to approach the alert and well equipped defenders in Spring City, the survivors had eliminated the obvious. No defender would welcome the approach of an rag tag pseudo military convoy. Protracted daylight negotiations at the foot of the wall of the smallish compound would only result in the inevitable arrival of hungry, less civilized visitors.

Jordan Robbins had suggested to her father that someone use a boat to approach Spring City from the river, in the daylight, unarmed. Then she volunteered.

"Not only no, but hell no. And take a lesson from the Navy," her father ordered. "Never Again Volunteer Yourself."

"She has a point," Kaplan said, interjecting. "If all they see is military-age armed males we'll look like a potential opponent, not an ally. If they see that we have kids and women with us they are more likely to accept our story long enough to let us talk."

"What part of 'we aren't sending my teenage daughter to negotiate' wasn't clear, Kap?" said Robbins Senior with a growl. "I can go."

"Maybe someone with better people skills?" Debbie Robbins said, cutting him off. "And someone who can run the boat."

∽◯◠

Kaplan found himself sitting with Debbie, nodding as she explained the situation to a very skeptical reception committee over welcome mugs of coffee and less welcome, but quite understandable gun muzzles. She had been persuasive enough that the convoy was permitted into Spring City at nightfall. A minor diversion attracted most of the visible infected to a point opposite the gate, and the refugees' vehicles slipped inside after full dark. The newcomers' convoy filled most of the open space that remained inside the CONEX shelter walls. Looking around from inside their trucks, the newcomers could see that scores, perhaps hundreds of standardized shipping containers had been adapted into as defense, stacked two high everywhere that an existing structure didn't already provide a barrier.

During the ensuing negotiation, Kaplan and the Robbinses made it a point to admire the security of the town, before addressing the real point of their visit. Meanwhile, the rest had been allowed out of the vehicles with the proviso that they leave weapons in the trucks and not wander out of the square.

"Look, my boss will be along in a few days," Kaplan said, explaining. "But, in a nutshell, he wants—we want—to find a defensible place on the river that can be used to jumpstart the regional efforts at clearing infected and reestablishing some sort of civil framework."

In addition to Mike and his aide Brandy there were several senior members of the community present. The most influential sat in the first rank of folding chairs that were drawn up in a circle inside the gymnasium of the elementary school. The surviving Methodist pastor, Jon Parrish, was a neatly dressed man with a drawn, wary face. Uniquely among the Spring City group, he didn't carry a firearm. In that particular he resembled all of the representatives of the convoy who were unarmed as a condition of the meeting.

"We can let you stay overnight, just on the basis of Christian charity," said Parrish, gesturing to his right. "But our little council extends beyond the concerns of the church. This is Mike Stantz, our expert on defense and technical matters."

"Howdy folks," Mike said, nodding amicably. "I already know the basics from our chat with Mrs. Robbins. You'll understand that our resources are stretched just taking care of our existing population. Frankly, the idea of absorbing a few hundred more people is both electrifying and terrifying. We need people, sure, but it only makes sense if you have something to offer. We have power, water, some security. No one inside Spring City is sick. You are strangers to us; what do you have?"

"Plenty," Kaplan said with a glance towards Rob. Receiving a nod, he went on. "Vaccine for one thing. A wide array of pharmaceuticals, medical aid and people that know how to use them. A trained, armed cadre that can bolster defense here. Engineering talent. And a plan to start clearing the Tennessee Valley to restore our civilization."

"What's the source of your vaccine, Mr. Kaplan?" the pastor asked gently.

"Human sourced," Kaplan said. He had expected the question and didn't flinch. "Specifically, the neural tissue of dead infected."

"We are familiar with this sort of... *vaccine*," Parrish said grimly, sitting back with his arms folded across his chest. "It is not my place to condemn such that use it, but as for our community, we will not."

"Why the f— why on earth wouldn't you?" Kaplan said, not quite stuttering.

"Please," Debbie said as she laid a hand on Kaplan's forearm and turned to face their hosts. "Surely the Lord accepts that saving life is a moral decision?"

"Saving life, yes. Harvesting 'tissue' from human beings, however ill, no."

"So even it meant your life, your family's life, you won't vaccinate?" Debbie asked softly, looking around the room.

"We do not deny that vaccines work, ma'am," Mike said. "We've engineers here that understand the science, even if we can't, won't make that vaccine. However, we choose not to profit from the illness. We fight zombies. We know that they are dangerous, lethal. When necessary, we send them to the Lord. But we won't harvest people."

"The infected aren't just ill. They aren't people anymore!" Kaplan expostulated. "The disease kills off the part of their brain that made them human. They're animals. Cannibals!"

"They are still the Lord's children, Mr. Kaplan," Parrish admonished. "As long as you are allowed to shelter here, you will not kill other humans for their flesh. Is that not the very cannibalism that you decry?"

"What are we supposed to do when they attack—negotiate?" Robbins said, contributing to the dialogue.

"Oh, we defend ourselves. And we kill zombies," Stantz said even as he noted the fixed look that he was receiving from Parrish. "I meant to say, we have sent a lot of the infected to their eternal reward. We have a few tricks up our sleeve and we are working on some interesting refinements. So there is a good chance that we are going to send a lot more of the undead to their final rest, soon."

He offered the room an *electric* smile.

Kaplan looked up from his notes and quirked an eyebrow.

CHAPTER 14

Dave Khorbish squinted through the binoculars. His small convoy of Gleaners had not cleared infected as they proceeded, so discretion and sound discipline remained the order of the day. Green had set his team to identifying which crossings of the Tennessee river were open. Or open-ish.

Khorbish was also to identify which dams were intact and where uninfected humans might be clustered.

They had started below Chattanooga.

Wheeler, Guntersville, Nickajack—Khorbish checked dam after dam from his list—either damaged by fire or entirely blockaded by large swarms of infected without any sign of recent human habitation. After a detour around the densest part of the city and despite the danger of being so close to Chattanooga, Khorbish had risked his little convoy to confirm that Chickamauga dam was also a wreck. A shift in the breeze had brought the reek of decomposing bodies, piled along the face of the upper basin, nearly stunning the Gleaner party.

Prior to his departure, Green had insisted that Khorbish study up on hydroelectric power plants in order to be able to report their condition more accurately. Despite their hasty retreat from Chickamauga, Khorbish had still noted the fire damage in the adjoining switching yard, which housed the towers and associated critical equipment such as transformers, rectifiers and regulators.

Shit, if he'd spotted that first, they wouldn't have had to get so close. Damage to the switching equipment was beyond their capability to repair. Any dam that they hoped to occupy and actually use had to be taken intact.

Farther upstream, the next few bridges were clogged with

wrecks and human remains. They were also well populated by scavenging infected. Away from the city, the density of zombies dropped considerably, so they were unmolested as they paused to scan the Sequoyah nuclear plant from across the river.

Khorbish checked the map again, noting that their vantage point was appropriately named.

Skull Island. Hell, all they needed now was a fifty-foot-tall gorilla.

"Hey Dave," his driver whispered in an unnecessarily low voice.

"You can speak up a bit, asshole," Khorbish said. "The zombies across the river can't hear you. Whatcha want?"

"How do we know that this place isn't radioactive?" the driver asked. "That place is a *nucular* plant, right?"

"Do you see all the live infected?" the convoy boss answered without lowering his binocs.

"Yeah?"

"Well, then there isn't any radioactivity to worry about, or at least not enough to kill you very fast."

"Oh," the driver said, keying on the qualifier "fast." "So we done here?"

"Yeah, let's cut further north," Khorbish said, consulting his map. "We can cross this spot off the list. It's intact, but boss said for us to check the dams. We don't have the smarts to run this place yet. Next up is Watts Bar."

He tucked the compact binocs into his new vest.

"Careful with that pallet, Jordan!" Robbins Sr. said loudly. Despite fatigue and irritation he was trying to coordinate the contribution of the newcomers to Spring City.

"I *am* being careful, Dad!" Jordan replied. This trip she was ferrying a pallet of literally priceless high voltage capacitors.

"She's doing all right, Robbie," Kaplan said. "Hasn't had a spill yet."

"We can't afford a single screwup," Rob said with a glare at Kaplan. "And I know my daughter, thank you!"

"No need to get so crisp," Kap replied, his hands held up placatingly as Mike Stantz approached from the other end of the TVA assembly building. Essentially a large gray cement auditorium that was adjacent to the fence transformer field, it was where Stantz was turning hoarded equipment into a new weapon.

"Problem?"

Robbins shook his head. "It's all good, Mike. Just keeping an eye on the kids. Howzit on your end?"

"Decent," Stantz said, taking off his grimy TVA ballcap to scratch his sparse iron gray hair. "We are producing two tested coils per shift. The bottleneck is that I am personally installing and testing each one."

Stantz hadn't really asked the Spring City council for permission when he had begun experimenting with Tesla coils as more lethal obstacles to infected. With Brandy's help, he had completed several prototypes, each increasing in size. However, without the skilled assistance of the former soldiers and a few of their dependents, he could never have assembled so many in the short interval since their arrival a week earlier.

"Is there any way to have someone else do some of that?" Robbins asked.

"The only surviving engineer with direct experience on the dam and the plant is Brandy," answered the short TVA engineer. "And I need her here to double-check critical steps in the assembly. Not to mention checking on our power plant, covering the positions of three people that we don't have."

"Well, you got us for that, no?" retorted Robbins.

"No offense, soldier boy, but what you don't know about electrical engineering, generation and distribution is enough to make one of these rigs blow as soon as I put power to it," Stantz said. "Since I'm already handicapped by doing my installs at night to avoid attracting even more infected, you're invited to guess at my enthusiasm for the risk of lethal electrocution. So, sorry but not sorry. Brandy or I will recheck each key component and then *I* do the installs. The toroids that your team are fabbing have a thirty percent reject rate!"

Each coil relied on a large aluminum-coated donut-shaped toroid with a foam core. Installed at the top of each tower, they were the surface from which the lethal electrical streamers discharged. Gross imperfections in the toroids dramatically reduced the length of the streamers from each electrical discharge, and therefore the hypothetical kill radius of each coil.

"Detkovic is busting his ass, Mike," replied Kaplan. "The crew's getting better, but a lot of them are kids. Still, we'll get them done—hell, we'll even have some spares in case the bad guys figure out how to disable a few."

Many of the Tesla coil parts could be readily adapted from stores that Stantz had laid in before infected began to mob the perimeter. Some things had to be hand made, among them the metal donuts.

And they were fragile.

"No way to make them bulletproof," Stantz replied. "We're gonna need spares for sure. As soon as these things fire up, any sane opposition is going to try to shoot them."

A few test runs using the first models of the Tesla coils had been mixed successes. Kaplan was surprised at the extremely loud snarling generated by the coils when they fired. The gossamer webs of energy were visible even in daylight, but the nighttime test had really been a visual treat. The down side was that the testing tended to attract more infected. As a result, they only fired them for very brief bursts.

Stantz had been finishing the assemblies during daylight hours but performing the actual installs at night, carefully screening the small amount of illumination required to connect the coils.

The existing design demonstrated the tendency of the coils, over time, to ionize a single pathway through the air. The more that the coil fired, the smaller the area of effect became.

But the coils worked.

Infected tended to simply drop to the ground in jerking piles while their nervous systems were interrupted by the powerful current. Even if the initial electrocution wasn't lethal, it was disabling and either subsequent discharges or gunfire would finish off the wounded. For a medium sized group of infected, the growing daisy chain of Tesla coils deployed near Spring City and the dam presented an impassable defense.

A bigger problem was dealing with the number of dead.

Stantz used heavy equipment to push bodies into the river below the dam, relying on the current to move the offal a safe distance downstream. It was a messy and ugly business, but the amount of carrion presented a significant risk of disease to the living.

"All right!" A squeal of tracks accompanied the feminine shout. "Check me out!"

Jordan had successfully drifted the unladen skip loader around a corner, gymkhana style. Her audience of younger teens oohed and ah'ed.

Stantz watched, amused, as the elder Robbins stalked towards

his daughter, who in turn immediately moderated her speed and
scooted around the corner and out of sight.

"Well, ain't that some shit," Khorbish said.

They were on yet another scenic overlook. But unlike the rest
whose vistas leaned towards burnt out buildings and dead people,
this one was different.

"No holes in the fence," commented his helper. "And we aren't
the first ones here. There are some car tracks fresher than a
couple weeks back where we moved our trucks."

"Keep the spotters awake," Khorbish replied. "This place is
virgin. They don't know that we're here yet."

The dirty water below the dam foamed brownish green, but
it was moving steadily away from the spillways. The chain-link
fence was still up as far as he could follow it with his binoculars. Farther along the cement buildings alongside the switchyard
were still closed, and like the electrical equipment visible outside,
nothing was blackened by fire.

As the head of the little expedition continued his scan, he
identified a boat on the beach, a few infected well outside the
fenced area and a series of curious looking constructs, roughly
resembling outdoor space heaters.

"I think we're in business," Khorbish told his subordinate.
"We'll get closer after dark. Let's just perch here a bit and see
what we can see."

"I don't care if you can't see!" Khorbish ordered, albeit very
quietly to his companion. "Watch where you put your hands!"

The Gleaner lieutenant was leading one of his least tactically
incompetent men towards the most recently added "space heater."
After full dark, he had spotted very small and brief light leaks
created when the group of survivors inside the wire, unaware of
their audience, worked on another one of the mystery assemblies.
They looked like fat umbrellas or space heaters and formed a line
stretching towards but not reaching the river.

If they were adding some kind of barrier or detection system
it wasn't finished yet.

He carried a radio to communicate with the remaining men
who guarded their vehicles and the two who had stopped crawling a little ways back in order to provide security overwatch. Not

that Khorbish exactly trusted then to shoot *over* his head once they got excited.

"What are those things?" muttered his subordinate.

They had already crossed the tall chain-link fence by the simple expedient of cutting a short flap that could be held out of the way. They had been crawling for several minutes, and the tension was mounting.

"We're gonna find out. Shut it," Khorbish said tersely.

"Why don't we just go back and tell Green what we got so far—why do we have to sneak up through the water, then crawl around and play Navy SEAL?" The whisperer had crawled up alongside his boss so that he could whine quietly. "We're never going to be as good as that, right?"

The way that this guy made everything into a question was really getting on Khorbish's last nerve.

He might have to have an accident after the mission.

Still, the man was among the better draftees available to Khorbish. He'd trained his group more aggressively than would have been possible at the start, installing a modicum of discipline and weeding out as many as he could afford to, screening out the weakest and most impulsive. Still, none of them were particularly good at planning ahead.

The big blue line of the Tennessee on Green's map should've been a pretty obvious clue.

Khorbish had the foresight to collect swim fins and children's boogie boards during the last few weeks. Even without much time to practice, his picked squad were able to make the slow flowing river an asset, evading infected and any patrols that the locals might have set.

"All the SEALs in the world are dead, you asshole," Khorbish said in a very low voice, directly into the complainer's ear. "We don't have to be better than SEALs, just a little better than the locals. Now shut your face and stay alert, we're working. Green expects information."

Distances were deceiving at night, especially to the men who tended to work mostly in the day. Khorbish was surprised when the tower seemed to suddenly loom overhead. He slowly stood and looked more closely at the device.

The amount of starlight was almost enough for Khorbish to read some small printed labels on the tower. He edged forward very carefully, and his foot touched something that felt like a garden hose.

A cable.

The bottom of the assembly was a square that was about an arm's width wide and deep. It supported a thick tube that was more than head high. Above that was some sort of donut, broader than the base.

"Up close, this thing looks kinda familiar," the meathead said, reaching out to touch the smooth metal.

"Don't touch anything, jackass!" Khorbish said, smacking the curious man's hand down.

"Hey, I'm getting a wiggle on mount thirty-two," announced Detkovic.

He was inside the Watts Bar electrical generation station watch office, which was built into a stout concrete blockhouse. Stantz had made it into their command center. All of the usual plant equipment as well as the more recently installed pieces could be monitored and operated from there.

The large observation windows were sealed with several sections of painted plywood that were currently down and latched, but which could be swung up and clipped to the ceiling. Gray rubber weather stripping lined the edges, compressing when closed and preventing any light leaks.

"Any cameras on that part of the line?" asked Brandy Bolgeo.

"Nope," Detkovic said. "Not that your cameras are worth a sh—" He cleared his throat. "I mean they don't work well at night."

Each coil had been fitted with a very simple tremble sensor. Moving the coil minutely would briefly close a circuit, causing a corresponding light to blink several times. The visual alert was necessary because of the crowded dashboard which confronted Detkovic.

He watched the board carefully.

"I only got a transient motion alert on the mount itself," he said. "It's gone now. Want I should test the coil?"

Seated at the central chair of the office, Detkovic's knees were squeezed under the built-in metal desktop that supported myriads of gauges, some computer monitors and several controls, including a scratch built transparent Lucite housing that covered an oversized red button.

He kept his hand well away from that. Next to it, a series of numbered analogue switches had been set into the desk.

"SOP is to give any mount that registers movement a five-second shot of juice, and repeat as needed," he added helpfully.

"I *know* the SOP," replied Brandy, briefly clenching her fists. "I *wrote* it. But I also know Mike. He approves all the live shots."

Detkovic tapped the desk surface next to the switch labeled thirty-two.

Brandy picked up the phone. The answer didn't take long.

"I just wanted to see if it was metal," protested the meathead. "You only wa—"

Khorbish didn't finish his sentence.

He very briefly registered a flash of light and a moment of intense pain before all his awareness stopped and his lifeless body dropped to the ground.

"Jesus God!"

Even a quarter mile away the crackling and buzzing was loud enough to make the overwatch team raise their voices to be heard.

However, the lightshow was the showstopper.

For what seemed like a hundred feet in all directions, eye-searing violet-white light snarled and crackled, drawing persistent and jagged lines of light across the sky.

The brilliant display lit the ground around each streamer of electricity. Momentarily they could make out doll-sized shapes that were outlined as they froze and then fell, vanishing into the shadows at the base of the tower.

"What the fuck do we do?" the sniper yelled into the suddenly quiet night.

The tower had gone dark. It didn't really matter since every Gleaner that had watched the lightshow was effectively night blind, their vision still obscured by brilliant afterimages on their retinas.

The Gleaner overwatch lead keyed his radio.

"Khorbish! Hey, Khorbish, are you all right?"

Standard operating procedure was to reduce the clustering of new infected by promptly removing any fresh carrion created by Watts Bar's evolving defenses. Usually the dozer-loader operator started the run closer to the main facility, but only the newest coil had fired overnight, so he started there.

The few people that rotated through dozer duty had *really* appreciated the closed cab and integrated air conditioner during the warmer days. The Southeast was cooling off during the fall months, reducing temperatures to the point where the pervasive odors of decomposition were merely overwhelming, not physically nauseating.

This was a new one, though. It was worth the nasty smell outside to be sure. He stopped and cracked the cab to confirm what he had found before he called it in.

Then he heard a metallic clang and a moment later the report of a rifle.

"Still in rigor," Brandy said.

"It isn't how stiff they are that bugs me," replied Detkovic. "It's the armor and the guns. These ain't zombies."

"No shit," Kaplan said, squatting on the floor of the small loading dock, looking at the two bodies still cradled in the dozer-loader's bucket. He pulled one body around and stared hard at the tan fabric that made up the vest of the dead man. There was a label under the pull handle. In all capital letters it read "DURANTE."

"Who are these guys?" asked Detkovic.

"Well, this is a Bank of the Americas' assault vest," replied Kaplan. "Bought it myself, and two dozen more just like it. And that makes this asshole one of the pricks that we ran into."

"How did he get your equipment?" asked Brandy.

"Pulled it off my dead friend," Kaplan said, surprising his audience into silence.

He'd stopped staring at the nametag and was briskly and thoroughly searching every pouch and pocket on the dead man. A small pile of equipment grew in front of him: a radio, a pistol and two magazines, first aid kit, binoculars; the accumulation of pocket plunder was extensive.

He passed the radio to Detkovic.

"What can you do with that?" he asked, pulling out a small spiral notepad and flipping through it.

"Looks like this crispy critter was scouting dams," Kaplan said. "Hmm."

He stepped inside the warehouse, pushing aside the canvas around the door.

"Did the folks in town call in anything new?" Kaplan asked Stantz and Robbins, who were both looking at spare parts for the Tesla coils.

The reconnaissance probe attack by what appeared to be a Gleaner detachment hadn't resulted in any casualties, but they'd cut a section of fence that previously kept infected from approaching the TVA generator house proper. At least one Gleaner appeared to be equipped with a decent big bore rifle, but the sniper's long range accuracy wasn't great. A few near misses during the early morning was keeping the engineers from repairing damaged coils and fence breaks until night fell.

"Nah, still quiet over there," Stantz said, examining one of the latest aluminum emitters. "And no more shots from the river side. The newest assholes are still leaving Spring City alone. The shooting has attracted enough infected outside the barrier so anything but a reconnaissance in force is dicey. I'll stay here when this shift ends. Ask them to send some food over with the night crew."

"Never thought I'd be glad for more zombies," Kaplan replied, squinting into the overhead florescent lighting. "But bad guys with guns are worse. If the infected are covering our flank, so much the better."

Even before the failure of their adversaries to directly threaten the town, it hadn't been a particularly tough sell to persuade the council that improved defenses were a requirement. The first Tesla coils had been installed there, each providing almost two hundred linear feet of coverage. That seemed like a lot, until Stantz added up the length of the perimeter.

"Town's started out with less fencing that we did and we can't make enough Teslas to cover them and the dam," Robbins said, still examining one of the toroids awaiting installation. "So they're trying out the newest bit of kit, courtesy of Jordan."

"I know she's your daughter, but your girl scares me just a little, Robbie," Kaplan said. "Her mod to the zombie grates is genius."

Resembling the large cattle grates that were used to deter grazing steers from wandering through open gates, the zombie variation was nothing more than a series of parallel steel beams set several inches apart, but close enough to support a vehicle tire. The area under was dug out to a depth of a few feet. These grates had to be traversed in order to access a few choke points on the approaches to key buildings, both in town and soon, at the dam.

"I'd ask you why you were scared personally, but I'm a little proud about that," Robbins replied.

It was Jordan's idea to use steel of a gauge sufficient to permit the "zombie grates" to deliver not only lethal current, but destructively powerful current.

"She must get it from her old man," Kaplan observed. "The test actually carbonized every infected that tried to cross. What was left just fell through the grate and presto, ready for the next customer!"

"Hey!" Stantz objected. "It's just horizontal fence—not nearly as cool as the coils! No style at all!"

"Hey, do you hear that?" Brandy had been troubleshooting a bench-mounted condenser and listening in the background. "That's the sound of me rolling my eyes."

"I like the coils fine," soothed Kaplan. "But they're damned fragile, even more so than the existing electrified fence, which enough zombies can both short and knock over."

Loud chatter distracted all three men. Across the loading bay, Karrin and the other teen refugees were assisting Jordan by unwrapping the heavy plastic weatherproofing from the just delivered condensers. The oldest teen was already wheeling the skip loader back to the truck outside, driving with much more care than she'd shown previously.

"We gonna actually have time to assemble all those into your special?" Brandy asked Mike Stantz. "Or have a need to finish it? We've got the coils, the fence, the grates and with the new people, now we have actual Army men that are decent shooters."

"That depends on how long we have until those assholes come back," Stantz replied. "And how many friends they bring along. So yeah, the Big Bad is *on*."

"Mr. Green will be back eventually," Eva said to her doctor. "I need to be up by then."

"I, uh, I'm pretty confident that my repairs will hold," the doctor said. "And as long as our supply of antibiotics holds out, I, uh, don't anticipate any complications. But you definitely need to stay off your feet for another week and give the wound time to knit."

Eva scowled.

The surgeon was sweating as he watched Miss O'Shannesy's severe expression. Jason Young stood alongside her bed, fully rigged out and lending menace to her mood.

They'd found both Green and Loki gone when their depleted patrol limped into camp only half a day after the disastrous fight. Only a few other trusted Guards remained in camp, the rest having either accompanied Loki or Green on separate tasks. With so much of the Gleaners' strength away from camp, it was important that Guards project menace, keeping the laborers cowed.

Despite austere medical conditions, their pet doctor had actually saved everyone that they'd brought back and Eva actually woke up on time after her operation.

Of course she wasn't in a great mood. Or talkative.

"Doctor, make a list of everything that you used," Young said. "I'll check that we don't need to move any items back onto the top of the gleaning chart."

Eva scowled even harder.

She wasn't looking forward to explaining her failure to Green. Using up more supplies wasn't going to strengthen her explanation. That asshole Khorbish wouldn't let her forget it either.

Even inside the air conditioned infirmary they could hear a vehicle briefly honk as it climbed the hill to their camp. Gleaners had learned to give the gate guards some early warning in order to avoid startling them.

"What exactly do you mean," Jason asked firmly, "when you say 'a lightning gun'?"

"How many different ways can I say it?" replied Khorbish's surviving team lead, uneasily shifting his weight from side to side.

Upon stepping outside, Jason had found most of river reconnaissance team debarking their vehicles, instead of Green. After he heard their initial summary outside he dragged the two senior surviving men inside to deliver their report to Eva and the other Guards as well.

"They were sneaking up on some equipment that the locals are using," the defiant Gleaner said. "I was watching through my scope. All of a sudden, this thing spat violet lightning in all directions. It was really loud and bright—bitched up our night vision good. When I could see again, it was too dark to make out anything, but Khorbish never answered the radio afterwards."

"Some kind of electric fence, maybe?" Jason asked, turning to look at Eva.

"Khorbish wasn't stupid," Eva replied. "He'd let someone else try any 'lectric fence before he did it himself."

"Okay, so you saw a lightning gun," Jason glanced back to the survivor. "And afterwards?"

"Next morning we could see two bodies right next to the thing," the shaken man explained. "Khorbish for sure. A bulldozer came out and I took a few shots but didn't do anything good. They have lots of these things, at least fifteen we saw. Instead of waiting for them to come after us, we lit out. Figured Green would rather have the info, you know?"

"Go get cleaned up," Jason said, slapping the man on the shoulder. "Hit the rec hall, whatever."

He looked first at Eva and then the other Guards.

"We're gonna need a plan for how to take those things out," he said. "And we better be ready to move as soon as Mr. Green returns."

CHAPTER 15

Radio watch wasn't just boring, it was really, really depressing. And that was saying something, because inside the locked radio shack, watch was boring as hell.

Cameron "Gunner" Randall, or as he had come to think of himself, Sergeant Randall, late of the Army of the United States, was the only RF—or radio frequency—literate person at Site Blue. Hell, it wasn't even Site Blue anymore since that power hungry bitch Kohn and her crew of townies, sycophants and hangers on had renamed the camp "New Hope."

A new hope for what?

Also, he had hated that they stole the name from the movie.

Probably they hoped for another new committee. There were only eleventy-something of the damn things. That number probably represented a critical shortage, according to some bureaucrat.

He once again balefully considered the rack of radios, power supplies and batteries arrayed inside the CHU that had been designated as the radio room. They had planted it next to the main administration building and he had both his long distance and intermediate distance antennas on a mast on the taller building's roof. They had a trickle of power from the solar panels—despite the field being rated for twenty kilowatts, the set up required full sun to generate that much power. Usually he began and ended the day on batteries. Those times coincided with last chance for decent radio propagation at lower frequencies, and right now Gunner was monitoring the Citizen's Band and rotating through the four-meter band which was used, pre-Fall, by American ham radio hobbyists.

Initially, he had busted his ass trying different ground based dipole antennas, hoping that he could reach a government or military organization from the site's relatively high hilltop location. The Executive Committee's prohibition on transmitting was probably a good idea, but afterwards he was reduced to listening for news. The news all pointed one way: downhill.

Eventually, the number of active broadcasters was almost zero. As a result, he rarely got a chance to transmit, other than talking to their own scavenging parties within a smallish radius.

There wasn't even enough chatter to rotate the radio watch apart from Gunner checking during morning and evening hours.

It had been nearly four months since they had all run from New York. Apart from Kendra, there weren't really any familiar faces anymore. Some things were familiar—the PC police were alive and well. In an ironic twist, one of the people that his team had saved from Washington Square Park was that skinny schoolteacher Christine.

She had become the most aggressive enforcer of proper speech, organizer of mandatory community meetings and more recently, had been trying to get Randall to support her notion to broadcast by radio that their camp location was a "beacon for a newer, better humanity."

Hanging a bloody steak around his neck and going for an indefinite unarmed stroll out the front gate was a simpler way to commit suicide, in Randall's opinion. Every time he happened to catch another heart-breaking final transmission from a station that went off the air, Randall considered his options.

He'd never been a quitter, but it seemed increasingly likely that he was never going to connect with Worf, any of the bank dudes or that hyperactive little psycho Cathe. She had been a pain in the ass, but she hadn't lacked for gung-ho spirit.

Randall hoped that she had sold her life expensively.

Hoo-ah, Specialist Astroga.

The CB radio speaker popped and scratched. Someone had broken squelch in range of his antenna. There weren't any foraging parties out at the moment so it might be someone screwing with a radio in one of their remaining vehicles.

He swiveled his head in time to hear a transmission so clear that the sender could have been in the CHU with him.

"Site Blue, Site Blue, this is Bank of the Americas' Unit Two, transmitting in the blind, how copy, over?"

Randall lunged for the radio, managing to knock over an adjoining table, spill his coffee and painfully bark his shin on a stool before he reached the mic.

"Station calling Blue, say again, over," he finally panted.

"This is Unit Two, Bank of the Americas' te— Hey, Gunner, is that you?"

"HOLE LEE SHIT! ASTRO WHERE THE FUCK ARE YOU?!"

Head wounds are funny things.

A tiny twenty-two caliber bullet can penetrate the skull and bounce about the interior, thoroughly and lethally scrambling the target's gray matter. A rifle round can strike the relatively elastic skull of a younger person and literally ricochet around the external circumference of the braincase before exiting on the opposite side, leaving the victim alive but suffering from a hematoma that might eventually kill them, or not.

And sometimes head wounds turn out to be the nonlethal, heroic grazes made famous in unrealistic Hollywood movies.

Luck, really.

Paul had woken up with a splitting headache, one eye glued shut, a pillowcase over his head and his hands still tied behind his back. He listened for a long time before he tried to move, but it was as silent as the grave. His thirst had eventually overcome his caution.

After what felt like several years of inchworming on the gritty floor, he had found the sharp edge of what had turned out to be a ceramic tile. Persistence, desperation and a willingness to abrade his swollen hands had resulted in the eventual parting of the nylon tie that had pinioned his wrists. After that it was a piece of cake.

Except for, you know, being abandoned alone and weaponless in a town that still attracted infected. Oh, and apparently he was a kill-on-sight target for the organization that he had been fighting to protect.

Groovy.

Once he'd cleared the cobwebs, Paul realized where he was. A glimpse at the street outside confirmed his location. He recognized the main thoroughfare of the hamlet a few miles outside the main gate of Site Blue itself.

He'd survived, that was the main thing. A rain shower had

provided enough water to get the crusted scab off his head and restore vision to both eyes.

He'd been lurking inside a small office building, very cautiously double-checking already cleared rooms for anything to eat when he heard a vehicle.

It took him a minute to screw up enough courage to carefully peek out.

"Why are we stopping here?" Cathe Astroga didn't yell, but she definitely wasn't using her "inside voice." "You all heard Gunner. He's alive!"

The battered silver blue Suburban slowed and rolled to a stop in the middle of road. No infected were in view, and the usual assortment of desiccated corpses, broken windows and wrecked vehicles occasioned no comment from the experienced members of the team.

The fourth rider was Luke Connor. He was the oldest surviving family member of one of the redoubt's families. His parents had died getting their kids almost all the way to the hideout when they became symptomatic. His father had done for his mother, and told Luke to drive his sisters the rest of the way to the camp where they had summered only the year before. Now the quiet, stocky red-haired high school senior rounded out their crew.

Everywhere he looked, he saw a new reminder of what everyone else in the car had known for a while. It really was all gone.

"Shut up, Specialist," Sergeant Copley said, fully back in Army mode. "Gunner ain't going anywhere. You heard what he said about the camp. We can wait here to give it a think and see if we can connect with Smith when he shows up."

"Now that we're mostly out of the valley, Tom might be able to hear the radio," said Risky. "We're only four miles from the Site. We're better off going to the camp together, if things are as...different as Randall said."

She looked at Copley.

"What do you think?"

"Well, Gunner is a pretty steady troop," Copley said, considering. "He isn't prone to making shit up. If something feels hinky, well, he's probably right. How long can we wait here?"

Before Risky could answer, Luke excitedly called out, "Zombie, right side!"

He began to lower his window to take a shot, but Astroga took in the "zombie" with a single glance and delivered her now patented head chop to the inexperienced, if keen-eyed teen.

"Check fire, hero," she ordered calmly. "Your 'zombie' is fully dressed. Which means that he isn't a zombie. Sheesh, you're more excitable than a second lieutenant."

She took another look.

"Hey, does that guy look familiar...?"

"You're saying that the bitch had you shot?" Copley asked Paul, not waiting for him to finish guzzling water one of their canteens. "Hey, slow down—you need to sip that or it's gonna come back up."

They'd given him some water and started cleaning up his nasty, if superficial, head wound, while he explained the current situation.

"Yeah," Paul gasped. "Sorry. It tastes so good!" He wiped his face with a dirty shirt sleeve, carefully avoiding the bandage work that Astro had taped in place. "Yeah, she had her crew dump me. I don't know who the shooter was or if he actually thought I was a zombie. I remember getting drugged and I remember waking up. The rest is guesswork. Kohn and her dog, Schweizer—they knew I wasn't a zombie. It's payback. She must've decided I was a threat after I turned down her *offer* to set her up as the permanent executive at Site Blue."

His rescuers muttered angrily, crammed inside the Suburban, which in turn was tucked into an overgrown side street, engine off and windows up.

"Kohn has full control," Risky asked, clearly considering the ramifications of what he'd already told them. "Kendra belongs to Kohn now. And everyone thinks that you're dead."

"Pretty much," Paul said. "Kohn won't tolerate any competition. As soon as someone from the Bank shows up, they'll become a threat."

"Gunner told us that it's been three days since they dumped you," Risky said, looking around her little audience and stopping at Paul. "And that a significant force of visitors has shown up."

"I don't know how long I was out exactly, Risky," Paul answered. "And I don't know shit about visitors."

"We need more information," she said, tapping the map opened on the dash. "If Tom reaches the camp before us, it would be bad."

"He *is* the worst possible threat to Kohn's legitimacy and she knows it," Paul said. "I don't think that she could have him shot out of hand though, especially if you were already there, visible to the camp."

"Why not just roll up and let them see Rune's still alive?" Astroga offered. "It would show that she's a lying, backstabbing, murderous—"

"Because *her* people would have to start shooting right away," Paul replied. "And there's still more of them than us."

"Not to mention we should try to save as many as we can," Copley added. "Even the sympathetic ones wouldn't be certain which way to jump, and they're going to be too scared as long as Kohn is sitting at the head of the table."

"Yes," Risky said. "Joanna Kohn is the main thing. So let's see about changing seat assignments."

"Leave your guns in the car!" an unfamiliar man in jeans and a red Pendleton shirt ordered the foursome.

"My name is Sergeant Copley," replied Worf. "This is Unit Two from Bank of the Americas. You know, the folks that own this camp?"

"I don't care if you're God himself," came the answer. "No one inside armed. Either leave the guns in the car or drive off. Try to stay there and we'll purely riddle that fancy ride of yours."

"Who's in charge?" demanded Risky. Coached by Rune during the day that they had spent treating his injury and debriefing one another while they waited in vain for Smith to show, she drew on the magic name. "Is Joanna Kohn here? Inform her that we've arrived."

"Umm..." the guard said, looking uncertain for the first time. "Look, no guns, really. Standing orders. Leave someone in the truck to watch your stuff, and I'll walk you to the meeting where she's at. Best I can do."

Risky exchanged looks with Worf. After the longest radio conversation with Randall that they had dared, all had agreed to conceal that they had been in contact. It seemed expedient to see how they were welcomed by hosts who believed them ignorant of recent history.

It would also give them the chance to distinguish between the guilty and the gullible by confirming who knew that Rune had been murdered and who merely believed him infected and then eliminated.

Worf pursed his lips and evaluated the defenses. In addition to the gate guard, two more men were visible at the top of the earthen berm that stretched in either direction, obscuring a view of the interior. An eight-foot wire fence was set along the bottom slope of the berm. Interestingly, there weren't any dead infected in view.

At ground level, inside the gate, two more men hustled up, breathing hard. Both had the same weapon as the rest, the ubiquitous AR. None of the men looked particularly at ease as they handled their weapons, but they did appear to be nervously determined.

With a final squint, he nodded to Risky and unslung his carbine, laying it on the back seat.

"Astroga, you are in charge while we go inside," he said. "If we aren't back in two hours, go back to our last rally point and wait for contact. Got it?"

"Copy that, Sergeant," Astroga said. For a wonder, she wasn't lippy.

The guards waited patiently as Risky and Worf continued to divest themselves of weapons, finally standing aside to allow them into the compound.

"Follow me, please."

Just before they completed their walk to the administration hall, Risky and Worf were met by one very relieved Specialist Randall.

"Man, am I glad to see you!" Gunner said, practically vibrating with excitement. "I thought you guys were all dead, it's been so long!"

"Good to see you too, Gunner," Copley replied as Risky exchanged hugs with Randall. "Glad that you made it!"

The two men exchanged pleasantries for a moment before Risky jumped in.

"Anything new?" Risky said, smiling for the benefit of the guard while eyeing Randall meaningfully. They had agreed to not reference Smith but to immediately alert each other if he came up on the radio. "Maybe something special on the menu?"

"Same old, same old," replied Randall, "But mostly, I am sick of MREs. Not much hunting is allowed anymore."

Risky began to ask about hunting as the entrance to the building hove into sight. The pair chatted casually, but Risky watched
Copley survey the scene carefully.

"Hey, Gunner," he asked. "Why isn't anyone armed? Zombie
apocalypse, yaknow?"

"Standing order from the Rules Committee," Randall said. "No
guns inside the compound. They're all stored in the armory and
guards or foragers draw them as required. The idea is to conserve
ammunition and prevent accidents, they say. I kept this."

He rotated one hip so that his kukri was obvious. "I don't
think that they like it, but no one has gotten around to actually
saying no. Yet."

"Who do you mean, *they*?" asked Risky.

"You'll see," replied Gunner.

They walked past two up-armored SUVs. The work looked
factory done, even if the paint job was obviously a hand-applied
rattle can treatment. Each had a large, capital "G" the doors.
Copley hooked a thumb towards the nearest one.

"Nice whip."

"Not ours," Randall said. "And with that..."

"Let's go," urged the impatient guard. "The administrator is
inside."

At first Risky thought that the inside of the meeting hall only
seemed dark because of the relatively bright exterior. Then she
realized that although there were electrical fixtures, they were few
in number. One of the brightest lights shone towards the head of
the space. It illuminated a long, narrow table covered in a rough
green cloth, behind which sat several people.

She recognized a few.

Joanna Kohn wore her familiar gray tunic, sitting behind a
neatly hand lettered sign that read "Administrator." To her right
was a vaguely familiar man that Risky had met during the indoc-
trination period at Bank of America before the Fall. His sign
read "Security" but his braided and beaded beard read "poser."
Additionally, the hapless female survivor that Tom had retrieved
during his escape from Washington Park was there, perched on a
folding seat behind a sign that read "Culture." There were others
in a variety of mismatched attire.

The opening of the outer door had interrupted the meeting.

"Administrator, these are the folks that just arrived," their escort announced them. "They say that they're from Bank of the Americas..." as eyes swiveled towards Risky and Copley, the guard belatedly added "...and that you know them."

Absent any reason not to, Risky strode confidently forward, paced by Copley a half step behind. Risky sensed something was not quite right.

She hadn't expected a welcoming parade or a party. She also hadn't expected complete silence. She schooled her features and scanned the room as she halted at the last row of seats, all of which were occupied.

"Miss Khabayeva, welcome to Camp New Hope," Kohn said, leaning back from where Schweizer had murmured in her ear a moment previous. "Are you traveling with Mr. Smith?"

"We're alone," Risky replied. "Just the four of us from the bank. We've been trying to reach this place for months."

"Administrator, this answers my question," a new, deep voice sounded to her right. It belonged to an enormous man who was standing to one side, in the shadows cast by the limited lighting. "I told you that our peaceful recovery party was attacked by a group that was from Bank of the Americas—and here they are, apparently allied with you. Interesting."

"Who the hell are you?" asked Copley angrily. "We haven't attacked anyone. Ever."

"My name is Loki," the hulking figure said, stepping fully into the light. He was dressed all in black, down to his clean plate carrier and its empty equipment pouches. A stained, buff-colored fireman's turnout coat was folded over one arm. "And my boss has twenty dead men who would disagree with your statement. If you hadn't killed them all."

He turned back to Kohn.

"Now we talk about the return of the girl." It wasn't a question.

"Girl?" Risky said, instantly making the connection. Her anger flared and she turned to squarely face the much taller man. "Was your imbecile that tried to steal her from her family? Was your group of murderers who killed Durante?"

"So you do have her," Loki said, carefully looking over his questioner before turning back to the table. "Kohn, I asked nicely already. Now, I'm telling you. Return the girl. Turn the head of this group over to us. Do it, and we'll leave you alone."

He looked at the two electric lights that struggled to illuminate the meeting room.

"We might even be able to trade for supplies that you could use..."

Risky watched the byplay intently, gauging the room and waiting for her moment. As she began to shift her weight onto the balls of her feet, she felt Copley firmly grip her elbow. She glanced back to see him staring at her intently.

She heard Loki finish.

"...or don't give me what I want, and we'll come take it anyway. And anything else we want."

At the head of the room, distanced by her desktop, Kohn met Loki's eyes squarely.

"I do not respond well to threats, Mr. Loki," she said acidly. "If you want to treat with us politely, you can return tomorrow. If you wish to trade, trade. If you prefer to fight, fight. That is all. You are *dismissed.*"

"Let's go, big man." Summoned by a tilt of Kohn's chin, Schweizer strode to just outside Loki's considerable reach and motioned with a drawn pistol. "Let's walk."

Scanning further, Risky saw that all the guards had drawn their weapons. Considering that the room was a jumble of people, she really hoped that no one began shooting.

Risky began to surge, but Copley had slid his hand from her elbow to her biceps. A surprisingly strong grip kept her anchored and he gave Risky an even more quelling look.

"No," Loki said before nodding to his aide, who stood. "We're done. You had your chance, Kohn. Next time you see me is the last time."

Without awaiting a reply, he walked briskly down the center aisle, the top of his head brushing the lowest beams. Both Gleaners ignored the weapons around them and strode briskly towards the door, trailed by three armed camp guards.

Risky got a good look at him as he passed. Loki returned the favor without breaking stride, his black eyes sliding over her appraisingly.

After they filed out, Kohn clapped her hands to regain everyone's attention, and Risky faced forward again, pulling her arm from Copley's grasp.

"Ms. Khabayeva, do you in fact have a young refugee with you?" Kohn asked directly. "And where is Mr. Smith?"

"Joanna, I've got only three people—" Risky replied.

To Risky's confusion, there were a few gasps from other civilian members of the camp staff.

Kohn held up an open hand.

"Please, be calm everyone," she said. Her smile was sad, even though her eyes never changed. "Ms. Khabayeva is not offering offense by omitting my title. She is clearly overwrought from her harrowing journey. She is unaccustomed to our cultured ways inside the camp, as we begin to restore civilization."

"Title..." sputtered Risky. "Culture? This little place? Cultured ways?"

She sought additional words but Copley placed a calming hand on her shoulder, making her twitch.

"Ah, Ms. Kohn. Right?" Copley said, stepping forward. "We've been looking for Mr. Smith but no dice. We four are pretty tired. Any chance that we could let the other two into the camp, maybe get some food and wash up? Afterwards, maybe we can relax and share our story and get this sorted."

"Sorted, Mr....?" inquired Kohn.

"Sergeant Copley, New York National Guard, ma'am." Risky listened to Copley glibly stroke Kohn's ego. "I meant, that we could sort out the details and figure out what to do next. This was our destination, like."

"Of course, Sergeant," Kohn said, turning to Copley. "But your idiom recalls the Commonwealth. You would not happen to be from Australia, would you?"

Her eyes glittered.

"No, ma'am," Copley replied, putting on his best shuck and jive. "I'm Army; we're from everywhere."

"Just so, Sergeant," Kohn said before pivoting back to face Risky. "Well, then. Welcome, Ms. Khabayeva and Sergeant Copley," she said, holding up both hands, palm up. "Does anyone in your party need medical care?"

Risky didn't trust herself to speak, so she limited her response to a quick headshake.

"Despite the challenges, we are happy that you have returned. Mr. Schweizer and..."

Kohn's gaze panned the room, and stopped on a tall, gaunt blonde with a crew cut.

"...and Ms. Jones will assist you to get oriented. After you have eaten and cleaned up, we will meet back here in two hours and we can answer any questions you might have and help get you settled. Ken, please stay for a moment. Kendra, perhaps you could show our guests to the CHU area."

Risky turned her head to look for the familiar figure of Kendra Jones and instead found a pair of empty eyes staring back at her.

"Yes, Ms. Kohn," Schweizer said as soon as Jones closed the door behind the last newcomer to file out.

"Ken, I need you to keep a very close eye on our latest additions," Joanna said, her hands clasped together on top of her desk. "I want to know how they relate to each other, if any are unhappy and if any might be persuaded to work with us."

"I understand, Ms. Kohn," Schweizer said.

"And watch Sergeant Randall as well," Joanna added. "We need to ensure that we can rely on our *loyal* team members."

Kendra had instantly recognized Risky the moment that she walked in. She noticed, in a detached, former intel analyst way, the condition of Risky's clothes, the fatigue in her stride and the way that Risky's eyes took in everything. Despite the obvious signs of an arduous journey, Risky radiated attractiveness, from the swing of her hips as she strode into the room to her long brown hair that appeared to have been washed only days ago.

If Kendra had been inclined to feel anything, she might have felt jealousy.

No one deserved to feel so normal.

Once the Suburban had been rolled inside under the supervision of camp security, Kendra turned to the four newcomers.

"Hi everybody," she said without inflection. "I'll show you guys to a temporary room that you can share. We'll put you next door to the guys. Clear all your guns and leave them locked in the truck for now. No one will bother them. If you stay, all the guns will go in the armory. Randall will take the guys over to their hut and I'll walk you over to yours."

She paused. "You're staying, right?"

"You got hot showers, girl?" replied Astroga.

"Hot water we have," Kendra said. "Long, hot showers are harder, but do-able. After you clean up, we'll feed you and then we can talk, if you're up to it."

"Why can't we keep the guns, Kendra?" asked Copley.

"Camp policy," Schweizer said, interjecting as he walked up. "If you stay, you follow the rules. We have our reasons. You might have had it tough out there, but there's plenty of tough times to go around. Get cleaned up and eat. Then we can swap questions and answers. Cool?"

Kendra watched all four nod.

"Great," she said. "Ladies, follow me."

She turned her back and walked towards the women's shower hut.

Schweizer fell in behind the men.

After cleaning up and eating, Worf felt almost human. Next door, the ladies hadn't even left the shower yet, so he lounged around outside, staying inside Schweizer's field of view.

"Hey, Worf," Randall said as he sidled up to his old Army boss. "Man, I never thought I'd say this, but it is good to have you around."

"Hey, Gunner," the sergeant replied. "I won't tell anyone that you said that. So, what's new?"

"Nada," said Randall. He turned to their current escort. "Kendra, Ken—would you mind if I talk with my old boss privately first? Might make things easier to understand, coming from me. The others are coming out, so I'm going to take them to get some food. When the administrator is ready to talk, come get us at the dining hall."

"Sure thing, Randall," Schweizer replied, looking over to Jones, who was watching the scene while she leaned against the hut, one foot's sole against the corrugated siding. "I've got plenty to do. You still need an escort for the ladies, though. Kendra will stay. She can grab a coffee while you chat. I'll come get you when Ms. Kohn is ready."

Worf watched the byplay as Kendra looked at Schweizer and nodded, seemingly bored. The Army National Guardsman watched Risky try to catch their old comrade's eye, but Kendra looked right though both Risky and himself before she kicked her weight off the CHU.

"Food is this way," she said. "Whenever you're ready."

Worf noticed that Kendra was still armed. So was Schweizer.

As she joined the table, Risky glanced toward Kendra, who sat well apart, staring into a white ceramic mug of cooling coffee.

"So what's the story with Jones?" asked Astroga. "That girl looks dead. And I don't like that Billy Idol thing she did with her hair at all."

They were sitting in a corner, enjoying the finest textured vegetable protein and rehydrated beans that pre-Fall Bank of the Americas dollars could buy.

"That bank guy we *talked* about?" Randall said before he paused as another camp resident walked past. "He and Kendra became a thing after we got here. Then they weren't anymore. Then Rune got himself infected, as far as *anyone* knows."

"How did Kohn sell it?" said Copley.

"Just the way it sounds," Randall shrugged, keeping his voice low. "An op for vaccine supplies went bad and Paul was in charge." Randall laid out the story.

Rune infected. Schweizer assigned disposal to the same townies that helped snatch Rune. Kohn's set up and Kendra's justice.

"... Kohn let Kendra do it herself. She put two into each dude less than five minutes later. Didn't even blink. Cut her hair super short that night and hasn't changed it since."

"Okay, that makes more sense," Risky said after Randall finished. "How tight was Kendra with Kohn before Rune died?"

"Not particularly," Randall replied as he looked around casually, before slowly letting one eyelid droop. "Not any more than most, but a lot less than the real kiss-asses like Christine or her toadies that made it here from the city. Until we *lost* Paul, she was sorta in the middle, helping make shit work. She was only on one committee."

"And what's with all the committees?" Astroga said. At the food line the daily, weekly and monthly schedule for meetings was posted for the convenience of the camp staff. Astroga rolled her eyes. "Worse than the Army."

"There's a committee for everything, including to boss around the other committees," Randall explained. "With Rune gone and Kendra basically doing special projects, each committee is run by a person who either owes Kohn or buys into her bullshit. As she likes to say: 'Everybody works, everybody eats.'"

"Well, that sounds draconian, but this is survival," Copley said mildly. "Seems legit enough."

"Except that Kohn decides who does what work, doesn't she?" interrupted Risky. "And for how long, and defines what's good enough."

"Yeah, exactly," Randall said with an interested look at Risky. "Lucky guess?"

"No," Risky replied. "Familiar system for anyone that has lived in Eastern Europe, or old Soviet Russia. What matters is we wait for Tom. We get as much information as we can. We play along. When—"

"Hey, hot stuff," Astroga said, greeting Schweizer unnecessarily loudly as he headed towards their table from across the room. She added a wink. "Looking good!"

"Hello, folks," Schweizer smiled back, unimpressed. He kept himself at an arm's distance from their table. "If you're all done, the administrator will see you in her office now."

No one made an immediate move.

"Thanks, I got this, Sergeant Randall," Schweizer said with a glance at Randall. "Why don't you head back to the radio hut and buzz yourself in? No one can run the watch like you."

"Well, actually boyo, we aren't—" Copley said as he began to shield his former subordinate, but Risky smiled back and spoke over her teammate's nascent objections.

"Sounds fine," she said with a bright smile at her table mates. "Let's all go visit."

CHAPTER 16

Joanna Kohn calmly awaited the newest arrivals to New Hope.

Her preparations were working exactly as intended. Her proxies chaired every important department. She had carefully, systematically converted the survival organization into a working model that they could grow into a better world.

Discipline and focus were needed. That was all. The former bankers could be quite valuable, if she could motivate them as she had everyone else. Kendra Jones was one of her most reliable people.

Now.

Even the arrival of the Gleaners, as they styled themselves, could be managed. She identified Loki for what he was, a simple murderer who was ruled by his hungers. His pathetically bad hair notwithstanding, she recognized his look because she could see its cousin in her mirror, peeking around the edge at her, now and again.

She'd been comfortable with that realization for some time.

Even if, when she gave Loki or *Governor* Green what they wanted, he wouldn't be satisfied. Yet, he wouldn't expect premature treachery from a woman, let alone an effete, urban bureaucrat.

Men had always believed themselves possessed of a monopoly on ruthlessness, and that had lasted for some time.

Before the Fall, one of her many interchangeable security types had been a reasonably presentable man. Not very biddable, but certainly possessed of *endurance*. They argued in bed, afterwards, over inconsequentialities. Enamored of all things military despite not being a veteran, he was very much known for carrying every gadget and widget for security that he could conceal under his suit jacket, including a dive knife.

When she had pointed out the futility of a diver carrying a knife to defend against sharks and on land at that, he had laughed.

The knife wasn't to stab the sharks if they came for you, he explained. It was for stabbing another diver and then slowly, calmly swimming away.

That was worth remembering.

Sharks came in all shapes, everywhere.

The knock on her office door was immediately followed by Schweizer stepping through and ushering in Khabayeva and the others.

"Welcome, welcome!" Joanna stood to greet them, stepping around her desk. "I hope that you are all feeling refreshed."

She waved them into four chairs that had been placed in front of her desk.

"Yes, thank you, Joanna," replied the dark-haired Russian woman. The other three made polite noises.

"While I am very glad to see that more of our old colleagues have reached our haven, you have arrived during a difficult time," Joanna sat on the corner of her desk, slightly above the sight line of her guests. As she perched, her figure obscured the gleaming white placard which read "Administrator."

"As you probably learned, we recently lost several staff during a recovery sweep for medical material. One of them was a longtime, trusted friend, Paul Rune."

Joanna watched all of their faces as she spoke. All of them nodded, nearly in unison. So they'd heard, already.

"When the sweep failed, Paul volunteered to test some vaccine that we recovered, previously," she went on. "It was tainted and his earlier vaccination failed him. As a result, it has called into question all the early vaccinations administered by Bank of the Americas."

"You mean that we could still be vulnerable?" Khabayeva stammered.

"Yes, you might be susceptible to infection." Joanna shifted from a polite smile to a concerned look as she reassured the shaken woman. "We have been considering protocols to keep those personnel safe." Joanna shifted slightly. "Does your party have any vaccine?"

"We got split up by an attack of infected about a week ago,

ma'am," the grungy-looking sergeant replied. "Haven't seen the other truck since then. They had a cooler of vaccine, but I don't know if it's good anymore. Same stuff that the bank made, so if it didn't protect Rune..."

"Yes, that is a consideration." Joanna favored him with a smile. "We now have a quandary apart from the vaccination and recent loss of staff. The party which you saw departing earlier is a new development. They call themselves the Gleaners and appear to be both well equipped and large in size."

"Where did they come from?" asked Khabayeva. "Honestly, we didn't know who they were when they started shooting at us."

"They tell a different tale, Ms. Khabayeva," countered Joanna. "And we need to have an answer for them. You don't have the girl or know where she is, do you?"

"We dropped her at a farm, several days away," Copley said. "Said she was family. Made sense at the time, we were in a hurry to get here and didn't have room for more people."

"A farm." Joanna decided to let that go, for now. "And Mr. Smith—well, Loki and his leader want him as well. If they do not get what they demand, they are threatening violence. Violence which we would be hard pressed to resist. And if we resisted successfully, we would do so at tremendous cost, wasting much of what we have accomplished to date."

Her audience didn't have an answer for her.

"So you can see, while I am very glad that you are safe with us now..." Joanna paused to emphasize her point "...everything comes at a cost."

At that moment footsteps could be head on the wooden floor outside her office. There was a brief snippet of tense dialogue, unintelligible to Joanna.

Then the door opened briskly.

Fat Ralph drove the entire way. After dawn, they found a spot where they could observe their back trail. Tom had told Ralph to pull over, and commenced assessing injuries. Once the adrenaline of surviving combat had worn off, the pain of their injuries sharply diminished the humorous chatter.

Pascoe's eyes were mostly swollen shut; Junior's leg gunshot wound was red and angry. The gouges and scrapes were dirty, and despite cleaning them, the red streaks up his leg were plain.

"I've got bad news," Tom announced. "The kid is bit, not just scratched."

"Aw, fuck," said Pascoe. "Motherfu—"

"The good news is that he had the primer," Tom added, looking directly into Junior's terrified eyes. "We'll get you the booster right now. Then again in twelve hours. This worked on my thirteen-year-old niece, and she had direct blood-to-blood contact. You're gonna feel sick as hell, but you are gonna make it."

"I don't want to be a zombie!" Junior said, shaken. "I'll eat a bullet first."

He reached a hand down to touch the pistol at his thigh.

"No one is turning into a zombie," Tom said, putting his hand on top of the kid's. "I personally guarantee it. You're going to get a relaxing break from working and fighting while you smile at pretty nurses at our camp."

Tom continued to reassure Junior while he pulled out both the small electrically powered cooler and the red folding tackle box that housed their first aid supplies. Despite the pain in his shoulder, for the next hour he did all the nursing, starting with the booster for the teenager and, after a pause, for Pascoe as well. After some first aid and rebandaging, Tom decided to press directly all the way to the camp.

They arrived just at dusk, pulling to a gradual halt inside the chicane that protected the direct approach to the closed gate. He'd visited Site Blue once before, during the initial assessment, but it was nearly unrecognizable now. The SUV's bright halogen headlamps were making the unfamiliar gate guards squint, so Tom instructed Ralph to shut them off.

"My name is Smith, and this is my camp," Tom announced, swinging his door open into the yellow illumination of their parking lights. "Who's in charge here?"

There was a brief unintelligible conference among the guards, and much consulting of a clipboard before they answered. Tom could feel his ire begin to mount, but he suppressed it, squeezing his anger down into the tight ball of rage that had been building for months.

This was not the time, just as he finally reached the gate of his own facility. He inhaled deeply and then exhaled very slowly through his nostrils.

"Howdy, Mr. Smith. My name is Bustamante, and Administrator

Kohn gave directions to pass you directly into camp if you was to show up," answered the central man finally, walking forward to shine a light inside the battered Suburban. "Y'all the second arrival today; another truck from the bank pulled in a few hours back."

Tom's eyes had narrowed fractionally when he heard Kohn's name, but his face underwent a transformation of relief when he heard that the others had arrived.

"They made it?" Tom asked eagerly.

"Yeah, and they're in better condition than you all," the guard replied, looking the entire party over. "Okay, y'all need to go the dispensary first."

The guard waved the gate open and jumped on the running board. "Keep y'all's speed down and follow where I point."

Ralph followed the ground guide's directions and a short drive later, the guard rousted out some muscle to help Pascoe and Junior out of the car.

"You got a doctor?" asked the teen.

"Well, what we got's a decent medic and a dental hygienist," said Bustamante, snorting. "Practically the same thing, nowadays."

"Kid needs an IV and antibiotics," Tom ordered. "While he gets seen, take me to the other folks that got there, then to Kohn."

"Let's head over now," the guard replied. He looked at Tom's torn sleeves and blood-splattered trousers. "They all in the same place, if you can walk."

"Try me."

There was a brief delay once they entered the building.

Tom recognized Ken Schweizer and began to pass him after a polite nod. Before he reached what was clearly the next door, Schweizer placed on hand on Tom's chest, barring his way.

There was a pause as Tom looked down at the palm that was flat against his chest. He slowly stretched, rolling his neck and shoulders before speaking.

"Is Risky inside?" he inquired very, very mildly. "Because if she is, you are going to want to move your hand before something unpleasant happens to it."

"Good evening, Mr. Smith," answered Schweizer. "Administrator Kohn is in a meeting. It's great to see you, but I can let her know that you're here while you wait."

Tom's face became even more composed and, with an apologetic smile, he used his good right hand to lock Schweizer's extended wrist in place and then suddenly leaned sharply down and forward, hyperextending the arm and wrist. Schweizer buckled at the knees, wincing in sudden pain as the small bones in his hands and wrist were torqued to the point of breaking. Tom stepped carefully around the suddenly kneeling man and swung the door open firmly.

If Tom noticed that the downed man had dropped a hand to the pistol on his belt, he didn't show it.

His eyes first sought out Risky, who was facing the desk at the front of the room. As Tom stepped through the door, he saw Risky turn and stare for a moment, and then there was a moment of confusion.

Almost instantly, Tom was hit from a distance of six feet by a guided missile comma brown haired comma female comma one each. Risky managed to wrap all four of her limbs around Tom, hugging him tightly enough that it actually hurt a little.

Tom wouldn't have moved her for worlds. She smelled clean and felt . . . just felt *right*. In the background he heard the inevitable peanut gallery.

"Damn," said Astroga observantly. "It's like she fucking teleported or something." Schweizer stepped through the door, rubbing his wrist while he apologized to Kohn, who raised one eyebrow but waved away the interruption. Kohn watched the couple without interference while her security chief explained about the truck and the injuries.

When Risky and Tom broke apart slightly to inhale, the administrator spoke.

"Well, Mr. Smith, it's good to see you," she said. "Would you like something to drink?"

"Water, please," Tom said, looking up to address Kohn as he took in the room. "Looks as though there have been some changes to the plan. Where's Paul Rune?"

"I'm sorry, Tom," Risky said, this time squeezing his hand especially hard. "Paul's dead."

"How?" Tom replied stiffly. His eyes blazed, as he looked down at Risky, then over to the others.

"They're saying that he tried out some bad vaccine," Copley waved a little too casually towards Kohn and Schweizer. "That he got sick and turned. That all of our vaccinations might be no good."

"Impossible," Tom said, looking directly at Kohn. "Can't happen that way. Paul had the primer and the booster less than six months ago. He can't contract H7D3."

"And yet he did," Kohn replied smoothly. "That is a big question and until we have the facilities and scientific staff it will remain an open issue which we cannot answer directly. Worse, we have another major issue which demands our attention."

"What could be more serious than Paul dying from the virus after he was vaccinated?" demanded Tom.

"Tom, listen to her!" Risky said, again squeezing his hand, invisibly grinding a few fingers together.

Tom looked at her for a moment, then back to Kohn, his eyes once again mild.

"You, Mr. Smith," Kohn leveled her gray eyes at him as Schweizer nodded to some people outside the door. Four more staff walked in, lining the wall behind the bank crew. Tom had accepted the request to disarm as they exited their SUV. Now he noted that these four all wore holstered pistols.

"You, and the fight that you apparently picked with one very large, capable and organized force," she went on. "They are here now, and their price for not attacking this camp is also you. You—personally."

It was nearly midnight before everyone had been settled, still disarmed, in their respective CHUs and most of the guards had been withdrawn.

Tom was visited by a delegation composed of Copley and Risky, who were admitted by one of Kohn's armed staff.

"Are the others okay?" Tom said, standing up from his seat on the bed as they closed the door behind them.

"They're fine," answered Risky. "We wanted to share what we learned so far."

"Are these rooms secure?" Tom said with a casual glance around the little prefabbed hut. The overhead florescent lighting cast dark lines across the faces of his companions.

"Gunner Randall says so," Copley said, twisting the door lock. "He's what passes for the electronics specialist around here. Just keep your voice down."

"So, what happened to Paul, really?" Tom asked. "You know the story about bad vaccine is bullshit."

Rapidly, the duo filled him in while he listened impassively. He initially brightened to hear that his deputy was alive, but as he considered the situation, any pleasure that he felt was swept away in calculation.

"So, we know Kohn runs the camp, right?" Tom asked, rubbing his chin contemplatively. "And now we have a name for the bad guys. Do we know what strength this Gleaner arsehole Loki has with him? And what does Kohn have here?"

"According to Schweizer, who said to tell you that his wrist 'still hurts like hell and was that really necessary,' the town clowns that pass for camp security now have seen five vehicles and twenty-five men altogether," answered Copley. "The camp has plenty of guns and a bit more than a hundred survivors, split between bank folks and local yokels that are firmly on Kohn's side. What they don't have are many trained shooters. There might be couple dozen who hunt, but soldiers? People that know how to fight? Me, you, Randall and Astroga and that's i—oof!"

He looked to his right where Risky held her fist cocked, ready to plant it in his ribs again.

"...and Risky, we got her too."

Risky smiled toothily at him and relaxed her fist. She reached out and grasped one of Tom's hands.

"And the Gleaners?" asked Tom. "We got hit by thirty or more about a three days ago. I don't know how many we killed, but except for Ralph, all of us are hurt. Add those to the force we saw at the first drama, then factor what Loki has with him—it's got to be a really large force, maybe hundreds."

"How do you know that?" asked Risky.

"Loki told Kohn that he works for a bigshot named Green, Governor Green," Tom said. "This Green has to be more than somewhat organized in order to field three separate bands of armed scavengers. I don't know what his tooth to tail ratio is, but he's got to have one. Even the pros still need two people behind every fighter. That means the Gleaners have hundreds of people."

"So, figure this guy is at best a skilled amateur," Copley offered. "We've seen maybe seventy-five shooters so far? Giving him a three-to-one ratio means that his organization needs at least another two-fifty in support for logistics, medical, admin, the usual."

"So why is this Loki here with so little force?" Risky asked.

"Because the rest are somewhere else?" replied Copley.

"They have the map," Tom said suddenly. He tilted his head downwards and exhaled. "They're not here because the real prize is getting a dam."

There was a long silence that no one felt like breaking.

"This is...bad," Tom said finally, looking around the plywood interior of the little CHU for inspiration. "No one else useful here in camp, Worf?"

"Not really. The bank people are financial analysts, traders and some of their families," answered Copley. "I kinda left ole' Ralph out of my calculations after his performance when we lost Durante. I saw one of yours here, Kendra Jones. She's pretty out of it. I don't think she's altogether present and correct, if you know what I mean."

"So what do we do?" asked Risky, plopping down on the bed. "What's the plan?"

"If Kohn decides to give Loki what he wants and we fight it out internally, it'll be a mess," Tom said, beginning to pace back and forth. He covered the short distance in only a few slow steps before pivoting and walking the opposite direction. "I'm not sure that we can win that scenario anyhow, given how few we are. If we lose, the camp's defenses are diminished and our wounded are at Kohn's mercy. Even if we win, we'll still have less combat power than the whole camp is starting out with, right now. And we're stuck inside the perimeter while Loki keeps us from joining up with the rest of our people, who are facing pretty crappy odds."

"I follow," Copley said, leaning backwards against the inside of the door. "I don't like it, but I follow."

"If I offer something else to Kohn, it has to look at least as attractive as giving me up," Tom said, still pacing. "What does she need?"

"All she wants is power and control," Copley answered, agitatedly. "And she already has both."

"Hmm," was Tom's answer.

"Maybe we make a run for the car?" Copley said, rubbing his trousers along the tops of his thighs.

"Can't," Tom replied. "We have people here, including Robbins's injured kid. Not to mention the bank folks that were the entire reason for Site Blue in the first place. We aren't leaving them to Kohn's mercies while we run to safety, assuming we could fight our way to the truck."

"Yeah, I'm just thinking out loud," Copley said. "Besides, Gunner told me that all the vehicles are controlled access items. Schweizer maintains control of all the keys and the access to the fuel storage. If we bust out, we do it with minimal guns. You got a holdout?"

He looked at Tom.

"Just a knife." Tom produced a large folder from his pocket.

Copley inclined an eyebrow towards Risky.

"Teach own grandmother to suck eggs," Risky answered, and then pushed Tom's shoulder to get his attention. "Is not the point. We don't give you up."

Tom walked half a step and hugged her.

"I'm pretty sure that we could blow out of here, maybe get most of us out except for our wounded," he said. "We'd have to kill or hurt a lot of people to do it, including people whose only crime is being desperate enough to follow Kohn. That would leave Site Blue wide open to the Gleaners. This isn't just about me and our group. It isn't even about the damn bank any longer. It's about keeping the largest number of uninfected people alive that we can. If I make a trade to Kohn, it would be for her to support the dam."

"No, Tom," Risky protested, squeezing him hard. "I won't give you up!"

"When you made me promise to stay alive, I said that I would try hard, Risky." He kissed her gently. "I didn't promise that I would pull it off."

They stayed, embracing.

Copley stood and made as if to leave quietly.

"Wait!" Tom leaned back and looked at Risky, then the sergeant. Copley froze with his hand on the doorknob.

"What did you say? What does Kohn want?"

"Power and control," Copley answered.

"What if we offered her more?" Tom said.

"More what?" Risky asked.

"Power. As much as she can imagine."

Risky woke up before Tom and carefully eased her weight from the smallish mattress without waking him. She elected to try out what passed for showers. Inside one of the nearby CHU that had been converted into bathrooms and showers, she found Cathe Astroga preparing to scrub-down at one end of the cramped space.

"You too?" the indomitable private inquired. "Never pass up a chance to pee, eat, shower or sleep is what my dad always taught me. Rule number four."

"Sounds like a wise man," Risky said, disrobing. She had the seeds of a plan. She began fiddling with the toilet tank while Astroga watched curiously.

"That thing works fine," she said. "Used the hell out of it yesterday. Fucking MREs."

"That isn't what..." Risky said, fishing around in her skirt. She took care of a minor chore. The toilet tank lid clanked into place. "...I had in mind."

"Oh," Astroga observed, puzzled but captivated. "Interesting. So you got some more ideas?"

Risky showed her another weapon, and explained how she'd use it.

"Hmm, sounds complicated," Astroga said. "What did Smith say?"

"My darling idiot thinks that he can negotiate with the snake, Kohn." Risky went on. "He's going to try for a deal and seal it with his honor."

"Well, Smitty's a straight up guy," Astroga said, then smiled as Risky turned around. "Damn, look at those hand prints. You been *busy*, girl!"

"What?" Risky replied, then looked down at herself and smiled ruefully. "Well, at least these are good for something."

"Oh, they are good for a lot of things, but usually for turning men into fools," Astroga reflected happily. She looked down at her own lean physique. "I have got to get me some of that. No other privates around to play with."

Risky raised an eyebrow.

"Privates, people of my same or lower *rank*," Astroga said, explaining. "I mean, I know that I am promoted and all, but what I wouldn't give for a handy-dandy E-2 right now. My guys are my bosses and senior in rank to boot, so that's a no-go. Maybe Junior, once the kid heals up." She grinned broadly and shook her hips. "If he's old enough to shoot, then he's old enough to..."

Now Risky held up one hand.

"Ah, yeah. Sorry," Astroga subsided and added. "But yeah, like I said. Smith. Straight up guy. Men are pretty hard over on the whole 'honor' thing. That can be pretty impractical. Me—not so much. I'm way too little to worry about shit like honor. I have to be Ms. Practicality, if you know what I mean. How about you?"

"Oh, I am quite practical," Risky said, assuring her. "Quite."

"Ooh—goody," Astroga said, brightening further. "Let's share some suds, then. Wash my back?"

"One thing at a time, please." Risky rolled her eyes.

Risky walked back to Tom's CHU. At least she had been able to change into fresh underwear. That, the shower and brushing her teeth had considerably lightened her mood.

Until she and Tom visited the wounded.

They found the Robbins boy and Pascoe in the infirmary. Pascoe's eyes were unbandaged. He could even squint out of the left one, revealing a bloodshot eyeball, but one which he claimed was working, mostly.

Junior was much worse, burning up with fever. Hampered by his sling, Tom talked Risky through the method to inject one of their few remaining doses of booster while a woman named Evelyn who had been introduced as a dental hygienist watched carefully. Risky tucked Junior back under the covers, assuring him that he was going to be fine.

The boy's big eyes still managed to get a quick look at her cleavage, despite the savage chills that shook his body, earning him another smile as Risky assured him that he would be fine.

Outside, Tom took her hand as they walked.

"You know that he probably is," he said. "Going to be fine, that is."

"He has terrible fever," Risky said. "Is that normal?"

"Same thing that my niece lived through," Tom said pensively, looking into the middle distance. "I wonder what they are up to. That dinky sailboat will be getting tossed around in the storms outside the Stream now."

"Hey," Risky said, shaking his hand to get his attention. "Hey. How about some food?"

"Hmmm," Smith replied before calling over his shoulder. "You want some food?"

Their armed minder shrugged indifferently, so they walked outside and turned along the gravel path towards the dining facility.

Inside, they sat over some truly bitter coffee. On the up side, it warmed Risky's hands and smelled nice.

"What have you thought of?" Risky asked. "All I have is trying to persuade Kohn to evacuate to the dam."

"I'm thinking that as bad as I feel, it's nothing like *her* personal hell," the banker replied. Risky followed his look towards the corner table, where Kendra sat, not drinking her coffee. "I'm going over to say hello."

He stood and moved to her table, mirrored by Risky.

"Hi, Tom, hi, Risky," Kendra greeted them flatly. "I'm glad that you survived."

"Hi, Jonesy," Tom replied. "I'm glad that you survived, too."

"I didn't," Kendra said, looking back down at her coffee.

After that conversation killer, Risky paused for a minute before taking her turn.

"Why's everyone so formal?" she said, prompting Kendra. "Miz this, Mister that. We're living in the outlands; camp isn't Wall Street or City Hall."

"Once you've been here long enough you can begin to see the similarities to those places," Kendra said. "Joanna and her closest people explained that survival is contingent on working together. Cooperation requires respect. Respect starts with speech. Respect, diversity, equality, all the things that the Executive Committee define as community—the camp is as much about that as it's about survival." She paused again, looking thoughtful. "Actually, New Hope is more about 'community' than it is about survival."

"I haven't recognized as many bank folks as I expected to," Tom said, picking up the conversation. "How many are here? I haven't seen a single senior person. Where are we storing the offline data?"

"That's actually kind of funny, Tom," Kendra said, pushing her coffee away. "Site Blue was never properly finished or staffed. This place isn't about the bank anymore. Once Kohn began organizing the place and she accepted external refugees, it was something else. Paul tried to . . ."

She abruptly stopped talking and went back to contemplating her coffee.

"Kohn has asked me to surrender to the Gleaners," Tom stated after a longish interval. "What do you think?"

"She's got a plan," Kendra said, looking directly into both their faces. Her normally bright eyes mirrored the darkness of the coffee that was slowly approaching room temperature. "She always has a plan. She makes it work. She protects the greatest number even if someone has to pay."

She looked back down.

"Maybe it's your turn to pay," she mumbled. "It goes around."

Schweizer entered, the bright light from outside shining behind him.

"Mr. Smith, I'm here to escort you to the administrator," Schweizer said with a nod to the other guard already in the canteen. "You can come with us. Ms. Jones will stay with our other guest."

Risky began to stand, protesting, but Tom laid a hand on her forearm.

"Stay and chat with Kendra, Risky," he said easily. "I'll be along presently." Schweizer nodded unctuously and held the door for Tom as he walked by.

Risky watched them both go. Then she looked over to Kendra and scooted a little closer.

Tom sat, seemingly relaxed, replying to the pleasant greetings as Kohn moved through the business rituals of an everyday meeting, though he knew full well that this was anything but that. Armed, Schweizer stood well behind Tom.

"This is a bit of a change from our first meeting at the bank. The four of us, views for miles overlooking the river," Tom said, looking around the shabby confines of the office. "Just us two, now."

"It was a good partnership," Kohn replied. "Whatever did happen, after you placed me on that flight?"

"Ding went crazy," Tom replied, studying Kohn's face. "He was convinced that Cosa Nova set up a hit on the police and their families at One Police Plaza. In the end he died trying to kill Matricardi and his men."

"I was aware of the strike on police headquarters," Kohn said, her lips quirked. "Did anyone turn up any proof that Matricardi did it?"

"No," Tom said, squinting at her. "But I'm pretty sure that he didn't. What's your theory?"

"I do not have any theories, Mr. Smith." Her smile sharpened. "So, Matricardi killed Captain Dominguez?"

"Again, no," Tom replied. "I did."

Kohn raised her eyebrows, surprised.

"Long story, but eventually Ding came to the bank, just like you did," Tom said. "We beat off the cops after they shot down the last helicopter and set the building on fire. Then we ran for the boats with what was left of Cosa Nova. Matricardi was murdered by one of his own. We cleaned house *again* and got offshore."

"Ah, that explains how you came to have some of his men in your party," Kohn said, tapping her pen on the desk blotter. "Reminiscing is very nice, but we have a more immediate problem. Actually, two."

"I'm listening."

"Your actions, no doubt *forced* upon you by circumstances, have led to a rather unfavorable standoff with this new group, the Gleaners," Kohn said, slightly adjusting the position of the nameplate on her desk. "This comes at a time when we are still too few to be certain of fighting off a significant threat. We would lose many people even if we won that fight. On the other hand, if we surrender you to Loki and his governor, all we lose is one person and we buy ourselves considerable time."

"The math seems compelling," Tom said, letting a faint smile play across his face, "but afterwards, you're no better off. Once you pay the Danegeld, it can be hard to—"

"I am familiar with the saying Mr. Smith," Kohn replied acerbically.

"What you don't have are numbers and fighting power," Tom said. He rolled one shoulder, but winced as the recent injury pinched something. He straightened out his leg, and winced again. "So trading away people, even a single beat-up specimen like myself, leaves you weaker than you were. In turn, that encourages the Gleaners to stick around. They'll keep making demands until you balk, and then they'll walk over any remaining resistance."

Kohn narrowed her eyes before replying.

"You think that you have a strong bargaining position," she said. "That is adorable. I could just kill you now and hand your body over to the Gleaners, and thereby satisfy their immediate hunger."

"Unlikely to impossible," he replied impatiently. "And we both know it. The Gleaner contingent already left. Moreover, the entire camp knows I'm in here. Kill me out of hand, and you'll have a fight. If you win—and as you pointed out, that isn't a certain thing—you'll be weakened enough to lose to Loki here and now instead of in a few months. On the other hand, if we work together on a different plan, if we're seen to cooperate, your power grows."

Kohn smoothed her brow, dismissing the frown that he'd prompted. Then she nodded before tapping her fingers on the desk blotter.

"Go on."

"Let's skip to the important bits," Tom went on. "What if there was an option which allowed Site Blue—"

"Camp *New Hope*," Schweizer spoke up, ending his long silence.

"Right, New Hope," Tom said wearily, turning his head to acknowledge the man behind him. "What if you could get more people? And power. Lots and lots of electrical power."

"And where would you get these things, Tom?" Kohn asked suspiciously.

"The Tennessee River is only about fifteen miles thataway," Tom answered. He felt his fatigue building but refocused and casually waved one hand in an easterly direction. "There are five hydroelectric power plants along the closest bit of the river. One of them will be operational or can be made that way. We take one, relocate our survivors and enjoy security, electricity, unlimited hot water, that sort of thing. And you'll be the administrator that made it happen. You'll be the one to restart civilization."

"I'm well aware of the location of the river," Kohn replied. "And equally aware of the very large number of infected which are drawn to it as a water source. Not to mention the enemies which you have made, lurking somewhere out there. Assuming that you can actually reach such a dam, and find it functioning, why would you just give this to me?"

"Not for you, Joanna," Tom replied. "For everyone here. I've been driving through the remains of civilization for three months. I won't pretend that I like you, or think that you're a particularly good leader. But you are better than all that."

He waved his hand around the room again, indicated the world outside.

"One of your injured men mentioned that you have a force outside the camp," Kohn said, changing the subject abruptly.

Apart from quickly flicking his eyes up to meet Kohn's level gaze, Tom didn't show any additional reaction, but it was enough.

"A young man, pain medication, fatigue, a pretty nurse," Joanna said, smiling thinly for Smith's benefit. "Interesting how much one can learn from a medical situation. So, there are another twenty or more people, friends of yours. They include soldiers. And they're already heading towards the nearest dam."

Smith was silent a moment longer, then shrugged.

"Well, I never said I'd take the dam alone," he offered casually.

"With so many resources, I am confident that you might actually succeed, Tom," Joanna said. "However, I *want* you to succeed."

"Or wear down the Gleaners in trying," Smith pointed out.

"Or that, Mr. Smith," she said. "Or that. But to either end, I will return a vehicle. I will allow young Mr. Connor to accompany you. You may even take your weapons with you, as well."

"Thank you—"

"In your absence, the soldiers will help us guard the camp," Joanna cut Tom off, while sliding her right hand into an open desk drawer where, out of sight, she kept a small pistol. "I will personally guarantee the best possible treatment of your wounded, who will of course need to remain. As well as Miss Khabayeva."

"What?" Smith said. Joanna watched his face shift from guarded confidence to surprise to anger in the space of a moment. It was delicious. She allowed him to continue. "No. No deal. They all come with me."

"I know you, Smith," Joanna replied smoothly. "You, and men like you, are quite irrational about women. We are weak, we need protection, we need you to decide for us. Well, no longer. For now, you will work for me. Oh, I know that you could find a way to make trouble for me, one way or the other. If you actually succeed in taking the dam, you would be motivated to move against me and you would have considerable resources. If you fail, well, at least you distracted Loki and his governor while we prepare here. So, I will retain assurances in the form of the person that you care about more than yourself. More than your precious bank or this camp."

She paused, savoring the moment, watching his face.

"Take the dam for *me*, and eliminate the threat from the Gleaners," Joanna said, before adding a little encouragement, "and you may have your lover back."

She watched the muscles in Smith's cheek bunch and his hands tighten on his chair arms. Behind him, her man Schweizer had readied his pistol in case Smith failed to maintain control. Smith's eyes flickered with an animal awareness of the trap, fully realized at last.

"Ah, yes, I am well aware of the relationship," Joanna said, using her free hand to tap the desktop. "Your little spectacle earlier was most indiscreet, for a man who usually conceals his relationships. But nonetheless, she is one of the survivors and you pledged to protect the survivors from the bank, Smith, did you not? You pledged a full measure of your devotion. You haven't redeemed that pledge, yet. Do this, and your mission is complete. You can do as you will. But..."

She stopped tapping.

"Take any action against me..." Joanna paused and smiled even more broadly, "...well, there is no need to be specific, is there? I will keep my part of the bargain, to the letter, just as before. And if, as you say in banking, the counterparty breaks the terms of the deal...let us just say that I will visit sorrow upon you, just as in the past I have visited sorrow upon *all* those who have broken faith with me. One way or the other, you will serve my needs. And my first need is that you explain to everyone here that we are friends, once again. Afterwards, you have a dam to secure. So put your 'happy-face' on. You are about to talk to the entire camp. Do be convincing."

CHAPTER 17

After Smith failed to show, Rune had made the next two communication windows, trying to raise Randall using Risky's handheld. He got through on the second attempt.

"Bravo, Bravo this is Romeo," Paul sent. Knowing the quality of any radio operators at Site Blue, apart from Randall, he decided to use military phonetics in place of names. Besides, if someone beside Gunner was listening, then the hangers-on wouldn't recognize his voice through the distortion of the retail quality CB radio speaker. "Comeback on channel two-one."

"Romeo, Bravo," Randall immediately replied. "You are go on an open channel."

"What the fuck over? Where's Sierra One? I've been sitting on my ass since the Two unit left yesterday."

"Umm, all I know is that my radio room is clean," Randall transmitted. "Anyone could be sitting on this channel."

"In for a penny," Rune said. "SITREP, over."

Randall hesitated before he replied, considering how to condense the information to a single transmission.

The word of Smith's decision to accept Kohn's deal had spread through the camp faster than the schedule of pre-Fall Pacific Fleet ship movements spread through the hostess stands in Guam and Singapore. Smith had addressed the camp in the dining facility to explain that the decision to buy time was solely his, that Kohn had his full support, and that he was thankful that his team could stay, heal and contribute.

Risky had been kept in a CHU, under escort. After she'd

fucked up one guard, Kohn had finally assigned Kendra, armed, to the task.

So to say that things smelled fishy was an understatement.

"Injured visitors held hostage," Randall sent. "Sierra One will depart camp for dam. Plan to link up in same location as first contact. Site Blue unaware of your status."

"Well, how truly good. Really wonderful," Paul said. There was a long pause as he digested the summary. "Pass to Sierra that I'll be there."

"Don't guarantee that we'll get access to Sierra before departure, so you need to be ready to signal him, Romeo," Randall said. Then, he sniggered a little bit. "Romeo. Sorry, I can't help it. You and Kendra. Get it?"

"Something's gonna get git," Rune said bitingly. "See you at the pick-up. Out."

"Out."

"We're nearly all set, Miss Kohn," Schweizer said, leaning a little more closely towards Joanna. "The Army personnel are segregated from the others, and both Smith and Khabayeva are under guard in temporary quarters."

Joanna looked up from the clipboard, using one hand to pin the papers that were being ruffled by the strong breeze blowing across Site Blue. She passed the clipboard to Christine, who was hovering nearby.

"Here you go, dear," she said. "Please get the cafeteria area ready for a short presentation and let the camp know that Mr. Smith will be addressing us later this morning." She ignored the uncertain nod from Christine as she turned to Schweizer.

"Very good, Ken," she replied. "Before that, I'd like your read on the two new soldiers, especially the young woman."

"She's the lowest ranking one, pretty junior," Schweizer summarized. "The men are foot soldiers, artillery branch. Her specialty is administration. Kendra, ah, Miss Jones says that she's high energy, lots of initiative and looking for something to do."

"Really?" Joanna asked, raising one eyebrow. "That sounds interesting. As soon as we bid Mr. Smith goodbye, please arrange an interview with her in my office. I'm always looking for new talent."

"Miss Kohn, she's a soldier," Schweizer half-protested. "Are you sure you want to try to recruit her? Military types tend to take the entire duty and oath thing pretty seriously."

"Precisely, Ken," Joanna replied. "And just who has a greater claim to be representing any sort of government that a soldier would obey? A washed-up banker or a member of the city council of New York? She will be looking for something to do, and is probably tired of listening to her sergeant anyway. Maybe she is interested in, what do they call it? Ah, yes—detached duty."

"Yes, ma'am," her dutiful subordinate said. "I'll set it up."

Risky was not having any of it.

When Tom had failed to return to his prefab hut and was instead replaced by a male guard, she decided that she wasn't going to stay inside, regardless. A bloody nose and a couple gouges to his face later, the guard was forced to contact tase Risky, which laid her out for a while. Eventually, she came to, one hand zip tied to the bed in her CHU.

Kendra sat on the floor with her back to the inside of the unit's door.

"Don't try to break the plastic," she said in a flat voice. "You'll just tear the skin, and then I'll tase you and you'll hate me even more."

"I need to see Tom, now!" demanded Risky. "Right the fuck now!"

"I know," Kendra said, leaning her head back on the door, "been there. Kohn's just letting things settle down. Smith is just wrapping up a little speech to the camp about how he's delighted to be working for the good of the camp. In the meantime, she doesn't want you getting everyone more upset or trying to change Smith's mind."

"Change his mind how?"

"Smith is going to take over some dam," Kendra answered. "He's going to get it cleaned up and working and give it to Joanna. In return, he gets you. You get to stay here, along with the old guy and the kid in the clinic."

"Can't believe that you're working for that fucking psycho," Risky said. She looked at her restrained hand and judged the distance to Kendra.

Too far.

"She isn't the one that insisted that you stay inside," Kendra said. She didn't even look back at her. "Smith's idea. Keeps you out of the way and safe. Kohn will send for you—she wants to persuade you—help you see things. There will be an after."

"After what?" Risky replied, as she felt around in the pockets of her skirt. "Hey, where's my knife?"

"Either after Tom fails and dies or he gets the dam for Joanna," Kendra answered flatly, watching Risky pat herself down. "The guy that tased you searched your stuff before I got called. He took anything that could be a weapon. Actually got in trouble for it—supposed to let females search females. Joanna was mildly pissed. If you had a knife, it's in the armory now."

Risky had frozen when Kendra mentioned the dam mission.

"Just let me see Kohn," Risky said. She tried to keep her voice steady. "Kendra, *please*."

"When she calls," Kendra replied. Seeing the look on Risky's face, she sighed. "And even if you beat me and got out, there's a guard outside. There are two with Smith, who's fine, by the way. He's leaving soon, with Randall and the other soldier you brought. There's another with Kohn. You don't have any weapons and you're tied up. I know it sucks, but it's over."

Risky eyed her speculatively and kept her hand on the prize in her pocket. They didn't find all of her weapons. And she knew where to get more.

Outside the CHU, Risky heard a brief cheer, but Jones didn't even twitch.

Tom kept the battered Suburban under twenty-five, carefully driving around the same car wrecks that they'd passed on the way into Site Blue.

The SUV felt strangely empty, but he could feel the tense silence that filled the space between himself and the others. His anger was red hot, and no one else seemed happy either. Rune had flagged him down a mile outside of camp and now he was riding shotgun while Luke Connor watched opposite side. Connor was jittery and Tom knew that the teen would be the first to talk.

"Mr. Smith, how long do you figure till we get to the dam?" he asked after a few miles had slid by.

"Fifteen miles to the dam on the map the Gleaners have," Tom replied curtly, keeping his eyes front. "Figure anything from a couple hours to half a day."

The reminder of his own culpability in the loss of the map made Tom's mouth fill with bile. Leaving Risky behind stoked his building anger even higher. He'd walked into Site Blue, blithely expecting to be welcomed and instead Kohn had outplayed him.

After their meeting, an armed-Schweizer had chivvied him outside to a podium facing the communal eating area. There, Tom had delivered a glad-handed speech, banker-style to a few dozen folks, mostly from the bank. He'd covered how glad he was to find them all safe, how he was going to scout the possibility of restoring a hydroelectric powerplant so that they could have electric fences, better food, more illumination and limitless hot water. The audience had seemed the most interested in the latter, perhaps inspired by Astroga's lusty cheer in the background.

"Where are we going now?" Luke asked from the back seat. "Why are we leaving Miss Risky and the Army guys behind?"

Tom ignored the teenager.

"Kid, we're heading for the nearest dam," Rune answered tersely. "Just like we told you already. Now shut up and watch your side."

Tom knew that he was radiating anger and that wasn't fair to a loyal teammate who'd just gone through his own version of hell, but he was mastering his rage and didn't trust himself to talk.

Tom could tell that Paul Rune was aggravated as well. If anyone deserved a break, it was Paul. His head had a lopsided bandage on it, held on with an abundance of tape: Astroga's signature.

Immediately after forcing Tom to talk, Schweizer had hustled Tom and Connor to one of the SUVs, under careful guard. Lastly, he'd passed over their empty weapons.

And Tom had meekly driven away.

While Tom hoped that the presence of the National Guard contingent encouraged Kohn to stick to the deal and keep Risky safe, he still seethed. He was fighting the emotion, knowing that he needed all of his experience and smarts to overcome the next challenge, but he continued to replay the scenario, recognizing that he'd been outmaneuvered from the very start. He'd failed to predict her hostage tactic. Now he'd left Risky behind.

There was still a mission ahead. When he finished it, he would return to settle Site Blue. He still had an ace in the hole and Kohn and her coterie didn't know.

∽ ⊙ ⌒

Harlan Green impatiently wiped the lenses of his binoculars, and refocused on the far shore. Despite the shelter of an umbrella held aloft by a flunky detailed to that sole purpose, the persistent morning rain immediately began to again smear across his field of vision. His lieutenant-on-probation, Mr. Young, was at his side, scanning with a set of his own binocs. His longtime lieutenant, Loki, stood glum-faced, flanking Green on his other side.

Green had been visiting the various towns where his Gleaners had already cleared the zombies and installed a small contingent to maintain control. These towns were sited at important crossroads or other nearby high value locations such as the National Guard armory where they'd found and repaired a very large, wheeled armored vehicle. However, the good news where he'd been was trumped by the disappointing news at his main camp.

Khorbish was dead, presumably electrocuted by some sort of advanced defense. Eva Green was severely injured and had failed to bring him any prisoners or new intelligence other than confirming the very irritating military proficiency of their new opponents. Worse, Loki had failed to win over the camp that Green himself had identified on the captured map. More than likely he had relied on brute intimidation rather than subtlety. Green suppressed a melodramatic sigh.

Good help was indeed hard to find.

Well, the banker's camp was secondary. He could return to it at his leisure. In front of him was the real prize.

The powerful binoculars brought the hydroelectric facility to within arm's distance.

Everything reported by Young appeared to be accurate. The facility was intact and operating *and* the defenses were considerable. Green grimaced. Between the first confrontation, the losses incurred by his scouting groups and general wastage, the Gleaners' supply of foot soldiers had become seriously depleted. Yet, the winter season was very nearly upon them and he could ill afford the time needed to recruit back up to strength and train to any meaningful standard.

If Biggs had killed off Smith at the first meeting, *if* O'Shannesy had mousetrapped the damnably competent ex-banker instead of getting herself shot, *if* Loki had secured an alliance with that viper Kohn just a day sooner, he wouldn't be facing the need for a direct attack against a prepared enemy who might be ably led and highly motivated.

No matter.

He had to get his group under cover and into winter quarters, and he'd made promises. Electricity, abundant hot water, fresh loot, *recreation*. Green didn't overestimate the quality of his organization and he understood the fate of any leader that couldn't deliver on promises.

"The obvious route's too obvious," offered the former cop at his side. "Attacking over the bridge would be very expensive."

"True," Green said, squinting at the dam and the pile-mounted bridge that ran directly above it.

It would still be less expensive than failing to take it, he didn't add, continuing his study.

Above the dam itself, and supported by concrete pilings, was the kilometer-long bridge for the state highway. The two-lane road was thoroughly blocked by a series of scuffed concrete Jersey barriers spanning the roadbed in multiple places. Getting a vehicle heavy enough to displace the barriers would be the only way to avoid the infected in view as well as provide shelter from the defenders' inevitable armed response. The length of the bridge would keep any vehicle under fire for a long time and clearing the barriers on foot, under fire would indeed be expensive.

Below the highway, the dam was topped by an access path, not quite wide enough for a single vehicle. Dotted along the walkway were sheds or storage huts. The upstream face was a sheer drop to the lake below but downstream, rotating cams blocked the spillways between the near-shore barge lock and the far-side power house. A modest amount of barbed wire and chain-link provided security, and no zombies were in view on dam proper.

He let his eyes travel to the opposite shore. A few distant uninfected humans had been briefly visible inside the obvious defenses. Slightly closer, an outboard-equipped boat was pulled up onto a small gravel beach, itself screened by tall chain-link. The steep path that led upwards through the riprap had several gates that would impede infected, and on the bluff above the water's edge was perched the original construction, a two-story concrete gray blockhouse. It was well supplied with windows protected by folding louvers. A tall auxiliary smokestack dominated the open area that surrounded the structure, and outside yet another ring of fencing, he could make out the unmistakable shapes of the previously suspected electrical defense.

"Are those space-heater looking things the lightning machines that killed Khorbish?" asked Dragon.

The mushroom-shaped devices were situated at even intervals, creating a visual barrier that was also demarcated by dozens of naked corpses. Green had nearly decided that his Triad recruit was excess to needs when the tattooed convict had returned from the meeting engagement outside the bank's camp considerably sobered and reflective. Pairing him with Young and Eva had perhaps matured him to a functional level of utility.

Green would afford the man a chance to prove it.

"Yes," replied Green, with a measured glance. "They're called Tesla coils. They were popular for entertainment purposes before the plague. Evidently they're also useful for eliminating zombies, but they're not dangerous to us if you don't stupidly walk within range. They do require a lot of materials and expertise to construct. Someone over there thought well ahead in order to stockpile that amount of supplies. We could use a person like that."

"Can't we just shoot them?" rumbled Loki. "The coils? Shoot everything that looks important?"

"We can," said Young, "and we will. They're fragile. But we'll want to keep our direction of approach hidden till it's too late. They might have mines and other defenses as well. And more importantly, we want to be careful about what we destroy. The entire purpose of this operation is to capture a hydroelectric power plant in *working* order."

"Just so," said Green, with an approving glance at the ex-cop. "So step one will be to deploy a little surprise that will occupy the attention of our friends across the river. We will force them to deal with as many zombies as we can lure into their preparations. Every mine, every bit of fence stomped flat and every bullet they expend on the zombies is one that we don't have to contend with ourselves."

There were a few grins in the group now. Softening up the defenses was a concept that they could get behind.

"So, if just charging across is too expensive, then how do we do this?" asked Dragon.

"Consider that," Green said, gesturing to the river itself and then upstream to the north side of the waterway.

"We're in a new era where we'll have to rebuild using the tools and practices of a much earlier time," Green said. "Given their focus on the defenses for the bridge and dam, I suspect that our technical geniuses across the way aren't avid students of history, or they would've considered what the father of the old United States did to defeat the Hessians on the Christmas eve of the revolution."

Most of the men could only muster a blank stare, and even Young looked faintly puzzled.

"You're saying that we'll sneak across the river in the middle of the night—" Loki chuckled evilly—"and murder them in their sleep."

"That's exactly what I mean," replied Green.

Now the grins among the Guard were universal.

"Mr. Loki, pass the word to move the rest of our convoy as soon as possible," Green ordered confidently. "Mr. Young, please organize this place to receive our men and equipment. If possible, I want to be able to attack tonight."

Robbins looked up at the interruption.

"Jordan, I didn't mean it!" protested Eric, as he was towed into view by one firmly clutched elbow, trailed by Katrin and Cheryl.

The boy was mortified at the manhandling being dished out by the surprisingly strong, though older teen.

"Doesn't matter what you meant!" Jordan replied angrily. "I told you and then I showed you all where you can't go and you went and did it anyway! That cliff is unstable. If you fall into the lake, you're dead! You were supposed to stay inside and you shouldn't even be here in the first place!"

"Please don't tell!" pleaded Katrin. "We're just really bored, is all."

"Besides," added Cheryl, "back at the ranch, Specialist Astroga told us that we should always try to build our understanding of the tactical environment."

Robbins watched from around the corner as Katrin and Eric nodded in agreement, and he could tell that his daughter was suppressing an urge to tear at her hair.

"I can't believe that she really made you call her 'Specialist,'" replied Jordan tartly. "Screw it, I'm definitely telling, and I'll make sure that you all go back to Spring City, or else I can't be responsible."

"Responsible for what?" asked her father, Robbins Senior, heaving into view.

"They belong in Spring City, Dad!" Jordan said. "I've got a real job to do and I don't have time to babysit!"

In the time since the first mud encrusted ranch truck had finally gained the supposed safety of Spring City, the youngest members of the party had been very excited with the hustle and bustle, breathing life into the boring routine that had dominated since their own arrival.

An opportunity to accompany her father on the latest inspection of the dam defenses had been an irresistible break in the tedium. In the eyes of 'tweens who had been cooped up for months, the seemingly zombie-free dam area was tailor-made for exploration.

Brandy Bolgeo stalked over from her ad hoc workshop desk.

"Jordan Robbins," she said forcefully, "what are you doing with those kids?"

"I'm trying to get them out of here, Brandy!" Jordan replied.

"There's nothing to do!" Katrin stamped her feet in her best Astroga style. "Can we at least go look in the woods?"

"No!" chorused Jordan, Bolgeo and Robbins.

"Why not? There aren't any zombies," said Eric.

"The rain has made the path to the woods unstable, and if you fall into the lake you're either zombie food or you get sucked into the turbine house," replied Bolgeo. "And if you little monsters make it to the woods, I've scattered half a dozen mid level industrial accidents just waiting to happen inside the treeline. So stay the hell inside this building unless you intend to lower the oversized rug-rat count."

"We aren't kids!" Jonsdottir, the ringleader stomped one foot. "We've been training and everything!"

"Jordan!" yelled Robbins Senior, becoming distracted as the warehouse phone rang. "Take control of your insolent Astroga-wannabes!"

"Robbins!" he barked into the handset that he'd just snatched up. "No shit? About time. Yeah, send him over in a boat after nightfall."

"What's that about?" Bolgeo asked.

"My guy Smitty is here from Site Blue and he's got news," Robbins answered.

"Good news or bad news?"

"Both."

∾ ⊖ ∾

Tom kept his own emotions off his face as he looked around the table, trying to gauge the mood.

Clustered around the waist high map table the representatives from Spring City, the dam and Robbins's prepper site stood looking at the layout of the dam's defenses. In the background, warehouse preparations continued, but the general plan was set. All of the adults were wearing some variation of combat gear over a combination of denim, surplus fatigues or hunting attire. The inevitable fidgeting and jostling created a constant rustling susurration as the rain gear rubbed and crinkled.

The dam's listening post at the fenceline had reported that several vehicles arrived at the rest stop across the river. Groups of men had debarked and a flurry of distant gunshots suggested that they'd cleared the immediate area of infected. More vehicles were now arriving. There was only one organized group in the area: Gleaners.

This matched what his gut told him. If their opposition was going to make a move, it would be soon. The debrief and inevitable questions about the happenings at Site Blue had taken an hour, and had been received stoically for the most part. Getting everyone else, including Tom, up to speed on recent events at Watts Bar had taken another hour. Tom was still trying to get a feel for the considerable defenses. The engineers had been busy, but no amount of sophisticated electrified barriers could take the place of sufficient numbers of people. Tom had precious few shooters that he could rely on.

"Is the rain going to be a problem with the coils?" asked Tom, glancing out the window at the intermittent drizzle. "I've used a lot of improvised weapons, but this is a new one."

The steel-colored sky outside had ushered in lower temperatures and a steady breeze that was starting to whip up little white caps on the lake.

"Probably increase the amount of ground conduction and ion channeling," answered Stantz, shifting his ballcap. "If the secondaries get wet, then the high voltage streamers from the primary might over-arc."

Tom glanced around and except for Detkovic, all he saw was a number of blank looks.

"Thanks," he replied following up dryly. "Perfectly accurate and yet totally incomprehensible. I swear it's like Curry just materialized here. Matt, can you translate, please?"

"Hard to say. I wouldn't run coils in the rain for a rock and roll light show," opined the grizzled combat engineer. "Could get anything from sparkly lights on the ground to burnt wiring to no change at all. Bottom line is you'll get partial effectiveness and probably shorten the life of the hardware."

"Roight, how bloody good." Tom's accent was starting to get noticeable again.

"What if the Gleaners attack Spring City?" asked Emily Bloome. She'd been taking a more active interest in the dam and had volunteered to stand watch. Even her former students had caught the helpful mood that was building in response to being under a roof, with power and supplies to spare. "All the noncombatants are there."

"Their defenses are better and they have the advantage of terrain," replied Tom, looking to Robbins. "Plus Robbie has been there for a week looking things over."

"Spring City has had months to prepare," agreed Robbins, wandering over from where he'd left Jordan supervising. "Fixed defenses, a sixteen-foot wall of shipping containers, reinforced brick walls, caltrops and the moral courage that comes of protecting their homes. Plus they'll have me. If that asshole Loki or his boss has any smarts he'll try to take this place first and deprive them of power before he hits the town."

"What if they double back to hit Site Blue?" Rune asked. "We got people there."

"We're not fighting Loki, however big he is," Tom answered again. "It's his boss, this Green, who's behind the Gleaners. He's the brains of the outfit. If Green really wants Blue right away, he can take it, but at a considerable cost. But if he does that, the most that Green can hope for is burned wreckage and he'll miss his chance to take the dam. And not to be brutal, but most of the folks we left at Blue are expendable. This place isn't."

He slapped the tabletop.

"Cold, Boss," Robbins said.

"Maybe, but it's true nevertheless," Tom said, noting hard looks from some of his team, especially Paul Rune. "And the folks we left there would agree. Green won't try for the site, though. The grand prize is here. His reconnaissance proves it. Now we know that he's putting in an attack, and soon. After getting a bloody nose twice, Green isn't going to try half-measures. He's going to throw everything against this place. And we're going to crush the Gleaners and return to Site Blue."

"Those assholes are screwed," Kaplan spoke up, as he unwrapped a wooden toothpick and lifted it to his mouth. "I've walked the ground. This place is tight. The bridge is impassable even if they have ten times our numbers. The perimeter is solid. The town, ditto. As long as we keep our nerve, even a dozen of us plus the coils can hold. I can't believe that Green is stupid enough to try for a frontal assault, unless he has competent crew-served weapons and indirect fire."

"He's not stupid," replied Tom. "That's part of the problem. But I don't see a winning strategy for him. He's smart, but he's an amateur."

"Still, it's better than fighting a professional, like yourself, right, Smith?" asked Stantz.

"Maybe," Tom looked at the map, and then up at the faces all watching him. "Intelligent amateurs can get lucky, and he doesn't have a playbook to work from. That makes him dangerously unpredictable. So let's get to the detailed planning."

"You've all heard the detailed plan," Green stood under the awning of an abandoned campground. His lieutenants, the Guards, circled around him, their faces displaying varying levels of indifference, eagerness or apprehension. "The fact is that once we begin it will become hard to coordinate, so you have to understand the plan. However, things will change, so you'll have considerable leeway to adjust to the unexpected as we go. But—"

He looked around the circle, making eye contact with each Guard.

"—leeway doesn't mean slowing or waiting or delaying. Our attack will have to succeed on the first try. That means leading from close enough to the front to keep our people moving but not so close that you die unhelpfully. I need you all alive in order to help me consolidate our new territory—"

A blatant lie, but necessary for morale.

"—and I am investing everything we have to ensure our success."

That much was true, at least. If this attack didn't succeed, he'd have to start over nearly from the very beginning.

"I'm deploying everything we have. The heavy vehicles and armor will be pushed up to provide cover, destroy obstacles and ensure your success. Dedicated snipers will disable their defenses and kill any armed resistance as you cross. But you must cross! Remind your troops that hesitation is death and all the good loot is over there! If that doesn't work, you may tell the less motivated that laggards and deserters will be shot."

Definitely not a lie, and yet still helpful for morale. He let it sink in for a moment.

"Very well. Group commanders, get your teams ready."

Jason stood in the shadow of the trees on the Gleaner side of the river, keeping Green's picked team clustered around the abandoned picnic tables. The little hill had been the east side overlook for the lake's campground and the narrow beach where they'd stashed their boats was below. Green had pulled the rest of the force inland, out of sight behind the promontory, after setting the usual anti-zombie patrols. The rest of the Gleaners were milling about in a disorganized fashion, eating, grab-assing, making parts runs to the supply truck and generally acting out their pre-battle nervousness.

The gray overcast prematurely deepened the gloom and the occasional shower kept Jason's equipment shiny with the damp. He *knew* the plan, and even he could barely discern meaningful movement in the entire cluster. It was deploying, with painful slowness mind you, into the different attack groups. Any observers would stay confused, should they be able to see this far.

Not that there was a lot of doubt about what would happen.

River, dam, bridge. Anyone could sort it out.

The sight of the power plant and its switching yard, perfectly intact and free of the stinking mounds of trash and loose paper that seemed to be everywhere, had braced Jason's earlier doubts. The power plant was the key. Get that, and Green could rebuild properly. Maybe this could be the last horror. Maybe afterwards they could make a fresh start. A clean start.

He scanned again, and spotted the unmistakable bulk of Loki, pushing the slight figure of a young woman towards Green's tent. She had been scooped up by the convoy en route. The woman walked slowly, slightly hunched over. Loki gave her a light shove and she stumbled.

Unbidden, a memory from the world-that-was surged up. Only a few years earlier, Jason had responded to a domestic violence call. They'd surrounded the house where a meth-head had barricaded himself with his wife as a hostage. They tried to talk

him out, and eventually provoked him to emerge. He'd shoved
the woman outside, holding her at gunpoint as a human shield.
Guns and blinding lights in front of her, a psychopathic gunman
at her back, the woman had moved the same way. The shuffle
of the condemned.

He blinked and the woman was gone.

Jason resolutely looked back to the dam.

Tom dispassionately watched most of the gathering force on the
far side of the dam withdraw out of sight. He lowered his binos
onto their strap and tried a scan with one of their remaining
sets of helmet mounted NODs. The deepening twilight was still
too bright for night vision and he grunted as he unclipped the
goggles from his helmet and slipped them into a pouch.

"Well, they in fact do have more than ten times our numbers,"
he commented, grim-faced. He kept his face to the front. "Where
do you put their operational level?"

Kaplan cocked his head to the side without taking his eyes
from the spotting scope he was using.

"DRoC army," he answered after a moment's thought, pronounc-
ing it "Dee-rock." "Not the irregulars, but the militia." Then he
went back to examining the enemy.

"Dangit," Brandy said, unhappily. "They're as good as an army?"
She was an engineer so she'd applied Stantz analytical counting
to estimate the number of bad guys. There were possibly fifteen
to twenty times as many of the Gleaners intermittently in view
as Tom had defenders.

"Democratic Republic of the Congo army," Tom pointed out,
raising his binos again. "It was not a compliment, miss. And
they're going to try a night attack. Bold."

"Controlled line of assault," Kaplan said. "Keep your regime
protection group at the back and push forward the fodder. Soak
up our ammo, cause casualties, then follow on with your primary
push. There's a really significant disparity of force. Could work."

"We've got a prepared defensive position," Tom pointed out.
"And as you noted it's a very narrow assault vector. The guy leading this group, Green, he's an intelligent bugger. Bugnuts and an
amateur, but he's not an idiot. He's got to know that a frontal
attack would probably fail, or at best, be a toss-up. I can't see
him banking on a roll of the dice like that."

"Whoever is leading them isn't an idiot," Kaplan responded, "but he's also not in view. Given the quality that this guy had to choose from they're pretty well organized over there, considering. While we had better light, Rune and I spotted the major players. We saw his second, that really big Loki guy is easy to spot. If he's close to Green, ID'ing the top dog should be easy. And I still haven't seen anyone that matches the profile. The officer types are all wearing that same franken-firefighter rig. But no Green."

"Which is what's bothering me," Tom said. "He's probably not a lead from the front fellow but for this he should be rallying his troops. Instead he's letting chief subordinates handle it."

"Not the primary assault vector maybe..." Kaplan said, lifting his eye from the scope and looking around. "Where then?"

"That's a major distraction force," Tom replied, also looking around. "They'll hit us from the side or flank while we're having to commit the majority of our defenders to this vector. Choice of downstream, upstream or direct rear."

"Downstream they've got to cross the nuke plant operational area," Kaplan said. "They don't know if it's still defended unless they've put in more recon than we've seen. Hard to tell if the guard towers are manned. Direct rear—they've got to get there first. That leaves somewhere upstream."

"We've got zombie defenses out there," Brandy said.

"They know about the Tesla coils," Tom said. "There's gaps up there. If they don't merely walk around, then they'll simply take them out with fire. The contraptions seem rather fragile."

"There's more than that," Brandy said. "Trust me, the peninsula is covered. We'll know if anyone or anything is moving through there and they or it *shall* not enjoy the experience."

"What about the bridge?" Kaplan asked.

"I let Mike play with Tesla coils and Big Baddie," Brandy said. "The bridge was mostly mine. There are...significant defenses on both the dam itself as well as the bridge."

"Mines?" Tom asked. "Explosives?"

"We're the technical team for the Tennessee Valley Authority with the entire output of a hundred and ninety megawatt hydroelectric facility at our disposal," Brandy said primly. "Explosives would be redundant."

❦ ⊖ ❧

"That's a *lot* more than I thought we'd see," Detkovic said on the tactical channel, a few hours later. "Looks like three groups, about fifty each plus so-called leadership in each group. Everyone's hanging back, just outside small arms range. There are too many to maneuver comfortably, which is why they're still jacking around in their assembly areas."

The engineers were hooked into existing security cameras that covered both the dam itself and the pylon supported roadway above its entire length. They'd also installed additional systems since taking over the facility. The small control room in the basement was covered with scavenged LED TVs showing dozens of different camera views. As a result they had an unfortunately detailed view of the approaching enemy.

"Say again the count," Tom asked, rolling one shoulder. He looked across the room where Kaplan was performing another gear check and last minute training on some of their first time fighters.

The sun had been set for hours at this point, but the moonlight filtering through the patchy cloud cover was enough to see the larger bodies of men and vehicles more than a half mile away. Barely. Turning on the still functioning lights all over the dam was a last-ditch choice. That much light would concentrate every infected within fifty miles on the facility, but it would also allow his marksmen to engage at a greater distance.

"Two bunches of infantry, call them reinforced platoons, positioned to advance along the top of the dam," Detkovic continued his description over the encoded radio. "One light platoon riding technicals with what looks like a no-shit MRAP are positioned at the foot of the topside bridge. One of the technicals is a semi-wrecker with a prow front. One hundred-fifty to two hundred, all up."

"Armament?"

"I can't make out any crew-served weapons at this time." Detkovic paused for a moment and then rekeyed the mic. "Boss, that MRAP's going to smash most of the zombie fences on the bridge. And we've got what, maybe a four or five real shooters and the rest civilians?"

"Don't assume the enemy is ten feet tall, Butters," Tom replied. "Just be ready in case they are. Figure that the grunts move along the dam top using the spillways and equipment bays for cover while the vehicles push across the causeway right over their heads," Tom said.

"Whatever you say, Boss."

"The causeway force will wait until we're fully committed against the larger force. We can probably deal with that. Then they ram the MRAP over. Question is: where's the buggery group?"

"Buggery group?" Stantz asked.

"Coming in from the backside," Detkovic said. "Figure they'll show when they think we're concentrated on the front."

"Staged already or crossing now?" Smith asked.

"Nothing on camera upstream or down," Detkovic replied. "But there's a bend upstream that's shielded by the peninsula. Can't see around it from here. Short walk up from there. Could be crossing now if they were in a hurry."

"Pity we don't have a gunboat," Tom said.

"Or air cover," Stantz muttered. "Or, I dunno, artillery? Or tanks. Or..."

"Got it," Detkovic said, then keyed the radio. "The drizzle is picking up and clouds are thickening up for now. We're getting degraded on visual."

"Stantz, Brandy," Smith said. "They're bringing a lot more blokes to the fight than I expected. Due to the visibility, our marksmen can't shoot accurately until they get much closer. We have a little night vision, but not enough to equip the number of shooters we have to use. Your dam, but...recommend we dismiss light discipline at this time."

"That will bring thousands, maybe tens of thousands of infected down on us, Mr. Smith," Brandy replied. "We've been trying to avoid that for months. You're the tactical expert but...that mass of bodies will bring down the fences."

"We've still got Big Bad," Stantz said, more than a little eagerly.

"Which is, we've agreed, a last ditch defense," Brandy said.

"If you've got near terminal cancer and suffer a heart attack which do you treat first?" Tom asked. "I'd say treat the heart attack and worry about the cancer later. Also, whether they will hold or not, we are *in* defenses. They are not. Ten thousand infected will mostly be a problem for *them*. At least at first. Recommendation stands."

"Go live," Brandy said.

"Got it," Stantz replied then hit a series of switches on the master control board. They were labeled in block letters: THOU SHALT NOT TOUCH, LEST YE SUMMON THE HORDE!

"Ballsy move," Loki muttered as both the roadway and dam access walkway were dazzlingly lit. In addition, dozens of flood-lights along the base of the bridge, designed to assist night work on the dam as well as provide security to the area, turned on. "And it's exactly what Green said would happen."

The level of chatter increased as the nervous group of cast-together Gleaners in front of him stopped moving forward and looked around, amazed at the sight of so much electric illumination after living for so long in pre-industrial darkness. Their entire side of the dam basin was bathed in golden light, leaving the Gleaners totally exposed.

The growls of just-roused zombies on their side of the river became audible, but Green had planned for that too. The perimeter security was pre-briefed, and the distinctive boom of their shotguns were the first shots of the battle.

Inevitably, there were lookie-loos on his side. One flinched away from a not-so-friendly ricochet.

"Stay in cover, you!" he shouted, gesturing with his carbine at the Gleaners who were rubbernecking. He lifted his radio and gave the next order. "Support groups open fire, work on the closest lights!"

On cue, a dozen of rifle-equipped Gleaners starting shooting. A few of the dam lights popped and went out.

"Get some fire on the Tesla things—shoot the lightning machines!"

More rounds began to crack out against the clearly visible electrical weapons, though there was no obvious result.

"Mr. Smith, they've opened fire and we can see on the monitors that some have started their advance," Brandy radioed. "If they're not distracted a few of the more clever may wonder at some of the modifications."

"Roger that," Tom said, switching to phone. "Designated marksmen *only* to open fire at advancing enemy forces."

That was the signal for Kaplan, Robbins and Rune to shoot from concealment, semi-auto only.

Very deliberate, aimed fire began to crack outwards towards the encroaching forces.

"What about me?" Jordan Robbins asked, peering through the scope on her rifle. She was located well back in the cramped room, lying prone on a stack of two metal work desks. She'd appropriated a decent hunting rifle from one of the Springers. Tom didn't even want to know how she'd accomplished that trade. The Savage 111 XP was chambered in three hundred Winchester Magnum, known for its flat trajectory, accuracy and muzzle blast. He had his doubts about her ability to ride the recoil of the famously powerful cartridge. Still, she was positioned competently and for once wasn't complaining about the teenagers she'd inherited.

"Only for a VIP, Jordan," Tom replied. "Look for the firemen's jackets. You've only got so many rounds for that cannon. We're pretty far back here and Miss Bolgeo recommends allowing them to close a bit because we don't want to scare them off yet. She has some surprises waiting. Meanwhile, look for blokes that look like they're in charge."

"Shooting officers," the young woman answered. "Astroga's gonna be jealous when she hears about it."

Tom just smiled and shook his head.

And then the horizon lit even brighter as bright red and green flares rose into the sky above the dam's defenses. The new lights outshone the floodlights on the dam itself, and turned night into day across the entire compound and fenceline.

As if on cue, the previously occasional growls and screams from the infected in view were augmented by a rushing howl that lifted the hairs on the back of Tom's neck.

CHAPTER 18

"That's a lot of zombies," remarked the usually taciturn Loki, watching the ground crawl on the far side of the river. "A lot of god-damn zombies."

The brilliant incendiaries and noisemakers that Green had deployed to attract the zombies outshone even the electric illumination that the defenders had elected to switch on. Of course, Loki knew that the entire point was for the zombies to mob the Tesla coils and burn them out, compel the bankers to use up their ammunition and distract the defenders from the obvious Gleaner assault to follow. He just hadn't considered what several thousand zombies might look like. The illuminated area across the river rippled with the movement of more infected than Loki had ever seen.

"Green's gonna be pissed. He wanted me save as many of the technicians and related families as we could."

Loki registered his batman nodding hurriedly. There was nothing that Loki could say that this moron wouldn't agree with.

"Well, maybe some are gonna make it inside the concrete structures," he went on. "We'll just have to recruit the rest after we clear out the fucking zombies."

Loki could tell that in the days since Khorbish's men had returned, the dam's defenders had been busy. In addition to the primary fence, the electrified fence and the Tesla systems the scouts had indicated on their maps, Loki noted a new physical barrier, now revealed by the flares that the Gleaners had fired into the fenced ground surrounding the blockhouse.

A hundred yards outside the main blockhouse was a short, narrow gauge, almost negligible, circle of pipe, perhaps set to trip the infected. Inside that, defenders had found enough metal drums to create a hip-high stockade around the bottom floor of the building. The barrels were topped with a single row of sandbags, providing them with both weight and some ballistic protection. Little bubbles of fine netting, almost like chicken wire, dotted the central area.

However, compared to the mob of infected that was flooding into the illuminated area, the fences looked like scant protection. Undamaged Tesla coils began arcing, whether manually controlled or automatically firing. Dozens of infected simply collapsed, but as the mounds of dead began to form, the brilliant streamers of electricity flickered over shorter and shorter distances. In some areas, adjoining coils were already dead, and a stream of zombies poured like a soccer mob charging the field.

"I don't think the barriers are going to do more than slow them zombies down," Loki added. He held a hand out for his binoculars and the flunky promptly slapped them into his palm.

The flare-illuminated view had actually grown brighter than the earlier overcast daylight. He studied the target. Outside the metal ring-and-drum combination and a second, presumably electrified, fence, was a third barrier. This was a simple head-high chain-link fence, laid in a rough circle some five hundred feet in diameter. It was centered on the gray, two-story control building. All around the interior the vegetation, tents or anything that could obstruct a sight line or deflect a bullet had been stripped away. What appeared to be four entry-control points, shielded by the thick-masted coil devices, were dispersed evenly about the circumference.

In the center of the cleared area a large smokestack, festooned with a regular pattern of scaffolding, emerged from the side of the blockhouse.

"What's that, sir?" Dragon asked, pointing to the stack.

"Smokestack," Loki rumbled. "Probably part of a backup power generation system. Looks like they were trying to repair it before our arrival. These are probably older, stronger buildings that accompany the original construction and the technicians have chosen those for their last stand."

Loki recognized the effort that had been invested in protecting the location. Green would approve. Loki knew that the most important next step in Green's plan was returning reliable power to the immediate area. With enough power, the Gleaners could consolidate their hold on the entire region.

The defenders' problem was that enough infected would rapidly overcome the chain-link, electrified or not. The mere three-foot height of the drum barrier was laughable. The blockhouse was sturdy enough, but once trapped inside, the survivors' options would drop to zero.

"What if they just hide inside?" asked the former Triad gangster. "They could just block the doors. That smokestack means they can burn something in there, make electricity, even if we cut the lines to the dam."

He stabbed a thick finger, clad in his trademark blue gloves, at the tallest of the remaining buildings. What appeared to be a spark arrester perched on top of the scaffold-clad tower.

"We'll find their fuel source and isolate it," promised Loki as he scanned the approaching storm line of zombies. Even at this distance, the building howls and screams were plainly audible, even over the popping of harassing rifle fire. "We only kill as many as we have to. Their boss has to go, of course. Anyone in a leadership role. But we can afford to starve them out. We'll have plenty to do just on the cleanup. Besides, it's time. Get back to your team now. Start the push."

Dragon nodded and headed for the ladder up to their side of the roadway.

The defenders were picking up their rate of fire, but so far all they had used were rifles. Hundreds of dead infected were visible, but upwards of fifteen *thousand* howling zombies were surging towards the outer fenceline. Using just their mass the mob of infected humanity was about to collapse the first barrier.

This wouldn't take too long. They might not even have to assault across the bridge. Loki wondered how Green was doing and began to consider the next steps in the plan. His men could clear the dam and use the funnel to kill off such infected as survived the onslaught of the defenses.

Anyone that survived the infected might actually be glad to see him.

For a little while.

⌒◦─⊖─◦⌒

"Too many to stop!" Kaplan shouted above the gunfire, changing magazines. "Way too many. And we're burning through ammo!"

The designated marksmen had been joined by every other trigger puller available, but even the rapid sustained aimed fire wasn't even making a dent in the onrushing horde. Empty magazines and brass littered the blue tile floor of the blockhouse. The attackers' fire had also heated up considerably, while most of Smith's team was compelled to focus on the infected swarming against the fence. At random and decreasing intervals, Gleaner rounds cracked through the windows of the blockhouse. The deadliness of the incoming was manifest.

Two of their number, including one of their spare engineers as well as one of the volunteers from Spring City had been killed. Their jacket covered bodies were against the wall, away from the remaining survivors.

"Changing magazines!" Jordan yelled, exactly as her father had trained her. Then she grunted and dropped the AR which she'd swapped for her bolt-gun. She stumbled back, bleeding. Her father immediately went to her aid, further reducing the defenders' fire.

Tom looked over to the bridge for another second. The reports on the number of infected were incredible, so he'd rushed forward to see for himself. It was worse than he'd planned. The combination of heavy, but mercifully inaccurate suppressive fire from across the bridge and the close assault by the infected wasn't something that he'd foreseen. The Gleaners weren't actually communicating with the infected for coordination, but the effect was the same. He'd have to show his hole card, which wasn't his first choice.

"Go hot on the belt-feds," Tom said, referencing the two remaining light machine guns that he'd been saving for the Gleaners. He turned to Stantz. "We're going to go live on the Big Bad. All right hotshot, here's your chance."

Stantz beamed.

"Brandy, open gate four!" he said.

The four gates around the inner perimeter were not designed to let anyone out, but to channel the infected when they approached. Brandy turned a key and hit the gate control, but there was no response. She cursed and repeated the procedure.

"No response!"

"What?" Stantz got up from his seat and looked over her shoulder. "Did yo—"

"I know the system!" she cut him off. "I built it! The generator's down!"

She picked up a phone.

"Damnit, phone's down!"

"I'll run to the generator house and tell Larry—" Stantz began.

"Nope," Tom said firmly. "We need you here, and serving as a runner who has to dash through rifle fire is why we have runners. Who's up?"

"Hoo-ah, sir," little Cheryl Blaine said, rising from where she'd been crouched on one knee. "Run to the generator house, tell them to unfuck the motor and return, got it!"

"Language!" Tom replied. "Otherwise, you got it in one!"

"Be careful, Cheryl," Brandy said worriedly.

"No problem, miss," Cheryl replied as she skittered out the door. "Specialist Astroga taught us how to channel our inner demon!"

"I'm going to have a word with Astro when we get back," Tom said more calmly than he felt. He heard a grunt of pain and looked over to see Robbins packing Celox gauze into a bullet hole in Jordan's side. "Robbie, I need you on a gun."

Robbins looked up angrily.

"Start thinning the herd with a belt-fed, Rob," Tom said. "If that fence doesn't hold, that first aid means nothing! Brandy, take over first aid."

"Ah, Boss, looks they're approaching the middle of the bridge," Kaplan called, never moving from his cheek weld.

Jason spent the second half of the paddle across the lake marveling at the lights that covered the entire span of the dam and the road above it. He'd seen some electrical equipment in operation back at the Gleaner camp, powered by the portable Honda generators that Green had scrounged. They kept the rec hall lit, and powered the TVs and gaming consoles. But this was magic.

Several hundred yards of river, almost bank to bank, were lit with golden light, just as though the Fall had never happened.

Jason's spirits lifted. Man could still banish the darkness!

As he watched, some of the lights on the Gleaner side went

out. One, two, then a handful all together. The far bank, where they had started, was plunged back into blackness.

He frowned, and then understood.

He'd made some choices. He decided to walk away from the Force when there hadn't seemed to be any point to policing anymore. He'd walked away from other groups that been on the edge of coming apart. He'd thrown his hat in with Green, because he liked cars and ice and showers. He'd chosen to accept that only the strong could regain a measure of civilization.

He'd chosen to work with monsters. He'd . . . done things.

But here was a group that still held back the night.

And his side was murdering them.

At once something like scales fell from his eyes. It was as if he was seeing clearly for the first time since he'd given Joe Paterno peace. Since he'd shot his infected partner.

Above, another light on the bridge shattered. In his mind, Jason could hear the glass tinkle to the cement, just like a single empty nine-millimeter case from a police-issue Glock.

Then the skies over the far bank were lit like the Fourth of July.

"This bunch might penetrate the perimeter," Kaplan raised his voice just enough to heard. His trademark toothpick was getting a workout. "You watching this, Boss?"

"I don't care if this thing is newer, I miss my own machine gun!" Robbins added, keeping his cheek on the feed tray cover of the hammering M240. "You gotta stop losing shit, Thunder!"

"Jesus, let it go, Robbie!" Tom yelled, squinting at the scene as he flaked out the next ammo belt. He'd run back with his shooters in order to add their weight to the fight. "That gun is state of the art."

"Art—shmart—just feed me!"

The ammo can next to the machine gun was nearly empty and the brass was piling up underneath the mouse-hole of their window shooting position. The noise was ear shattering, fed by chattering weapons fire, the snarl of the remaining Tesla coils and over it all, the roars and hunting screams of a mob of zombies numbering in the thousands. Apart from a rapidly splintering toothpick, Kaplan wasn't showing any obvious signs that he was nervous, and continued cracking rounds out from his personal weapon, but that the laconic veteran was talkative at all said volumes about his mental state.

Since normal speech was impossible Mike Stantz leaned closer from his position near the control panel.

"Even noisier than the crowd at Ozzfest when the band wouldn't play an encore," he remarked offhand, sipping one of his remaining Budweisers. "You know, your boy is shooting the shit out of the fence that is all that's holding them zombies back, right?"

The entire circumference of the fence was covered in infected, and at the end gate nearest the main door to the blockhouse, the crowd of zombies was packed tightly enough that the sturdy chain-link was literally bowing inwards under their combined weight. This was hard on the zombies up against the wire mesh, some of whom were being squeezed through like Play-Doh. Despite their screams of pain the remainder of the cohort behind them kept up the pressure, gruesomely crushing the individuals in the leading ranks.

A loud *zing* from a parting wire was audible over the gunfire. It caught the defenders' attention and the fence jerked as the reinforcing wire guyline parted.

"If we don't move the fence or get the weight off, it is going to drop any second!" Kaplan yelled matter-of-factly, while still snapping out aimed rounds. "Without the coils or the Big Bad, we can't hold this line and either we retreat inside to be trapped or we run like hell to Spring City, *now!*"

"Wait for it," Tom said. He leaned his head to one side, slowly rolled one shoulder and then adjusted his plate carrier. "Just a little longer."

"I'm dry!" Robbins announced, lifting the feed tray on the smoking machine gun. "Tom, we can't hold back that many—unless you want to meet your Aussie gods, we gotta unass now!"

Smith stood fast.

"Tom, we got to go, now!" Robbins repeated, shouting now to be heard over the howling mob of thousands of zombies only a few hundred meters distant.

The guylines that stabilized the fence had begun to pop with ever greater frequency and the chain-link barrier was moments from being knocked over.

"Just another minute, Robbie," Tom said, watching the fence quiver under tension. "Just a bit more."

"I think we're fucked, Boss."

Tom couldn't tell who said it, but it didn't matter.

Black smoke suddenly burst from the stack on the generator building, causing all of them to jerk their heads to stare at it.

"Nah, we're good," Stantz said, clapping Kaplan on the shoulder and passing him the can of Bud. "Hold my beer and watch this."

Tom nodded, and Stantz placed his hand on a series of large switches set into the panel. Eyeballing the growing mob, he deliberately flicked each one in succession while carefully watching the corresponding gauges. A deep, low frequency hum became audible above the already high background noise level. With each switch, it grew louder, resonating a heavy bass note that pulsed through their bones.

"You're gonna want your eye pro in a second," Stantz offered.

The exhaust had been spurting irregularly from the generator building while the diesel warmed. As it settled into a steady rhythm the exhaust began to change color in the glare of the flares and electric light, gradually thinning from a heavy black cloud into a light gray as the motor that powered the draglines burnt fuel more efficiently. His ear cocked to one side, Stantz considered the exhaust and the dials before him before throwing a single final switch.

The nearest gate suddenly jerked, not down, but sideways. Metal squealed as the weight of the infected increased the friction against the fence guides, but the aperture opened inexorably, jerking under the weight of the infected clinging to the barrier.

Precisely like water spurting through the emergency spillway of a dam, the infected began flooding into the open space inside the final fenceline. Hundreds of zombies raced towards the tempting morsels visible through the control window, separated only by distance, a flimsy shin high metal ring and some barrels. They ignored the oddly shaped metal teardrop that rode the short metal ring.

The shuttlecock of polished aluminum responded to the dial under Mike Stantz's hand, and it spun to sit between his position and the densest portion of the approaching mob.

Stantz lowered dark glasses over his eyes and opened the clear lucite box that covered the object of his affection.

It was *finally* about to happen.

He depressed the Big Red Button.

The remaining lights all around the dam dimmed.

CRACK. CRA-CRACK! CRA-CRACK!

The report of the new weapon firing was a series of impossibly loud detonations that were spaced closely enough together to be perceived as God's own novelty joy buzzer.

If that joy buzzer was powered by the firing of an infinite number of overlapping Army howitzers.

Blinding light illuminated the entire area as arcs of blue white electricity spanned the space between the top of the "smoke stack" and the metal ring. The eerily beautiful loops and whorls of pure energy flickered from infected to infected, seizing scores and then hundreds in a deadly embrace. Where the wrist-thick spark actually touched individual infected, the target instantly ignited, flashing aflame and then to charcoal in a moment. Occasionally, the tissues of the infected actually blew outwards, but more commonly the zombies suddenly froze for meters around each strike, their bodies first straining in the galvanic clutch of the coils and then falling in windrows, en masse.

Time elapsed: two seconds.

Stantz's "smoke stack" was anything but.

As a final backup to the now mostly quiescent line of Tesla coils, he had built a very, very large Marx generator. Using designs nearly a century old and consuming much of the stock of equipment intended to maintain the upper third of the Tennessee Valley Authority hydroelectric power plants, Stantz had constructed a powerful artificial lightning machine, dwarfing the output of the much smaller Tesla coils.

Marx generators had been used for esoteric purposes before, such as testing pre-Fall passenger jetliners for lightning strike safety, or Mike Stantz's personal favorite, testing the ignition sequence of a plutonium fueled bomb.

But as Tom witnessed, the Marx generator was a peach when it came to large scale zombie disposal.

Electricity from the dam's five generators, each pushing nearly forty megawatts, powered multiple arrays of powerful industrial-sized capacitors set vertically into the side of what had in fact actually been a smokestack, charging them in parallel. Each time that Stantz depressed the firing button, a mechanical armature changed the circuit architecture. The capacitors in successive arrays were instantaneously aligned in serial, and discharged violently along a waveguide that led towards the top of the tower. The energy desperately sought a ground, and so the spark was attracted to the metal shuttlecock more than a hundred feet away. The spark appeared to last only a second but in that brief instant of time the waveguide discharged at twice the base frequency of the electricity that powered the entire array.

Stantz had designed the array to operate at sixty Hertz so the spark struck the impact zone not sixty but one-hundred and twenty times per second.

Delivering almost two hundred thousand joules per strike.

Aiming was somewhat haphazard. The metal shuttle-cock attracted the hundred-foot-long spark, but the actual strikes lit the area around the target, stroboscopically outlining the zombie mob while the discharge lasted. The energy was bright enough to be visible in the still brilliant illumination of the Gleaner flares.

"Now that's worthy to be the weapon of Zeus..." Tom said, exhaling appreciatively. No one could've possibly heard him because the deafening thunder from towering Marx Generator absolutely blanketed all other sound, leaving everyone's ears ringing despite the ear protection they all wore.

"Absolutely beautiful."

As the entire first wave of infected dropped, the array automatically shut down, and began recharging the capacitors. The menacing bass hum again became audible, presaging the release of more power.

Tom could hear Stantz carrying-on jubilantly, something about his machine being hungry, but he wasn't sure.

The surviving infected at the edge of the affected area stumbled on the bodies of the fallen, slowing their progress. A few saw the chance for an opportune snack, further slowing the progress of the wave front of infected.

But in a few seconds, the pressure of thousands of zombies restarted the hungry flood.

Fifteen seconds after the first shot, the "ready" light illuminated on the panel.

Stantz slammed the button again without waiting for direction.

Once again the glowing fist of God danced along the impact area. Everywhere it touched it created catastrophic burns and interrupted normal cardiac function. More zombies poured into the fire sack, only to be caught by the same arcs as their fellows. Less than two seconds later, the killing ground was still and smoking. The capacitors instantly began recharging and the angry hum of the god of lightning filled the almost deafening quiet.

More than a thousand infected lay before them, perfectly still. Some were charred beyond recognition and others had massive, sizzling wounds where electricity had explosively exited from their bodies to ground, but most were still and unmarked.

Dead.

Looking at each other and the carnage, the defenders began to remove their hearing protection.

"Hole-lee-shit," Kaplan said, awed. His toothpick dangled from one lip. "I thought that I'd seen every way to kill a zombie, but this is just..."

"Perfect," Tom said, finishing the sentence. "Absolutely aces. Absolutely. Fucking. Aces."

More infected flooded onto the killing ground.

The light next to the Big Red Button glowed again.

"You're gonna want to keep that ear pro in," Stantz said, laughing exuberantly. Then he depressed the firing stud again.

"YES!" he screamed again, overpowered by the thundering reports of his weapon.

Tom couldn't make out the rest of whatever it was that Stantz was yelling, but the normally taciturn engineer was certainly letting it all out. Tom could feel the harsh buzzing discharge of the Marx generator resonate through his very bones as he watched the powerful yet eerily beautiful man-made lightning dance across the killing ground, reaping an ashen harvest.

Glorious.

"Okay, okay," Brandy said with an aggrieved sigh. "So maybe that is pretty cool."

"Pretty cool?" Detkovic said. "*Pretty* cool?"

"Okay, so it's very cool," Brandy said with another sigh. "But you have no clue how hard it was to build the damned thing *in the middle of a zombie apocalypse. Stantz used everything!*"

"Worth every bit," Detkovic said, watching another zombie disintegrate into a charred pile of smoking meat. "Whoa! That's gotta HURT!"

USSTRATCOM
Offutt Air Force Base
Omaha, Nebraska
The Hole

"Whoa!" Airman Charles Barner said. "What the hell is *that?*"

"What?" Master Sergeant John Doehler said, glancing up from a magazine that he hadn't reread in at least a week.

Prior to the Fall, the U.S. Strategic Command maintained a continuous watch, serving as a backup to the backup for American national level command and control facilities. Since it had been designed during the height of the Cold War, the facility was built deep underground in order to ride out a barrage of Soviet nukes which, mercifully, had never come. That location had earned it the sobriquet, "The Hole." Despite the lack of a view or a nightlife, its air handling, filtration and overall security made it the home of the senior surviving representatives of the U.S. Government, insofar as it could be ascertained.

Of course, those representatives were pretty far down the seniority list. The enlisted staff still standing their posts were even more so, which meant that although the Russians were mostly preoccupied with their own problems, it being a zombie apocalypse and so forth, someone had to watch the remaining satellite feeds.

Those feeds had been pretty dull, unless your thing happened to be watching the tide of infected spread across the face of the planet, extinguishing civilization. Recent events in the Caribbean had begun to brighten the mood in The Hole.

And now there was this, whatever *this* was.

"One of the launch warning birds—SBIRS 7 Delta, Master Sergeant," Barner replied, referring to what the U.S. military discreetly labeled "overhead assets." "Older vehicle, was scheduled for de-orbit. Just pinged an anomaly in southeastern CONUS. Very high energy flux. The lat-long shows as...shows as Watts Bar Dam in Tennessee. I'll route the optical feed to your station."

"What the hell is that?" Master Sergeant Doehler asked, unconsciously aping his subordinate. He studied the image and then pulled up a database of anomalous photonic signatures as he continued to observe. "That's no launch plume. We don't have missiles in Tennessee anyway. But that's one hell of a lot of photons."

"So much for *one* point of light," the airman said with a snicker.

"We weren't sure before, but I think we can definitely say that something in Watts Bar is operational," Doehler said, making a note. "And damn that's a lot of freaking photons. Call Commander Freeman."

After the first three firings, Stantz had to pause for longer and longer intervals to allow enough infected into the killing ground. After a dozen shots, the infected crowding the fence were all dead and the thousands thronging the open area had begun to recoil from the brilliant discharge and overwhelming man-made thunder. The infected were predators, and hungry, aggressive hunters at that, but somewhere deep in their remaining predator reflexes lay the recognition of a greater, more terrifying killer. Slowly, increasingly alarmed by each firing of the terrible weapon, the zombies halted and began to retreat towards the apparent safety of the treeline.

CRACK-CRACK-CRACK!

A fresh line of dead fell or were consumed by the light.

The terrifying god of day had awoken, and it was *hungry.*

As the elated defenders watched, the zombies began to retreat even more rapidly.

The pitch black night was safer, as long as it lasted.

The number of bodies was actually impeding the view of the killing ground in some places. They mounded as high as the fence in a few spots.

The shuttlecock had been blocked by corpses more than once, but the concentrated discharge of the Marx generator had actually burned and disintegrated the bodies to the point where the aiming system could traverse freely once more.

"Brilliant!" Tom clapped Stantz on the shoulder, repeating himself. "Absolutely fucking aces!"

"Well, that was certainly—" Kaplan said, blinking beneath the dark glasses which he had belatedly donned. "—very bright and very, very loud."

He handed back the beer to Stantz before cocking his head sideways and again plucking out his safety orange foam ear plug.

"Hey, anyone else hear that?"

CHAPTER 19

"That's unexpected," Loki said musingly, watching the tremendous lightshow across the river. Even at this distance, the intensity of the electricity coming from the "smokestack" was too bright to observe directly. He blinked rapidly, trying to clear the afterimages that impaired his vision. It was akin to staring at a welding arc and probably about as good for you.

"Don't look directly at it!" he yelled. "Pass it along! Don't look directly at the light!"

Once he could hear the order being passed along, he stuck a finger in one ear and called Green on radio.

"Governor, it's Loki, did you see that?" he transmitted.

There was a pause, lasting about as long as it would take to stop walking and operate a walkie-talkie.

"Mr. Loki, I think the entire country saw that," Green answered, asperity plain in his tone. "What's making that light?"

"Smith has some kind of super lightning weapon built into the smokestack at the dam," Loki said, wincing as yet another shot of lightning snarled into the ground near the target. "It's killing zombies by the hundreds, but the regular lights are out."

"Ah!" Green exclaimed. "They don't have enough power to do two things at once. Push all the way across the bridge immediately. We're going to initiate our flanking movement now."

"Got that, sir," Loki answered, waving at his people to get their attention. "We're starting now."

He lowered the radio and switched channels before making a second call.

"All groups maximum advance. Roll the trucks. Shoot anyone with a gun, then anyone at all and if you can't see anyone, lay into the blockhouse and fighting positions. Nobody stops!"

Shots began to crack out along his front. He tapped the shoulder of the designated marksman lying down next to him, who was still looking though his scope.

"That means you, dumbass."

"It's starting to get pretty hot," Kaplan said over the radio. "I think that they're starting the push in earnest now."

"I can see that," Tom replied, watching from inside the blockhouse. "Pass the word. Keep returning fire, but nothing heavy till they reach the midpoint. The point is to keep their heads down and concentrated on us and deny them a chance to move across the dam quickly."

Rounds snapped overhead with ugly, distinctive cracking sounds. After the sounds of the Marx generator, they weren't too intimidating. That itself could be a problem. A single bullet in the right place was every bit as fatal as a few thousand megawatts.

"Got it," Kaplan said, and then stopped, listening to the volume of enemy fire increase steadily. "It's picking up, gonna get worse before it gets better."

"Good," Tom said. "That means they're following the plan. Let's allow them to feel confident. I'm heading back to the reserve."

"Keep up the fire," Loki said, patting one of the shooters on the back. "Keep them pinned down."

They were about a quarter of the way across the dam top. Besides the equipment boxes, railings, stairways, portable cranes and other equipment, the walkway was interrupted by regular zombie barriers including a mix of barbed and chain-link fencing. Teams had to slowly nibble their way through that. The absence of lights was reassuring, but inexplicable, now that the big lightning machine had quit. Even better, the machine gun fire had mostly stopped as well.

Of course, the defenders' marksmanship was still pretty dangerous.

"Mr. Loki, we just lost another man!" came the cry from ahead.

"Keep moving or you're gonna lose some more!" Loki shouted back. The casualties were making the group wary. Retreat wasn't an option anymore, and he needed the bullet sponges to keep leapfrogging up. He and the few picked men had probably killed more of the defenders than the rest of the idiots combined.

But they were doing what Green wanted. Being a really, really good distraction.

His radio clicked twice. He barely caught it over the fire; it might not have been the first time. A glance at the channel told him who it was, but he acknowledged then keyed the radio again.

"Dragon," he growled, bottling his irritation. "Where are you? Roll the vehicles all the way across, now!"

"Dragon's rolling the tank," the Gleaner replied.

Finally! What had that unreliable Triad jackass been doing all this time?

The radio clicked again then was silent.

Above them, on the causeway, Loki could hear the snarl of diesel engines revving.

After this fight, he'd have to have a little meeting with Dragon.

Green took a knee in the gravel of the short, curved beach, while a couple of underlings pulled the motley collection of aluminum skiffs all the way out of the water. The thick brush of the northern peninsula screened his perimeter while he considered the situation. The entire group of camouflage-clad, face-painted, Gleaner "special operators" could hear the crackle of fire from the embattled dam defenses. The brilliant, overwhelming loud lightshow had ended and the lights on the dam were still out. The Gleaners were about to decisively engage the defenders from the rear end and roll this engagement up.

It was perfect.

Which bothered Harlan Green. Loki's radio calls, audible over an earbud, were calm and indicated things were going more or less as planned. His landing and sneak to this point had been straightforward, almost routine. The defenders were preoccupied with the mob of infected that he'd baited into the area. His group remained undetected and Green hadn't even seen zombie one, or even deer, on the approach.

The entire peninsula was silent, empty and appeared entirely undefended. There was even an old, overgrown access road that made for a convenient path.

Other than the intermittent rainfall, it was just too damned easy. Smith was, supposedly, some kind of military expert. There was no way a professional would leave this area entirely uncovered.

And with all the light, zombies should be waking up and moving all over. There weren't any. They'd run across a few old skeletons but no fresh kills.

Something was badly wrong. If there had been any way to hit the pause button, he would've retreated and reconsidered. But with the main force so totally committed, it would be organizational suicide. It was win or die at this point.

"One of those fucking coil things," Freddo said, whispering and pointing.

"As I said," Green said, using the reflected light from the dam lights to spot the shiny Tesla coil, "use your normal voice, pitched low, if you please. It carries less far than a whisper. And, yes, good eye. But we're out of range."

"You're sure, sir?" Freddo said nervously. The entire group had heard the lurid story of Khorbish's death.

"Positive," Green said, holding out his hand to hold the Gleaner in place. "We'll move that way," he added, pointing down the road. "You've shown considerable improvement since the unfortunate incident in Virginia, Freddo. You can take point."

Freddo gulped, stood, and began to poke his way uphill.

"I've got a strong spike on inductor four," Brandy said, as an open laptop started pinging. "More than flesh. Has to be metal."

"Where is . . . that?" Detkovic asked, flipping through the maps that littered the desk. He'd been rapidly briefed on the defenses the electricians had put into place but . . . these guys, and one lady, were *more* paranoid than most SF troopers. There were *a lot* of defenses. It was giving him wonderful ideas. For now though, he scrabbled among the layered papers on the ops desk.

"Back on the peninsula," Brandy replied, gesturing with her chin. "Right on the old campground road."

"That's our boys," Detkovic said then keyed his radio. "Thunderblast, it's Butters. Buggery on campground road, over."

"Roger," Smith replied. "Rolling."

"You *sure* you don't want me to come along for old times?" Detkovic asked a little wistfully. He was annoyed at being remaindered to the control center.

"What advantage do superior numbers afford the commander, Butters?"

"The opportunity to pursue multiple avenues of attack, Tom," Detkovic replied.

"And that's what these assholes are doing," Tom said. "I'll buy you guys the time to clear the bridge. Stay on station."

Tom didn't have many options. On the positive side of the ledger, he did have Rune on the team. He would have much preferred to add Kaplan or Detkovic as well. Or the National Guardsmen who were cooling their heels, however unwillingly, back at Site Blue. Any available professional, really. However, there was too much perimeter to cover and only so many people that he could trust to hold the line at the dam. Pascoe was down. Both Robbins kids were down, and wasn't *that* going to be a fun conversation with their mother. Most of the families from Robbins's ranch were back at Spring City, stiffening their defenses in exchange for technical support at the dam.

What he'd started out with at the beginning of the defense of the dam was a pick-up team of a dozen shooters, counting himself, plus four engineers, including Mike and Brandy. Given the narrow frontage of the bridge and dam, their defensive preparations and their motivation, Tom had been confident that he could inflict casualties beyond the Gleaners' appetite to continue, and force them to withdraw. However, Green's little zombie surprise had significantly eroded their defenses. Worse, Green had brought more men to the fight than Tom's worst case scenario.

The casualties so far had cut the margin too thin. So, what they didn't have was flexibility.

If Tom was "lost," as in the nice euphemism for the southern word "kilt," then Kaplan, Robbins and Detkovic could continue to help the dam people with defenses. This wouldn't be the last battle and while their resources were considerable, the engineers needed people with tactical background. As Detkovic had demonstrated with his last transmission, he was one of the few with that knowledge. All Tom's forlorn hope had to do was delay the newest assault and buy the main defense time to launch the second surprise of the night. The survival of the rear guard was optional.

Somebody had to go and somebody had to stay.

He knew at a certain level that it should be Kap going and

him staying. But he was tired of being the boss. He was tired of running away. He was done with letting others face the greatest risks. He was ready and past ready to stick it to the bastards that kept presenting an endless succession of problems when all Tom really wanted to do was put stuff back together. His anger had built all this time, and Tom was ready for payback.

In short, it was time to just operate.

Unfortunately, he didn't have much in the way of a bench.

He looked around at the scratch team and tried to think positively.

Rune was right in his shadow. He'd made the deal, and he was going to put the mission first. He was rigged up and committed.

Luke Connor. Teenager, nearly man-size. He'd been steady enough during the second team's advance to Site Blue.

And that was it for "experienced" personnel. He was so short on personnel he'd dipped into the NYC refugees.

Emily Bloome. The more balanced of the two schoolteachers. Loyal, earnest. Likely to respond well to threats against her students.

Katrin Jonsdottir. She was the steadiest of the teens and had plenty of moxie. If nothing else, she was an ammo bearer.

Eric Swanson. Except for shitting himself he hadn't fucked up on a trip where plenty of older and wiser people had made one balls up after another. Like Tom himself, for instance. Eric's face was grim, and he had something to prove. Worst case, another ammo bearer and not to put too fine a point on it, another target for the hostiles to deal with.

That was it, a scant fire team.

The last three had a few days of weapons training and should be reasonably steady shooting from behind solid cover in a fixed position. All they had to do was give the appearance of a strong firing line. He wasn't confident that all of his team could actually nerve themselves to shoot at a human target. The reality was they were all amateurs and most of all, they were disposable. If his entire scratch team was wiped out buying time, it wasn't going to make a bit of difference in the long run. Between Kaplan, Robbins, Detkovic and the rest, there were plenty of highly trained, tactically proficient personnel to finish the Gleaners, as long as the defenders could deal with one attack at a time.

And that meant stopping or at least slowing the suspected

Gleaner push that threatened their flank. Green would've brought his best.

Bloody buggery was right.

"I'll go over this one more time," Tom said carefully, looking around at the camouflage-clad, rigged-up group of tyros. "We move into ambush position. You line up a target. You take your weapon off safe then. Not before. You wait for me to open fire. Then you fire one magazine. Try to stay on the target. Then we leave the way we came in, but much, much faster. If something happens to me, Paul is in charge. If something happens to Paul, Luke is charge. If something happens to Luke, drop your bloody gear and run back. Do not *fall* in the water. If this group catches you, the ladies at least will be raped to death and probably the lads. Do not hesitate to fire. God will not miss these misbegotten sons-of-bastards. Are we all clear?"

He took in the series of nods, wide eyes and a single wink.

The Regiment, this was not.

"Then we roll," Tom said. "And may victory anoint the right."

Freddo knew that point was the most dangerous position, but he also considered himself ready. He'd been talking to Loki before the mission about what to look out for, so he was careful in his steps, trying to feel for tripwires that might indicate mines. The lights from the dam gave considerable vision to eyes adjusted to months of darkness. He scanned left and right, out to the limits of vision and hearing, taking his time just as Loki had coached.

There weren't any ambushers waiting for them in the darkness. Things were clear. The brush was thickening though, and combined with his caution, traversing up the hill was taking some time. He continued his deliberate scan.

Like most people Freddo tended to rarely look up.

Even if he had, he would've probably ignored the uninsulated ten gauge copper wire strung between two trees. Green, who did look up, had seen it and dismissed it. The area they were moving through had once been a campground and he assumed, like the many old foundations, that it was a remnant of that facility.

It was not. It was a recent installation, much easier to make than a Tesla coil and, if less sparkly, just as dangerous. And it was capable of both delivering a message and sending one.

There was an easy walkway across the roadbed and onto the peninsula. However, it was potentially under observation. There was another way out, though, which crossed near the top of the dam, not actually in visual of the approaching force, then up onto the peninsula. Unfortunately, it was a very steep climb up onto the peninsula from the top of the dam. Tom's squad had to traverse a crumbly slope blanketed in wet leaves that hid the loose rocks underneath. On the upside, the path would be easy to find on their way out, since it was literally the last thing before the cliff's yield to the ledge.

Tom squinted into the intermittent rain.

They made their way cautiously, holding onto trees to keep from slipping until they were about fifty meters beyond the road. There, by a straight bit of cliff wall, Katrin suddenly stumbled and began to slide over the edge. Tom stepped wide in order to grab her arm, and arrested her fall. He waited until she'd regained her footing before he let go.

The turbulence of the near-shore generator intake was directly below the cliff. The swirling surface only hinted at the violence of the water as it entered the generator house. Katrin would have surely been sucked into the intake and made into bird food. The lights had begun attracting insects and awakened the terns and other seabirds so that during short breaks in the crackling weaponsfire, the birds' twerps and tweets of delight provided a surreal counterpoint to the sounds of violence.

"Watch your footing, lass," Tom said, grinning in the dappled light. He shoved her back onto the path. "Be a bit of a b—"

His well-planted foot slid out from under him as the wet soil gave way, and like a shot, he slipped immediately over the cliff. One scrabbling hand managed to grasp a tiny sapling for a bare moment.

In the now clear light he looked Katrin in the eye for just one second then said:

"Bugger."

With that he slipped over the edge into darkness.

"Smith!" Paul yelled, ignoring noise discipline. He didn't care if they were spotted by the entire enemy force. He scooted up to the middle of the group and dropped to his stomach and looked over the edge into the black waters. "TOM! TOM!"

He felt herself slipping as well and for a moment just didn't care. Suicide mission. If they were all going to die *anyway*...

Below, the dark waters swirled, throwing back highlights from the lights.

"Mr. Rune," Luke said. "What do we do?"

Paul realized the only reason he wasn't slipping over the side with Tom was that the teen had his hands firmly around one boot.

"We gotta get on mission," Luke said, more calmly than any teen should be in the situation. "We gotta push. We just gotta push."

Hanging head-down over the water that had just swallowed his commander, Paul gave himself a mental shake and then started wriggling backwards. It was a little embarrassing that the kid had to remind him.

"Luke, grab my plate-carrier," Paul said, scrabbling at the rocks. "Emily, grab Luke. Somebody else grab that somebody and a handy tree. Last one keep watch."

Gasping, he finally dragged himself up to reasonably stable ground. With the prospect of immediate death eased somewhat, he registered that the gunfire on the dam was picking up. He also saw the wide-open eyes of his new command staring back at him, waiting for his instructions.

"We push," Paul said when he was back upright. "Everyone back on the trail."

"But..." Emily said. "This is crazy. I know I said I'd do it, but without Tom this is crazy."

"We push," Paul said, his voice firm. "Mission continues. Luke, take rear security. I'll be up front."

"Roger," Luke said. He carefully grabbed a tree and stepped of the trail to allow the next two to slip by.

"Everyone watch your footing," Paul added. "The first place that we can set up is just a bit further."

On the far side of the dam, the terns broke into excited squawking.

Tom took a maximum breath just as he executed a semi-controlled entry into the tenebrous depths. The hundred pounds of guns, ammo, armor and sundry nastiness that he bore immediately sucked him under. In combat slow-time he engaged in a rapid inventory of his issues and assets.

Issues:

- Entering deep water while wearing full combat kit.
- Entering deep water in the immediate vicinity of a generating hydroelectric dam's primary intake during near-flood conditions.
- Entering deep water in an uncontrolled fall.
- Generally, just entering deep water.
- Also, a slamming gunfight only a few hundred meters away.

Assets:

- Extensive water experience. Grew up on station on the Australian coast. Former commander of the Australian SAS swim-unit.
- Extensive experience in high stress situations including out-of-breath situations.
- Profound desire not to be mince. Secondary desire to not die ignominiously of drowning. Tertiary desire to return to the unit before they all bloody killed themselves.

He could feel the suction of the dam's intakes from the moment he hit the water. It tugged him in precisely the direction he did not want to go.

He was not entirely sure of the location of the intakes nor their precise design. There'd been a brief. Something about thousands of gallons of water per minute and missing trashracks. Still immersed in the long slow moment that occasions utter terror, Tom had the time to contemplate all the questions he'd failed to ask the TVA operators about the exact configuration of the dam. Trashracks sounded *ungood*. He had to admit the questions hadn't really seemed germane in the short time they'd had to plan the op. Doing an upstream water entry was a third or fourth order contingency.

Wrong again.

Was there a large concrete lip? How far above the bottom of the lake did it extend? How deep was the lake in this immediate vicinity? Would he be fed through and minced or pinned to a grate until his breath ran out? Glorious and hopefully fast death by turbine or ignominious slow and torturous drowning?

His immediate, trained, reaction on hitting the water was to ditch his gear. The advanced armor had a single-point quick release and his hand gripped it for a moment, then paused.

If he hit the release now, he'd lose the weight of gear that was making him massively negatively buoyant—and potentially dragging him under, past the danger level of the intakes. If he were to suddenly stop sinking, well...he was a strong swimmer but the current was ferocious. Mince presumably. Very last choice. Perhaps drop a bit and hope for the best?

His eardrums began to hurt which meant he was passing five meters or more. He swallowed and worked his jaw, performing the Valsalva maneuver that equalized the pressure.

As he dropped, he felt the sideways suction reduce until he was in free-fall. The intake appeared to be shallow and placed near the surface of the lake. Ergo, he needed to be deep before trying to free swim.

Might as well take the ride to the bottom then extract.

As he continued to sink, he ran through his points of performance for his Free-Swim-Ascent, performing each as he thought of it. A textbook FSA this was not.

- Ditch cranial. Done.
- Ditch primary weapon to avoid entanglement with the sling. Done.
- Retain plate carrier with heavy strike plate and full magazines to maintain his rate of descent, but prepare to ditch once on the bottom. Check.
- Ditto secondary and pistol belt with Surefire and spare mags. Check.
- Tomahawk on baldric under the plate. Stays. Oh, yeah, the RMJ stays.
- Locate quick release with fingers of right hand. Done.

Feet together, elbows in to streamline and speed up the bloody, how-long-is-this-going-to-go-on descent. Done.

- Determine overhead obstacles. Massive bloody current suction into maw of death. Check.
- Determine safe exit route. Go upstream away from aforementioned massive bloody current suction into maw of death. Still check.

As he cleared his ears the second time, meaning he was passing about ten bloody meters plus, damnit, he considered his available breath-hold time. He determined that there might be a bit of a difficulty.

HOW BLOODY DEEP IS THIS BLOODY LAKE?

Remain calm.

Note to self: In future when operating in potential water-hazard environment, include flotation equipment.

Addendum, safety briefs might not be as stupid as they often seem.

Well, it seems we've time to put a spare Surefire in our bloody cargo pocket.

Clear ears again...Jesus!

If it were only you know, not tenebrous depths and less, you know, wet, he'd consider reading a book. Say, *War and Peace*. Plenty of time, my lads...

HOW DEEP IS THIS BLOODY...?

As his feet hit the bottom, he almost breathed an assuredly fatal sigh of relief. Then the "bottom" took off from under said feet and he was swept off his legs while something very large struggled beneath him.

Just one bloody thing...

Then again, sometimes when you have several problems...

"They're going to get out of the trap zone soon," Brandy said. "And the ambush team doesn't want to hit them in there. It would be...bad."

"Right," Detkovic said. "Thunderblast, Butters."

"Rune," Detkovic heard Smith's right-hand man reply. "Thunder unavailable."

"Location?"

"About Phase Line Two," Rune said. "We got held up."

"Hold," Detkovic said. "Going sparkly."

"Roger," Rune replied. "Out."

"That sounded...sharp," Brandy said. "They okay?"

"You keep military messages short," Detkovic replied, but he was bothered by the tone and that Smith had been "unavailable." "They're outside the hot zone. Fire it up."

"Not as much fun as my toys," the engineer said. "Not going to be anything to see here."

"Probably not much to see there, either," Detkovic said. He understood the physics and it wouldn't actually be "sparkly."

"Not so much see as, you know, *feel*," Brandy replied, raising one eyebrow. She flipped a toggle switch.

"For a very brief second," Detkovic said, grinning ferally.

∽ ⊖ ⋐

Americans had long been accustomed to the familiar towers and wrist thick cables that carried industrial amounts of electrical current across vast distances. The movement of this current generated, or induced, an electrical field which, by the time it reached ground level, was perceptible only because of an audible but mild buzzing. Attenuated by the height of the towers, these weakened fields could impart enough charge to an ungrounded metal fencepost to startle the unwary civilian with a mild tingle. However, one of the preventable pre-Fall causes of death among high-tension linemen, accounting for an average of twenty fatalities annually, was exposure to induced current.

Usually, high-tension cables were safely overhead and induced current was a low threat. When powerlines downed by storms weren't noted in time, linemen could stumble into an induced electrical field and unwittingly serve as a bridge between two points of radically different electrical potential. They would then be trapped and killed, as would anyone else who happened along until the downed lines were de-energized or shorted out. What Brandy Bolgeo had done was to recreate this very situation, *intentionally,* in order to plug gaps in their perimeter. Wherever Tesla coils couldn't reach, she'd connected thick copper and aluminum wires to the high tension cables that led from the dam's electrical switching yard. These unobtrusive wires were lowered to ground level, radically strengthening any induced electrical field once the wires were energized.

A savvy lineman would've been both well trained to note the position of transmission towers and alert to downed power lines.

The Gleaners were neither.

Freddo the First Time Point Man was twenty-five meters in front of the main body where Harlan Green had placed himself. Ole Freddo never got the chance to recognize the fact of his own death since the current that coursed into his body disrupted every electrical pathway in his brain even as it permanently interrupted his cardiac rhythm. All four remaining scouts imitated Freddo, simultaneously freezing in place and then falling like stones as their bodies strained, rigid and immovable. Stiffened by muscles galvanically locked into place, the bodies remained frozen in place, involuntarily serving as resistors in a circuit containing nearly four hundred thousand volts. In moments, clothing smoldered and then ignited. The water saturating the tissue inside Freddo's head rapidly heated, then steamed and finally expanded, causing his cranium to lift with a soft *pop*. It wasn't the last.

"Okay, we should probably stop here for a moment," Harlan said, as another skull popped a few meters ahead. He wasn't sure of the details, but he recognized cause and effect. He was pretty good with electricity but very high voltage wasn't a specialty. However, he did know a bit about electrical physics, and reconsidered the naked copper wire. From a *distance*.

"Oh, you *clever* bastards," he muttered.

"The fuck is going on?" Berb asked. "What the fuck killed them?"

"That copper wire," Green said, pointing carefully. It was hard to see in the dark. "It's conducting electricity through the air. Somewhere around here is a buried ground. Since they walked under it for a while then it activated, the power plant people presumably know we're here."

"Then we gotta go," Berb snarled. "Back I mean. I'm not walking into invisible death for anything, man!"

The gunshot was muted but not "silenced" by the suppressor on Green's MP7.

"Then you don't have to," Green said to the corpse. "That's fine. I'm entirely okay with your decision. Anyone else in agreement with the late Mr. Berb?"

There was a chorus of "Naw, we're good, sir!" and "I'm fine" from the group.

However, his law enforcement recruit seemed frozen in place.

"Mr. Young?" Green asked carefully.

Jason knew that he needed to keep his head in-mission, but he couldn't stop thinking about the beautiful, radiant illumination that bathed the dam until Green's marksmen started shooting out lights in order to cloak their attack in darkness. What was he doing?

The Gleaners as the apparently best option. Civilization had come apart. Horror ruled. It made sense that only the most horrible would rule. It was order of a sort. Things were getting together even if they were doing so...horribly.

But here there was...hope. Light. He knew that civilization existed before electricity but electric light defined, for modern man, civilization. The gleam of golden light revealing the horror of the advancing undead, the swirling nimbus of electricity cast from each of the Tesla coils, the hundred-foot-long spark of energy dancing above the dam, they were all markers that civilization still fought on. And he was fighting for the group that wanted to erase the very survivors who had maintained one small patch of civilization.

Even the weapon that had just erased a fifth of Green's little strike group was more technologically advanced than Green himself could contrive.

The ex-cop had reluctantly gone along with the plan but without any heart or hope. But here was hope. Light against the dark.

The fuck if he was going to help the dark one more second.

Jason could feel Green behind him. That man never allowed anyone at his back, save Loki.

"Mr. Young?" came a soft call over his shoulder.

Green would kill him in an instant. Jason knew it. Their mad leader wasn't in position to be able to afford disagreement. To resist would be to die.

He no longer cared. He would no longer be part of the darkness.

He would fight for the light.

Jason clicked the safety on his modified Colt to fully automatic and moved without further hesitation.

Warned by something in his posture, or perhaps Jason's hesitation, Green shot first, his rounds cracking into Jason's armor before the officer's first shot cleared the muzzle.

But Green was too late.

Jason wasn't trying to aim at the commander of the Gleaners. As the high velocity MP7 rounds cratered and then penetrated his armor, Jason kept his trigger depressed, dumping an entire magazine into the backs of the thugs and former prisoners that made up Green's special operator group, the very men he was supposed to be leading.

Fully automatic weapons are difficult to aim accurately, even at very short ranges, but fortunately his group had closed up when Freddo and the leading element hit the electric field. The cop's rounds ripped into the backs and sides of all four of the Gleaners in Jason's team. Two dropped limply to the ground. Another suddenly knelt as if overcome with a need to pray, before slumping over. The last spun, clawing at his back, before dropping.

Young fell to the ground, bleeding out. He was hit...a bunch. Give Green credit: indecisive he was not.

Jason didn't even feel his hands relax, dropping the rifle to mingle with the leaves blanketing the ground. His throat filled with blood, and he coughed reflexively.

"Well, I guess I gauged that one wrong," Green said, again enjoying the feeling of euphoria that accompanied any enforcement of his authority. Working to keep calm, he walked over to the police officer and drew his pistol. "What exactly were you planning to accomplish, Officer Young?"

"Just to fuck you over," Young coughed. He smiled through red gore. "Light against the dark."

"Really, you come to this after all the choices you've already made?" Green said, his control slipping. "You're already committed. You're no hero. You die here and it Just Does Not Matter. I will still win and nobody will ever know what a fool you just were."

"God knows," Young said. "I give my soul to God."

"Your God wouldn't have you, Mr. 'I Do What I Must To Survive,'" Green said, the volume of his voice increasing further.

Still smiling, Officer Jason Young of the Williamsburg Police Department, badge number 19076, closed his eyes for the last time.

Green shot the fallen man in the face and paused, then shot him several more times.

"I HATE RELIGIOUS FANATICS!" Green screamed, his controlled facade cracking under the intense pressure. He tried to master his anger, reloading his pistol. It didn't work.

"You could have screamed 'Allahu Akbar' or SOMETHING. Fucking JESUS FREAKS."

He shot the officer a few more times just to express his displeasure then walked over and assessed the dead and wounded operators.

"What good are you now?" Green snarled, before turning to the remaining men. "Grab their ammunition and let's go."

"I'm right with you, Boss," one of the Gleaners said nervously. "But...how are we going to get around the magic fields of invisible death?"

"There's one of those Tesla coils over there," Green said, pointing towards the river. "Noise discipline is forgone anyway. Just shoot it."

"Yes, sir," the Gleaner said, taking careful aim, then shooting the bright silver power-head. "And again sir, not wanting to get shot, there's no invisible field of death over there?"

"You can't have one of these and a Tesla coil in the same area," Green said, gesturing in the direction of the destroyed coil. "And before you ask why, it's because . . . science, understand? Are you going to aggravate me and ask for an in-depth physics explanation, Charlie?"

"No, sir, Mr. Green," Charlie said hastily.

"Good call," Green replied. "Move out, we're almost there."

CHAPTER 20

Frederika had lived a long and fruitful life.

That is, for a blue catfish.

She was unusually long lived, even by catfish standards. For more than two decades she had survived in Watts Bar lake. She'd dodged anglers or thrown their hooks. She'd detected the sting of industrial pollution and moved to a new hole on the muddy bottom, while her fellows washed ashore. Floods, droughts, heavy construction, she'd outlasted it all.

She'd spawned uncounted clouds of eggs and passed along her champion genes. In fact, only a few moons past, she'd selected a feisty male and after a gratifying tussle, laid her clutch in the shallow depression he'd prepared before she swam off, leaving her suitor to his guard duty, just as she'd done each time before.

And the payoff was now.

She'd felt the rainy season approach, which usually brought with it nutrient rich water and prey from upstream. However, life had been especially good recently. An entirely new food source, made up of tasty baitfish, was prolific in the lake and their numbers steadily growing. She could eat her fill by moving only a few meters closer to shore and slurping down dinner. Since moving her five-foot-long bulk, which exceeded one hundred-and-forty pounds, could be a tedious chore, the short distance to her feeding grounds was a tremendous boon.

This night, she felt ravenous, and started to rise in the water column, seeking her favorite food.

Suddenly, a tremendous weight struck her back! Indignant, she spasmed, trying to slap the intruder with her thick body and tail, but a disgusting protrusion invaded her mouth!

Grabbed her gill cover!

Punched her flanks!

Panicked as she had never been before, she swam for her life.

"Hold here," Paul said quietly as the earlier burst of automatic fire was followed by a series of individual gunshots. They struck a nearby Tesla coil. In the rain and wind the shots might have gone unnoticed. The actinic deconstruction of the charged coil, however, was unmistakable.

The coil was the landmark Smith had marked as the point to put in the ambush. To the west were various induction traps for the infected. They would be hard for the Gleaners to remove, if they could even detect them. The Tesla coils were more vulnerable, another argument against them. As predicted, the Gleaner team lead, whoever it was, had taken out the coil and thus would be pushing in their direction.

"Take positions behind the trees. Hold your fire till I shoot."

The team spread out with a bit more talking than he liked.

"Keep your voices down," he said, sotto voce. Paul gestured for Luke to go left as he went right.

"It's going to be fine," he whispered to Emily Bloome as she filed by nervously. "Just think of them as targets in darkness."

"They're people," the New York schoolteacher murmured back. "Not just targets."

"They're rapists and murderers and you're protecting your students," Paul said, "Just shoot the targets."

He continued on and moved Eric Swanson over to a tree.

"We don't want to be bunched up," he said. "Just shoot the targets."

"I . . . will," Eric said, gulping. "Sorry to say this, Mr. Rune, but I wish Mr. Smith was here."

"Me too, kid," Paul said. "But it's gonna work out fine. Wait until I fire."

He moved to a likely tree and took up a kneeling position, peering through the precious IR monocle.

Movement.

"Go to the Tesla coil," Green said. "Then turn right and head for the lights."

"Got it," Charlie said. He was nervous as hell. He wasn't sure whether he was more nervous about another invisible wall of death or catching a bullet from the psycho boss standing at his back.

The Tesla coil was on a tall metal pole. It was easy enough to see through the night vision goggles. But the rain was doing something funky with the goggles. They weren't very good, which quality should have been obvious from the name of that gadget maker that advertised inside an in-flight magazine. There were ghosts or something from the rain getting on them. Almost human figures...

He paused and wiped at the goggles. It made things worse. He was trying to puzzle out if they were actually people or just smears.

"I think there's something..."

Paul realized they'd been compromised when the point stopped. The Gleaner team must be using night vision also. It was the only way the small team could have been spotted with the rain and wind.

The Gleaners had been following a road that according to the TVA team dated to the construction of the dam in the 1940s. That was where they'd hit the induction electrical trap. They'd turned towards the Tesla coil, which was in an open area between two sets of trees, one of which had paralleled the road, the other of which was cover and concealment for Paul's team.

If the Gleaners had come into the open area it would have been one thing. Most of them would have been at short range and sitting ducks.

In the trees and fifty meters away, the situation was not as great. His team's marksmanship was not all that good. He'd wanted to get the Gleaner group to within no more than thirty meters before opening fire.

For that matter, having Smith and the rest of the Army guys with him would have been nice. Might as well ask for a Reaper overhead while he was at it.

As Smith used to say, there was a time to think and a time to act.

Paul carefully targeted the point man and rapidly sent three rounds at the target.

Everyone else immediately followed suit. Some of them might even have made hits.

❦

Green jumped behind a tree as the first pops of rifle fire signaled the presence of the enemy. He risked a quick look. He couldn't see the adversary, but he watched as his latest point man twitched and died. Again. On the other hand...

Finally somebody, on the other side *for once*, to kill.

"Team Three," Green yelled. "Lay down a base of fire! Team Five, move forward!"

His men immediately began shooting, emptying their magazines towards the trees and muzzle flashes across the clearing.

As Tom broached the surface of the river his flailing left arm landed on a decayed infected body. The bloated abdomen burst, releasing a mass of noxious gases and rotten intestines.

He inhaled the fetid air in a massive gulp as his head rose above the foam and scum at the water's surface.

It was the finest of fine wines. No breath from the pine-scented Alps, or fields of wheat in Queensland ever tasted as sweet as the rotten, polluted mix he breathed in. Tom coughed out the stinking water and inhaled again.

"Farewell, fine fish," Tom gasped, drawing his arm out of the catfish's mouth and releasing the massive cat to return to its watery home. "I wish thee well."

He struck out for the dimly seen shore and in what seemed like moments, his hand brushed the weeds and brush lining the shore. He allowed his body to rotate vertically and found his feet on the knee deep, uneven rocks below a towering cliff. Still hyperventilating after his extended breath-hold, he paused to listen. Several hundred meters to his left, the firefight at the dam was in full swing. Red tracers crisscrossed, and Tom could tell that the attackers were well onto the dam and the roadbed itself. Somewhere above him near the clifftop, Paul and the team should be slowly retreating after making first contact, but he couldn't distinguish between the sounds at the dam and any over his head. Tom knew that he should be thankful for his narrow, improbable escape, but instead he harnessed his accumulated anger that he couldn't more rapidly reach his team's position.

The adjacent bit of cliff was still too steep to climb without specialized equipment, but Tom could see the slope ease only a few hundred meters down the beach. He started splashing in that direction.

Unlike his more laid back brother, Tom Smith had a slight mental issue. It might have been nature, and he was just born different from his relaxed sibling. It might have been nurture, and his time in the Squadron, in combat and on Wall Street. Regardless, his little brother Steve would grow calm, even jocular as already tense situations went for a ball of chalk. Not Tom. Tom got angry. Very, very angry. Under the tutelage of their heavy-handed father and later in Regiment, he'd learned control. Without control, he could lose track of the mission because the worse things went, the angrier he got.

Things had been going very poorly so far this night. In fact, things had been going wrong for a good long while now. The ball of rage that he'd squeezed, suppressed and stored away was now descending across his vision like a red curtain.

He was, therefore, less than fair dinkum. He'd been considering how to properly describe his mood while wondering if he was ever going to find the surface of this bloody lake.

He had considered a number of synonyms for perturbed.

Angry.

Upset.

Exasperated.

Fucking pissed didn't really convey it.

After far too long to consider, he had decided the perfect word was: Wrathful.

It felt well on his tongue. Wrathful. Full of wrath. It just needed the right weapon to accompany it.

Tom reflected on his inventory as he reached the bit of cliff that looked climbable. He might not have pitons or cams, but...

Tomahawks had many uses. In fact, the basic design of the tomahawk had not changed in millennia, created and recreated by civilizations founded from Oceania to Asia, from Africa to Europe. Chopping, cutting, fighting and digging, 'hawks were the original multitool. The example that he'd recovered from the devastated grocery represented the pinnacle of the art. He drew the tomahawk, reversed it and hooked the lanyard over his wrist. With a single overarm lunge he drove the weapon into the crumbly rock over his head. The tempered spike of the RMJ buried itself deeply into the decomposed granite that made up this particular shelf.

He pulled on the nonslip grip, performing a sort of one-armed pull-up while his off hand scrabbled along the sharp-edged rock until he found good, solid hand- and footholds. He squeezed his fingers on the stone shelf, looked at the cliff overhead and repeated the procedure.

Some people just needed killing. By good fortune, he was in a wrathful mood...

"Which team are we?" Jeff Paquet asked, trying to see who was shooting at them as he hid behind a tree.

Jeff had been a forklift operator in a home fittings manufacturing plant before the plague. It wasn't much of a job but Jeff wasn't really Harvard material. If he had enough money for food, booze and dope, he was happy. The rent would get paid eventually.

Then the Plague came and his comfortable life went sideways. The Gleaners just seemed like the best of many bad choices. As someone who knew which end of rifle the bullet came out of, and had enough training to not accidentally shoot teammates on a regular basis, he'd been promoted to the "special operations" part of the Gleaners.

That he was not Harvard material nor operator material was proved by his current position crouched with his back to the enemy behind a tree and just as willing to stay there, thank you.

"Uh," his team lead replied, crouched behind the bare cover of some sort of house foundation.

Marcus Clemons had been a theater manager before the Plague. He'd never really seen himself as someone who would get into "rape, loot, pillage and burn" but there were benefits and it was better than trying to survive on his own.

As someone who not only knew which end the bullet came out but also had management experience, he'd been appointed team lead. After a brief, blissful moment of shooting at their enemy, he'd used all the ammo in his gun and he'd gotten a little confused.

But combat has a tendency to make all thoughts other than "I need to LIVE" go out of your head. One forgets one's name, personal history, loved ones and even what country or state you happen to be in, much less which scratch team you'd been put in charge of.

With shots now peppering his position, he was just trying to remember the answer to the question.

"Uh..." Clemons ordered, while fumbling to reload. "We need to maneuver on them! Move left!"

It sounded like the right thing to do. Maneuver, right?

"Fuck you!" Jeff shouted. "I'm fine where *I* am. *You* maneuver!"

It was possible that Jeff was smarter than his team lead.

"Reload, Katrin!" Paul shouted, looking over at the teen. "You're pulling a dry trigger."

The teen continued to look carefully through her scope, clearly aiming at what she thought were targets. The problem was, she'd shot through her magazine and wouldn't seem to respond no matter how much he yelled.

"Katrin!" Paul yelled. "Katrin..." He tried like hell to remember the girl's last name. "Katrin!"

No response. It was like the girl didn't even hear him.

Paul took the risk, and dove from cover to cross to the girl. It took shaking her shoulder violently to get her attention.

"What?" Katrin yelled. Or thought she did. She actually was still whispering.

In combat the simplest things also become massively complicated. The brain goes to very strange places. Displacement activity becomes common. Believing you're in some other place, maybe playing a video game. A feeling of absolute unreality. Victims of violent crime often report similar experiences.

This can't really be happening.

In addition, strange things happen to the senses. Sometimes noises fade away to the point that you cannot hear your own rounds going off and yet you'd hear a pin drop behind you. Your vision often zooms—"tunnel vision" is one of the greatest dangers in combat. This last is one of the reasons that flanking attacks are so deadly: people under fire or firing rarely look to their left or right, up or down.

Military training, particularly for infantry, is mostly about preparing soldiers for the experience of combat. By placing people under the most extreme stress allowable, it partially inoculates them against the stress of combat. By requiring repetition of tasks to the point of utter boredom, preferably under stress conditions, it teaches the military person, male, female, soldier, Marine, sailor, how to just keep doing their job even when everything is going to hell around them.

Just a few months before, Katrin Jonsdottir had been a twelve-year-old student at an elite NYC prep school. Guns, per se, were anathema. Guns were icky, evil, bad. They were only good for school shootings and should be banned.

There were police to keep the bad people away. Sure, there was the occasional jerk on the subway. There were random muggings. Girls sometimes got raped. But if you knew when and where to go and not go, bad things happened to other, generally bad, people.

She'd never in her entire life expected to be in a position where bad people were shooting at her and she was supposed to shoot back. Yes, she'd taken the firearms training from the adults at the ranch, including the hunky but scary Mr. Smith and the funny but cool Cathe Astroga. But since then they'd barely had time or opportunity to practice and she was still somewhat afraid of her own gun much less that there might be actual bullets coming at her.

And she was scared so spitless, she hadn't even heard Rune yelling her name. Or could remember it.

When Mr. Rune grabbed her by the shoulder she jumped in fear and started to swing the barrel around.

"KATRIN!" the man shouted at her, blocking the swing of Katrin's weapon. "KATRIN! RELOAD!"

"Who?" Katrin whispered as she was shaken. She wasn't even sure where she was. She didn't know who was shaking her.

"KATRIN!" Paul shouted, leaning down and screaming in her ear. "KATRIN...SOMEBODY DAUGHTER? YOU! YOU'RE KATRIN! DO YOU HEAR ME?"

I'm Katrin, Katrin thought, dreamily. *Katrin Jonsdottir.*

"SHOOT THE BAD PEOPLE!" Paul shouted, actually pulling the trigger once for Katrin.

The initial fusillade from both sides had died off and now there was an intermittent crackle of shots. For his part, Luke Conner was trying to remember all his drills that he'd learned from his Special Forces dad and later practiced at the ranch.

Acquire the target, front sight focus, squeeze the trigger to a surprise break, maintain your sight picture and service the target again as needed.

His optic didn't have night vision, but the bright red dot in the Aimpoint was clear. Place the red dot on the target and squeeze...

Lather-rinse-repeat. And again. Again.

The enemy had gone to ground and wasn't even laying down much of a base of fire. Didn't mean they couldn't kill you.

He carefully targeted a shoulder that was sticking out from behind a too-small pine tree.

There was a yelp and the shoulder jerked out of sight.

"I'M SHOT!" Jeff screamed, landing on his side and dropping his shotgun. "SOMEBODY HELP ME!"

He whimpered from the pain. The bullet had entered his side and it burned like fire. He could feel the blood pumping out of the wound, exactly like you'd think a super-soaker would feel like if it was inside you and pointed outwards. Pump! Pump! Pump!

"I'M SHOT!" he repeated. "HELP! I NEED HELP!"

Paul reloaded and targeted the guy writhing around on the ground. It took four rounds to get him to lie still and be a good Gleaner, but it was worth it. It sounded like he and maybe one other person on his team were actually shooting.

None of the remaining Gleaner soldiers in Green's little task force were as well trained as the late Officer Jason Young. One of the teams constituted Green's reserve. It was led by one Timothy McFadden, one of Green's prison recruits, five years, armed robbery, rape and assault with a deadly weapon. Team one was as close to elite as Green had left.

McFadden wasn't elite, but he could do math. They'd started off with twenty-five men in five teams.

One team had been taken out by the invisible electrocution trap.

One had been taken out by that asshole ex-cop.

That left fifteen.

When Green had ordered team three to lay down fire and team five to move forward, it had been orders to his two front teams to engage. Instead they were all lying down behind any cover, such as hadn't already been shot by the defenders, and firing more or less blind. McFadden's opposite numbers were dug in, and firing back with accuracy and enthusiasm.

Worse, they seemed to have plenty of ammunition, or at least it felt that way to McFadden, who had zero experience in actual combat.

Tim McFadden liked the benefits of the Gleaners. A career criminal, the average Gleaner work day was basically what he'd done his whole life. All he had to do was threaten or hurt people and take their stuff, enjoy the occasional rape, and then he got paid, sort of. All that was required was not pissing off the guy in charge or one of his even crazier Guards.

What he did not like was being under fire from what was obviously a real operator team. They were putting out more rounds than Charlotte PD SWAT.

As soon as it was clear that Green's plan had gone totally to shit, he jumped up from his own position behind a tree and took off into the wet, dark woods.

McFadden wasn't exactly sure where he was going next, but it was anywhere but here. Mrs. McFadden's boy knew when to cut his losses. Worst case, he'd just claim that he got lost and rejoin Green after a victory, which in his opinion looked pretty unlikely at this point.

He didn't even tell the rest of his guys. They could take care of themselves. Or not. Fuck 'em.

Then again, looking around, he didn't see anybody else nearby. Those shitters had already bolted, the cowards! The irony of his indignation was completely lost on him.

He'd just about made it to the road, trying to figure out how to get the hell out of these fucking woods without poking his eyes out on low tree branches, running into one of those invisible electric chairs, or a zombie or another Gleaner, when he felt a tug on his collar. It turned into a massive force that jerked him off his feet and nearly dropped McFadden to his ass. Before he could recover, a powerful vise around his throat levered his upper body upright.

He tried to shout but the hold on his neck was choking him into silence. Whoever was holding his jacket was massive and the painful grip slowly forced his head to one side, affording him a brief view of another man, a Gleaner by his equipment, lying facedown at their feet. McFadden felt his weight leave his feet as he was lifted up into the air like that guy that Darth Vader choked and killed.

But it wasn't the Force that killed him. McFadden felt a burning hot line drawn across the side of his neck. A flood of heat spread across the skin of his right shoulder and arm, pulsing in time to his heart.

In his last conscious moments he heard a new voice say, "That's four."

∽ ⊙ ∾

Emily Bloome hadn't fired a shot.

She understood the concept of bad people. She wasn't in denial about the existence of evil or the reality of the new world, like her ex-girlfriend and fellow teacher. She knew history. But now that she was in a gunfight with people whom she'd never met and yet were trying to kill her, she was starting to mentally stutter. The noise was awful. The screams were awful. Her pants were soaking wet, whether from the rain saturated loam or from peeing herself, she didn't know.

She didn't want to know.

She wasn't sure why she'd agreed to this. It was completely and totally insane. Especially after losing Smith. They should have turned back, then. But... they hadn't. And now here she was, getting shot at, and being expected to shoot people she'd never even met because they were "bad" people. Which they were, but the reality of personally shooting, killing, was almost as shattering as the booms of the guns of the men trying to kill her, and cracks of their bullets as they passed by or crunched into her log shelter.

A glance over her shoulder revealed Eric carefully aiming and shooting around the edge of another heavy log. Emily's mind wandered, seeking traction. What did "bad" mean after all? How did you define it? Criminals could be rehabilitated. They should be trying to persuade them that their actions weren't the right actions.

On the other hand, they were shooting at her and her students. Conversation didn't really seem possible at the moment.

But killing people?

Maybe it wouldn't count if she just shot towards them. To scare them. Make them leave. If she didn't have to watch. Yes, she would shoot, but not at them. She wasn't even looking, see? Emily crouched up enough that although her head was still well beneath the log top, her rifle was now more or less parallel to the ground and aiming, as far as she could tell, towards and over the "bad" guys. In their general direction, sure. But with no real intent of harm.

She started squeezing her trigger rapidly, and flinched as the hot casings pattered on top of her hood and jacket. She didn't stop though, letting the recoil of the weapon move the barrel at random between shots.

∽ ○ ဆ

Marcus Clemons decided he had to do something. Most of his guys were down, he was pretty sure. Jeff sure as hell was dead. He was pretty sure Jeff was on his team.

Clemons peered around the tree as he reloaded his Winchester Model 1100 shotgun. This wasn't the right place for a shotgun, but at least his was a semi auto with rifle sights and not some fudd-gun. He'd wanted to tell Green they needed ARs but... you didn't tell Green stuff. You just did what you were told and tried not to get killed.

Maybe he could get close enough for a kill shot, like *Call of Duty*, and then get a better gun.

Time to get bold!

Despite Emily's nonlethal intent, resting an AR-15 style rifle on a fallen tree and firing blind, "over their heads," wasn't an actual aiming concept. One could point well up into the air, but if you just leaned around like Emily, and most of the Gleaners for that matter, had been doing, and tried to fire blind... well, you were firing blind. The tree log didn't care about her intent and it was actually doing a good job of keeping her rounds traveling at the same height.

As a result, her shots were consistently passing through the Gleaner area at about chest height to anyone who happened to be present and standing.

Or someone choosing that moment to starting charging forward.

One saying among experienced infantrymen is "It's not the one with your name on it you've got to worry about. It's all the ones that say 'To whom it may concern.'"

Emily had not, as Katrin had, put a name on her rounds. There was no particular target.

Nonetheless, one of Emily's bullets, intended to send as nonviolent a message as it was possible for rounds from a combat rifle to do, cracked right through Marcus's pistol-grade plate carrier, pierced his sternum and then severed his descending aorta before tumbling, as light rounds are wont to do, and broke his spine before embedding itself in the light backpack he wore.

Good bye, Marcus.

The Skirmish of Watts Bar Point would one day be described in a history book as "a small but decisive action that was one of the foundational battles of post-Plague civilization." Many legends made it into a latter-day Alamo with a better ending.

The reality was it was one shambolic clusterfuck of a battle featuring the seriously deficient versus utterly incompetent, with a merest edge going to the former.

Thankfully, that would be enough.

"ARE ANY OF YOU LAZY BASTARDS GOING TO *DO* ANYTHING?" Harlan Green screamed.

Half the team had slowed, and then receded behind him so they were hidden in the darkness and barely firing. The other half was either lying low, or dead, like that idiot that had just charged across the clearing. Harlan wasn't even sure how many were still there, but he was certain that no one replied to his yell. He hated being out of control! "YOU'RE ALL FUCKING USELESS!"

The dark that surrounded him deigned not to answer.

"Intolerable," Green muttered to himself. "I've got to start recruiting a better class of thug..."

He leaned around the tree, risking his own precious hide, and used his superior night optics to scan around. There was a figure prone behind a tree but enough of the figure was in view to target. He aimed carefully and squeezed off a single shot.

"Mr. Rune!" Luke yelled. "I'm hit!"

Luke wasn't sure how bad it was but it was bad. The round had punched into his side, hard.

Another cracked near him and he tried to determine where they were coming from. But he couldn't find any valid targets. Most of the Gleaners seemed to be down already.

The wound was really starting to hurt, and he began to feel lightheaded, almost nauseated.

"Help! I'm bleeding bad!"

Luke felt himself slipping away, and the world grew even darker. He didn't feel the weapon slip from his hands.

When Marcus had charged forward, he'd left his Winchester off safe, which wasn't a surprise considering the overall weapons handling skills of the Gleaners. But as a result, when the man fell he performed, without volition, a last, small but crucial action.

The pain of the round hitting his chest caused his trigger finger to spasm, and his shotgun discharged one last round of buckshot.

By equally sheer bloody bad luck, one of the unaimed pellets struck Paul right in his unarmored buttocks, burning like fire.

"Well, shit," he muttered. He tried moving experimentally, but he discovered that moving his right leg created stabbing pains that radiated from the deep muscle in his hips and ass all the way up his spine. Running away was going to be a problem.

He tried to listen for Connor, for the teen's voice rapidly faded.

Most of the fire had fallen off. There apparently weren't many of the Gleaners left to shoot, but a few rounds still snapped overhead or slapped into the trees around him. But a single shooter was enough in a situation like this one. Paul took a deep breath.

"Emily!" he yelled. "Emily! Can you hear me?"

"Yes!" Emily shouted back as she continued to trying to force a backwards magazine into the underside of her rifle.

"I'm going to provide cover fire!" Paul yelled. "Don't shoot. Get..." He fumbled for the boy's name. "The kid next to you! Get his attention! When I start shooting, you grab him and Katrin and get the hell out of here. I'll cover you!"

"Okay!" Emily shouted, sounding almost relieved. "I can do that. Eric! Eric! Can you hear me...?"

As the rest of the team started to pull out, Paul rocked his selector switch from semi to full auto. He squeezed the trigger for short bursts, laying down fire on every spot that might hide a remaining Gleaner. He could see some vague shapes in his night vision, despite the rain and he concentrated on those positions. He rapidly emptied two magazines, then a third, smoothly reloading each time.

The last one ran dry and he dipped into his hip pouch, finding it empty. He checked the magazines in his chest rig. There was one more and he rocked it into his rifle. Paul couldn't hear anyone else shooting, and there were no sounds of movement behind him, so the team had already retreated a safe distance.

He flexed his leg, and bit back a scream at the burning, stabbing sensation as the great muscle above his thigh moved the shotgun pellet around. Nope, he wasn't walking out of here.

But if they'd slowed the Gleaners long enough and the rest of the team made it back to the dam alive, he'd call it a win. He peered through his sights and scanned for targets.

❦ ⊖ ❦

CRA-CRA-CRACK! CRA-CRA-CRA-CRACK!

Harlan crouched lower behind the tree as somebody on the other side began firing short bursts on full auto, peppering each likely hiding spot with three to four rounds before moving to the next. After several bursts, there was a longer pause, presumably as the shooter replenished their ammunition. There'd been shouting, and then the sounds of movement and now this. He was no tactical expert, but even he knew that expending that much ammo on auto, in this visibility, was wasteful. That was one of the reasons that he'd limited weapons capable of automatic fire to his lieutenants who he trusted to judiciously use the increasingly scarce ammunition.

Like Young.

Harlan frowned at the memory as a few rounds snapped close by, refocusing his attention. He peered carefully around and spotted the sustained muzzle flashes. Whoever it was seemed to have plenty of the needful. The shooter was still using bursts, not just panic firing. That suggested a certain amount of intelligence and self-control. That could be a problem, especially since Harlan seemed to be about out of people. He noted that the stay-behind was remaining in one place, judging by the sound and muzzle flash. Better, there seemed to be only one person and he was pulling one of those "I'll stay put to cover you" things.

That was the kind of stupidity that made Harlan certain of victory.

Because the shooter would run out of rounds sooner or later, and now Harlan knew exactly where he was.

Paul ran through a final string of fire and went dry on his rifle so he laid it aside and drew his Glock. He couldn't hear any movement on the trail behind him, so maybe Emily had successfully extracted the survivors. He leaned around the tree and scanned the area. He could see one figure in the distance, farther back than most of the Gleaners, and he targeted it with the pistol, firing a few shots just to keep the shadow at a distance.

A much different timbre accompanied the next string of shots from the hold-out.

Pop—pop—pop.

Harlan smiled.

The last of the group was down to pistol and the shooting wasn't even in the right direction. That suited him just fine. He'd maneuvered farther to one side, finding a couple of fresh Gleaner corpses, and one stranger, a very young teenage male. The age of the victim was good news, if it meant that the defenders were down to high school kids.

He leaned around and tried to figure out which tree hid the shooter. His goggles had the same drawbacks as all night optics, and in this case the very limited field of view required him to move his head slowly side to side, panning around to spot the bright spots in the night.

His remaining men were where? . . . well, that was a good question. However, his target was *right there*.

Harlan lay down in the prone and fired an economical burst at the tree hiding the shooter. Then he jumped to his feet and ran forward and to the side, hip firing in the general direction to cover his movement, just as the books said to do.

Paul cursed as the rounds cracked around his position. Okay, so maybe staying behind sucked a little harder than he expected.

He tried to cover the open area with the pistol and banged some blind rounds around the tree but he wasn't sure if he was even firing at the remaining Gleaners.

Harlan made it to cover and considered his next move. One enemy left, pistol only. If only he had a grenade this would be easy. He needed to find grenades. Harlan made a mental note.

He reloaded, considering how many magazines he had left. Not many. Finding mags for an MP-7 was tough. The previous owner had had only one. He considered reloading ammo from his backpack but he'd been dropping his empty magazines as he went.

He'd just have to go with what he had.

Or, maybe, talk? Whoever was left was probably thinking about how they'd not like to die.

"Hey! You listening?"

Am I? Paul wondered.

Sure. The longer this jackass talked, the longer the team had to escape.

"I'm listening!" he shouted back.

≈ ⊖ ≈

"Hey, listen," Harlan muttered, considering his options. More loudly, "We don't have to do this. You're down to your pistol. That's a losing proposition for you."

"So why you talking?" the voice yelled back. "Why not just shoot?"

"You could get lucky," Harlan said, admitting nothing that wasn't obvious. "Besides, you're still alive, even if you're alone. That makes you a survivor. Hard. I need people like you. I reward talent. Why take the chance on dying? Just change sides."

"Eat shit and die," the man yelled. "I'm not a mercenary for hire!"

"Oh, are you a believer?" Harlan said. "You're a rare breed now. Sure you don't want to live through this?"

"Bring it, bitch," the target said, sounding confident.

Harlan liked the attitude, even if it was mere bluster.

"I like your spirit," Green said, wondering if maybe he didn't really want to try to recruit this guy. It seemed like all of his own people had run away and here this guy was standing his ground, fearless. Worst case, he could get a little closer before he finished this guy off.

"Look, let's keep talking. I'm coming up so we don't have to yell at each other. Don't shoot."

What the fuck? Paul wondered. *Hell, keep this asshole talking.*

In the near distance, the rifle fire that had been steadily increasing was joined by the sound of overlapping explosions. That was either very good or very bad, and there was no way to tell from here. He could hear deeper reports and the roar of something that sounded like surf, which made no sense since they were nowhere near the ocean.

Paul looked at his pistol. He didn't harbor any illusions about his chances. Lamed, alone and low on ammunition was not a winning hand. He made up his mind. One mag in, one out, let this guy get close and then take the best shot that he could.

"Okay," Paul said after pausing long enough to appear that he was seriously considering the Gleaner's offer. "Come on up."

"No shooting," the man said.

"Sure," Paul said. "Word of honor of a banker. We'll just talk."

He waited until he heard the crack of a branch then leaned around and dumped the mag towards the sound.

The volume of return fire was unpleasant. Paul was struck twice in quick succession. The round that skidded off his back plate felt like a hammer, but the near miss was worse. It opened the sleeve of his jacket as neatly as a fresh scalpel, skimming along the length of his left forearm and burning like hell. The moist forest loam had already soaked through the material of his trousers, and now fresh blood added a new note to the smell of mud and decay. The arm wound numbed his left hand, and the instant-on sensation of pins and needles made him sag.

Paul half rolled to one side and went for a one-handed pistol reload. Using his injured arm to pin the gun to his hip, he used his right hand to eject the spent magazine and replaced it with the last one. He got ready to lean around the tree for one last try.

Harlan had noted that the shooter favored his primary shooting hand, always going to the right, so he dodged in the opposite direction.

Bingo. Intelligence over guts, every time.

"Why, hello there," he said to the man sprawled on the ground. "Let's get acquainted."

"Aw, fuck," Paul muttered as he felt the barrel of the rifle touch his skull.

He relaxed his grip on the handgun, and it dangled from his forefinger before falling to the ground. Paul raised his hands and rolled onto his side, but motion used his injured ham, where the damned shotgun pellet was buried deeply in the muscle. He gritted his teeth.

"Shot?" his captor asked solicitously.

"Not by you. You can't shoot for shit," Paul said. "Just shot in the ass by some random clown."

"And where did you put your head that it was unwelcome?" the gunman said, painfully banging his rifle muzzle on the bandage that covered Paul's existing head wound. "Maybe you should work at not shooting when you promise to talk!"

"I promised as a banker," Paul said, chuckling despite his situation. "You'd trust a banker? We fuck anyone over for enough money. You? I'd fuck you over for free."

"I'm sorry to hear that," the man answered, then kicked him squarely on the dark gooey stain that was seeping across the seat of Paul's trousers. "I just wanted to ask you a few questions. Wait—you're a banker? Would you happen to be from Bank of the Americas?"

The standing man added a kick for emphasis.

"Ahh," Paul groaned as the pain in his legs, ass and back soared higher. He braced himself with one arm to avoid rolling sideways. He glanced at the Gleaner and considered his gear. Even in the partial-darkness, Paul could tell that the man was well equipped and lightly built. A shadow moved in the trees behind his captor, who was taking his sweet time looking at Paul down the length of a thin nose, the looks of which would be greatly improved if Paul could just smash it flat. "Maybe. You must be the team lead."

"Governor," the man said, correcting him. "Harlan Green. Pleased to meet you, Mister 'Used-to-be-a-Banker.' If you worked for Bank of the Americas, you must have worked for a man named Smith. His little group has become a thorn in my side, and it's been a pleasure killing you off one at a time."

"Oh, god," Paul groaned. "You're a talker. Jesus, not that. Just shoot me and end it."

"Soon, Mr. Banker. First, where's your boss? I'd like to talk to him."

"Fuck off and die," Paul said. "Save your time and end it."

"How many are at the dam?" Green asked persistently.

"More than enough to stop you, prick," Paul said. He saw the shadow move behind Green again, drifting closer.

Harlan's radio broke squelch, and though he'd already turned it down to avoid giving his position away, it was still too loud and distracting. He reached down with his left hand and twisted the volume knob till it clicked off.

Though the battle was out of sight behind the forested peninsula, the firing at the dam had built to a thundering crescendo. Harlan knew that he had places to be and people to kill. However, any information that he could get from the wounded man might help. Time to get a better look at what he had to work with.

He fished around in a pocket and withdrew a Cyalume, snapped it and dropped it in front of his catch. They'd seen zero zombies since crossing the river, the defenders had all withdrawn, and let's face it, he really wanted a look at his captive.

Below him, the soldier rolled all the way over and returned Harlan's gaze.

"Hey, asshole," the bleeding man said. "You *really* should look behind you."

"I admire your optimism," Harlan said as he raised his rifle and aimed at the one leg that wasn't bleeding. He felt the beginnings of the delicious rush that accompanied each demonstration of his power, each time that he consummated his will. "Does that ever work?"

His captive stayed silent. Pity that he couldn't take longer to enjoy this, but needs must.

"I'll start with the legs, then each forearm and go from there until you are more cooperative," Harlan warned the man, knowing that no matter what he learned, he'd add this one to his collection. *The lack of hair would be a challenge. Hmm.*

"You just going to stand there?" his captive asked.

"I'm pointing a rifle at you," Harlan answered. "That's hardly just 'standing here.'"

Without warning, Harlan Green felt a point of burning cold just barely kiss the skin under his Adam's apple. He froze, perfectly motionless.

"Mate," a gravelly voice whispered intimately in his ear. "He wasn't talking to you."

Green very carefully thumbed the MP7 on safe and slowly allowed his weapon to sag until the sling held its weight.

CHAPTER 21

Dragon had received Loki's orders to advance across the bridge with ill grace, but he did it. No one disobeyed that big fucker. Still, no one had said that Dragon had to be on foot when he did it. The governor had found a working armored truck somewhere, something surplused to a local yokel cop after the war on terror. Loki called it an emrap, whatever the hell that meant, but Dragon called it bad-ass! The big gun was removed, but there was a turret, and lights, and it still had armored windows and everything. The six huge tires lifted it way up in the air, and he had a great view over the sides of the bridge. Ahead, muzzle flashes were visible and the occasional bullet struck his armor before wheeling off into the dark. The vehicle lurched and Dragon's helmet smacked the turret interior. He suppressed a curse as the driver inexpertly slowed, preparing to ram an obstacle. A crunching sound signaled that he had breasted yet another concrete barrier and was taking advantage of the machine's bulk to shove the obstruction out of the way.

Dragon spun the turret to look backwards for a look-see. Behind them, the now darkened bridge was littered with zombie corpses both old and new, jumbled Jersey barriers and improvised metal wire fencing that had been crushed flat by his bitchin' ride.

Closely trailing his tank was a big dark blue semi tractor set up as a towing rig. A couple of pickup trucks were well to the rear, dismounting their troops. One of Green's tame mechanics had welded a bunch of shit to the eighteen-wheeler, Mad-Max style. It was supposed to help push the lead vehicle if needed, but so far it was just something that the upper deck assault team of fifty could hide behind, and they were doing a good job of staying tightly clustered in the shadow of its tailgate as the little convoy crept across the never ending span. The defenders' rounds clanged off the armor of Dragon's pseudo-tank or skipped off the pavement and whirred past, but the troops were safe from anything to the direct front.

Dragon estimated that they were just about halfway across. He'd been shooting one of their few machine guns, the one that he and Young had captured in fact, but it wasn't as much fun as he'd hoped. The damn thing was heavy, the controls were stiff and the thing kept jamming. It seemed like every twenty or thirty rounds he'd have to open the lid, fiddle with the belt of bullets, then align everything, then smack the lid down again, work the handle and see if it shot. Talk about a pain in the ass.

Still, when it ran, it was fucking great to watch his bullets hit the target building with little puffs, or best of all, when the ruby tracers ricocheted up and away at crazy angles. For the moment, he wasn't shooting. He was saving an entire belt to blast the concrete blockhouse from close range, or maybe that crazy lightning-shooting smokestack. He sure as hell wasn't gonna get within a football field of that fucker until it was knocked flat. Screw Loki and his plan to save any technology!

To be fair, there really wasn't anyone to shoot at, just flickering little lights that he thought were muzzle flashes, and not many of those. It was actually really noisy and confusing. Worse, it was taking a long time, because the driver wasn't in any hurry. Hitting a barrier too hard could bust the truck, which sucked, because these things were supposed to be invulnerable or something. Still, Dragon appreciated the care that his driver exhibited. The last thing they needed was to get high-centered in the middle of the span.

Still, they were nearly there. There was only one more row of barriers and then he could ram the buildings, push the troops up and it would be the same routine of killing, looting and raping all night, like they always did. He smiled a little in anticipation, stroking the spade grips of the captured weapon with his blue-gloved hands.

The semi flashed its lights, and his radio squawked.

"Hey, Dragon," the second driver said, almost whining. "I

musta run over some wire or some shit, I gotta stop and clear it, or we're gonna lose the rig."

"God-damnit!" Dragon cursed. Loki was going to have his ass if they didn't get across.

Fuck it, time to shoot up some rounds.

"These guys are attacking blind," Kaplan remarked coolly, changing magazines. "They're putting down decent amounts of fire but they aren't hitting anything."

"Are you complaining?" Detkovic asked, peeking above the barricade. "Or suggesting that it's finally time?"

He'd ceded the control panel seat to Brandy, who was inside, looking at her monitors.

"So..." asked Brandy.

"Smith is offline, and now Rune isn't answering calls," Kaplan replied. "I think it's probably about that time."

"Gents, what it is, is use it or lose it time," she said. "The elements on the bridge are through more than half the barriers and traps, and if we don't go live now, some of them are going to get through. As it is, I can't do anything about the trucks, they're naturally electrically isolated already. Judging from these—"

She gestured at the dials.

"Most of the Teslas are down and Big Bad is getting shot up."

A fresh burst of fire stitched across their building. A single round whined into their room, burying itself in the interior opposing wall. Everyone flinched away, except Robbins, who punched out another shot from the deer rifle he'd appropriated from his daughter.

"I'll take care of the MRAP," Kaplan said. "Butters, give me a hand, but keep your head down."

"On it," the girthy engineer replied.

The two squatted and lifted their only heavy weapon, the grenade launcher Smith had salvaged from their flight out of New York.

"Wondered when you were gonna use that," Stantz remarked. "We gonna take turns?"

"We've got just one partial box of ammunition, so gotta go with 'no' on that one," Kaplan replied as they dropped the heavy mechanism on the pintle mount inside the door. Detkovic stumbled for a second, tripping on the sandbags that were heaped around the legs of the mount. "Not enough ammo to dent the infected, but it should be enough for a couple oversized trucks. Once I flush the infantry, you get on them and look for any obvious leaders."

"How are grenades going to stop a tank?" Brandy asked.

"Well, for one, it's not a tank," Detkovic answered, kicking the sandbags back into place. "It's really a lightly armored truck. Two, it doesn't really shoot grenades in the John Wayne sense. They're actually high explosive—dual purpose. Each one is a little shaped charge combined with regular explosive. They should do a number on anything but an actual tank. I wish we had more of 'em."

"This very gun did for the FBI's trucks in Manhattan," Kaplan added as he lifted the end of their only belt of grenades towards the open action of the gun. "Butters, distance to target?"

"Range four-fifty, target vehicles and troops in the open," Detkovic said, peeking above the window rim for an instant. It was a moment too long. There was a wet smacking sound and instantly afterwards another heavy bullet smacked into the far wall of their shelter. Detkovic stumbled back and then fell to his side, utterly still.

Kaplan glanced down at the fresh corpse without expression and Brandy cried out, "No!" Robbins glanced up, then reacquired his cheek weld without comment and sent another round downrange.

"Everyone keep your damn heads down!" Kaplan said, adjusting the launcher's feed slide assembly before smacking down the cover. "Stantz, get over here and get this belt straight!"

"Ah, Kaplan?" Brandy asked, almost hyperventilating. Still, she kept her hand hovering over the system controls. Unlike Stantz's elaborate firing system, she had a simple on/off button highlighted on her laptop's screen. "Now?"

"Now."

Loki stayed well to the rear, urging his men forward with shouts. Very few wanted to be close to him, so as long as he moved from cover to cover, the assaulters stayed mostly ahead of him. Mercifully, the amount of fire that had held up their advance was now dropping off. As far as he could tell, the two machine guns that had alternated between spraying his force and the vehicles over his head were now either out of ammunition or broken.

"Move up, keep moving!" he yelled. He noticed a pair of men lagging, hiding behind a the lip of a maintenance stairwell, gripping the metal rail. He jogged forward, equipment rattling.

They had to move all the way across before the defenders came up with a new surprise, and these two slow pokes clearly needed a little encouragement.

Before he could reach them, bright orange and yellow sparks popped all around him. Several screams of surprise sounded ahead of him. He crouched, and checked for incoming fire. There was none. He looked ahead to see the pair of laggards slumped, nearly lying on their sides. Curiously, they kept a firm grip on the railing. Small wisps of smoke rose from their hands and Loki made the connection.

They were electrocuted. The defenders had wired the dam.

Well, fuck.

Ahead of him a few more men screamed in fear, though fewer than before, as their fellows were fried in place. More than one Gleaner dropped directly onto a live contact, where their clothing smoldered and in a few cases, burst into flames. There were some further flashes and pops as humans involuntarily served as electrical resistors, but mostly there was an eerie silence as all of the shooting from his team died away.

"Fuck this shit fuck this shit fuck thi—" a Gleaner said, shouldering past Loki on his way to the rear. The big Guard was so surprised that he made no immediate move in response, which saved his life. As the fleeing Gleaner stepped between a pair of metal studs set on each side of the walkway that Loki had just used, a finger-thick spark snapped, dropping the man to the rough concrete, where he twitched for a moment.

Loki considered pushing up, but warily looked at every surface. There was metal everywhere and absent a correlating Gleaner body, there was no way to tell what was now coursing with deadly electricity and what was safe. The strong smell of ozone was present, overcoming the slight breeze over the river.

"Governor, this is Loki," he transmitted. "I've got a situation."

There was no reply.

He looked over his shoulder at the dark river bank behind him. Hmmm.

He heard Dragon's voice and carefully reached for his radio, avoiding brushing against anything metal.

"This is Loki."

Hopefully things were progressing a little better above.

꩜ ⊖ ꩜

"That's it, the dam is hot," Brandy reported. "I'm already getting about sixty percent shorts on my traps, so the bad guys just ran into a wall."

"Electrical shorts are good?" Robbins asked, searching for his next target.

"They are if they're made from the bodies of your enemies," retorted the TVA manager.

"Speaking of going hot," Kaplan said. He depressed the butterfly trigger between the spade grips of the Mark Nineteen.

"Okay, that's the last one," the driver said over the intercom as they slowly scraped past a final concrete barrier.

"Finally!" Dragon replied, reaching for the radio. "Loki, it's me, we're moving up."

He waited for a moment and repeated the call before he heard Loki reply, asking for a report on what the defenders were doing. He shrugged and spun the turret to the front, just in time to see two small explosions strike the causeway in front of him. The next two struck the front of his "tank," and for a moment his world stopped as the blast and concussion rattled his head.

He glanced down past his feet. He could see the driver's arm bent back at an unnatural angle, but the man wasn't moving.

"Shit-shit-shit."

Another series of explosions rocked the vehicle, which ground to a complete stop.

Because the big gun burped out five to six rounds a second, Kaplan *carefully* squeezed another sub-second burst. Mindful of his limited ammunition and the relatively high rate of fire of his weapon, he was trying to be economical with his ammo. A glance at his remaining supply revealed perhaps a third left. Fortunately, he'd already stopped both vehicles, which had sustained several hits each. The Gleaner infantry was clustered around the back of the farther truck, a large eighteen-wheeler with ad hoc plating that covered the engine and most of the windshield. It might have been a morale booster for the Gleaners, but in practice it had merely provided enough resistance to arm the projectiles that he was lofting.

"Robbie, the rest of you, get ready, I'm going to scatter the ones at the back," he warned. "When they run, cut as many down as you can."

"Set." "Yessir." "Oh, hell yes!" came the replies from Robbins and company.

Kaplan carefully sighted, guided by the orange flames licking underneath the punctured fuel tank on the converted truck. He loosed a longer burst and waited another second for the slow projectiles to reach his target before releasing his final rounds.

Dragon had kicked the warped rear hatch of his tank open, and then fallen out onto the rough concrete. His ears were ringing, his vision was blurry and his legs wouldn't work properly. Using only his arms, he pulled himself the rest of the way out.

"Hey!" he tried yelling to the other survivors that were dimly visible, peeking around the end of the wrecker. It was stopped a couple of lengths behind his own wrecked vehicle. There were actual holes visible in the windshield armor. Both front tires were flat and a growing puddle of diesel smoldered sullenly beneath the cab. He tried again, but couldn't hear himself. "Hey! Hey guys!"

He began to crawl, but before he made it halfway to the next vehicles, several explosions trip-hammered across the causeway, making it flex like a trampoline. The explosions lifted him from the surface and lofted him forward. Dragon landed squarely in burning diesel, and began screaming. He flailed with his arms, ignoring the sound of shrapnel as it *whickered* over his head and pinged off the chassis of the now destroyed semi.

Fresh screaming sounded from his men, and then a second string of explosions blew that to hell as well.

Dragon rolled himself out of the fire, smothering the flames on his trousers. Terrified, panting, he kept his face down. He could make out the snap of high velocity rounds overhead, their cadence as steady as a metronome.

Maybe if he held very, *very* still, the defenders might overlook him.

As it turns out, dual purpose shaped charge grenades will also do a number on unarmored troops in the open. Two grenades from Kaplan's last string burst on the concrete within five meters of Dragon's position, fragmenting his body so badly that any identification, if someone had cared enough to bother, would have relied on the tattered and scorched TSA-approved blue gloves he loved so much.

Loki heard the explosions overhead, and that decided the matter, right there. Green was out of contact, Dragon was out of contact and the dam assault was obviously a failure. It looked like nearly his entire force was wiped out.

Waiting here was a sucker bet. He'd have to chance any remaining electrical defenses behind him and get back to the take off point. Without a backward glance, he began to jog back the way his force had come.

"I think that's about the last of them," Robbins said, peering through the variable optic on his rifle. His left hand was curled under his chest, meeting the stock firmly tucked into his right shoulder. He reached up with his right hand and rotated the scope's bezel, increasing the magnification to 8X. "Hey, isn't that big guy the one that Smith pointed out?"

"Looking," Kaplan said, snapping his rifle back up to scan the dam walkway. The poor lighting made it hard to find his quarry, and by the time he caught the running figure in his sights, the man was six hundred yards out. "Contact! Robbie, high value target, spillway number nine, ENGAGE!"

"Running away, easy peasy," Robbins replied. He was sprawled on an elevated table in the back of the room where Jordan had set her shooting mat. A small, red plastic ammunition box was open at his side and the serried rows of ammunition were nearly empty. The rifle moved minutely on the sandbag, and he fired.

"Miss," Kaplan barked. "Low and right. Reengage."

Loki heard the ricochet and the snap of the round as it sped by. Still running, he still had time to register the two sounds nearly at the same time and understand the significance.

Still supersonic when it skipped. Heavy rifle, very fast round.

He began dodging as much as his running would permit, first moving towards the center, then towards the railing on his left, and back again. The remainder of the dam stretched in front of him.

Robbins ejected the spent case smoothly, maintaining his sight picture.

"Wind?" he asked, sliding the bolt forward and locking it down.

"Left to right," Kaplan directed, watching the figure dwindle in his own optic. "Gusting to ten. Holdover five."

"Set," Robbins said, barely whispering as he exhaled, balancing the little chevron of the crosshair above and to the left of the running man's head.

"Send it."

Robbins finished staging the trigger and just thought about completing the trigger stroke.

The three-hundred Winmag barked, punishing his shoulder.

Loki had put another fifty meters between him and those persistent defenders. He was still randomly jerking his stride right and left. He couldn't see any Gleaners ahead him, but he knew that there would still be a handful of friendly snipers as well as the zombie patrols keeping the staging area clear.

Those fools had better not shoot at him!

If he couldn't reach Green on radio and the boss didn't show up soon, they would pile into the vehicles and head back to camp. There was no way to get the dam before winter, but next spring, they could ret—

Robbins's round was fired from a hunter's rifle, one intended to one-shot drop large North American game animals that could weigh up to half a ton. The very high muzzle velocity and streamlined shape helped it retain considerable energy even at long ranges, which was why the military used that caliber for distant targets.

However, bullets can shatter on bone, such as the human spine. When that happens, the bone fragments become further projectiles, enlarging the area of destruction within the body. A side effect of such a spine shot is that nerves are instantly severed, sharply reducing all sensation of pain below the injury.

Lucky Loki.

The round easily penetrated the ceramic plate designed to stop slower and lighter bullets. It did deform considerably, which only served to make the wound channel wider. However, as luck would have it, the next thing that happened to the slug was fragmentation. Loki felt a massive sledgehammer blow, perfectly centered between his shoulder blades. Nerveless, his hands opened and his weapon began to fall the length of his sling. His legs abruptly stopped working and he felt a tremendous pressure in this throat, but he couldn't cough. Very, very slowly it seemed to Loki, the dirty gray concrete of the dam walkway floated up to meet him.

∞—⊖—∞

"Hit," Kaplan reported. "Target down. Reengage."

Robbins cycled the bolt and fired again. The bundle of black rags didn't even twitch.

"Hit." His spotter reached over and smacked Robbins's shoulder. "Rounds complete. Nice job."

Tom kept the beard of his tomahawk on the Gleaner leader's throat as he used his left hand to methodically strip Green of weapons. A tidy pile accumulated. A pistol clunked onto the rifle already on the ground. A small knife from inside Green's waistband tinkled on top of the pistol.

"You're late, Boss," Rune said. In the background, small arms fire had increased. Tom could make out sustained automatic fire. The final assault was underway.

"I had to find a friendly catfish," Tom replied absently, reaching around to pat his prisoner's pockets with his left hand. "There are catfish a many, but friendly catfish are few."

"I have no idea what you mean," Rune said. "What catfish?"

"A noble steed, a veritable horse of the river," Tom said with artificial jocularity. "Give me moment lad, I need to deal with our company, here."

In his peripheral vision, he could see Rune shrug, but Tom kept his eyes on the locus of his wrath.

Green was still holding preternaturally still, perhaps sensing Tom's mood, or maybe he was just deeply concerned about Tom's blood-soaked 'hawk, which continued to hover just below Green's chin. A simple rearwards pull would hook the lower point of the blade in the prisoner's throat, just like gaffing a fish.

"Roight, mate," Tom said, still facing his prisoner's back. "If you want to live a little longer, you'll hold very still while we relieve you of the unpleasant weight of your kit. And if you think that a few more minutes of life aren't worth living for, then give it a try. I'd really, really enjoy it if you resisted."

The prisoner just nodded, so Tom slowly reached around to one side to unclip Green's combat vest.

"When I tell you, you are going to shrug your left shoulder and let the vest slide right down your other arm. Here's the trick: don't move your head, because my tomahawk is thirsty and it might just nick something vital."

"Look, if you j—" Green tried to speak but Tom applied just

a bit more pressure to the RMJ, making the Gleaner inhale in sudden pain as he felt the searing kiss of the blade just above his Adam's apple. A trickle of dark blood ran down his neck into his collar.

"Uh-uh-uh, *Governor*," Tom said warningly. "You don't get to talk yet. Just ever so slightly nod if you understand about the vest."

Green's head barely moved.

"Good, now do it."

The vest thumped to the ground and Tom continued to talk Green through losing his belt, and emptying his pockets. He ran his hand up Green's inseam, squeezing the prisoner's crotch and then down the opposite inseam. He ended by having the man very slowly turn around, hands interleaved on his head.

They locked eyes, and without warning, Tom used a bladed hand to deeply jab Green's abdomen, just below the point of the xiphoid process. Green bent, gasped and fought his paralyzed diaphragm for a breath. Tom struck again, his stiffly cupped hand coming from underneath to fork Green's neck, making the Gleaner involuntarily stop choking and arch his back. Green's hands fluttered like birds at his own throat.

"So, you enjoyed killing us off one at a time?" Tom asked, batting Green's hands to the side with a quick left-right motion, before firmly grasping the Gleaner by his right elbow. "You wanted to meet the guy in charge? Well, here you are. My name is Smith, late of Australian Special Air Service and formerly chief of security for Bank of the Americas."

Green just goggled at him.

"I was under the impression that an erudite fellow like yourself would be aware of the Special Air Service and its reputation. No?"

Tom straightened his arm, raising Green's arm above his head and pinning it to the very tree where Rune had sheltered. Tom was so angry that he shook slightly, and the Gleaner vibrated in Tom's grip, barely supporting his weight on his toes. Little rasping sounds started as he recovered from the blow to his throat, allowing him more air.

This brought them face-to-face, and they shared bad breath laden with the by-products of exertion, fear and rage.

"Whoa, mate," Tom averted his head slightly. "You really need to floss... Wait."

Tom paused and considered the arm that he was pinning

against the tree. The light from the dam was striking highlights from a collection of thin, woven bracelets. Tom twisted the arm a bit, turning it back and forth before the objects snapped into focus. They were circlets of hair, in various shades. As he watched, they slid downwards, bunching up on the thickest part of Green's forearm.

"Is that... is that *human* hair?" Tom asked, puzzled. Then he got it.

"Does that terrify you?" Green said, his voice rasping unevenly but arrogantly.

"Nooo..." Tom growled dangerously. "Clarifies some shit that I've heard about you. Pussies keep trophies. Professionals just do the job and go have breakfast."

"Professionals are overrated," Green said, struggling to free himself from the viselike grip. "I cleared two dozen towns and I'm rebuilding civilization. What have you done, besides kiss the ass of your Wall Street masters?"

"Who's dangling who in the air, Green?" Tom said, slapping him with nearly the full force of his arm. "Hold still, unless you want to start bleeding prematurely."

Tom hooked the RMJ over the clump of trophies and yanked upwards, using the sharpened inner edge of the weapon to sever the bracelets, letting them fall to the ground.

"No!" Green cried, ignoring the oozing, shallow slit in his forearm and redoubling his efforts to free himself and recover the lost bracelets.

Tom slapped him briskly, forehand and backhand. Slapping was simply an ad hoc prisoner control method. Yep.

Definitely not because he felt like it though. Nope, just keeping the prisoner subdued.

"Can we get a move on?" Rune asked from behind him. "How long were you standing there, listening?"

"Had to make certain this arsehole was alone," Tom said, briefly noting that his own respiration was accelerating, becoming deeper *and* faster. "Give me a moment, Paul."

He reconsidered Green, still pinned to the tree trunk. "You. You're nothing but a stain that's been plaguing me for a fair bit. Thanks to you, friends of mine are dead. Thanks to you, my girlfriend is a prisoner in my own camp. And now, I'm in a wrathful mood."

"Smith, no, wait," Green gasped.

"Something you want to add, you piece of shit? You want to admit your guilt? Confess that you're ashamed?"

"Ashamed? Shame is for people that don't live up to what they can be!" Green said, his voice hoarse with pain. "Look at what I've accomplished, the towns I've liberated from the Plague, the roads I've cleared. I'm not making the mistakes of the old system. I'm making something new! With this dam, I can do even more, enough power to make a new beginning. I'm proud—"

"And no," Tom said, cutting him off. "Bo-ring. By the way, if that was the start of your monologue, it was weak. I've heard Indonesian Jemaah-Islamiyah shite-eaters using English as a second language who did a better job on rhetoric and strophe—ah, no, no!"

Tom swung the flat of the tomahawk and broke the Gleaner's wrist just as Green attempted to reach one ankle. Green's boot knife thudded to the leaf litter at their feet.

"Fuck!" Green said, grunting and grimacing. "Fuck you, you barbarian! This is how you show that you're better than me?"

"Not better than you," Tom continued, bouncing the RMJ in his right hand. "Wrathful. But now I've got wounded to attend to and professional responsibilities. We've got a great murthering battle still going on and I'm not abandoning my friends. I don't have time to properly discharge my *wrath*. I could kill a half dozen of you with my bare hands and it wouldn't be enough. It's like... Marmite and crisps. I could chew on you all night."

"So... you're going to just let me go?" Green said, unable to keep the hope out of his voice. "Bygones be bygones and all that?"

"Oh, fuck no," Tom replied, smashing the flat of the tomahawk against the arm he was holding.

Green started to scream shrilly. Instead of simply being suspended midair by a mostly intact arm he was now suspended in the air by a broken elbow.

"Wrath-ful," Tom said carefully. "W-R-A-T-H-ful. Wrathful. I'd say look it up, but you won't really be given the opportunity."

Tom swung and buried his tomahawk in the tree next to his prisoner's head. Green flinched automatically, and Tom let the man fall forward far enough to pull the Gleaner's head into his chest.

He braced both hands and squeezed hard.

"If... I... can... just..." Tom said, grimacing in effort. "I know it's nearly impossible to crush a fresh skull with your hands. They're too flexible. But . . ."

Harlan Green kicked ineffectually at the monstrously strong former SAS officer. He'd have created what were termed "defensive wounds" in the forensic world but now he had compound open fractures of the left wrist and right elbow. Scratching was out. As he was twisted back and forth as helplessly as a baby, the pressure on his head caused him to first whimper in pain and then scream, as deep in his heart something bloomed for the first time: an honest fear he'd never really experienced. He might actually . . . die.

"Tom," Rune said weakly. "*Tom.* Green is shit, but you're not. Kill him and be done."

"He needs more!" Tom said, through a curtain of red. He tried a tournament-disapproved variation of krav maga, causing Green to switch from screams to an inarticulate keening. "I have more to let out."

"I've seen enough bad things that people do to each other, Tom, and it's all ugly," Rune replied, his voice now raspy with pain. "Kill him. Besides, I'm bleeding here. Getting shot really hurts."

Tom angrily grunted in precisely the manner of an irritated silverback gorilla. A last hammer fist flattened Green's nose to his face. After a moment's thought, Tom dropped Green to the ground and looked left and right, seeking inspiration. He looked at Rune again. Paul was starting to shiver. At Tom's feet, the battered and terrified Gleaner commander had curled into a fetal ball, trying to master his own pain and fear. There was no punishment that Tom could levy against the man that could possibly balance the Gleaner's crimes.

Trying to balance Green's actions with the suffering that Green deserved would only serve to smear that evil on Tom's own hands. Tom knew that he didn't have time for reflection, not now. Even so, several of the hardest decisions that he'd made rose in his memory, unbidden.

His own blood-drenched hands processing the very first infected human that he had captured for the bank.

Staring into Durante's eyes and then leaving his mortally wounded teammate to stall the Gleaners' advance.

Shooting police and FBI agents that had been driven mad by the slaughter of their families.

Getting mousetrapped by Kohn, enduring her lecture as she explained how she'd visit sorrow on all that Tom held dear if he broke her deal to free the dam.

Tom's eyes widened.

Kohn.

Her deal with Captain Dominguez. The deliberate infection of the cops' families at One Police Plaza in New York City.

Kohn.

And the bitch was holding Risky hostage while Tom did even more dirty work for her.

He shook himself again, mentally and physically, becoming aware that he was breathing like a bellows. The bloody, rocking ball of diseased humanity at his feet was the sideshow. The true enemy, Tom's real problem, was the spider at Site Blue, and every minute Tom spent here strengthened Kohn's hand.

He didn't have time for Green, not anymore. He had somewhere to be.

Only ten meters distant lay the edge of the same cliff where Tom had begun his earlier, very deep, unplanned descent.

"Perfect," Tom said, before adding for Rune's benefit. "I'll be right there, Paul. Just a short chore."

He dragged Green almost all the way over to the edge before picking him up. A few steps later, he propped up the formerly haughty man, letting him teeter at the very edge of the precipice, bleeding from multiple wounds.

Tom paused with his hands bunched on the bloody lapels of Green's camouflage jacket, letting the wobbly man get a good look over his shoulder at the churning water below.

"I've got things to do, Green, and I doubt that your victims were ever afforded such a chance," Tom said matter-of-factly, pitching his voice to carry over the dwindling gunfire at the dam, "but I'm going to let you die quickly. I'm not going to do anything spectacular, or save you for trial and execution. Nothing that would memorialize your name. You're going to die unmourned, unimportant and unwitnessed. I'm going to erase your organization. Then I'm going to forget that you ever existed. And so will everyone else."

"But wait, we— I—" Green began but then Tom gave him a sharp push.

Tom heard a brief, thin wail, the sound of some rocks banging together and then a loud splash.

Below, the current snatched the maimed Gleaner leader and pulled him under.

There was no audience when less than a minute later, the dam's return loop downstream was once again discolored, if only for a moment, belching out a well-mulched corpse. In seconds, the remains of Green mingled anonymously with the polluted river water. The baitfish swarmed and the birds' cries sounded grateful.

CHAPTER 22

"That went very well," Joanna said, looking down at her notes. "Are we agreed, Ken?"

"Better than I expected Miss Kohn," Schweizer answered. Joanna detected the merest hint of truculence in his tone. "But I wonder if we shouldn't start Miss, pardon, Specialist Astroga out small and work up to full trust."

"Of course," Joanna answered pertly. "I tested her by requesting that she perform some basic, even menial administration duties, and suggested that rapid promotion was possible. She is going to be straightening some of the offices later. Unarmed, of course."

"Of course, Miss Kohn," her man replied, standing tall in front of her desk. "And the others? I still think that Randall is a question."

"His technical communications knowledge is still valuable," she said. "But we should remain alert to opportunities to add to that specialty, just in case something should happen to him. However, with luck, that will not be necessary. My meeting with his superior was productive."

"Did Sergeant Copley accept your authority, Miss Kohn?"

"He did not reject it, Ken," Joanna replied. "And he seemed persuadable given the truth, which is that I am the seniormost government official that has survived so far, discounting the desperate impostors that have broadcast on the radio."

"The flag behind your desk was a nice touch," Schweizer said, looking at the red, white and blue colors that stretched nearly the width of Joanna's office wall.

"Soldiers adore symbols," she answered. "Like Smith, they swore an oath, only in this case, to a constitution. Whether Smith succeeds or fails at the dam, I have planted the idea that these soldiers owe allegiance to their country, not a Wall Street has-been. By the time Smith returns, *if* he returns, the seed of doubt that I am planting about the true direction of their duty will suffice to sever their direct obedience to Smith. And of course, if they should fully join our organization, they will be useful symbols for such new recruits as we gather."

"Yes, ma'am. And Smith's woman?"

"Khabayeva will get her chance to decide, as well. Please set up the office for a special interview, say, well after evening curfew. We will want to avoid witnesses, just in case she chooses poorly."

"What did she offer you?" Randall asked Worf.

It wasn't a casual question.

Kohn had talked with Worf for almost an hour, probing him for the history of the group's escape, about Smith's decisions and about the long-term goals of the camp. She hadn't offered him a job, exactly, but she'd made it plain that accepting her leadership as a government representative would work out a lot better for Worf than if he stayed loyal to Smith.

Worf had coached Randall to scrape off their guard outside, leaving him to smoke in the gravel lane that ran along the "street" of housing unit ("no smoking around the radios, see?") while they enjoyed some privacy in the comms CHU. Though their separate meetings with Kohn had been hours earlier, this had been their first chance to talk without Astroga, and Astroga had become a question.

"Kohn didn't make an offer, Gunner," Worf replied, stretching in his chair and looking at the radio rack. "She just reminded me about my oath of service and that she was the last known government official that anyone knew about."

"I'm not worried about you, Worf," Randall said, snapping and unsnapping the catch on his sheathed kukri. "I'm worried about Astro. She was in with Kohn longer than either of us, and came out whistling like she just got laid before disappearing for an hour. Then she waltzes in here with a camp guard and ratfucks the desk for admin supplies."

"Did she say what she wanted them for?"

"Something about doing admin for the 'new boss,'" Randall

answered, shifting uncomfortably in his seat. "Worries me. I know that she's junior as hell, she's young, and Kohn is a good talker."

"Astroga is solid, Gunner," Copley said. "You didn't see her in the last three months. She's shot the shit out of the Gleaners and the infected, she's been shot and she's been a loyal troop. I'm more worried about Risky."

"You mean Smith's girlfriend?" Randall replied. "Rowf!"

"Lock it up, Randall!" Copley snapped. "Yeah, Tom Smith's girlfriend. The one that Kohn is using as leverage. She's live ordnance and she's not going to wait to be saved. Kohn won't do anything permanent until Smith gets back. But then, we gotta be ready to back Risky's play."

"So what's the play?" Randall asked. He stopped fiddling with his big knife and leaned forward intently. "What do we do? Do we wait for Smith to come back? Do we guard the common frequency? Do we soldier for Kohn in the meantime?"

"What does any good NCO do when there is thinking to be done and shit details to avoid?" Copley asked. "Let's get some coffee and keep our ears spread."

When Tom had entered the dam compound with Rune over his shoulder in an uncomfortable fireman's carry, he'd noted the bodies that lay outside the powerhouse, covered with jackets and blankets. Compared to the literal heaps of dead infected that began only a few dozen meters from the walls, they were a tiny number, but the little cluster represented pain that Tom wouldn't process until he had more time. He simply added it to the list and felt his anger build anew.

Inside, the glad cries and excitement generated by his return had briefly overcome the dismal stink of gunsmoke, blood and charred meat.

Robbins was their primary medic and he'd immediately started an IV on Rune, who was now lying on his side, hoarsely complaining as his bullet wound was packed in preparation to move him, and the other seriously wounded, to Spring City. However, Tom noted that Rune had energy enough to lead the argument against Tom's plan as soon as Tom had explained the next steps.

"Tom, at least wait until morning," Rune said from the tabletop where Robbins had improvised an aid station. "Site Blue will be there in the morning, after you've gotten some sleep."

"Kohn has Risky," Tom said, looking up as he reloaded magazines and stuffed them into a replacement plate carrier. "And I'm not waiting until morning to get her back. You, of all people, know the why."

"I'll bite," Kaplan said. "Why not wait? Everyone's tired, the defenses are shot to shit and we have dead and wounded."

"Kohn gave me an impossible task and threatened to kill Risky if I don't do exactly as she says," Tom explained, as he slid another full mag into his vest. "But I think that she might not wait for that. Remember Dominguez?"

"Who's that?" Robbins asked, tightly taping down a dressing on Rune, to the accompaniment of a pained grunt.

"Precinct captain in New York," Kaplan said offhand, the expression on his face clearly suggesting that he was thinking back to the operations of the vaccine cartel that Tom himself had organized. "Dominguez represented the cops in the unofficial vaccine cartel that we organized. Four players: Ding for the PD, Matricardi for the mob, Smith for the banks and Joanna Kohn for the city council. Ding and the rest of the cops went nuts and starting killing everyone after the Jamaican Queens gang put a hit on their kids inside the cops' own safe zone."

"Not the Jamaicans, Kap," Tom said, as he unstuck from the tomahawk the clotted blood and mud that caked its sheath. He walked over to the tiny bathroom but left the door open as he ran the sink. "Kohn. Kohn put the hit on Dominguez because he'd become too big a threat. Remember how we couldn't figure out how the hitters made it inside One Police Plaza, the hardest target in New York? Why they chose the kids' dormitory to start the infection? Kohn had access to all the information on entry protocols, building layout, credentials—you name it."

"And you know this how?" Stantz asked.

"Kohn all but bragged about it as she shoved me out of the camp under guard," Tom answered while rinsing blood and hair from his tomahawk before hitting it with a spray of lubricant. "She warned us—me, personally, I think—that she won't tolerate any rival, and I *know* that Risky will not respond well to being threatened. So I'm going, tonight."

Tom walked back into the main room, ignoring the discomfort of his mud-encrusted clothes.

"I marked the best route on the way here," he said, reaching for the AR that was lying on the main control panel. "Whose rifle is this?"

"Detkovic's," Robbins answered. "He's outside, under a blanket."

Tom closed his eyes, motionless for a moment. Then he performed a chamber check and dropped the sling over his shoulder.

"I'm leaving now for Spring City," he said, scanning his audience's skeptical faces. He didn't want to ask for more, but he had no choice. "Then I'm driving to Site Blue. It's going to be dangerous. I know that you're all tired. I'm tired too. But the op isn't over, not yet, and it has the potential to get worse. Who's in?"

"I think that the coffee is getting worse," Randall said, staring balefully into the brown-stained mug.

The door to the mostly empty cafeteria opened too swiftly for the blackout curtain, letting electric light leak into the night sky, and someone growled a reproof. Worf looked up to see Astroga in new civilian clothes, headed for the coffee urn, trailed by one of Schweizer's deer-rifle armed goons.

"Hey Worf, is the coffee fresh?" Astroga chirped.

"That's Sergeant Copley to you, Specialist!" Randall grated, staring hard at his former teammate. "And you're out of uniform!"

"Wow, aren't we regulation!" Astroga said, pointedly looking at her guard for a moment before giving Randall a big, cheesy smile. "Good thing I don't work for you anymore. I just wanted a favor from *Worf*, is all, since I'm gonna be wearing more civvies now." She addressed Worf directly. "I left my favorite Cardinals ballcap in the ladies latrine and I gotta go clean Miss Kohn's office. Can you grab it for me before it walks off? I'll come find you in the radio shack later."

"Lock it up, Pri—" Randall began to stand up but Worf grabbed his forearm in a strong grip, quashing the other man's anger.

"It's all good, Astro," Worf said with deceptive mildness. "Happy to get it as soon as I finish my coffee."

"Ain't you a peach, Sarge!" she said, snapping a plastic lid onto her cup before briskly striding towards the door, still shadowed by the bored guard. "Gunner, you not so much! Gotta go!"

Worf kept sipping his coffee for a few minutes before Randall simmered over.

"What. The. Fuck. Was. That, Sergeant?" he whispered harshly.

"Astroga doesn't follow baseball, Gunner," Worf said softly, reaching for extra dairy creamer. "So we're going to go fetch her cap for her."

Randall stared at him like he was a crazy man.

Astroga had shown up hours earlier to deliver dinner and assurances that she was just being practical. The empty trays hadn't yet been retrieved and Risky was balefully staring at the nylon zip ties that anchored her to the bed frame when the CHU door rattled under someone's knock.

Risky watched Kendra open the door for Schweizer, who soundlessly hooked a thumb towards the main camp building. Kendra got up and snipped the zip ties with a wire cutter.

"We're going to talk to Joanna now," she said.

"Can I persuade you to let me pee first?" Risky asked, standing up and smoothing her rumpled clothes.

"Sure," Kendra answered, after getting a shrug from Schweizer.

It only took Worf a moment to locate the pistol and the plastic baggie with a note scrawled by Astroga, while Randall watched the door.

Worf read the note twice.

What the hell?

As they walked around the corner towards the CHU where she'd showered earlier, the trio led by Schweizer almost ran into Copley and Randall, who came to a complete halt to avoid the collision.

"What are you guys doing out?" Schweizer asked, looking irritated. "There's a reason for curfew, Randall. We stay dark, we stay quiet and we stay inside to avoid attracting attention. You know it as well as I do. This isn't the time to remini—"

"We just got some coffee," Randall said. "That's all."

Risky darted a look at Copley, who was wearing his "bland" face.

"We're heading back to the comms shack now."

"Can I go?" Risky said, striding around the group towards the bathroom hut. "Have been damn CHU all damn day!"

"We have a meeting," Schweizer said as he watched Risky pass. Then he motioned curtly for the two soldiers. "Go back to the radio room. I'll be there in five minutes, and you better have a better explanation, Randall."

Risky ignored the exchange, walking rapidly to the bathroom CHU, trailed by Kendra, and let herself into "her" stall.

Lifting the toilet tank lid, she was greeted by...nothing.

"*Kak chertovski zdorovo!*" she said under her breath. "How very fucking great!"

She patted her pocket to double-check that she still had one weapon.

"Through the door," said Kendra in a firm voice. She'd kept a safe interval between herself and Risky during their walk over.

That was a compliment of a sort, Risky realized.

She strode confidently into Kohn's office, her feet wrinkling heavy plastic that obscured the wooden cabin floor. She looked down and smiled.

Subtlety was supposed to be Kohn's strong suite.

Behind her desk, in her high-collared gray tunic, Kohn was reading. The pages quietly shuffled as she leafed through the red-spined binder.

Kendra slipped through the door behind Risky and closed it, maintaining a double arm's distance. The muzzle of the pistol didn't waver, forming the vertex of a triangle defined by the three women. She waited a beat. Two.

"Joanna, Ms. Khabayeva is here to see you," she said.

"Mmmm?" Kohn murmured unnecessarily as she looked up. "Ah. Ms. Khabayeva, so glad that you came." The binder closed with a snap. "I have to make a great number of decisions that will decide the future of the colony of New Hope and those that shelter within."

Risky stood easily, but silently. She looked at the seated woman, giving away nothing.

After a pause, Kohn plucked a fountain pen from its holder.

"As you may have learned, Mr. Smith has accepted his duty to secure for the camp a functioning hydroelectric dam that may be nearby," she said patiently. "Further, he will likely have to confront the Gleaners, who may have the same objective. In either event, there remains the likelihood that we will have to surrender the child in order to buy us more time to prepare."

Risky bared her teeth. She wasn't smiling.

"It would help me a very great deal if, like Mr. Smith, you publicly recognized my authority. He is doing this of his own will, for all of us," Kohn said, her tone becoming persuasive. "Further divisions among the...contributors of our colony can weaken us all."

"Don't you mean that with Tom out of the picture, there is no one to challenge your job?" Risky said, jamming her hands in her pants pockets. "What is title you adopted, Administrator, yes?"

"I am the Acting Administrator, yes." Joanna was unruffled. "But anyone could be nominated to the permanent role, once we resolve the current crisis. A crisis precipitated by the incautious actions of our friend, Tom Smith. That he accepts responsibility for this crisis and is prepared to make amends, even at great personal risk, had a certain..." the fountain pen tapped the desk once "...symmetry."

"Joanna, I know how your type craves power," Risky said. "Crave power like fat man crave food he doesn't need. I know scared people will trade a little of themselves for promises of safety, or food. Or freedom. This isn't sacrifice that *we* need. But it gets rid of person that *you* don't need. So less, how you say, *bullshit*, please."

"I am not asking for your gratitude," Joanna said, tapping the desk again. "What I am trying to explain is that this is the only way. If you are part of the solution, then Mr. Smith gets a better chance to survive. If he does not survive that will be a great tragedy, but New Hope will remain strong, unified. Yes, I intend to be in charge. All there is of a civil society is this colony. I mean to ensure that I can direct its success."

She paused and resumed a more conversational tone.

"I know something of your personal history, Risky. I know that you are a survivor, too. How can I persuade you to trust me that this is important?"

"I have no trust for you, Joanna," Risky said. "Was raised by Russians, and I know that everyone lies. Let us trade truths, instead. You say that if I cooperate, Tom lives. Prove it."

"Ah, the mark of Cosa Nova," Kohn said. Risky watched her lean back in the soft office chair, assuming the "power position." They eyed each other speculatively. "Always bargaining, just like your previous lover. Matricardi was a dangerous man. Dominguez was a dangerous man. And still I manipulated them, defeated them. Just as I have outmaneuvered Smith. Come now, Miss Khabayeva, are we so different? Already you have moved easily from one strong leader to another. You can do so again. Do the Russians not appreciate a winner? Consider the advantages of cooperation. Consider how my interests are served if both you and Smith ally yourselves to me. Of course, that assumes that Smith is as good as he thinks he is, and actually secures a hydroelectric facility, despite all obstacles. He might fail, and you might lose your chance to bargain with me now, tonight."

This bitch loves to talk. Time to irritate her a bit more.

"Tom will not fail," Risky replied confidently, measuring her moment. "Does not know how. When Tom returns, he will bargain from outside gate, with forces you cannot stop. He will have soldiers. He will have a victory to persuade your camp."

"I do not appreciate your tone, Risky," Joanna said, anger creeping into her tone. Her pen continued to beat against the desk. "You seem to believe that I have not thought this through." Tap, tap. "You are here now. Not Smith. This could work to your advantage, personally. The path of the future is set, and what remains to be determined is if you will be in it. No longer will the privileged few, chosen by economic lottery, impose their rule on our new society. Women with my . . . perspective . . . are better suited to guide a new society as it rises from the wreckage of the old system. It is my turn now." Tap, tap. "Maybe it can be your turn too, Risky."

Risky looked around the room. Down at the plastic sheet. Back up at Kohn's smug expression.

"No, don't think so," she replied confidently. "If you want to persuade his friends to give up Tom, must find someone else to, how did they say on Wall Street? Ah yes, *shill* for you."

"You are close to Tom." The pen tapped again. "Your feelings are understandable. Everyone has sacrificed. I lost many of my most trusted people. How many of our foragers have failed to return from supply runs? Even Kendra lost someone special when Paul bravely volunteered to test the new vaccine on himself, and turned. But she has come to understand."

Risky looked at Kohn and decided.

Now.

She reached into her pocket for her secret weapon.

"Are you sure about this, man?" Randall asked as they crunched along the gravel path.

"What part of this isn't clear?" Worf replied. "Kohn has built a tidy little cult of personality. Risky is gonna run a de-cap op. Astro is helping her. For this to work, we gotta take out a couple levels at once."

"Schweizer isn't going to play along," Randall said. "He knows that as soon as Kohn is out, his goose is cooked."

"So we wait for him to come remind us that it's curfew," Worf said, surreptitiously raising his shirt to display the pistol under his belt. "He comes inside and that's that. Then we get to the admin building and back Astro's play."

"Works for me," Randall said, patting his kukri. "You did say it was a decapitation op, right? Rune would approve."

"What?" Risky turned around to face her escort. "You really believe Paul is dead? I thought that you were playing—Paul Rune is fine, he isn't dead."

Kendra had remained quiet during the interview so far, keeping her pistol at the low ready, her two-handed grip firm.

She didn't say anything in reply, yet somehow the silence became freighted with meaning.

"Of course he is!" insisted Joanna. "We all saw him turn. Once we were certain, he was taken outside the wire and humanely extinguished."

"Extinguished," Risky said with a snort. She looked to Kendra, ignoring the gun. "Is new way to say murdered? I saw Paul two days ago. He's healthy, and working for Smith."

"How?" Kendra's said huskily. "How do I know that you aren't lying?"

She wasn't talking to Kohn.

"Of course she is lying, Miss Jones; she will say anything," Kohn said, her anger plain now. The fountain pen beat a brisk tattoo. "If she persists, shoot."

Kendra's eyes flicked back and forth between the other two women.

"Miss Khabayeva, this is your last chance," Joanna said, standing decisively. "Support me. Help me guide the others, Copley and Randall, for example. They can take over the military aspect. We will find something safe for Smith. Even you can have a place here on my staff." The pen tapping paused and Kohn eyed the plastic sheeting meaningfully. "Or you can end up in a ditch."

"Didn't know that you guys were a thing, but now this makes sense," Risky said. She completely ignored Kohn, directing her words to her erstwhile guard. She stood even more hipshot, and her left hand, finding the item that had been left in her pocket, slowly withdrew it. "Paul asked me to give you this. He said you would understand."

Risky held a fine gold chain out at arm's length, letting it dangle. The desk lamp struck a single golden highlight from the medallion as it spun slowly.

For a moment, all three of them just looked at.

The woman behind the desk looked puzzled, lacking comprehension. The woman who dangled the pendant smirked with satisfaction, but held very still, watching her target. This weapon was for the third member of the audience, the woman holding the gun.

Kendra stepped forward with her left hand outstretched, palm facing Risky, guarding the pistol that she now held low against her right hip, safe from any lunge or grab. The little Saint Joshua medallion that she'd returned to Paul was unmistakable. Slowly she rotated her outthrust hand until it was palm up. She felt the familiar pendant touch her skin as Risky lowered it all the way, the weight kissing Kendra's palm.

"How...?" she stuttered.

"They didn't give him bad vaccine or live virus," Risky said. To Kendra, it seemed like Risky's eyes glowed like little suns as the two stared at each other, and then the amulet. "Was synthetic drug, K2 or Spice or some shitty Chinese import. Something that one of the scavengers brought back early on. Primary symptoms look just like second stage flu." Risky finished lowering the medallion into Kendra's hand. "Would be convincing and involuntary performance."

Kendra continued to finger the medallion, feeling the texture under her fingers as Risky slowly turned back to face Kohn across the desk.

"This amateur dictator fancied Paul from start, apparently," Risky said, finally turning back to face Kohn, her wide grin feline. "Had plans for him. He declined and that was *unacceptable*. Wasn't it, Joanna? Or do you insist on 'Acting Administrator'?"

Kohn stared back at the taller woman, finally getting it. She wasn't impressed.

"Fine," Kohn said, hissing the word. "Kendra, shoot her now."

Kendra heard the command, but her mind was racing ahead, following the logic, one step at a time.

Paul was alive? Could this be a trick? The Russian woman would say anything to protect her man. Any woman would. Was Kohn lying? She'd lied before. This really was the medal. The actual medal.

It had to be true.

The office door jerked partially open and then closed itself with a loud clack, surprising all three women. It opened again, and Kendra shifted her aim, waiting to see who entered. Cathe Astroga awkwardly stepped through, her load banging the door frame, making even more noise. The little specialist grinned at everyone and then looked at the floor.

"Oh crap, you already have plastic," she said, dropping her bundle. However, her unbalanced load swung and this time she banged a wooden shovel handle against a wall. "Sheesh. Didn't need all this."

"What are you doing here?" Kohn demanded. "What is all this?!"

"This?" Astroga said, waggling the hand carrying a bottle of bleach. "I'm here to help clean up. You know, for after we kill you!"

Kendra thought it through. There was no way for Risky to have the medallion that didn't begin with Paul giving it to her. And Paul had it when he was infected.

When he was *set up.*

"Fine, I will do it!" Risky heard Kohn declare, and the woman darted a hand into a drawer, withdrawing a pistol. That hadn't been part of the plan. Risky began to react before she heard Astroga laugh delightedly.

It was so incongruous that the two other women froze for a moment, looking at the new arrival, before Kohn aimed the Glock pistol at Astroga and pulled the trigger.

Risky winced, and heard an audible click.

"Well, what do you know?" Astroga said happily. "The loudest sound in a gunfight is the sound of a gun going 'click'!"

Risky exhaled with relief, then darted a look at Kohn to see her reaction.

Kohn looked flustered and fumbled a moment, slapping the magazine and manually cycling the pistol. One round flew out and clicked on the floor as Kohn aimed again and pulled the trigger, squeezing the gun so hard that the muzzle perceptibly jerked downwards a bit.

But the gun didn't shoot.

"Hey Kohn, you forgot that I told you I was a *combat* administrator," Astroga said, waggling a small tube of adhesive. "Krazy glue. Bonds anything, even firing pins!"

Risky and Astroga both turned to see how Kendra was taking it.

Kohn followed their eyes and stared in horror when she saw Kendra's pistol was aimed squarely at her own face.

"Kendra, she is lying to you!" Kohn said, her voice rising a full octave. "Paul died for us, but he did die. Shoot her! Shoot her now, right now!"

Risky could see that the knuckles of Kendra's left hand were white, the chain of the medallion dangling from her fist.

"Really?" Kendra said, almost sobbing. Then her voice became even and strengthened with each word. "What, she dug up a grave at random, happened to find Paul's body, saw this medallion, intuited that Paul and I talked about it, *and then* saved it just in case, because she predicted that you would have me do your dirty work?" Kendra lips twisted. "You lying, backstabbing murderous cunt!"

Risky noted with professional interest that despite her emotional response, Kendra's one-handed shooting stance was remarkably steady.

"Kendra, stop!" Kohn urged, her voice breaking. "She lies! This bitch is lying to save herself." The pen made a flat sound as it hit the desk blotter. "Give me the gun, I will do it."

Kendra didn't react.

"Listen to me!" Kohn insisted. "Everything I said was true!"

"Nothing you say is true," Kendra said and carefully lined up the front sight. As she slowly, carefully squeezed the trigger Risky could see the hammer easing back, a moment away from slipping off the sear and sending the well-deserved bullet home.

Risky raised a hand in Kendra's line of vision.

"Stop!"

Kendra's gun muzzle was unwavering.

Kohn's shoulders had slumped a bit in relief when Risky had intervened, but she sobbed when she saw the dark eye of the gun still staring, holding the promise of oblivion even more surely than the poisonous hate in Kendra's bright, feral eyes.

"Kendra, no!" Kohn almost sobbed. "We are on the same side! We can skip the same mistakes that others made for us! Please listen, this way is better. My way is better. We can—"

"SHUT IT, BITCH," Kendra's replied flatly, but no less venomously than her earlier profanity. "This little slice of heaven has sucked but I hoped that you were real. I really *hoped*. As long as there was a chance, any chance, that your patter about a better world, from each according to ability and to each according to need might come true, I was willing to wait. Christ, I even hoped you had an alternative to the shit system that I was a part of. I *murdered* for you. I don't like Smith, particularly, but at least he never lied. He never blew sunshine up my hoo-ha."

Again, her trigger finger tightened on the double-action pistol.

"Don't shoot!" Risky repeated. "Really!"

"Why shouldn't I?" Kendra replied. Her eyes never left Kohn. "Give me a reason."

Risky reached for Astroga's shovel.

"Russian lesson. Shovel is quieter."

"Hoo-ha?" Astroga said with a grunt, adjusting the slippery plastic-wrapped bundle. "Who the hell calls their lady parts a 'hoo-ha'? Way too Rangerific, if you ask me."

The bundle slipped from her grip, almost dropping.

"Would you just shut up, hold the roll steady and walk?" Risky said, her voice strained. "We don't need to attract attention."

"Who the hell knew this bitch was so heavy?" grumped Astroga. "Coulda sworn she wouldn't fetch more than a buck twenty, wet. Here's a bright idea, why don't we ALL carry?"

"Someone has to carry the shovel and the bleach to wash down with after," Kendra replied primly. "And keep watch."

"Keep watch for what?" asked a new, deeper voice.

Kendra leveled her pistol, and Astroga dropped her end of the bundle, reaching for her waistband. Risky held on, but glared as Tom Smith loomed out of the shadows. Kaplan paced his boss, backed by Copley and Randall, who was carrying a bucket.

"Um, for..." stuttered Kendra.

"For zombies, sir, zombies," caroled Astroga. She stopped pawing at her blouse hem and looked guiltily down at the slumped bundle that trailed from Risky's grasp, then looked up again brightly. "So...you made it back. Uh, where are the guards, Gunner?"

"Not an issue, if you're doing what I hope you're doing," Smith replied, taking in Risky's little group. "We took the dam and then Kap and I hauled ass here. The gate guard was persuaded by Schweizer to sit this one out."

"Where is Schweizer, Tom?" Risky asked urgently.

"Ken Schweizer is in the bucket," Tom replied. A smiling Randall held a blood-smeared bucket up and gave it a helpful shake. "The next few folks we saw decided that they didn't want to get caught in an intramural fight. Which brings me to... where are you three going at night?"

"The night air is refreshing?" Risky said, trying for "butter wouldn't melt in my mouth." The butter melted. "The humidity isn't so bad."

Tom looked pointedly at the thick, tapered roll of plastic that was still carried by Risky, half slumped to the ground. Astroga was suddenly fascinated with her own boots.

"What's all the plastic for?"

"You were taking too long to get back and I was tired of the color of my, how you say, CHEW interior," Risky said, shifting her grip on the bundle as the slippery plastic threatened to unroll. "Joanna said that I could paint it. Before you ask, the bleach is for cleanup, after."

"And the shovel?" Smith asked.

"I like shovels," replied Risky quickly, a sparkle in her eye.

"For a smooth liar that was surprisingly bad."

Two of the women just stared at him. The third, still gripping the heavy plastic-wrapped roll, leaned her head back and laughed merrily.

"In the history of illicit corpse management," Tom said, putting his hands on his hips and fighting a smile that was threatening to bloom across his tired face, "no one has looked more like they were about to surreptitiously get rid of a dead body than you three. You impatient gits just couldn't wait, could you?"

"Am strong independent woman," Risky said, squinting at the bundle and then at her audience. "I don't need prince to rescue me. I pick prince. Also, Cathe, come over to me. Help me on this side."

Tom glanced at Kendra's load of tools and bleach as Cathe trudged over to stand beside Risky. Kendra just stared back, wide-eyed.

Risky blew her bangs back from her face and grinned at Tom.

"Okay, prince, now we have someone for the heavy end. Grab the head, would you?"

As another gray dawn lit Site Blue, Tom stood in the dining facility. He was flanked by Paul Rune, Risky and a rebandaged Sergeant Major Pascoe. One bloodshot eye was visible in a puffy but cheerful face.

Tom's audience was nervously attentive. There had been some changes in the last twenty-four hours, not least of which was the number of weapons in view.

And who was carrying them.

Fully rigged up, Astroga, Worf and Gunner had made the circuit, waking the occupants of every CHU and announcing the camp-wide meeting. After that chore, they had deposited the remains of the previous management team in the open pit beyond the wire that served the camp as a garbage dump.

"My name is Smith," Tom said. "I'm the person responsible for the establishment of this facility. Please hold your questions till I finish my statement. At this point, you could say that Joanna Kohn is no longer in charge."

"You could say that," Astroga said not so quietly to Randall. "You could also say she's wrapped in eight mil vinyl acetate and buried outside the perimeter."

For once Randall didn't perform the head chop, instead offering her a fist to bump, to the horror of a few of Kohn's former cronies within earshot.

Smith continued as though he hadn't heard the exchange.

"Next to me is Paul Rune, whom all of you should recognize. He's not infected with H7D3 and never was. The attempt on his life was an elaborate scheme intended to further isolate any remaining bank personnel and entrench Kohn in power—"

"What did you say?" yelled an angry committee chairwoman in the back row, who hadn't quite heard the byplay. "Where's Miss Kohn?"

"Dead," Tom answered, not mincing words this time. "Which might be better than she deserved considering her manipulation of this camp in the months since the Fall."

"You killed her?" Christine yelled, genuinely aghast. "You bastard!"

"My mother would be surprised to hear it," Tom looked to his right. "And no, I didn't kill her."

"I did," Kendra Jones said, standing up in the front row. She spat. "Fairness. A new start. A better world, eventually. All these things Kohn promised. Well, *now* maybe we can get them."

Tom watched as Kendra stepped towards Christine. The little group around the former administrator's head of the Culture Committee shrank back from the object of Kendra's ire.

"Y-you?" Christine stuttered. "Why? We were about to have everything."

"We had *nothing* and we were on a path to even less," Kendra said, looking towards the low dais where Smith's party stood. Her eyes sought out Paul. "I believed in her. We all did. She took everything she could and killed anyone that she couldn't manipulate. Which is why she had Paul killed. Then to cover up her murder, she aimed me at the expendable men who carried out her orders. So, in the end, I stove her head in with a shovel, while you all slept."

"How could you!" Christine was genuinely in shock. Her face was white and drawn and she trembled. "You've killed us all! Don't you feel anything!?"

"If I'd killed you, you'd know it." Kendra looked back towards Christine. "As for feeling? Kohn made me a murderer. I don't much feel anything anymore. Wanna see?"

She stalked a few steps closer to the suddenly isolated Christine.

"Kendra, why don't you and Paul talk about...things," Tom said, electing to interrupt the early stages of a homicide in progress. Risky had given him the whole story regarding Kohn's demise, and as attractive as it was in the short run to eliminate problems like that, it came with a downside too.

Sooner or later, the rule of law would have to return. It would be easier to reclaim if the spilled blood didn't lie any deeper than it had to.

"As I was about to say," he said, raising his voice to address the group once more. "We have a potential enemy that has threatened to attack this facility. Fifteen miles away is a dam and a hydroelectric power plant. They have electricity and a town secure from the infected. We're going to move the camp there. You can stay, or you can come with me. If you stay, you're on your own. If you come with me, you're committing to Site Blue."

"What makes you different from Kohn?" a voice called out.

"For one thing, you can call me out and the worst that will happen is that I will reply," Tom replied. "Which should answer your question. However, if you come with me, there will be work. It won't be easy. It will be about rebuilding civilization, not about building a bank. That means access to electricity, it means more people, and it means a different plan."

Loud murmurs greeted his announcement. Below, he could see Paul and Kendra hugging each other tightly.

"For the moment, the Commissary Committee will remain in charge of the dining facility operations. Rations are doubled, effective immediately. All other committees are suspended. Paul will run security. Members of the Bank of the Americas team will post new information here throughout the day and we'll meet again at the noon meal. No other questions for now."

EPILOGUE

Watts Bar Dam
December 1st

"Thank God for the cooler weather," Tom Smith remarked to his companions, passing his binoculars to Kaplan. "Even so, we need to keep getting as many bodies underground as we can."

Below the balcony on the third floor of the powerhouse, an unbroken chain of Tesla coils guarded the repaired fenceline. Beyond that, a yellow, medium-sized backhoe was digging yet another long trench adjacent to one that was already in use. As they watched, a grimy skip loader, its white paint mostly covered by a disgusting blend of muck and other organic debris, was dumping a load of corpses into a communal grave. Tom couldn't make out who it was; the driver's identity was hidden by a full face mask and coveralls. Despite the discomfort of working long shifts completely covered by protective equipment, no one had complained. Each driver had learned the hard way to avoid raising the bucket overhead. They tended to . . . drip.

Behind the action, several more dark stripes of soil scarred the earth, marking previously filled trenches.

"The ones in the river are bad enough," Kaplan said, scanning the field in front of them. "And no, I'm not volunteering to clean them up."

"Speaking of clean up, we're still getting a couple dozen kills each night," Brandy offered. "I know that they're working as planned, now that we're baiting the coils and induced-current traps with strobes. Still, we're going to need more trenches."

"How about we bait the trenches and set up traps inside them?" Kaplan asked.

"Sure, but we'll need power to do that, which means running even more cable. Which we don't have," she answered, reaching for the binoculars. "Gimme."

"Speaking of which, did you review the surveys on Nickajack and Chickamauga?" Tom asked, referring to the next dams downstream. "We need to get as many plants back into operation as we can before spring, if at all possible."

"Fires at both, according to Mike," she replied. "Fixable, if we have enough parts, time and talent."

"Tell Mike to ask me for anything but time," Tom said, sighing. Mike Stantz had cautioned the rest of the consolidated team about the expected conditions at the other dams. Neither had been in working order and very few surviving personnel had been found. Despite that, Stantz's daily messages had clearly signaled his glee at eventually having two further multi-hundred megawatt dams under his control. "Paul, get with Brandy and figure out what they need, then do a search on any records for bits and pieces that we can repurpose from anything else."

"On it, Boss," Paul replied, rubbing his stubbly, but mostly bald head. Tom could see him carefully avoiding the inflamed, stapled crease that started at the corner of one eye and splashed diagonally upwards. The intelligence expert paused before adding, "Anyone else think that the river is even higher than yesterday?"

Tom, like the others, looked upstream. The brown water that was swirling a mix of branches, brightly colored plastic garbage and dead bodies against the stained, upstream dam face did in fact look a bit higher than before. If it wasn't one thing, it was another. They had to get the dams back into operation in order to generate power, and they needed power in order to get the dams fixed. Both had to happen in order to continue clearing out the infected and reestablishing a permanent, defensible city.

None of that could occur if this dam failed or flooded. He fought the urge to sigh again.

"Brandy, can you look into a way to get more of the spillways back in operation?" he asked. "Just in case."

"So long as you can loan me some of your soldiers for security," she replied. "Just because we haven't seen them doesn't mean that some of those psycho Gleaners aren't still around. I'll need to access the far end of the dam and the lock system."

"None of the Gleaner prisoners seem particularly loyal to their organization," Robbins offered from the end of the group that was looking over the gray cement balcony. "I think that they will likely just drift apart without a leader like Green. Without organization, the bits and pieces that are left are a nuisance, not a danger."

"Not right away," Tom said, flicking his eyes over taller man. "But they will be if we leave them alone long enough. They stay on our to-do list, but meanwhile we provide heavy security for the lock repair team."

Before Robbins could reply, Tom heard Kaplan carol out, "Hey, look who decided to join us. Something at breakfast not agree with you two?"

Smith turned to see Risky and Astroga approaching. Risky looked a little pale, but both women were smiling.

Tom felt his heart give a little lift, like it always did when he saw his woman. Even wearing her hair in a simple ponytail and bereft of makeup, Risky was the most beautiful thing in this world.

"Hello gorgeous," he said, holding out a hand. "You're late."

"Yes," Risky replied, her smile widening. "I am."

"What?"

APPENDIX

~~Private~~ Specialist Cathe Astroga's Do's and Don'ts
RULES FOR A ZOMBIE APOCALYPSE

1. The Private shall never impersonate a rigger to give parachute rigging instruction to a Chief Warrant Officer rigger.

2. Even if the Warrant Officer is clueless.

3. Just "shall never impersonate a rigger."

4. Like my father the colonel says, always take advantage of a chance to eat, sleep or pee. You never know when you'll get the next chance.

5. The moment that you run out of sanitary products is the moment that you will most need them. Dad forgot that one.

6. When receiving a battle fatigued squad of National Guardsmen as they reenter the wire, the Private shall not suggest, "Next time, just pay the Girl Scouts for their damn cookies and they won't beat your ass."

7. There is no condition of HMMWV cleanliness that the Private can achieve which will satisfy Top.

8. The Private shall not describe the impossibility of
    cleaning unit vehicles to the Top's standards by
    claiming that "even waving my Hitachi Magic
    Wand at the problem fails to clean this Hummer!"

9. The Private shall remind junior officers that if they
    ask about the "why," "how," and "where," they lose
    all deniability.

10. There is not a Joint Meritorious Fraternization
    ribbon awarded for performing the Happy Dance
    of Combat Administration for Navy or Marine
    reservists.

11. The Private may not use her authority as a Combat
    Administrator to establish new awards in the forward
    operating area.

12. Combat Administration is not a valid Military
    Occupational Specialty.

13. Clipboard mounted documents are less likely to be
    questioned as unofficial.

14. Once ammo cans are used as field expedient latrines,
    they shall not be resealed and stacked at the
    ammunition resupply point.

15. Telling a Second Lieutenant "Sir, hush, the adults
    are talking" while within the hearing of the First
    Sergeant is not recommended.

16. That is why you encourage the dickhead Private from
    supply who denied your Lost Property Report to
    do it.

17. The use of duct tape and straight back chairs during
    counseling sessions is not authorized.

18. Even when the counseling is being delivered by the
    Command Private Major.

19. Removing two rockers and two chevrons from
    a Command Sergeant Major's insignia is not

justification to claim status as the Command Private Major.

20. General officers in emotional shock will sign anything that the Specialist presents on a clipboard.

21. When persuading general officers to sign official documents, it is beneficial to coopt the participation of nearby senior noncommissioned officer. This is also known as "leave some meat on the bone for the Sergeants."

22. Large formations of zombies are best viewed from inside armored vehicles.

23. The Specialist shall not attempt to make ATM withdrawals during a zombie apocalypse.

24. Working with contractors from a financial institution is insufficient authority for establishing an apocalypse-specific currency.

25. No matter how much you sweep concrete, you still get dust. Fighting zombies underground in New York City is like sweeping concrete.

26. Yelling "Get some, get some!" is not approved for engaging large bodies of enemy troops, zombies, whatever.

27. The Specialist is not allowed to rename the Vehicle Checkpoint as "Hadley's Hope," even if it's perfectly descriptive or improves morale.

28. "Remember LV-426!" is not an authorized battle cry.

29. The Specialist shall not encourage the homicidal teenager to slap around VIPs.

30. Even if it is intensely reassuring.

31. Army regulations do not recognize the use of Kipling's "Loot" to justify post-combat resource allocation of abandoned cultural treasures.

32. Broadening the allocation of post-combat resources decreases command resistance to the preservation of abandoned cultural treasures. Or you know, stuff.

33. The Specialist shall avoid the use of skyscraper elevators during combat operations, helicopter crashes and large scale building fires.

34. The Specialist shall not remind scaredy-cat bankers that jet fuel does in fact melt steel I-beams when we are standing inside a New York City burning building.

35. Ass slaps to encourage the cuter dudes still count as sexual harassment.

36. Even in combat.

37. Little black cocktail dresses are also not approved for combat operations.

38. While in combat, the Specialist shall not criticize the driving skills of the scary, secret SOCOM old guy.

39. The Specialist shall not try to cleverly guess at the career path of the clearly former Delta shooter who is only a civilian now.

40. Because he carries a lot of guns.

41. Getting shot on your armor hurts. It hurts less than getting shot not on your armor.

42. Knee strikes to the head and torso are not approved methods for adjusting the position of restrained prisoners-in-custody when officers are within line-of-sight.

43. Tasers may not be used to preemptively enforce internal team discipline and morale.

44. When dictators take over after the end of the world it is better to be on their side, and armed, than not.

45. Pick good dictators.

46. The Specialist shall not refer to rescued middle-school students as Organ Donors, Involuntary, Single-Use, Do Not Rough Handle When Frozen, One Each.

47. The Specialist shall not instruct members of the Global E-4 Apocalypse Mafia in the Dark Arts of distracting officers and more senior noncommissioned officers in order to avoid onerous additional duty.

48. The Specialist may not hold unauthorized swearing-in ceremonies for the Global E-4 Apocalypse Militia.

49. Particularly for inductees under the age of consent.

50. Bayonet kills on zombies are not "just the way grandma used to make kebobs."

51. It is decreed that "Dragula" by Rob Zombie is the "Universal Anti-Zombie Anthem of the E-4 Mafia."

52. Unless replaced with "Bodies" by Drowning Pool. Or "Down With The Sickness" by Disturbed.

53. During target identification training for volunteers and irregular forces, the Specialist shall not label running targets as zombies and standing targets as well-disciplined zombies.

54. Even if she's a HUGE Warren Zevon fan, the Specialist shall not refer to any junior officer as "an excitable boy."

55. The queen of the E-4 Mafia may not unilaterally change the age of consent in the state of Tennessee to seventeen, despite the clear absence of controlling legal authority.

56. The Specialist shall not perform preventative maintenance function testing of Tasers on friendly targets.

57. Taunting the soon to be dead is not encouraged immediately prior to application of high speed sleeping pills.

58. Officers will always misread the map and should rely on E-4 navigational expertise.

59. The Specialist shall refrain from giving the officer in charge navigational corrections unless directed by the NCOIC then present.

60. Any instances where the Specialist's navigation is incorrect shall immediately be attributed to erroneous officer input.

61. Using a disarticulated skull as a ventriloquist's dummy to imitate the NCOIC is not approved.

62. The Specialist may not use said skull to conduct partner training for Immediate Action Drills.

63. The Specialist shall not hit on the commanding officer's girlfriend.

64. Especially if she seems kinda into it.

65. Illicit corpse management is not authorized.

66. The Specialist is always designated to carry the heavy end of the body. Upon promotion to Sergeant, transport of the light end of the body is authorized.

67. Apparently, the shooting of officers is authorized, as long as they are the right officers.

68. The development of woman-portable lightning guns is a priority for the apocalypse R&D department.